THE SPIRIT ROOM

A NOVEL

MARSCHEL PAUL

Wasteland Press

www.wastelandpress.net
Shelbyville, KY USA

The Spirit Room
by Marschel Paul

First Printing – May 2013
ISBN: 978-1-60047-847-5
Library of Congress Control Number: 2013904528

Cover designed by Phil Kovacevich
Cover Photograph: Library of Congress, Prints & Photographs Division
[Reproduction number LC-USZ62-110206 DLC]

This is a work of fiction. While, as in all fiction, the literary perceptions and insights are based on experience, all names, characters, places, and incidents are products of the author's imagination or are used fictitiously.

Printed in the U.S.A.

0   1   2   3   4   5   6   7   8   9   10

For my Mother

and

For Margaret

BOOK I

One

RIGHT AFTER MAMMA DROWNED, Papa took Izzie and her sister Clara aside and told them he was going to make them famous like the Fox sisters. He was going to turn them into mediums who could speak to the spirits and dazzle believers and non-believers alike. They might even become rich, he'd told them. Papa had always been a man of pipe dreams, but this was the first time she and Clara had been drafted to be part of them. Izzie knew that Mamma—if she were alive—would have never gone along.

It had only been a few weeks since Izzie had found Mamma floating face down, lodged between some rocks in the shallow water at Kashong Point. And here they were, waiting at the entry of an elegant brick house for Spiritualism lessons. Izzie stepped off the landing and took a few steps toward the street, away from Clara and Papa. The house was enormous—one in a long row of other enormous houses on Main Street, all perched high above Seneca Lake. Snowflakes began to drift down. Izzie held out her palm and captured one, then made a fist around it. She wondered how they were ever going to get through a long, cold northern winter, their first winter in Geneva, New York, and their first winter without Mamma.

"Look, Papa, it's snowing," Clara said and smiled up at him.

Clara was wearing Mamma's black hooded cape. Izzie wasn't quite used to seeing her in it yet. Mamma's cape, but no Mamma.

"That's right, Little Plum. Soon the sleighs will come out." Papa rapped the doorknocker, harder this time.

Right then, a carriage jangled by, a runabout with its folding top down and a single dapple horse. A man in a stovepipe hat rode beside a woman in a ruby red wide-brimmed bonnet. The reins were in the woman's hands. The man's head tilted downward and bobbed. Something was wrong with him. Perhaps he was ill. Otherwise the woman wouldn't be driving. Izzie wanted to be the one holding the reins of that smart new buggy so she could ride away, away from the lake—the smell of it, the dank of it, the very sight of it.

The door clicked open and there was a smiling woman of forty years or so in a blue, shimmering dress. She was hardly taller than Clara and even more wiry than Mamma had been. Izzie darted back up the steps to the landing.

"Are these your girls, Mr. Benton? I'm Mrs. Fielding, girls." She clasped her thin hands at the base of her throat, where a brooch of red and blue stones was pinned to her collar. Her hair, pulled back neatly, had probably been a full red in earlier years, but was now pale, laced with silver.

"This is Clara, my thirteen-year-old daughter." Papa held his hand over Clara's head as though blessing her for the new undertaking. "She's the beauty of the family and brimmin' with talent." He winked at Clara.

Clara grinned up at him like he was the sun and the moon rolled into one. That was far too much adoration, thought Izzie. She felt the urge to shake Clara and slap Papa at the same time.

"And this is Isabelle, my seventeen-year-old, the one I told you about, the one with the gift." His flat hand hovered over her head.

She cringed. "Papa, there is no gift."

The lines around Papa's mouth twitched, though he didn't speak.

Mrs. Fielding's expression fell for the slightest moment, then returned to a gracious smile. "Well, girls, are you ready to learn to speak for the spirits?"

Pulling back her hood to reveal shiny brown hair, Clara nodded politely. But Izzie wasn't ready to be polite.

"I'm not sure, Mrs. Fielding. It's kind of you to offer us lessons, but we don't know if spirit-speaking work is something we're capable of. Besides, my mother always said it was something that should never be paid for."

"Isabelle!" Papa snapped at her.

She braced herself for more, but Papa restrained himself.

Mrs. Fielding studied him a moment. "Your father told me about your mother's passing. I am very sorry, dear."

Fighting tears, Izzie looked down the street through the snow flurries, searching for the runabout with the woman driving, but it was long gone.

Papa nudged his spectacles up the bridge of his nose with a forefinger. Ordinarily he would have done a lot more than bark at her for speaking out like that, but he hadn't been himself since Mamma died. Izzie couldn't tell when he was going to rile and when he wasn't. He was sure trying to make a good impression on Mrs. Fielding. He had just hired Adele Fielding, the renowned Spiritualist, to apprentice her and Clara for the week she was in town on her tour of New York State and New England. Papa said he had chosen her because she was well known and because she was from New York City. There were other mediums in Geneva, but he said, "Better to learn from an outsider. An outsider won't get competitive later on if things get goin' for you two. Maybe there're even some angles to learn that the locals don't know about."

"Come in, come in," Mrs. Fielding beckoned to Clara. "Mr. Benton, I'll see you tonight at the séance?"

"You sure I can't be in on the lessons?"

"Mediums only. I explained all that. You and I will speak privately later and you are welcome to observe my séances while I am in Geneva."

Without waiting for Papa to say more, the short spry woman turned and led Izzie and Clara through a long hallway that stretched from the front door to the rear of the house. As they followed the sweeping bell of Mrs. Fielding's blue taffeta dress, Izzie glanced back to see Papa waving goodbye and closing the front door.

"The house belongs to my dear friend, Mrs. Carr. She's in Italy just now," Mrs. Fielding said.

They passed large mirrors with gilded frames and oil paintings of ships and of stern-looking men. Every few feet there were oil lamp sconces with sparkling cut crystal glass dangling down like icicles. *A palace*, thought Izzie. They arrived at a large sitting room with tall bay windows looking out over Seneca Lake. In the middle of the room sat a large oval table dressed with a green cloth.

A young woman with black hair in coils, black eyebrows, a hint of a dark mustache, and wearing what was called a bloomer costume or reform dress—a short dress over baggy trousers tapered at the ankle—swept into the room.

"This is my assistant, Anna Santini." Mrs. Fielding gestured toward Anna as she took a seat at the end of the table.

Clara jabbed her elbow into Izzie's arm. "Nineteen since Ohio," she said.

Anna laughed and approached them. "Nineteen what?"

"Clara counts all the bloomer reform dresses she sees." Izzie felt a smile coming, but stopped herself. She needed to stay annoyed and skeptical all afternoon. If it took all week, she would find the perfect reason why she and Clara couldn't become Spiritualists.

"The trousers do allow me to move more freely." Anna gestured toward the oval table. "Here, please sit. I think the dress reform people are right. Have you ever tried it?"

Izzie shook her head as she headed for the nearest upholstered chair facing the lake. She peered out the bay windows at the water. The thought of Mamma out there in the night, alone and lost, wrenched her insides. Turning away from the lake-view chair, she instead took a seat with her back to the windows. Clara followed and sat near her.

As Anna took the seat she had avoided, Izzie looked her over. Anna was probably about her own age, sixteen or seventeen. Except for her very dark, mysterious features, she seemed sweet—almost ordinary. Could she truly talk to spirits?

Spreading her thin hands rather dramatically out on the table, Mrs. Fielding looked at Clara for a moment, then Izzie. "Girls, you are on the verge of being indoctrinated into a new religion. This is a profoundly serious undertaking." Her voice was strong without being loud. "We have no churches with tall spires, nor altars, nor shrines." She paused, then thumped the table with her palms. "We have God—eternity, truth, and everlasting life and love." Blue eyes aglow like a clear morning sky, she stared deep into Izzie's eyes, then Clara's for a long and painful amount of time. It was as though she was planting seeds, then patting the loose soil down.

Finally, Mrs. Fielding took a deep breath and began to tap her fingers on the table in double-quick time. It was going to be a long afternoon and far more complicated than Izzie had expected. Tricks making bells ring, tables knock and instruments play music in the dark were one thing. Religion was another.

Clara squirmed in her chair. She was surprised too, thought Izzie. Suddenly Mrs. Fielding bolted up and thrust her hands toward the chandelier. *Oh, Lawk-a-mercy. What now?*

"Sacred." Mrs. Fielding glared at them. "Sacred, girls. That's what this work of communicating with the spirit realm is." She strode around the table and stood directly behind Izzie, then pressed both hands firmly on her shoulders, forcing her down deeper into her chair. Clara looked fixated. "And because it is sacred, those of us who are the messengers have a divine role, a role..." Mrs. Fielding pressed harder still. It seemed she was going to plunge her right through the chair and onto the floor. "A role to be taken as radiant, as pure."

Then, finally, the pressure on Izzie's shoulders lightened.

"Before I teach you girls to speak for the spirits, who are dearly longing to be with us, you must swear yourselves to secrecy. Once you learn the lessons I have to teach you, you will join a new family of mediums and believers. This new family has rules. No... laws."

Releasing Izzie altogether, Mrs. Fielding slid between her and Clara. Then, placing a palm on each of their heads, she was silent except for the sound of inhaling and exhaling big, noisy breaths. Scalp warming under Mrs. Fielding's boney hand, Izzie started to feel giddy.

With eyebrows raised high on her forehead and biting at her lower lip, Clara looked a little panicky. Izzie winked at her, trying to let her know they were all right. If Mrs. Fielding was trying to anoint or baptize them in some way, or cast a witch's spell, she wasn't going to succeed. After a seemingly endless moment, Mrs. Fielding's breathing quieted and she lifted her hand from Izzie's head.

"Do you swear yourself to secrecy, Clara?"

Clara's face opened into a smile. "Yes, ma'am."

"Very well. And you, Isabelle?" Nostrils flaring, Mrs. Fielding looked down at her.

Izzie had no idea what this promise meant because she didn't know what she was about to learn. Was she joining a secret society or simply agreeing to not spill the beans about the tricks? She glanced over at Anna who was nodding and grinning at her, egging her on.

"What about Papa? He's going to hound us about it all," Izzie asked.

Mrs. Fielding clasped her hands together, wrung them a moment. "Yes. Yes. You will have to confide in him, but no one else. Not a soul."

Izzie nodded, but her heart wasn't in agreement at all.

Mrs. Fielding joyfully clasped her hands under her throat. "Now, before we go any further, I think we should have refreshments while I learn something about the both of you. Anna, will you bring in the tea?"

Anna glided from the room. Something was so very odd about this pair. They were both altogether too happy, thought Izzie.

"Tell me, Clara, what do you know about séances?" asked Mrs. Fielding as she took her seat again.

"Are there ghosts?"

"First of all, they are not ghosts as you are thinking of them, Clara. They are as real as we are. They're the spirits of people who once lived on this earth with us. They're just in another sphere now, a sphere of eternal spring. It is harder for them to talk to us from there. That's why we need mediums. Do you think you might have the medium's gift?"

"I don't know."

Mrs. Fielding looked into Izzie's eyes and held her gaze a moment. "What about you, Isabelle?"

"No."

"Well, why take the lessons?"

"My father insisted. He wants to make money and thinks Clara and I could conduct circles like you and Anna do. He wants us to become the famous Benton sisters, even more famous than the Fox sisters."

"Yes. He is ambitious, isn't he. He led me to believe that you might have some ability."

"No. It's not true."

In her plaid bloomers and flashing that hideous radiant smile, Anna appeared with a tray and set it on the green tablecloth, then began to pour steaming tea from a silver pot.

"He told me your mother had visions and spoke with spirits frequently."

Izzie felt as though she had been punched in the chest. As far as she was concerned, Mamma's spirits had killed her mother, drowned her—ultimately betrayed her.

Mamma had talked to those spirit voices her whole life. Just two months before this, Mamma had dragged her, Clara, Clara's twin, Billy, and their little sister Euphora by wagon from Homer, Ohio in pursuit of Papa. He had been charged with arson in Homer and fled the family and the town leaving no word of his destination. But Mamma had always listened to her voices and they told her to go to Geneva, New

York where she and Papa had lived long before. To no one's surprise, Mamma and her voices were right and she got their Benton family back together.

But in the short time they had been reunited with Papa in Geneva, it seemed Mamma began to lose herself and that the spirit voices took her over more and more each day. She had disappeared four times overnight. On the fourth time, she had somehow gotten hold of a small sailboat in the dark and taken it out on the lake all by herself. Mamma knew nothing about sailing or boats, but Izzie was sure it had been the voices that led her each step of the way.

Seneca was a deep lake with powerful currents fed by springs. It was dangerous and it swallowed Mamma and her boat up and spit them both out not far from the Seneca Indian graveyard. After a two day search with Papa and some of the sheriff's men, she and Billy were the ones who found Mamma tangled in her gray homespun dress stuck between those boulders at the water's edge.

"Isabelle." Like a black-haired angel, Anna was leaning over the table and offering her a cup of tea. "My mother was very gifted as well. What was your mother able to do?"

Blazing like a relentless, scorching August sun, Anna passed her the cup. Perhaps Anna was intoxicated with something, Izzie thought. Laughing gas. Opium. No one smiled this much.

"I'm not sure exactly what she did. She'd drift away from us and then tell us she'd been speaking to her spirits. I never understood it exactly." Hoping the conversation would turn elsewhere, Izzie took a sip of warm tea.

Mrs. Fielding set her cup down, then rose and approached Izzie.

"What do you think she saw or heard?" Her voice was gentle.

To tell these strangers what she truly thought about her mother, that she was somewhat touched, perhaps even loony, would be disloyal. Izzie wanted to yell at Mrs. Fielding and Anna, "The rotten voices killed my mother!" But instead she looked down from their gaze and waited. The fire crackled, spitting sparks at the screen. Clara and the others kept their attention on her. Izzie could feel them waiting for her answer. No, it would be better not to talk about Mamma outside the family, even to these two.

Izzie stood, suddenly overwhelmed by the urge to leave. "Perhaps we can talk about Mamma later."

"Of course, dear. I apologize. I know you are mourning." Mrs. Fielding patted her shoulder. "Let's have the ginger cake, Anna." Mrs. Fielding beckoned to Anna with a wave of one hand and, with the other, pressed down once again on Izzie's shoulder, more gently this time. Izzie gave in, sinking back into the chair.

"Perhaps we should go now," Izzie said, wanting to flick Mrs. Fielding's hand away.

"Clara, would you like to continue with the lessons?" Mrs. Fielding asked.

Having just taken a large bite of ginger cake, Clara chewed for a long moment, then looked up toward the glass chandelier over the table and then gulped down her cake. She glanced over at Izzie and squinted again. That squint was a bad sign. Clara was afraid of something and wanting something at the same time. Clara looked at Mrs. Fielding.

"Yes, ma'am."

Oh, rubbish and rot. Clara wanted the lessons, ghosts and all. Well, that was going to make getting out of Papa's scheme a lot harder.

"And why is that, dear?"

Clara fidgeted in her seat. "I want to learn something new." She grasped the edge of the tablecloth and began to twist it. "And I want to help our father. He needs us."

Papa's girl again. Clara needed some talking to. Papa had run away from them. He had deserted his family. Why wasn't she angry at him for that?

"That's very noble dear, but this is special work, sacred work. I'm sure you and Isabelle can find other ways to help the family."

"There's something else," Clara said. "I think Izzie is like you and Anna."

Mrs. Fielding, blue eyes sparkling, examined Izzie.

"Papa got you thinking that way. It isn't so." Izzie shoved her teacup and cake plate away. "It's ridiculous."

"Izzie says things sometimes that no one else knows. When someone knocks on the door at our rooms, she always guesses who it is."

"That's nothing, Clara. I just know how people knock. Mrs. Purcell knocks three times firmly. Miss Mary Carter and Miss Jane Carter both knock very lightly but Mary keeps going and Jane is short with it."

"Girls, I can return your father's money to him or we can continue and see if your transcendent powers develop. It may very well turn out that neither of you have a gift. If we go on, I expect your utmost dedication and concentration on the exercises."

Egging them on with nods and smiles, Anna rose and stood by her fancy tea tray. These women certainly knew something extraordinary. Whether it was about religion or theater or death or artful deception, it wasn't entirely clear. Izzie clenched her hands together in her lap. If they got their money back, Papa could return it to whomever he borrowed it from and there would be less chance of trouble later. If they went on with the lessons, she and Clara would be mediums, either true ones or charlatans, as soon as Papa set them up.

Mrs. Fielding stroked Izzie's hair lightly.

"Isabelle, I think this is up to you."

Suddenly Anna was making a terrible ruckus, her shoulders gyrating, her arms flailing about. Eyes closed and neck craned back, Anna lifted her face toward the ceiling. At first her breathing was belabored, then she yipped piercingly like a wolf cub.

"She's in a trance," Mrs. Fielding whispered as she extracted one of Clara's hands from its grip on the tablecloth and held it, then she reached down for Izzie's hands and tried to unclench them, but Izzie refused. "I think she is going to speak for her spirit now. Don't be afraid. He's a kind gentleman."

Anna opened her mouth and a low, scratchy voice poured forth. "Clara, Izzie, your mother wants to speak to you."

Izzie's heart cramped. She glanced over at Clara who was sitting rigid with thunderstruck eyes. This was certainly an inventive way to get them to take the lessons, but it was cruel.

"She says your life will not be complete until you embrace Spiritualism, Isabelle." Anna's voice was sweet and soft again. "She didn't know how to use her gift. You will. You will learn." She hesitated a moment. "You will understand. Listen to these women. Learn from them."

Feeling a cold draft at the back of her neck, Izzie turned to see if a window was open, but it wasn't. Mamma's spirit. Ridiculous. Did they think she was a half-wit? If she could show Clara this was a silly act, maybe Clara would see how foolish, how disrespectful, this all was. It wasn't right to portray Mamma as present in some way. Mamma was lost to them forever. Lost. This is what mediums did—dangle the hope of eternal life at people who were deep in pain. An imaginary, delicious meal set before the hungry. It was plain cruel.

"Mrs. Fielding, may I ask Anna, or her spirit, a question to prove that my mother is really there?" Izzie asked.

"This kind of proof does not always work as one desires, Isabelle. You shouldn't be disappointed if you don't receive the message you are seeking. It can take many attempts before the proof, as you say, is satisfactory."

"I'd like to try."

"All right." Mrs. Fielding looked at Anna who still had her eyes closed and head tilted up. "She can hear you."

Izzie had to ask something that only Mamma could know. The white horse. That hot summer night back in Homer when Clara was little. Clara refused to use the chamber pot in the house and insisted that Izzie escort her to the privy in the backyard. It was a starry night with a crescent moon and just enough light to see by. When they were nearly to the privy, they heard strange, hollow breathing and snorting. Alarmed, they grabbed each other and squealed. Not twenty feet from them, a white horse, luminous and eerie, pounded frantically out of the bushes. It reared up, then darted off, its hooves thundering as it sped around the side of their little house. After it left, it took Izzie until dawn to calm Clara down.

"Mamma, can you hear me?"

"Clearly, like a bird in the early evening, Isabelle."

"Do you remember that night when Clara was only three and I took her to the privy? There was an animal out there and we scared it just as much as it scared us. Can you tell me what it was so that I'll know this is really you, Mamma?"

Placing her hands over her chest, Anna stilled. There was no way Anna could answer this question, absolutely none.

"You mean that old white horse that broke loose?"

Every hair root on Izzie's scalp prickled. The back of her hands tingled. Leaning back in her chair, she noticed that Clara's precious brown eyes were petrified and she was sitting up so tall it seemed she was going to levitate.

The mean monster horsey was all she talked about for weeks and weeks after that night.

Anna patted her chest lightly. "I love you both. Do not worry about me. I am not in pain. It's beautiful here in Summerland."

Izzie was dumbfounded. This wasn't possible. They couldn't know about the white horse. Could they?

Clara, whose eyes were now more fearful than surprised, looked up at Mrs. Fielding, who was standing between them and smiling brilliantly.

"Do you see Mamma, Mrs. Fielding? What's Summerland?" Clara asked.

"Shhh. Wait." Mrs. Fielding lifted a finger to her lips.

Anna stepped away from the table, then began to pace back and forth. Suddenly she froze and looked straight at Izzie.

"There are many who want to talk to you."

The prickling sensation on Izzie's scalp shot down her spine. "Who are they?"

"I'm not sure. There's a large group all asking to be heard. It's confusing me." She stood motionless and appeared to be listening to something.

"Whoever they are, I don't want to talk to them," Izzie said.

"Wait," Mrs. Fielding said.

Anna was breathing steadily and looking off at some point high on the wall. Several moments passed. Izzie was concentrating so hard on Anna, standing there in her green plaid bloomers, with her perfect olive skin and radiant black hair, that she began breathing in rhythm with Anna.

Finally, Anna closed her eyes, then blinked a few times.

"I'm sorry. I had to stop. It was too baffling, too many voices at once. That happens sometimes."

"I don't want to speak with them," Izzie said.

"Why not?" Mrs. Fielding asked.

"Because that's what my mother did, talk to people who weren't there." Izzie's face burned and tears started to stream down. "Sometimes my mother stayed in that world with her spirits for long periods of time. This last time she didn't come back to us." She took a moment to compose herself and wiped her eyes with her dress sleeve. "I won't be like that."

Izzie knew she had to leave. It was dangerous here. She shoved her chair back and rose.

"Come on, Clara. Leave with me." Izzie glanced from Anna to Mrs. Fielding who both looked concerned.

"Are you sure, Izzie? What if Mamma wants to say more to us?"

"Mamma is dead. She's gone."

Clara stood, picked up Mamma's black cape from the back of her chair, walked to Izzie, and took her hand. Then Izzie turned quickly and, pulling Clara along, started down the hallway for the front door.

"Wait, please, Isabelle. Anna gave you a very special message. Please, don't run away," Mrs. Fielding said.

Halfway to the door, Izzie stopped and whirled to face Mrs. Fielding who was again calling for her to wait. Anna, watching them, remained behind in the parlor. Clara's hand trembled in Izzie's grasp as they waited for Mrs. Fielding to get closer. Mrs. Fielding held out a thick book toward her. Without thinking, Izzie dropped Clara's hand and accepted it.

"Isabelle, one great lesson I have learned is that life is never what you expect it to be."

Mrs. Fielding's blue eyes narrowed as she spoke. She tapped the brown cloth cover of the book. "Your father says you love books. This one is our sacred scripture. Read as much as you can tonight and tell me your thoughts tomorrow."

The Principles of Nature, Her Divine Revelations, and a Voice to Mankind. Izzie pushed the volume back toward Mrs. Fielding, but Mrs. Fielding raised an outward palm and shook her head.

"No, please, just read some of it and return it to me at your next lesson. If you choose not to take the lessons, we will return all of your father's money."

Izzie was torn. She did want to know more about how Anna spoke of the white horse, but she was afraid. The weight of the book and the texture of its embossed gold title tugged at her. She had never refused a book and she knew the book itself couldn't hurt her.

With the big bright windows behind her, Anna's face was just visible, but Izzie sensed the now familiar encouraging smile. The glass chandelier sparkled above Anna's head as she waved calmly at them. Clara returned the wave.

"Tomorrow then," Izzie said to Mrs. Fielding. Tucking the book under one arm and taking her sister's shaky hand again, she led Clara to the front of the house and then out into the snowy evening.

Two

L ATER THAT NIGHT, after they had met with the mediums, Clara perspired by the fire as she sat sewing at one end of the long pine table in the Blue Room. While she worked the needle, she was missing Mamma and trying not to cry. At the other end of the table, near the foolish, giant fire her brother Billy had stirred up, Papa and Billy were playing checkers. Izzie was downstairs in Mrs. Purcell's library reading the big fat Spiritualism book that Mrs. Fielding had given her. Her younger sister, Euphora, was playing alone with her wooden horses on the girls' bed. Everyone had been settled like this for hours, no one saying much of anything. Clara's heart sank every time she looked over at Mamma's empty rocker.

The Blue Room upstairs in Mrs. Purcell's boardinghouse, with its sky-colored walls, was both their family parlor and bedchamber for Clara and her brother and sisters. They had a long table with six ladder-back chairs by the fireplace in the middle of the room and two beds with cotton mattresses—a skinny one for Billy and a broad one for the three girls. They also had Mamma's rocking chair, which no one wanted to sit in now, brought with them from Ohio.

One Blue Room door led out to the top of the stairs and another led directly to Papa and Mamma's bedchamber, now just Papa's room since Mamma died. Tonight the Blue Room was full of a broken-heart heaviness, hot and stuffy because of Billy's mutton-head fire, but there was no place else Clara wanted to be. She wished Izzie was here too, but Izzie was always downstairs reading. Since they got to Geneva and Izzie and Mamma found Papa passed out in the rat-hole hotel down near the train station, Izzie didn't like being around Papa much. She said she was never going to forgive him for his running off on them. And since Mamma died, it was worse. She hardly spoke to him at all or even stayed in the same room with him.

Billy jiggled his knee while he waited for Papa to make a move. "I heard John Brown went down to Missouri and stole eleven slaves right out from their masters' plantations and took them a thousand miles to freedom," Billy said.

"That Brown's goin' to get himself shot," Papa said, keeping his eyes on the board.

Clara pulled the glass candle lantern closer to the shirt she had taken from the pile of seamstress work Mamma had left unfinished. Fifty shirts. Fifty collars to finish. One hundred cuffs to sew to one hundred sleeves. One hundred sleeves to sew to one hundred shoulders. Only eleven shirts, eleven collars and twenty-two cuffs done. Until Billy got his first pay at the tree nursery in a few weeks, this pile of shirts was the only earnings anyone in the family had. Clara studied her loose and uneven stitching on the cuff. "Inferior," she could hear the tailor saying. Should she tear it out and start over? No, they needed the money now. If she were lucky, he wouldn't notice.

Billy jumped up for the ninth time and added a log to the fire. The fire was already burning so furiously it looked as if the flames might lick their way up onto the walls and catch the whole tarnal house on fire. Every time he made a move on the checkerboard, he popped up and stoked again.

"That makes thirteen logs, Clara," he said.

"Twelve."

"No, thirteen."

She ignored her twin and went back to her sewing. He might be right. He might have used thirteen logs. She might have missed one. Using that much wood, he was surely borrowing trouble with Mrs. Purcell. She pulled the thread through the sleeve cuff and felt tears try to push out from inside her eyes. When she and Billy were four years old, her brother had taught her to count everything in the world. Now neither of them could stop.

"Billy, are you trying to cook us like pigs on a spit?" Euphora, red-faced and weary looking, clutched her two painted wooden horses. She hadn't picked up those little blue and yellow horses since they arrived in Geneva. She was too old for them now.

Billy sneered at her. "Go back to your toys."

Once Billy settled down and fixed himself on the checkerboard again, Clara dropped her mending on the chair, wandered to the window, and opened it. The cold air soothed her. She breathed in the smell of new snow. Euphora left the bed and came and leaned against her side.

"Did you and Izzie really talk to Mamma with the mediums?" Euphora asked.

"We did."

"You did not. It was some kind of trick," Billy said from across the room.

She put her arm around Euphora's shoulders. Even though Euphora was eleven, two years younger, she was lanky and nearly as tall as her. By next summer, Euphora'd shoot past her like a stalk of corn at the end of August.

Clara looked up at the white stars in the black sky and thought of Mamma somewhere out there and then thought of how few people were at her burial. If they had been back in Homer, half the town would have come to Mamma's burial, but since they had only been in Geneva a short time, there were only seven besides their family: Mrs. Purcell, who knew Mamma when she was young, the two spinster sisters, who were the only other boarders, the man Mamma did the seamstress work for, and Papa's friends, Mr. Weston, Mr. Payne, and Mr. Washburn, and not even Mr. Washburn's wife. It was a puny service and the reverend's high voice reading scriptures had given Clara a headache and it wasn't like any headache she'd ever had before. It hurt in her head but also made her peaky in the stomach.

"Maybe Mamma is out there looking down on us," Euphora said. "Maybe she's sailing in her sailboat around heaven."

"Maybe she is."

If Anna and Mrs. Fielding were real mediums, Clara could talk to Mamma properly and thank her for bringing them all back together with Papa. She wished she hadn't whined so bitterly about the exhausting, rainy wagon journey from Ohio. If only she had told Mamma that she was right and brave to bring them all that way.

Refreshed from the night air, Clara closed the window and returned to her sewing. Euphora went back to her wooden horses, but instead of playing with them, she lay down and held them to her.

Lifting the whisky bottle by the checkerboard, Papa poured his fourth drink and shot it down. Not all of it made its way past his lips, trickling instead down his chin into his new fuzzy beard. He better stop drinking that whisky now, she thought. Four drinks were usually all right. If she brought him some tea, maybe he'd stop and go to bed.

"Papa, I could make tea. Would you like that?"

Reaching across the checkerboard, Billy took one of his black discs, plopped it over one of Papa's reds, which he snatched up, and then added to the red wobbly stack in front of him.

Papa slammed his hand flat down on the table. Billy's tower of red checkers careened over and the rest on the board jiggled, slid, and hopped. Clara's head pounded.

"Damn you, Billy. You changed it when I wasn't lookin'."

"No, sir. I'm beatin' you fair and square." Billy's voice cracked high as he stacked the red checkers up in front of him.

Papa poured a fifth whiskey and clunked the bottle down hard. He took a swig, swilling it round and round in his mouth, then he swallowed and bared his teeth like a mean dog. That was five. Too late for tea, thought Clara. They were all in dutch now. Picking up the shirt and needle, Clara started sewing the cuff again. No sooner did she push the needle carefully into the white cotton than Papa smacked his fist down on the table.

She drove the needle through the cotton and into her index finger. "Ack!" Drawing the fingertip to her mouth, she glanced at the board. Not one red left on the board. Billy had won again.

"Damn you, Billy." Papa braced both hands on the table like he might roll the whole thing over.

"It's just a game, Papa, that's all," Clara said.

He shoved the checkerboard toward Billy, spilling the red discs into Billy's lap. Billy flew out of his chair, arms straight out, like the checkers were hot coals. Then Papa lurched out of his chair and came around and gripped Billy's neck in one hand.

"Papa, it's a game!" Clara said.

"You think you're the man of the family now because you got a man's job up at that Maxwell's tree nursery?"

Papa squeezed Billy's neck until Billy's eyes swelled. Then Billy grabbed Papa's arm in both his hands and yanked it down hard, breaking free.

Stepping back, Billy pushed his long sandy hair out of his eyes with one hand and held up his other just near Papa's chest. "You're drunk, Papa. Stop." He glimpsed the fireplace irons near him.

Papa followed Billy's eyes. "Oh, I see, you're goin' ta hack down your old man with an iron." Roaring like a lion, Papa rammed at Billy and shoved him backward all the way across the room. Then he pinned Billy against the wall.

Clara ran over to the bed and plopped down next to Euphora, who was completely hidden under the blanket. This never happened before. Not this. Papa yelled and slammed things, but he never slammed Billy like that.

Reaching down into his trouser pocket, Billy got out something that looked like a rusty nail or old key. He thrust it up into Papa's arm with enough spike to startle Papa and make him fall back. Rapid-fire, Papa grabbed his arm like a bee stung him. In that slightest second, Billy slid out the door. His footsteps rumbled down the stairs and then the front door crashed shut.

Clara's heart was thumping hard. Holding his hurt arm, and snorting and sweating, Papa glared over at her and Euphora on the bed. Euphora had wrapped herself into a tiny ball against Clara's back.

Izzie suddenly appeared in the doorway, her gray-green eyes darting, her light brown hair flowing down her back, and

her wide shoulders higher and wider than ever. Izzie looked at
Papa a moment, then all around the room, and finally settled
her gaze on her and Euphora on the bed. Izzie's eyes calmed
down a little and her shoulders dropped part way. She didn't
say a word. She squared off toward Papa and just stood there
in the doorway watching him. Papa stared right back at her
for a long time while he caught his breath. If Izzie said the
wrong thing like she was sure to, he'd probably knock her
clear down the stairs. Euphora was quivering against Clara's
back.

Izzie stayed silent a while longer, then finally stepped
right past sweating Papa like he wasn't there at all and walked
over to the bed.

"I've come up to say goodnight, girls. Are you ready for
bed?"

Clara sighed. Ready for bed? More like ready to hide
under it and not come out for a week or two. Lucky stars.
Izzie knew to hold her tongue once in a while.

Still clutching his wounded arm, Papa watched Izzie cross
the room. Then he muttered something Clara couldn't hear
and drifted back to the table. He picked up his bottle and
glass and, still mumbling, shuffled away to his bedchamber.

"Izzie, I wish you wouldn't stay downstairs so much."
Euphora's blue eyes were just peeping out over the top of the
blanket. "Papa heaved Billy clear across the room."

Looking over at Papa's door, Izzie took a deep breath and
held it in like she was under water. Clara counted slowly to
seven before Izzie sighed it out.

"Come on now, time for bed. I'll read *The Deerslayer* to
you." Izzie pulled the quilt back onto Euphora's shoulders
and stroked her red hair. Picking up the James Fenimore
Cooper book, Izzie found the page where they had left off
and began.

"Judith, in the main, was a girl of great personal spirit, and her habits prevented her from feeling any of the terror that is apt to come over her sex at the report of firearms. She had discharged many a rifle, and had even been known to kill a deer, under circumstances that were favorable to the effort…"

Euphora snuggled next to Clara and fell asleep almost immediately. Clara heard some of the story, but her thoughts drifted away from Izzie's soothing voice as she worried about her twin out in the cold, snowy night.

LATER ON, BEFORE DAWN SOMETIME, Clara woke to a groan, hollow and horrible, coming from Papa's bedchamber. Then the groaning came again and rolled on and on. She gnawed at a place inside her mouth just underneath her lower lip. Each night, since Mamma had died, Clara lay awake in bed for hours listening to Papa cry. Hearing him like that was slow torture. When he finished, she would sleep. Usually Clara slept on one side of the girls' bed, Izzie on the other, and Euphora in the middle. Tonight Izzie wasn't there, though. After Izzie had tucked them under the quilt and read for a while about Judith and Deerslayer, she told them she had to go downstairs and read more of the Andrew Jackson Davis Spiritualism book.

Clara had been listening for Billy to come back and slip into his bed, but he hadn't. Papa had scared him badly this time. Was he wandering out in the snow or hiding under an awning or in a doorway somewhere? Maybe he was curled up in the parlor downstairs on the sofa. If he didn't show up soon, she would go down and see.

Papa was sobbing hard. The soft skin inside of Clara's mouth was sore from her biting it. She tried to stop, but couldn't. Papa would be all right without Mamma in due course, she thought, and so would Billy and Izzie and Euphora. They would all take care of Papa. She and Izzie would become mediums and Billy had his job at the tree nursery. They could keep up with their room and board until Papa found work. Mrs. Purcell, the landlady, would feed them well and they would stay in her beautiful house with the gardens. She and Izzie might even become famous like Papa wanted and make him as proud as he ever was in his whole life. Then he wouldn't shove at Billy or drink so much liquor. Everything would be all right. If she could just make Papa believe it.

"Almira!"

Papa was so loud this time that Euphora stirred. Grabbing the pillow she shared with Euphora out from under their heads, Clara pressed it over her left ear. But Papa's moans filtered through, straight into her. What if he decided to run away and leave them like he did before? The taste of blood spread onto her tongue. If she told him things would get better maybe he would believe her. She had to try.

She slid from the bed and tiptoed across the cold floor toward his door. It was nearly pitch-dark and, besides following the sound of Papa's wailing and weeping, she had to feel her way, brushing the end of the bed, then one ladder-back chair, then the family table, then a second ladder-back.

She jammed her toes on the runner of Mamma's rocking chair and grunted at the pain. The chair set off rocking, thrumming on the wood floor.

"Mamma, is that you?" Euphora said.

Clara lurched toward the chair and seized both arms to halt it. "No. It's me. Clara."

She let go of the chair. It resumed a gentle rock. She swallowed. "Mamma?" Waving her hand in the air over the seat, she searched the darkness. Nothing. She let out a sigh.

That would be just like Mamma to come back as a spirit and sit in her own rocker. Then Papa moaned again, this time horrified, like someone was forcing poison down his throat.

She made her way in the dark to the door and nudged it open, then stepped inside Papa's room and shut the door behind her.

"Papa?"

"Little Plum? That you?"

"Yes."

She shuffled straight ahead to the foot of the bed. The room smelled like whiskey and sour dishrags.

"Come here, by me."

In the dark, Clara inched her way along the side of the bed aiming for Papa's sniffling and coughing sounds. When she reached him, she accidentally stuck her searching hand into his chest and found he was sitting up against the headboard. Crawling onto the bed and sitting alongside him, she leaned her shoulder into his arm. He took her hand in his and held it, resting it on his thigh.

"My Almira ain't never comin' back." He squeezed her hand and began to cry in choppy snorting fits.

Tears streamed down Clara's face.

"I know, Papa, but don't cry so hard. Everything will be all right. We're all sad now, but Mamma is at peace, isn't she?"

"I don't think I'll ever feel like livin' again without her. I've got nothin'."

But he had her, she thought. She pressed her tongue against the bleeding spot in her mouth. If he thought she was nothing, she might as well go ahead and die with Mamma.

"You have me and Billy and Izzie and Euphora. We all love you, Papa. We'll take care of everything."

He was silent a moment.

"You are my precious one."

His voice sounded more like himself. This was much better. She was his precious one, not nothing. He was only saying terrible things because he was missing Mamma. Clara put her head against his shoulder.

"If I sit here, will you sleep some, Papa?"

He didn't answer, but in a moment, she felt him slide down on the bed, turn his back to her, and rest himself lightly against her stretched-out leg. She reached over and placed a hand delicately on his head. After a few minutes, he became quiet, then began to snore softly. He needed to sleep and forget his pain for as long as he could. She'd stay right there, still as a stone as long as she could so as not to wake him. Papa would feel better in the morning. After a long time, she tilted her head back and drifted off.

Three

IZZIE HAD LEFT THE DOOR to Mrs. Purcell's library open after the ruckus with Papa and Billy. If anything else happened upstairs, she wanted to hear it right away. Billy hadn't come back, but she wasn't worried. Even on a snowy night like this, her little brother could take care of himself. Still, she longed to hear the front door open and his footsteps bounding up the stairs skipping two or three at a time.

Before the yelling, before Billy raced out, Izzie had scarcely started reading the introduction of Andrew Jackson Davis's book, which was written by a scribe for Davis, a Mr. Fishbough. It discussed the history of the world and humankind and its progress toward unification as well as Mr. Davis himself, "amiable, simple-hearted, truth-loving, and unsophisticated."

It was going to take a lot more than a single night to grasp Fishbough's and Davis's ideas. She rose from Mrs. Purcell's reading chair and carried the eight hundred page book, one of the heaviest volumes she'd ever hoisted, over to the library shelves. She held her book up near the books lining the wall to compare it to the others. This book's spine had to be at least three inches wide, perhaps the thickest. Mrs. Purcell's volumes were bound in red, black, brown, and green, written by Ralph Waldo Emerson, John James Audubon, Mason

Weems, Lydia Maria Child, Washington Irving, Noah Webster, Mary Wollstonecraft, Charles Dickens, Frederick Douglass.

Books about ships, history, cooking, philosophy and science filled her landlady's shelves. While many had belonged to Mrs. Purcell's late husband, many were Emma Purcell's personal collection, including the ones about herbal medicines. On many occasions, Izzie had found Mrs. Purcell taking notes at her desk from *The English Physician Enlarged, Containing Three Hundred and Sixty-nine Receipts for Medicines Made from Herbs* by Nicholas Culpepper. Izzie ran her fingertips over several of the leather bindings. She hoped her family would be at the boardinghouse a long time, long enough to read all the books in the room, every last beautiful one of them. But with Papa acting more desperate, more harsh than usual, she wasn't sure how long they'd be at Mrs. Purcell's or even in Geneva.

Sinking back into the chair, she draped Clara's red woolen shawl over her lap and settled Davis's *The Principles of Nature, Her Divine Revelations, and a Voice to Mankind* over it. She wished Anna hadn't brought Mamma forth in her trance and hadn't known about the white horse. How could Anna have known about that? Impossible. She flipped the book over and opened the back cover. Seven hundred and eighty-two pages. The fire spat an ember at the screen. She glanced up at the mantle clock. It was nine. Mr. Andrew Jackson Davis would surely put her to sleep within minutes.

Resting her head against the pink upholstery at the side of the chair, she smelled the concoction of rose water, jasmine, orange, and vanilla that Mrs. Purcell brewed to wash her hair with.

Except for the sporadic crack of a beam or wall, or the ticking of the clock, the house was winter quiet, the street without horses, and the trees without wind. She tucked her feet, cozy in wool stockings, under her, and flipping the book over, opened the cover.

She began to read, at first lazily, expecting to be lulled under. As the scribe turned to the biography of Andrew Jackson Davis, she struggled to keep her eyes open.

"Neither father nor mother was particularly inclined to intellectual pursuits and hence felt no anxiety to bestow an education upon their son extending beyond the simplest rudiments that may be acquired in a common school...From early youth, therefore, until he entered his clairvoyance career, he was mostly kept at such manual employments as were adapted to his age, during which time his little earnings and affectionate attentions contributed greatly to the support of his immediate family connexions."

At least he'd gone to school for the "simplest rudiments," she thought. She hadn't even done that. She continued reading the biography. Davis was only nineteen when he started the book and he finished at twenty-one. He didn't actually write it himself, but instead recited it to Mr. Fishbough while in numerous trances. Over a period of fourteen months, he was magnetized daily, fell into a mesmeric trance in which a spirit would inhabit him, then dictated the words of the spirit. One hundred and fifty-seven sessions later, he had created a tome covering the entire story of civilization and he claimed he had only read one book in his life.

"The fact is, however, it is known to an absolute moral certainty to Mr. Davis's most intimate acquaintances, that he was, while in his normal state, totally uninformed on all the great leading subjects treated in this book, until he perused the manuscripts of his own lectures."

Izzie laughed. Magnetic sessions. *Oh, Mr. Davis. Ridiculous.* She slapped the book closed and placed it next to the shiny daguerreotype of Mrs. Purcell's husband, Richard, on the round table at her side. The photograph of Mr. Purcell made her wonder if there was a picture of Davis in the book. She snatched the volume back and thumbed through it until she found a plate depicting him. Huge black eyes, long nose and forehead, wavy swarthy hair, a perfect fuzzy line of beard from ear to ear, but no mustache over his thin upper lip. Fine coat and tie. Handsome.

Picking up a handful of her long hair, she began to twirl it in her fingers. Well, maybe she'd try just the first chapter. Someone at nineteen, only two years older than she was, writing about spiritual leaders and astronomy and the origin of language and something he called the seven spheres had to be interesting, even if absurd.

Curling deeper into the chair, Izzie poised the book under the light of the oil lamp and began to read. Every five or ten pages, she'd think about going upstairs to see if Billy had returned safely or getting up to lay more coal for the fire, but instead of doing those things, she turned the next page. Finally there was nothing else except the words before her. There were far too many of them, sometimes their meaning muddy, but she kept on.

"Your fire is out."

"Oh." Izzie startled at the voice, then saw it was Billy standing in the door, his coat collar up around his neck and his cap pulled low. Snow coated his cap, shoulders, and boots. His trousers were caked white half way to his knees.

"It's three in the morning," he said.

"Did Papa hurt you?"

"Na, but he was about to. I got out before he could." Billy took off his cap, shook the snow from it, then combed his red cold hand through his straight hair. Crossing his arms over his chest and pinching his shoulders up toward his ears, he shivered. He glanced around the library. "I'll start the fire again. I'll sleep on the floor in here for a few hours. Are you going up?"

"No. I want to read this book Mrs. Fielding gave me. Where were you?"

"I snuck onto the P.H. Field, the new steamboat down at Long Pier, and rolled myself up in a rug, but a night watchman found me. He kicked at me and hollered for me to get out. It didn't hurt, though. The rug was thick." Billy walked passed her to the fireplace. "What's the book about?"

"Eternal life."

"Will it tell you whether Mamma was loony or one of them mediums?"

"I don't think so."

As Billy knelt and piled chunks of coal, Izzie realized she was cold. The fire had probably been out for hours. She had been reading about liquid fire forming the cosmos, the sun, the planets, and of man rising through celestial spheres, but she still had no idea how Anna Santini knew about the white horse or how Mamma heard voices. She guessed that Davis would say it was a man or woman in one of those seven spheres telling Anna outright about the horse, or telling Mamma how to find Papa in Geneva after he disappeared, or how to take the boat out sailing on Seneca Lake.

Davis was either the biggest hoax of all hoaxes or there were unseen spheres inhabited by spirits. She had to test Anna again. She would go back and take the lessons. Humbug or eternal life. Mamma's sanity. She wanted to know. She and Clara would take the lessons, but she would never become a medium like Papa wanted. Never.

Four

I ZZIE FOLLOWED CLARA AND PAPA into the small parlor at the Carr house where they had their lesson the day before. Just like Papa, Izzie was sure she'd see trickery at Mrs. Fielding's spirit circle tonight. Even though Papa believed Mamma had spirits visit her and talk to her, he never believed any of them could move an object or make anything physical manifest, and they never did that Izzie saw.

This time the scarlet velvet curtains were closed and the room was dimly lit by oil lamps. At the oval table, four men and three women sat around in formal attire. The dresses Izzie and Clara wore were plain, like rags compared to what the three women wore with their colorful sheens, flaring flounces, and lace collars. Standing at the end of the table near her seat, Mrs. Fielding wore a silver dress that shimmered like the moon.

Mrs. Fielding gestured in their direction. "These are the Benton girls, my new apprentices, and their father. They'll be observing tonight."

A few of the people nodded. Others looked at them vacantly. With her arm and palm outstretched, Mrs. Fielding directed Izzie, Clara, and Papa to take three chairs near the fireplace. The burning coals radiated a welcome heat. Just as Izzie removed her winter shawl, Anna, who she hadn't noticed before, was suddenly before her offering to take it. She smiled as she took Clara's shawl and Papa's greatcoat, then vanished. When Anna returned to the room empty-handed, she stood like a sentry by the curtains. Instead of a bloomer costume, she wore an emerald-green wool dress with white lace trim.

Standing over the group at the table, Mrs. Fielding pulled out a gold watch from her dress pocket and explained how the séance would go. The watch was to keep time, not of the spirits, but of each mortal. People tended to go on too long and interfere with the chance others might have to talk to their spirits.

Then, as if perfectly rehearsed, Anna nodded to Mrs. Fielding and soberly moved about the room extinguishing the lamps until there was only the soft glow from the coal fire and a single candle lantern in the center of the table. Izzie wondered if Anna would go into trance again.

Once Mrs. Fielding took the empty seat at the séance table, she closed her eyes and placed her hands palm down on the surface. Everyone did the same. Sixteen hands, pinkie fingers touching, formed a ring around the table.

A gentleman, sitting with his back to Izzie, began the session without being asked.

"Is there a spirit here wishing to communicate with me?"

Izzie concentrated hard, watching for tricks, listening for people outside the room, or even nearby. Someone could be behind those huge velvet curtains, she thought. Several people could easily hide in the immense folds.

Three loud raps sounded sharply. No one's hands had moved from the table, but Izzie was certain someone close by had produced the noise. One of the women in the circle crouched over awkwardly and looked under the table but said nothing, then she returned to her upright position, hands again firmly on the table.

After the woman resettled, the man went on to ask if the spirit was his little son. Three solid, quick knocks thumped. It seemed to be coming from the table. Clara had been swinging her feet in swooping arcs under her chair, but now she began to swing faster, almost violently.

"Are you with me all the time?"

One rap from the table.

"Only tonight?"

Three raps. Yes.

It was maddening that the man's face was out of sight. His expression might tell more about his belief in the raps than his voice.

"I want to know if it is really you. How old were you when you died?"

Five raps.

The man paused for a long moment. "That's right."

Several at the table chimed, "Ah."

Clara bolted up from her chair, but Papa nimbly grabbed her wrist and forced her back down.

"I knew you would be here tonight, son." The man's shoulders fell a little and his voice softened.

Izzie felt her sister's elbow dig into her upper arm. Using her bulging eyes to point to Anna, Clara silently directed Izzie to look over at the young medium. Anna's arms were twisting, her shoulder's rotating. On her tiptoes, Anna wove about in tiny haphazard steps. She careened toward the table, lodging herself between two of the sitters. Anna slapped her hand on the table repetitively, convulsively. Izzie held her breath. Clara leapt up again. This time she escaped Papa's grasp by sliding sideways and down onto Izzie's lap. As Clara's weight plunked down on her, Izzie grunted. But then the wall of Clara's body was a reassuring buffer between her and the séance and she slid her arms around her sister's waist.

Head jerking about, mouth hanging open, Anna's eyes rolled wildly. Clara swung her heel into Izzie's ankle.

"Ouch."

Mrs. Fielding darted a scolding look their way. "Don't worry. Anna will not hurt herself." She looked back at the man. "It appears your son's spirit has taken possession of her, Mr. Gaylord."

Anna struck her hand brutally in a great swat against the table. That must have smarted, thought Izzie, possession or no possession. Anna's lips fluttered but she did not speak. Clara shivered against Izzie. Tightening her grip around Clara's waist, Izzie looked over at Papa. Thoroughly amused, he was smirking and quietly pummeling his thigh. Clara was terrified and Papa was thrilled. *Rot.* This medium venture was dreadful rubbish.

Suddenly, Anna's voice broke out high and clear. She sang:

Heaven is a bright land,
Spirits are rejoicing,
There are wings for all
Who shout their love.

Weep not, father dear,
My song brings you love,
Heaven is a bright land,
Spirits are rejoicing.

Anna huffed, wiped her brow, then stood limp, her head hanging down. An elderly woman in a blue paisley shawl whispered to the man next to her, "She sounds like Jenny

Lind, the Swedish nightingale." The man shifted in his chair and looked at Anna with concern.

Either because Clara was soothed by the song or frozen with fear, she had actually stopped quivering and was still.

"Are you with my mother and father, boy?" The man's voice cracked. He was probably crying. If only Izzie could see his face.

Three raps from the table. Yes.

"Will you grow into a man in the spirit world, or stay a boy forever?"

No answer. No raps. Anna stumbled away from the table and fell into a chair by the curtains. She slumped over and appeared to be asleep.

"I doubt we will hear anything else through Anna tonight. She is depleted. It's very exhausting being possessed, even for a moment." Mrs. Fielding turned toward the elderly woman wearing spectacles and the blue shawl. "I sense a tug in my chest toward you, Mrs. Tracey. I believe a spirit wishes to speak to you. Would you like to ask for a communication, my dear?"

The old woman straightened up, pursed her thin lips, and spread her fingers out on the table. She looked toward the ceiling, then closed her eyes.

"Is there a spirit here who wishes to communicate with me?"

No sounds.

"Try again. Take a deep breath. Everyone, drain your minds of thought."

"Is there…?"

Three raps.

"Is that you, Timothy?"

One rap.

Mrs. Fielding reached toward a large piece of paper that had been sitting on the table near her and positioned it squarely before her. It had writing on it, but Izzie could not make it out from her vantage. Papa leaned across Clara's empty chair and put his whiskey-smelling face near Izzie's ear.

"It's the alphabet," he said.

Mrs. Fielding pointed to one letter after another, her finger hovering a few inches in the air above the paper. Suddenly, the table knocked three times.

"S." Mrs. Fielding's voice sounded even and breathy. She went on with the pointing and rapping until the word "sister" had been spelled.

"Oh, my." Her jaw dropping, the elderly woman shifted in her seat.

"Don't say anything more. Write the name of your sister on one of the small pieces of paper in front of you as well as four other names on four separate pieces. Then we will see if she is truly your sister."

The woman dipped a pen into a glass inkbottle and wrote, one after another, on five pieces of paper. Mrs. Fielding and the other sitters watched intently. Anna had risen quietly from her stupor and was standing again. Turning her face toward the table to give the appearance of looking at the old woman, Izzie cast her eyes to the side to study Anna.

From her position, Anna could definitely see the papers the woman in blue was writing on and, although Anna had to be too far away to read them, she could at least identify which paper had been written on first.

"Now mix them up and hold one up at a time so only you can see it," Mrs. Fielding said.

She lifted up the first paper. Silence. The second. Silence. On the third paper, Anna crossed her arms over her waist.

Three raps from the table. Was the arm crossing a signal to someone?

"Yes. That's right. My sister is Susan." The woman looked at Mrs. Fielding, then at the paper to verify again, then closed her eyes. "Is Timothy with you my dear?"

Three raps.

"Are you—" Before her question was finished, Mrs. Fielding's right arm started to fly about spasmodically over the table, apparently with a will of its own. Using her other hand to control the flying one, she picked up a pen. She wrote rapidly, reading along in a croaky voice.

Do not be afraid. Do not be lonely, sister. Stay out of the kitchen. There is no danger around you, only sweetness. Many of us wait for you over here.

Susan

Mrs. Fielding's arms flapped like restless bird wings before finally coming to rest. All were hushed for some time while the old woman cried and Mrs. Fielding composed herself.

"My sister and I always fought about who was going to cook. She hated my cooking. Do you think that's what she means about the kitchen?" Her chest caved and she drew a handkerchief from her lap and held it over her mouth.

Mrs. Fielding nodded. "I haven't had a spirit possess me for writing in a long time. Your sister was insistent."

"Susan." A woman's warbly voice spoke.

Izzie glanced at the faces around the table. No one moved.

"Which one said that?" Izzie whispered into Clara's ear.

"What?" Clara lifted her face up a bit and breathed in.

"Susan. Which one said Susan?"

"No one."

"Yes. Someone said Susan."

Clara shook her head. Izzie would ask Papa later. Surely he heard it.

Five

A FEW DAYS AFTER OBSERVING THE SPIRIT CIRCLE, Clara sat quietly at the dining table at the boardinghouse with Izzie and Euphora, Mrs. Purcell, and the two spinster boarders Mary and Jane Carter. They were waiting for supper to begin, but were delaying because Billy and Papa weren't there. Mrs. Purcell, who always sat at the head of the table nearest the kitchen, glanced at Billy's and Papa's empty seats. Clara was sure her twin was out with some chums getting into trouble and Papa, even though he was skunk drunk when he told her, said he was going traveling on business.

Mrs. Purcell frowned at Mamma's empty seat for a lickety split and it made Clara picture Mamma there for a moment. She felt a pinch in her heart.

Untying her apron behind her back and removing it, Emma Purcell glared at Izzie. "I've got a substantial amount of food here. I made two apple pies. I wish you or your father would tell me when he and Billy won't be here for a meal." Her voice shook a little. Mrs. Purcell was going to find out sooner or later that Papa liked to wander off, and since Mamma died, his liquorizing was getting much worse.

Since the night of the checkers game Papa was drunk many more times, and each time, Billy had to fly out and stay out in the cold. On top of that, it looked like Papa was returning to his old ways, staying gone for a night or two or three. Things were unquestionably on a downhill slide around here, Clara thought. What if they got booted out of the boardinghouse? Then what?

Everyone's head turned toward Izzie standing near her chair. It was dandy not to be the oldest. If Papa wasn't around, Izzie always had to answer the questions and make the decisions.

"Papa left town this morning to look into a business arrangement."

Izzie was good at being the oldest. She had that sure-as-rain tone and knew not to mention certain things, such as Billy and two other boys being chased from the back door of a saloon yesterday by the sheriff for some betting scheme they had going on with the men inside.

"What about Billy?"

"I'm not sure. I apologize for both of them, Mrs. Purcell. Your meals are wonderful. I think we are the luckiest family in the world to be staying with you."

Mrs. Purcell's face relaxed.

"Well, it's just red flannel hash. We can have it again tomorrow."

The two silver-haired Carter spinsters leaned their foreheads together and said something to each other with their nods and eyes. They were always doing that. Clara still didn't know which one was Mary Carter and which one was Jane Carter. She had simply started calling them both Mary Jane to herself and if she asked them something she'd say, "Miss Carter" and one or the other would answer.

Mrs. Purcell left the table, put her apron on the hook on the back of the kitchen door, and came back to sit in her chair. She had a nice grandmotherly shape—a bit plump, like she'd made ten thousand apple pies over the years and had a good part in eating them. She picked up a large white bowl heaping with sauerkraut and passed it to the Miss Carter on her right.

"Euphora, I've spoken to your father. You are going to help me with the cooking from now on. I'll teach you how to cook and you'll assist me with whatever needs to be done in the kitchen."

Red hair down her shoulders, nose pinched, Euphora blinked several times, then looked at Izzie who nodded in agreement.

Euphora gave her freckle-faced grin. "Thank you, ma'am."

"Well, you're eleven and that's quite old enough to learn. You gain something from it. I gain as well, a fair exchange. I'll teach you to be a domestic. You'll have a skill."

Then Izzie, who for some darn reason still wasn't sitting yet, stepped away from her usual seat, placed a hand on the top rung of Papa's vacant chair at the end of the oval table, and Holy rolling Moses, she sat down erect and broad-shouldered like it was her own place. Clara clenched her teeth. What had come over Izzie? She was acting like the Queen of Geneva.

"Dear, how long will your father be away?" One of the Mary Janes raised her silver gray brow, then squinted at Clara.

"He always comes back," Clara said, "even if he takes a while."

Clara looked past the Mary Janes to the windows and lace curtains to the winter night behind them. Not always. He didn't come back last summer after his gristmill burned to the ground. Looking down at the bits of potato, red beet, and stringy meat piled high in a discombobberated mound, Clara felt her hunger dwindle.

That's why they were here in this house with these spinsters and Mrs. Purcell. That's why they had to travel from Homer for an entire month with that rickety old horse and that creaky buckboard wagon in the pouring rain. She shivered as she recalled the chilling downpour soaking her like a piece of laundry in a tub. Papa would have come back to them in Homer if they'd given him half a chance. They left Ohio too soon. Mamma was too impatient. He would have come back. He didn't truly run away. It was all the confusion about his gristmill and the insurance and his partners.

"He'll return soon then, won't he?" The Mary Janes both smiled. The one who spoke had a small black mole on the side of her chin with a few spunky white hairs growing out of it. She decided this one was Mary. The mole would be her marker. Mary mole. She could remember that.

Izzie was pushing the hash around her plate in that polite way she had, but she probably wasn't hungry either, thought Clara. Izzie never cared about Papa being gone, so it had to be that she was missing Mamma. Clara took a bite of her hash. It was warm and soft in her mouth, but she didn't want to swallow it. She chewed it for so long that it became thick like glue. She had no choice. She gulped it down.

"I find it interesting that a man, who doesn't allow his daughters to go to school because he thinks it is worthless for girls to spend their time with books and doesn't allow a son to go either, because a boy's place is work, would pay money to give his daughters special Spiritualism lessons." Mrs. Purcell shot the spinsters a look, as if Papa not letting them go to school had been talked about in private, maybe more than once. "Clara, why don't you tell us about the lessons you two had this week with that famous medium?"

The Mary Janes nodded and chimed, "Yes. Yes. Did you levitate anyone?"

Suddenly, all eyes turned toward Clara. She took a deep breath and sat up.

"We had four lessons. Then Mrs. Fielding and her assistant, Anna, had to go to Rochester. They're on a tour of nine cities and towns. In the first lesson, Mrs. Fielding explained the usual ways spirits communicate." Clara enjoyed the way the large word rolled off her tongue. "They speak through things around us. They tip tables, ring bells, rattle things, or rap or knock on something hard." Clara knocked on the table for effect.

One of the Mary Janes chuckled and drew a hand over her mouth. Clara took a bite of hash and swallowed it quickly.

"Could they tip this big table?" Euphora asked.

"Maybe. It depends. Mrs. Fielding said when mediums are just beginning to develop their skills they sometimes have to fix things to happen in case the spirits aren't able to perform as hoped. Even if they are advanced, sometimes tipping things just doesn't go right."

"Clara, we swore not to speak of the mechanics," Izzie said.

Double rot. That was right. She'd forgotten.

"Isn't it all a hoax?" Mrs. Purcell asked.

"No, it's not. Mrs. Fielding said you just can't overdo the effects because it hurts the reputations of all Spiritualists everywhere. She said one has to be reasonable, that's all."

"That's enough about it, Clara. We promised," Izzie said.

"Mrs. Fielding says it's only a hoax if they go too far like The Davenport Brothers." Everyone was watching Clara, not Izzie. Izzie was pure sour grapes tonight. "The Davenports make fiddles, guitars, and banjos fly about the room and the instruments play music by themselves." Clara danced her hands in the air. "Mrs. Fielding says they're downright liars and hoaxes. One day they'll be found out and it will be bad for true mediums like her and Anna."

"How do they make the instruments fly?" Euphora asked.

"They darken the room and use special lightweight ropes and pulleys. Helpers hide in the room and operate everything."

"Do you think Mrs. Fielding and Anna are true mediums, Isabelle?" No-mole Jane asked.

"I don't know what a true medium is exactly," Izzie said.

Then Izzie got the grumps all over her face and started stirring her food around again. She didn't want anyone asking her anything. That was darn sure.

"The next lesson we learned how the spirits speak through letters and words. Anna showed us something from Paris called a planchette. It's shaped like a heart, has a pencil sticking out of it, and little tiny wheels on the bottom. If a medium touches it properly, it writes on a paper beneath it." Clara demonstrated with fingers suspended gently over an imaginary planchette. "I hope we can get one. Mrs. Fielding says it is hard to get them. But, you don't have to have one. You can use an alphabet and just let your hand drift over the letters until the spirit tells your hand to stop."

Clara could feel how curious everyone was. The more she spoke, the more excited she got remembering Mrs. Fielding's words and demonstrations. She glanced at Izzie to see if she was going to rile, but Izzie was staring at her hash and seemed to be off in her own sad thoughts.

Clara stood up next to her chair, sliding Billy's empty seat away so she had room.

"There's deep trance and light trance. In a deep trance, a spirit can take over the medium altogether and speak with her voice." Clara closed her eyes. "I am here to visit my great great granddaughter, Euphora." Clara opened her eyes half way to see Euphora laughing hard, then opened them all the way and laughed along with the ladies. Izzie still had the grumps and was now scowling at her. "But I don't think I'd like that to really happen to me. And in a light trance, it's more like you are listening to the spirit and reporting back what they say."

She fully closed her eyes again. "Euphora, your great great grandmother is here. She says "hello" and something else…" Cocking her head and pretending to listen, Clara waited a moment. Everyone was silent. "She says you will travel the world."

The Mary Janes applauded.

"Anna Santini can do both kinds of trance. Izzie asked her if she ever worried about being insane. But Anna just gave Izzie a kiss and told her hearing spirits was absolutely the most wonderful gift a person could be blessed with. She said, 'Izzie, never for one minute in my entire life have I worried about sickness of the mind. My purpose on this earth is to help people reunite with their loved ones.' "

"Clara. That's enough," Izzie said.

Izzie looked strange, like she was about to vomit or freeze to death. She rose and excused herself politely, saying she was not feeling her best. As she turned to leave the table, she took one last look at Mamma's chair then left with a rain cloud over her head that Clara could almost see.

"And was there more?" Mary mole asked.

Trying to ignore Izzie and her rain cloud, Clara went on describing the third and fourth lessons, how she and Izzie could become true mediums, how they'd behave with the seekers, how they could go into trance by draining their minds and breathing deeply. While people finished eating, she told everyone how to organize seekers in circles using the principles of electricity with men positive and women negative, how to use trances for large audiences, and how to help just one person at a time, and finally, how some mediums could look inside a person's body and actually see their ailments.

She'd been standing and talking for a long time and no one had budged or spoken or even looked away from her. They weren't even eating their hash. So she went on.

"During the final lesson, Mrs. Fielding did nothing but talk for two hours without stopping. I thought she was practicing for her lecture in Rochester. She strode about the room." Clara began to march around the table, imitating Mrs. Fielding and trying to make her voice vibrate. "Spiritualism is the only religious sect in the world that recognizes women as the equal of men. Mediums communicate the divine truth because they can hear what the spirits say to them." She stopped behind the Mary Janes. "Every time Mrs. Fielding said 'divine truth' her voice quivered like that. Divine Truth." She continued around toward Mrs. Purcell. "Spiritualism itself is proof of the immortality of the soul and because the proof is spreading far and wide," Clara shot her arms straight up, "...the entire world is on the cusp of a new era."

Clara returned to her seat and tried one more time to make her voice quiver like Mrs. Fielding's. "Divine Truth!"

She bowed. Everyone was smiling like sunrises at her.

"After the lecture, Mrs. Fielding gave Izzie a journal called *The Spiritual Telegraph* and told her to subscribe to it when we made enough money and Izzie said, 'Even if we believed in Spiritualism, wouldn't Clara and I be just like the Davenport Brothers if we practiced being mediums but had no gift?' " Clara pretended to be Mrs. Fielding again. "'Not if your gift is forthcoming, my dear, and you are preparing for that day.'"

"Mrs. Fielding told Izzie she could come to New York City and observe their circles and maybe even go on a tour with them someday. They didn't offer all that to me."

"But you said they thought you might both be true mediums didn't they?" Mary Mole asked.

"Mrs. Fielding said if I used my intuition, I would be able to more or less know what the spirits *might* say rather than actually hear them say things. She said I would be good at that." Clara grinned. "Like a gifted actress."

"Yes, I believe she was right about that," Mrs. Purcell said. "Would anyone like apple pie?"

Six

CLARA POINTED AT THE HATS in the milliner's window. "This is the place. Papa said upstairs, above the hat shop."

A black flat-rimmed bonnet with a large bow the color of over-ripe cherries held Clara's attention. Then she glanced at the others—the blue silks, the red velvets, the shining delicate brown feathers. There were twelve in all. She longed to go inside and try every blessed one of them on.

"Come on, Clara. Papa is waiting for us. I'm freezing." Arms tucked under her plaid shawl, Izzie had gone ahead to the stairwell door and was leaning against it, holding it open.

They climbed the dim stairway to the first floor landing. What on earth did Papa have to show them? Clara wondered. While Izzie knocked, Clara rose up and down on her toes. She felt like a kettle about to boil over. On the way here this afternoon, Izzie had told her she was afraid Papa was up to no good and he'd spent even more borrowed money on some surprise. "He'll get us all in trouble," Izzie had said. She might be right, but maybe not. She never gave Papa a fair shake. If only Izzie and Papa could get along, everything would be more cheerful.

The door opened and there he was, standing tall and smiling like he had just caught the biggest trout in Seneca

Lake. His coat was brushed off and tidy, his spectacles wiped clear of smudges, and his sideburns trimmed neat. He looked like he did the day his gristmill had opened for business in Homer. He and his friends had celebrated by drinking ale inside and outside the mill building all day long. He got so tipsy and silly that Mamma finally came and dragged him home to bed. Before he finally went to sleep, he sang to her for an entire splendiferous hour.

"Come in, my two peaches."

Stepping away from the door, Papa swung his hand out into the room and bowed, welcoming her and Izzie like they were two princesses coming to court. Two peaches. Bowing like that. He had something big in mind, all right.

The winter sun spilled brilliantly in through three tall, narrow windows on one wall. The room was longer than wide, smelled a little smoky, and was warmed by a fire blazing in a hearth opposite the door. The wood of the mantel was fancy, carved with ribbons, bows, and bunches of grapes. There wasn't any furniture at all except for the empty ceiling-high bookcases along the walls to their right.

But what was the surprise? There was nothing here except cleaned-up Papa, and a fire. She looked at Izzie to see if her sister understood what Papa was up to, but Izzie was like an iceberg stuck at the door. She hadn't even stepped inside yet.

An odd smirk on his face, Papa watched them carefully. Suddenly he strutted across the room and leaned on the fireplace mantel, stretching an arm along the top. He held still for a long moment, like he was posing for an ambrotype. Tarnation, what was it?

"Well, girls." He swept his arm around. "This is where you'll become famous mediums. This is where the spirits will come and visit all those who enter. It's your very own place. We'll call it the Spirit Room."

"Just for us, Papa?" Clara spun around. "Izzie, we're going to be famous mediums!"

But Izzie, still the iceberg, wouldn't budge.

"Where did you get the money for this, Papa?" Izzie asked.

"None of your business. You ought to be proud I'm backin' you, givin' you a real chance to do somethin' with yourself besides marryin' the first thing in trousers that asks."

Clara cringed. That did it. They were both going to rile now and, just like night comes after day, a yelling fit was about to explode. Clara turned her back to them and walked toward the windows. She'd wait it out over there where she could see the comings and goings below on Seneca Street. But before Clara even got half way to the window, the door slammed.

She swiveled around. Izzie was gone. Papa stood still, his mouth hanging open a little. He kept his pose at the mantel, almost like Izzie had never been there at all nor said anything at all. He stayed like that a moment, then, shoving his hands into his black frock coat pockets, he rambled across the bare floor to her. "Your sister will come around. I'll bet my boots on it." Breaking into his Papa grin, crooked teeth showing, pewter-gray eyes clear, big ears rising up, he pointed back toward the fireplace. "Come back over here, Little Plum. Let me tell you what I have in mind."

A FEW DAYS LATER, Clara sat with Izzie and Euphora at their pine table in the Blue Room. After Clara had finished the fifty shirts, she got a new tall stack of seamstress work from the tailor. They were going to be sewing for at least a week, attaching petticoats to chemise tops and ruffles to the bottoms of pantalettes. When they left Ohio, Mamma decided to leave their spinning wheel behind. She said, "My girls, the days of spinning flax are coming to an end. That's the future. But the days of sewing will never end. Women like us will sew until we're too old and too tired to lift another needle, but then our daughters will sew and when they are too tired, their daughters will and on and on."

Clara was already tired of jamming the needle over and under, over and under, over and under. Fifty-one ruffles done. Sixty-one still to go.

Papa burst into the Blue Room. "I need Clara down at the Spirit Room. Billy's already there. Isabelle and Euphora, you keep at the sewin'."

Flying out the door behind Papa, Clara felt like a parakeet let out of its cage. When they got to the Spirit Room, which was a short walk from their boardinghouse, Papa took a few items from the bookcase. Gray eyes twinkling behind his spectacles, he presented them to Clara.

"Billy and I are goin' to work on some mechanical things. This is what you'll need to make the alphabet sheet like Mrs. Fielding had."

He handed her a small stack of folded papers with a few inkbottles and metal tip pens sitting tentatively on top.

"There's some handbills the letterpress man gave me that you can trace over to make the letters look nice. Can you put them in an arc like Mrs. Fielding did?" He drew a curve in the air.

Splendiferous, thought Clara. This was much better than sewing. She smiled and nodded at him, then looked around at the vacant room. Hands in trouser pockets, Billy was stomping with his boots lightly on different spots on the wood floor, like a square dancer, but slower. She carried her materials near the center window, settled herself on the dusty floor in a warm patch of sunlight, and began to unfold the papers.

Papa wandered about the room, tapping on the blue and green striped wallpaper, speaking loudly, then softly, saying, "Hallo there spirits," and "Dead people, come here." Clara laughed. He said he was "scrutinizin'" the way his voice resonated. Then he got on his knees and pounded with his fist on a few of the floorboards.

Suddenly he shot up like a firework and started rattling off instructions to Billy. Go down to the waterfront. Get this. Get that. When Papa had finished giving orders, Billy raced back and forth from the Spirit Room to the foundry, the carriage maker, the cabinetmaker, the blacksmith, and even the shipwright, and each time he returned with an assortment of things—pliers, a drill, iron rods, hinges, levers, screws, and other odds and ends, mostly metal.

Papa was going to rig up a secret knocker. He wanted the sound to come from some place in the room far enough away from where the table would be that people wouldn't think about the rap noise being made by her or Izzie. So he came up with the idea of removing a floor plank and running a long pole out of sight underneath.

He stood near the imagined table. "You or Isabelle will sit here. You'll step on a pedal under the rug." He stomped his foot down onto the floor. "The pedal will be hooked to a long rod by a hinge and a spring. It'll have extra punch, like the trigger on my old Colt Walker." He held up his hand up, finger pointing, thumb flexing, like a pistol. "Bang. The metal plate on the far end of the rod will hit the floor joist way over there." Smiling like he just shot a wild turkey, he blew at the tip of his finger, then pointed toward the three windows. It was surely the cleverest thing Papa had ever come up with.

Papa was full of sunshine those few days of fixing up the Spirit Room, not drinking at all as far as she could tell, and singing and whistling like the old days while he cooked up his ideas and tried them out. When he found out that Mrs. Beattie, the milliner landlady from downstairs, had some extra wallpaper, he dug a small hole about shoulder height in the wall near the back of the room and then carved out a skinny tunnel from the hole straight down to the floor. He installed a sweet little bell in the hole, hooked it to a black cord, and ran the cord down the tunnel and then under several floorboards. It ended up at the very spot where he said he would stand during séances. He tied it to his boot, crossed his arms, and just moved his foot a little. Then, ring, ring, ring.

"The spirits're chimin' away like boys in a choir," Papa said.

Then he pasted a fresh strip of the green and blue striped wallpaper over the damage he'd done to the wall. He and Billy swept up some dust and blew it off the palms of their hands and made it look just as dirty as the rest of the wall.

Every time something went right like the bell, he'd grin and slap Billy on the shoulder. Then, every time something didn't fit right or do what he wanted, he'd blame Billy somehow and cuss at him.

Papa'd say, "You got the wrong damn one," or "I told you the smallest," or "Why ain't you smart like your sisters?" Pulling back her pen from the alphabet paper, Clara clenched her teeth each and every time, waiting for something awful. But just when Billy looked like he was about to yell something back or throw a tool on the floor or maybe stomp out, Papa would break out his grin again and say, "Come on then, my Billy boy, we'll get it right."

It was a good thing Papa didn't kick up too much of a stink, because Billy had been different since they'd come to Geneva. He wasn't as likely to cast his brown eyes down and wait for Papa's storms to pass over him, unless of course Papa was pickled, then he just skedaddled. But now, if Papa wasn't liquorized, Billy'd raise up his face and look right into Papa's eyes and stare at him.

Mamma always said, "A father and son have to work out between them whether the father is going to let the son be a man and sometimes it ain't easy."

Between Billy, who must have finished with being a boy on the road between Homer and Geneva, and Izzie, who had her own mind about just about everything, there weren't too many quiet times when Papa was around.

Clara slowed her hand as she darkened a letter. She wanted it to be perfect and handsome. And besides that, she didn't want to go back to the sewing. Those few days of getting the Spirit Room ready were like summertime in the middle of winter. Even though Izzie wasn't there, the famous Benton Sisters were being born. A new beginning for all of them. It was just what Papa needed. As soon as Izzie saw how clever the secret knocker was, she'd come around. Papa was right about that. Papa was mostly right about everything. Except Billy, anyway.

WHEN THE SPIRIT ROOM was finally fixed up for their circles, Clara showed it to Izzie. Papa had told her it was her mission to get Izzie to agree to go ahead as the Benton Sisters, talented mediums. He could make Izzie do it, he'd said, but if Izzie was too ornery she wouldn't be a charming medium and charming was important. He said that the medium business was the only way he could figure to make money for now and she and Izzie had to do it. Clara had to convince her sister to go along.

After Clara gave Izzie a demonstration of Papa's floor knocker and the secret bell and showed off her alphabet, she stood with Izzie at the window looking down onto Seneca Street. It was bustling with walkers, horses, wagons and carriages. Except for a patch here and there, snow and ice had melted in the recent warm spell. Fidgeting with a dirty red and white checkered hair ribbon that she held in her hands, Clara leaned against the wall facing Izzie. The wind blew against the window, forcing cold air in.

"We have to work anyway, Iz. Papa has no income. We can do more seamstress work or be chambermaids or maybe shoe binders, but we would have so much more fun and money doing the spirit circles. What are we going to do if not this?"

Izzie was quiet a moment then looked at Clara. "But what if I start hearing voices like Mamma? I heard someone say the name Susan that evening at Mrs. Fielding's séance. I heard it clearly, but you didn't and Papa didn't. What if that was the beginning of being like Mamma? Maybe insane. Loony. Wouldn't it be better to do something dull and necessary, something honest?

And what if we both could do better than being seamstresses? I could get a governess position with one of the families on Main Street or even up in Rochester or Albany." Izzie gazed out the window. "Back in Homer, you know my friend Julianna's family educated me beyond what any girl's seminary could have. I know I could find a governess position. I should at least try. The hoax shenanigans might turn real for me and make me like Mamma."

Down on the street, everyone heading into the wind had a hand on their hat and was bent forward. Everyone going the other way was bent back.

"Izzie, you're nothing like Mamma. You're smart and strong and can do whatever you want to. You'll never buckle to anything. That's the way you are. I don't want to be a seamstress either. Never ever. I want to be an actress and maybe travel the world."

Izzie chuckled and looked at her. "You have a lot of growing up to do. If that's what you want, you better marry above your station then, Clara, and I don't mean a little above. I mean quite well above."

"Why don't you find a wealthy, smart gentleman and I'll marry his brother?" Clara laughed and slid closer. "There!" She pointed outside. "What about those two?" A bearded man wearing a fine greatcoat and holding a stovepipe hat and cane climbed into a plum-colored runabout hitched to two dapple, gray horses. He leaned over the side of his carriage and spoke to another man on the walk who was also well dressed in a fitted black coat.

"You saw them first. Go ahead, Clara. Which one?"

Clara shook her head and twisted the ribbon around her finger. "Not yet."

Izzie looked down. "I'm afraid of that spiritual world. Why did Anna Santini say those things about me?"

"Are you sure you don't have a gift for spirits?"

"I don't. I don't."

"Well then, see, you don't have to worry about being like Mamma or Anna. Besides, we won't have to always be mediums. Just for a while. If we're good at it, we can make money like Mrs. Fielding and travel to different cities. The Benton Sisters of Geneva. That sounds just as good as the Fox sisters of Hyde Park. You won't be like Mamma, Izzie. You won't."

But Clara knew there was something for Izzie to be at least a little afraid of. Izzie sometimes did know things in a mysterious way and Mamma used to tease her when she was little and tell her she would have spirits visit her when she got older.

Clara wrapped the hair ribbon she had been playing with around Izzie's wrist and tied it with a bow.

"Izzie, I'm afraid. I'm afraid Papa will leave us again if we don't make some money right away. Please, Izzie, for me?"

Izzie looked at her a long moment, then sighed. "Only for you, Clara. Not for Papa, not for Mrs. Fielding, not for Andrew Jackson Davis and his Harmonial Philosophy." She looked into Clara's eyes. "If I don't like it, I'll quit, Clara. I don't care what Papa says. I'll defy him. I'll leave. I'll do whatever is necessary to end it if I hate it. I'll be a governess."

Clara bounced up and down on her toes. "Oh, Izzie, you'll see. Being mediums will be thundering fun, much better than being a governess."

"I swear, Clara, you could charm a fish out of a stream. You'll certainly be a better medium than a seamstress. You'd be wasting yourself with a needle and thread. Maybe those pompous people who say that reading novels is bad for girls are right. Once we girls have visions of the world outside the home, we're unwilling to stay put and happily perform our domestic duties." Izzie gently untied the red and white ribbon, wrapped it around Clara's wrist and tied it again. "We can't go back. We've already read too many books. Julianna taught me to read. I taught you and Euphora to read. We're corrupted."

The plum runabout was on the move and caught Clara's eye. Slapping his reins on the backs of his gray horses, the fancy man's carriage began to climb Seneca Street. Clara waved at it.

"Goodbye. We don't need you now. We're the famous Benton Sisters," she said and then she extended her hand to Izzie and they shook like gentlemen partners.

Izzie pushed up her dress sleeves. "This place is foul with dust. Let's clean it up."

Seven

CLARA WAS READY FOR THEIR FIRST SPIRIT CIRCLE. This was the most excited she had ever been in her entire life. As Papa drew the new muslin curtains across their three windows, she took her place opposite Izzie at one end of the heavy oak table in the center of the Spirit Room. The room was cozy, lit by a fire in the hearth, the dull glow from gas street lamps filtering in, the candle near Izzie, and two oil lamps on the mantel. Also on the mantel was the small mahogany clock that Clara had found left behind by the previous tenant of the room. It was broken, stuck at eleven o'clock. Dead silent, it added something mysterious to the Spirit Room so they kept it. Izzie's face was buried from sight behind her small notebook. She was going over what she wrote down the night before, things Papa told her.

Papa's friends were coming any minute. The spirit circle was going to be a rehearsal, the way actors do in the theater. A "dress rehearsal" Papa had called it.

"You girls have to practice what you learned from Mrs. Fielding before we can charge money," he told them.

From Papa, she and Izzie now knew something about each of the men coming. He kept her and Izzie up half the night telling them personal things about the men, then making them repeat it back. Sam Weston was a canal contractor. Herbert Washburn owned three canal boats all himself, and John Payne was a barkeeper at Ramsey's, Papa's favorite saloon. Washburn and Payne were both married but Payne's wife died several years ago.

Papa said that Payne being a widower was significant, and she and Izzie should look to fit the dead wife into their trances. Weston never married, but was engaged once. The woman went off with someone else at the last minute before the wedding. Papa had lots more about brothers and sisters and where they grew up, things like that, pieces of a life puzzle.

When Papa and Izzie worked out the plan for the séance, they had decided that Izzie was going to imitate a serious deep trance. She was the oldest, not to mention smartest, but Clara could try out a light trance or a little song about heaven if she felt inclined.

While Papa paced up and down in front of the fireplace, Izzie shuffled and shuffled through the pages of her notebook. What on earth was she looking for?

Trying to get rid of the twitters in her stomach, Clara sighed noisily. She decided to remember the most important things that Mrs. Fielding had taught them. The very most significant thing of all was making people think their loved ones on the other side, in Summerland, were happy as could be. That's exactly how she said it. The spirits were spirits, not human, not suffering at all. These spirits loved their dear ones left behind and were looking forward to the day when their earthbound family members and friends died and came over to Summerland, although she and Izzie weren't supposed to say outright that the spirits were eager for the loved ones to die. *Lawky Lawk*, so much to remember, thought Clara. She stared up at the fine cracks in the ceiling.

"Happy as could be. The departed ones are happy as could be." Whispering out loud, she churned the rule over in her mind so that nothing could make her forget it. Grabbing the seat of her ladder-back chair, she pulled as close to the table as she could, pressing her chest against the weight of it.

Three loud knocks rattled the door. Clara flinched. Papa stopped pacing and stared at the door. With a smart little slap, Izzie shut her notebook, slipped it into her dress pocket, and then winked at her.

Clara took a deep breath and nodded. In the candlelight, Izzie looked calm and ready for something new. If anything went wrong with the three men, if they got angry or sad, Izzie would steer things the right way. And Papa would be nearby, too. Clara exhaled and put her moist palms on the bare table.

"Here we go, my young mediums." Papa tugged down on each of his jacket sleeves. He glanced at Izzie and Clara, grinned, and strode to the door. Clara bit down on her lower lip so that the fluttery feeling in her stomach might not turn into laughter.

Papa opened the door and the three men entered bringing in a cold draft with them. The men greeted Papa as Ol' Frank and laughed about something that had happened on the way to the Spirit Room. They hushed down lickety-click though, when they looked over at her and Izzie standing in their good dresses near the table.

"These are my talented daughters, Isabelle and Clara." Papa stepped toward the table and the men followed.

He placed a hand on the shoulder of the man next to him. "This is Sam Weston."

Clara could hear Papa's instructions in her head. Notice everything you can about every customer. Try to understand them by the things they say, the way they look and dress, the way they move around, and even what their posture is like. It would all come in handy. So, when Weston took off his hat and while Papa was introducing him, Clara noticed that his slicked-down hair had far too much pomade in it. Even from where she stood, several feet from Weston, his hair smelled like over-ripe apples. He was the one whose fiancée had run off. He looked older than thirty years, though, his eyes hollow and tired with dark circles below and the skin on his face sagged like the gravity in his world had more pull on him than other people's gravity did.

He dressed fancy for being in Geneva. His clothing was like the pictures in those magazines Mrs. Beattie, the milliner, had downstairs. His coat was the prettiest brown color and had a thick, soft look to it. It fit him to perfection.

"This feller is John Payne." Papa, gripping his lapel like a statesman, pointed at the man in the middle of the three.

This one was the widower, Mr. Payne. Payne beamed like he just won a bet. He was short, but his neck was thick and his shoulders were wide as a wagon and he looked strong enough to pull one if he had to. The top of his right ear was gone. Darn sure there was a story to that, but Papa hadn't mentioned the ear. Mr. Payne's eyes were blue and his hair light blond like a Norwegian's, but Papa never said anything about Norwegian either.

"And this last feller is Herbert Washburn." Now with both hands on his lapels, Papa indicated Washburn by nodding at him.

"Miss Isabelle, Miss Clara, a pleasure," Washburn said.

This one was polite, but he wore no smile. He was the married one with the boats. He was the plainest of the three, plain clothes, plain hair, plain eyes. Was there anything about him to notice? Clara stared hard at him, but then all of a sudden Izzie stepped a little away from her chair.

"Good evening, gentlemen. Thank you for coming to our very first spirit circle. Will you sit with us, please?"

Holy rolling Moses. Izzie never spoke like that. It was Mrs. Purcell, Mrs. Fielding, Anna and that Jane Austen all in one.

Washburn walked by Clara. He smelled like steaming vegetables, maybe beets. That was the best she could do for now. He went straight for the chair by the fire. Was he cold? Weston and Payne took the places opposite him, with Weston next to Clara and Payne, the little Norwegian, closest to Izzie. Even from two seats away, Payne smelled like his saloon—cigar smoke and ale. Papa smelled just like that many a night.

The men stood a moment looking back and forth between Izzie and her. Finally Mr. Washburn went over and put a hand on the top of Izzie's ladder-back chair. Izzie smiled at him and sat down. He was treating Izzie like a lady. *Lawky Lawky Lawk*. Before Clara could take her seat, Weston grinned and imitated Washburn's courtesy by shifting Clara's chair for her. Clara bit her lower lip, but a giggle slipped out anyway. Finally everyone was sitting at the table. Except Papa, of course.

That was planned ahead. He walked over to his shadowy corner near the tie up for the secret bell and folded his arms across his chest. Although he said he was itchin' to test the bell in the wall and for Clara to try out the new knocking device in the floor, he had said they weren't going to do anything tricky this time. They were to work on the alphabet.

Izzie reached for Clara's handmade alphabet sheet in the middle of the table and drew it toward her. It was nothing to be sneezed at, that alphabet sheet. Hardly a drop of ink in the wrong place and the curve of the letters only a little lopsided.

"You ready to be hounded by your ghosts, Washburn?" Sniggering, the little Norwegian, Payne, slapped a square hand on the middle of the table.

"What about yours, Payne? I'm sure they'll come and collect moral taxes of some kind from you." Washburn seemed almost angry, like they'd been having a bull and cow before, but Weston laughed and looked over at Izzie.

"Tell us what to do. I promise they'll behave."

"Well, the first thing is, we all put our hands out on the table and spread them out so that our little fingers are touching." She put her hands on the table to show them. "This lets the magnetism that's naturally in us connect with one another and gives us enough strength to draw in the spirits. It would be better if we had equal males and females, but I think we are close enough with three and two."

Lawk-a-mercy. Izzie sounded like she had done this a thousand times. The men placed their hands as they were told and Clara, spreading her much smaller hands out, touched fingers with Weston and Washburn. Her heart kicked up with excitement. These men needed to understand she was a medium in training too, not just the young sister of Izzie.

"Yes, I think three and two will be fine. Equal men and women is because equal positive and negative works best." Clara glanced at each man, and then looked at her sister. "I'm ready, Izzie."

But no one looked back at Izzie. Everyone kept looking at Clara with stone faces. They seemed tarnal fixated. Maybe she hadn't explained it correctly. Her stomach was twittering wildly.

Then, Weston burst out laughing and got the others laughing. He looked toward Papa in the corner. "You've been hiding these daughters from us, Ol' Frank. Your Clara is a rare and extraordinary beauty. And Isabelle is charming."

Clara felt a big smile break out on her face and craned her neck to see Papa. He pushed his hand into the air toward Weston, as though shoving him, but didn't say anything.

Then, by making her face as blank as an empty wall, Izzie showed how serious she was and she waited like that, wall-faced, until it was quiet again.

"Now, once the spirits are here, it's not as important to keep the fingers linked just so." Izzie raised both her little fingers in the air and wiggled them like tiny snakes coming up for a look. "Clara and I will have to move about. Everyone close your eyes until one of you wants to ask if there is any spirit here who wants to speak to you. The spirit, if there is one, will use my pointing finger to spell words on this alphabet paper in front of me." Izzie rested her hand on the large sheet a moment, then touched Payne's little finger again, snake nose to snake nose. "Clara will write the letters down and we'll see what it spells as we go."

Taking a huge, deep breath and releasing it, Izzie closed her eyes. Clara did the same, but then Clara tilted her head up and slowly, carefully, slightly raised her eyelids to see if everyone really had their eyes closed. Weston, with too much stinky pomade in his hair, had his eyes half open and was staring right at her. *Double rot.* He was going to ruin the whole thing. Just as Clara was about to say how important it was to be still and concentrate the way Mrs. Fielding had taught them, she heard Papa.

"Weston, come on, now, shut your dang eyes. I told you I'd buy you drinks later."

Everyone opened their eyes and looked over at Weston. He chuckled and apologized. While everyone did as they were told this time, eyes closed, fingers touching, Clara waited impatiently for one of them to ask for a spirit and for Izzie to perform. The fire crackled. Now and then a carriage or a wagon jangled by outside. Then Clara felt Weston raise his pinkie finger and tap it around randomly on hers. That wasn't right.

"Couple a sissies." Payne's voice was gruff and loud. "I'll ask for the spirit. Any spirit here want to talk?"

Well, if there were any spirits coming by, he'd have scared them off with that kind of tone. Weston's finger settled down.

Izzie kept rock still, eyes shut. Finally, oh finally, she got going. She started breathing heavy and rotating her head just so. Clara wanted to burst she was so proud of her sister. She wanted to stand up on her chair and say, "Papa, look! She's just like Mrs. Fielding! Like Anna!" But she didn't. She held her arms stiff, her back straight, and looked down at her paper, pen, and ink, ready to break from the circle and begin writing at the perfect moment.

After a while, Izzie raised her right hand ever so slightly, shook it around in the air, jittery, then let it fall back like a dead bird. Now everyone's eyes were open and watching the show. Izzie did this with her hand, not two or three times, but ten. That was too many. These men were going to want to go get their free drinks if she didn't get on with it. At last, she popped open her eyes and snapped out her pointing finger in a funny jerk and swept it over to the H in one rapid-fire move. Scrambling for her writing tools, Clara dipped the metal tip pen into the inkwell, and wrote the H. She knew the rest already. It was Hilda, Payne's dead wife. She had to wait for Izzie, though.

I-L-. Before Clara even wrote the D, Payne smiled. "Ah, Hilda." Grinning, the Norwegian looked over at Papa. "Frank, a big surprise, it's my wife Hilda here come to talk to me."

Clara stayed with her ink and paper, didn't turn around to see Papa this time.

"You can ask her questions, Mr. Payne." Clara said.

He tapped his fingers on the table. "You all right over there, Hilda?"

Y-E-S, then J-O-H-N.

"You got something to say to me, dearest?"

I-A-M-S-O-R-R-Y. Izzie paused while Clara finished.

"I'm sorry," Weston, leaning toward Clara, read it out. But, that was her job. She'd have to speak up faster.

"What for?" Payne's smile simmered down. Now he watched Clara's paper.

S-T-E-A-L-I-N-G

"Stealing," Clara blurted out before inscribing the G, proud to get it so quickly. But Hilda Payne stealing wasn't anything Papa had told them about. It was supposed to be something like "Sorry for leaving you so early." Izzie was going to get Papa hopping mad for this stealing business. Clara's temples grew moist. Their first try at being mediums and Izzie had to go in her own muttonhead direction.

Payne took his hand off the table and scratched the back of his neck. He was quiet a minute. The others were waiting for him. It was like one of the card games Papa used to let her watch when she was a little girl. No one was going to say a word until Payne played a card.

"You mean stealing my heart, dearest?"

Then Izzie started up like lightning crackling on a hot night. Clara's heart raced as she wrote the large letters.

N-O-S-I-L-L-Y.

"Noisily!"

Patting Clara's hand, Weston leaned close again. "I believe it says, No, Silly." Then he gently pointed toward Izzie who was at it again.

F-R-O-M-Y-O-U-R-F-A-T-H-E-R.

Clara read the words more quietly this time and looked at Payne. What was he thinking by now? He scratched his neck at the same place as before, but much longer and harder. Then suddenly he slapped the table and started laughing like it was a big joke.

He looked toward Papa in the corner, then stood up. "Awh, Frank, it's gibberish from the girls. No one is going to believe any of this. It's a little parlor game, is all." He tucked his chair against the table. "Fellers, I've got to get back to the saloon. Tom can't handle it more than a short while. You stay on and talk to your spirits without me." He chuckled, but he gave the back of his neck a good hard scratch.

Once more, Izzie made that empty as a wall look and watched Payne. When Payne turned to walk out, Izzie stood up and rushed toward him.

"It was my first time, Mr. Payne. I apologize if my communication was wrong. Maybe my trance wasn't deep enough to get her true message."

Well, that was splendiferous. Her true message. Holy rolling Moses. Izzie was born to this.

"Come on, then, Johnny, give the young ladies another chance. We want to hear about Hilda and your father." Greasy hair Weston reached toward Payne.

"No, boys, I don't have time for parlor games. I've got to get back to the saloon." He turned and left.

Clara twisted around to see if Papa had instructions for them now that the spirit circle was broken. He strode out of his dark spot and into the lamplight.

He had one of his big Papa grins on, but his eyes were squinty behind his spectacles. That meant the opposite of happy. "Come on, Sam, Herbert, let's go with him. I'll buy you them drinks."

Weston and Washburn thanked Izzie and Clara on their way out, but Papa wouldn't even look at Izzie. After he closed the door behind them, their low men's voices rumbled away down the stairs.

When Izzie returned to her place at the table, Clara got up and slid into the chair near her.

"Izzie, what in tarnation were you spelling about the stealing? Mrs. Fielding said the first thing above all else was the spirits had to make the people feel good."

Izzie cocked one eyebrow and smiled like a fox that just had a hen supper.

"I thought the smartest thing to do was to give the impression of having a real spirit message come through. That kind of thing would get people more interested in us, the Benton sisters. If you want to really be a famous medium, Clara, I don't think you can just make people feel good."

Now, out of nowhere, *Lawky Lawk*, Izzie knew more than Mrs. Fielding.

"But where did you get that about the stealing?"

"I found it out on my own."

The sound of footsteps running hard and heavy up the stairs drew Clara's eyes to the door. It flew open and banged something fierce against the bookcase. It was Papa. He was at Izzie's side in less than a breath. Grabbing the seat of her chair underneath herself, Clara stiffened, ready for war.

"If you wasn't my own daughter, I'd knock you down." His right hand was shaking in a knuckle-tight fist.

Scowling back at Papa, Izzie bolted up so fast it tipped her chair over behind her in a terrible crash. "You strike me and you'll never see me again. This Spiritualism hoax is your idea, Papa, not mine."

He got close to Izzie, staring straight into her eyes, but she stared right back. She seemed almost as tall as he was too. He swung his arm toward the door, pointing.

"You made Payne crawl out of here like a wounded critter lookin' for its hole. Is that stealing nonsense how to git the customers to pay you and Clara?" Nostrils flaring, Papa got his face up close to Izzie's. "Where'd you git that anyway?"

Clara's heart was beating fast. There wasn't anything Papa hated more than Izzie or Billy outsmarting him.

Backing away from him slowly, Izzie walked over to the fireplace. Good idea to get some distance from Papa. But when he followed Izzie so quickly, Clara's heart banged even harder. She slithered off her chair and eased around to the other side of the table where she'd be safe from any blows.

"I asked around town."

"Asked around town? Who on earth do you know in this town? We ain't been here that long." His nostrils kept flaring, but he let his tight fist relax.

Sighing quietly, Clara fell into a chair. It was bound to happen sometime. He'd let that fist fly right into Izzie's face. Then Izzie'd run away. Clara felt her eyes well up. How could a girl of seventeen run away though? If anyone could figure it out, it was Izzie. Good thing Papa wasn't drunk tonight. She wiped her eyes with her dress sleeve.

"Our new neighbors on William Street. Mrs. Purcell. The baker across from here. Mrs. Beattie, the milliner, downstairs. It's not a very big town. People know things." That little fox smile crept back to Izzie's face.

Finally, Papa simmered down. He lifted his arm onto the mantel and leaned into it. "It's true, then, about Hilda, the wife, stealing from Payne's father?"

Izzie nodded.

Papa looked over at Clara. "Did you know about this?"

Clara shook her head. "I thought Izzie might be getting a real spirit talking to her."

He smiled and pushed his spectacles up on his nose. He studied Izzie a moment, then raised a scolding finger at her. "Don't ask around town for secrets anymore. The whole town's gonna know how it is your spirits're so smart. I've got someone who knows everything in town and won't snitch on us."

"Who?" Izzie asked.

"None of your business."

Papa winked at Clara. "Weston thought you were purty. I always told you that, Little Plum. It's gonna help us. People'll want to come by our Spirit Room. You'll see."

Clara bent over the table and spread her arms out straight across the smooth surface. Everything was all right. There wasn't going to be any fist fighting, or bruises, or anyone running away. Papa walked around to her side and patted her on the head. Feeling like a fat old cat getting a good scratch, she almost purred.

Then he left to go and drink with his friends at Ramsey's Saloon.

Eight

IZZIE READ THE SIGN FOR THE THIRD TIME as she stood on the snow-covered sidewalk. "The Benton Sisters. Talented Genuine Mediums. Private Consultations and Spirit Circles. First Time Free. Inquire Second Floor, 28 Seneca." Papa had a big stack of these handbills printed on the press at the *Geneva Gazette* office and got Mrs. Beattie, the milliner landlady, to let him put one up on their street door. Then he got himself a bucket of glue, took Billy out, and the two of them plastered the bills all over town, on walls, in alleys, everywhere.

Even before they started being mediums, she and Clara were famous because of Papa. The Benton Sisters. Talented Genuine Mediums. It didn't matter that they weren't actually genuine. She hoped that would never be true, but Mrs. Fielding said girls often became true mediums once they began to conduct spirit circles. Their gift would just show up one day. Izzie wanted to be done with the spirit circles before that ever happened.

She looked up and down Seneca Street. It was busy with bundled-up men and women in scarves and muffs and coats and double shawls, walking briskly, and with carriages rolling and sleighs sliding on the icy street. Eventually, some of these people would be their customers. They'd had half a dozen circles already and didn't really need Papa's friends to come anymore, although Sam Weston liked to come and had been at every single one of their séances. Papa called the customers "seekers" because they were seeking answers to the great questions of life.

Mrs. Fielding had explained all that to them, too. Some people wanted to know for certain if there was immortality of the soul and some people just wanted to know if their dead brother or mother was in pain. No matter what the facts of eternal life might be, the answer she and Clara were supposed to give people was always the same, yes to the immortality and no to the pain. Mrs. Fielding believed in these answers, but to Papa it was business plain and simple. Give the seeker what he wants. That was the rule of all rules to live by, according to Papa.

Tonight Clara would pretend a trance for the first time. Clara had been begging to try it and, since Izzie wanted to be rid of that part of it, she convinced Papa that Clara's charm would make her better at it than she was.

AN HOUR LATER, the Spirit Room was prepared and Izzie and Clara were settled at the table with all their seekers ready, except for Sam Weston, who was late. As agreed, Izzie had taken Clara's usual chair with the lever for the knocking device under foot.

Papa announced they'd begin without Weston and so Clara got up and dimmed the oil lamps on the fireplace mantel, carefully leaving just enough light to distinguish the letters on the alphabet sheet. Papa explained to everyone about the spelling and the rapping and the touching of hands.

Once recently, when Papa had taken off for several days, she and Clara had no secret information about their seekers.

Since Papa's secret source of knowledge was only known to him, Izzie got Billy to ask questions about the seekers at his job at Maxwell's Nursery. "Be as casual as you can," she'd told Billy. "Act like you are interested in knowing people around town since you're new here." He came home with just a tidbit but it was enough for them to entertain their seekers.

But this evening, Papa was here and prepared. Earlier in the day, he had come back to Mrs. Purcell's and given them information about Mr. Isaac Camp who would be with them. Only two months ago, Camp had become a widower and his deceased wife was Jane. She had died in childbirth and the baby, a son, had lived. "That'll make it as easy as cherry pie," Papa had said.

A knock rattled the door and Clara swept over to open it. Sam Weston, dressed in a pale gray knee-length frock coat and a broad-brimmed Quakerish hat, came in holding a small paper-wrapped package. Smiling down at Clara, he removed the silly hat and presented the package to her sister.

"This is for you, my dear, to wish you luck tonight with your spirit communications and trance. You may open it later." He glanced at the table where everyone watched him and Clara. "I see I am late."

Smiling, Clara accepted the offering and led him to his seat next to hers. Then she put the parcel over on the bookcase and returned to the table. Izzie tapped her foot nervously. Why hadn't he brought something for her too? By mistake, she hit the knocker under the rug. It whacked twice.

"Oh, no." She covered her mouth.

"Well now, the spirits want to start right away." Papa began striding around the outside of the table. As he passed each seeker, he introduced them, even though some of them knew each other. There was Sam Weston, the latecomer, next to Clara, and Isaac Camp on her other side. There was Izzie, then an Edward Barnes and a Mrs. Mullen. Since the seekers had arrived, their banter had been cheerful and light, almost inane. They were brimming with anticipation, especially young Mrs. Mullen, with her thin lips and auburn hair braids wrapped in big loops around her ears. Mrs. Mullen looked to be about twenty and was observing every movement with the keen eye of a hawk.

This evening's sense of expectation seemed more heightened than usual. Papa had told her and Clara that the word was beginning to spread throughout Geneva. The Benton Sisters were truly gifted, but it was all making Izzie weary. The more excited people were, the more she felt trapped.

As Papa spoke and spun his made-up stories about how the Benton Sisters were talented since birth, Izzie, feeling tired, was glad to rest quietly. Izzie noticed how Clara was taking the moment to stare at Isaac Camp, who sat between them. Camp was fair and young and handsome, but not handsome in a rough way. He had a lightness about him. Unaware of Clara's intense stare, Camp kept his attention on Papa. She'd have to remember to let Clara know she must be more discreet.

"Is everyone comfortable? Let me put another log on the fire before we begin." Papa took a log, knelt down, and lodged it onto the flames. Then he stood and faced the group. "We may be in for something surprising tonight."

"My goodness, what is it?" Mrs. Mullen, in her handsome black wool jacket, lifted her shoulders and shook her head a little, feigning a shiver of exhilaration.

"Yes. Tell us," Edward Barnes said.

This was the already familiar, drawn-out monotone of the skeptic in the group. There was always at least one, one who was eager to find a fallacy. Tonight it looked like it would be old Edward Barnes.

"Well. We can't promise anythin' and it ain't right to get your hopes up." Papa nudged his spectacles up the bridge of his nose.

"Yes? Well, what is it?"

If he held back another second, people would be irked, and now even Clara herself dropped her study of Camp and turned to Papa in expectation.

"Shall I tell them, Clara?"

Beaming at Papa, the firelight making her pretty face glow, Clara nodded eagerly.

"Clara had her first speaking trance just the other day and we're hopeful she'll have another." Taking his lapels, Papa showed his crooked teeth in a sweeping smile.

Though Clara shined, as everyone turned toward her and made soft sounds of exclamation, there was a little surprise in her eyes. She had probably not expected such a grand introduction.

"My two girls have been developin' their gifts, but Clara's made a sort of jump deep into the spirit world."

Succumbing to a little dizzy spell, Izzie grasped the edge of the table. As she steadied herself she noticed that Weston, with an odd smirk, was watching Clara intently. He never seemed to entirely believe the Benton Sisters, but he never challenged them either. With the oil lamp and firelight behind him, Weston's narrow face was in shadow. His tired eyes looked like entries to black caves and he appeared to sway ever so slightly.

"Let's begin," Papa said.

Papa walked away from them to the dim side of the room near his bell. All six at the table put their hands flat out and made a circle, little fingers touching, eyes closed. They sat in silence for a long time. Occasionally, outside on the street, horse hooves clomped, harnesses jangled, wagons rattled. In between, there was nothing to listen to but the fire burning and Edward Barnes breathing laboriously next to her. If Izzie had been producing the trance, she would have been spelling away by now, but Clara had to make her own choices. Izzie felt another spell of dizziness, this one stronger and longer. Wondering if she was becoming ill with something, she took a deep breath and blinked hard a few times. She wouldn't ruin the circle or the mood before Clara had her chance.

After a while, Izzie felt Edward Barnes's fingers twitching slightly on the table and heard him shifting about in his chair. *It had better be now, little sister.*

"There's a spirit here. She wants to speak to Isaac."

Finally. If Clara had waited another minute, they would have lost all the enthusiasm at the table.

Izzie opened her eyes. Pushing her chair back, Clara stood and crossed her hands over the dark green stripes of her dress bodice.

"It's a female spirit."

Clara left her seat and walked smoothly and quickly past the fireplace, past everyone at the table. Izzie twisted around to watch. What in *tarnation* was Clara doing? She wandered to the far corner of the room, near Papa. She stood a moment in the corner, her back to the room. Arms crossed, Papa smiled and kept still a moment, but as soon as Clara was on the move again and all eyes were on her, the bell tinkled from behind the patched-on wallpaper.

Eyes turned toward Papa. To show he had nothing in his hands or attached to them, he held his hands up over his head. Clara suddenly dashed across the room to the opposite corner by the windows. She spun and faced everyone. The bell jingled. Every which way, the seekers darted glances, at Papa, at each other, at Clara, Izzie.

"I am hearing a name with a "J" sound. Is that someone you know, Mr. Camp?" Clara said.

"It could be my wife."

"Jane. Is that her name?"

Clara's timing was excellent. He had nearly given it to her.

"Yes." Camp's eyes narrowed and his mouth crimped.

"Just a minute." Clara returned to her ladder-back chair, but rather than sitting on it, she climbed onto the flat seat and stood towering over all. Surprised, Izzie gulped, which left an odd burn in her throat.

Clara swayed slightly from side to side. What the dickens was she going to do next? Whatever it was, Izzie decided to join in. Digging her heel into the lever, Izzie rapped off eight or nine knocks in a random sequence. The clunking wrenched everyone's attention to the area where the knocker was buried under the floor.

"She is here. She is a strong spirit. Wait." Clara leaned sideways and cupped a hand over her ear. "She is telling me to go to sleep so she can speak directly to you."

Shutting her eyes, Clara loomed motionless high above them. Weston and Camp arched their necks to watch her as though she were an angel. She seemed only to be missing the halo, the white gown and the little harp. Slowly, Clara elevated her arms part way and reached out toward the table.

Izzie struck the lever a few more times with her heel, the first strike thumping solidly, the others lighter. Young Mrs. Mullen flinched. Swiveling toward Izzie, Barnes glared at her rather than dwell on Clara the angel. Had he sensed her effort making the knocking? If she wanted to flex her heel again, she'd need to hold her upper body as still as a tombstone and keep her hands steady on the table.

Now Clara extended her arms straight up over her head and began to twirl gradually on the chair seat. Like a little child, she was almost silly, but she had everyone, even Barnes, gawking at her as though she were a death-defying act in the circus.

"Isaac. Isaac." Clara stopped spinning and lowered her arms.

That was a relief. The twirling was making Izzie lightheaded again. Clara went rigid and sat down. Then she began to breathe heavily, caving in, blowing up, caving in, blowing up. Izzie carefully pressed the knocking lever, but only once before Barnes could tear himself away from Clara's theatrics. The bell jingled.

"Is she all right?" Mrs. Mullen leaned toward Sam Weston.

"She seems fine."

Her brown eyes fixed in the air, Clara settled, then said, "Everyone, hold hands, please. It will help me speak to my beloved husband."

Splendid. Clever. My beloved husband. Everyone's hands came quickly back up on the table and clasped all round, Izzie taking Barnes and Camp.

"I was in pain when I left earth, but I am not in pain now, dear Isaac. It is beautiful here. I am in an advanced sphere, a place close to perfection." By deepening her voice, Clara sounded older.

Camp looked at Izzie. "How can I know it is really her?"

"I assure you. Clara is momentarily gone. This is your wife. Ask her a question," Izzie said.

Grinning ear to ear, Papa suddenly appeared by the fire behind Barnes and Mrs. Mullen.

"Yes, ask her a question," Barnes said.

Barnes's hand was cool and dry, whereas Camp's was growing hot and damp.

"Are you with your father over there?" Camp asked.

"Not a question like that, Camp. Ask something to test Miss Benton." Barnes bent forward.

"Let him speak to the spirit like he wants," Papa said.

Izzie was stunned. Papa had never come to the table before and he rarely spoke during a spirit circle. It was better that all attention be on the famous Benton Sisters, he'd always said.

Clara was tranquil. That was best, but now Camp's gaze was fixated on the table as though his head was stuck between the spokes of a wagon wheel. Perhaps it was all too painful for him. If he didn't want to speak to his wife, the séance would come to a dead end. Izzie rammed her heel into the foot lever as hard as she could. Bang. Through the rug, the floorboard vibrated under Izzie's foot.

Tick, tick, tick. Izzie looked over at the mantel. The broken clock had started up. The old clock that Clara had found and put there on the mantel, which had never worked, even though they had wound it and cleaned it and begged it, now suddenly tick-tocked off the seconds.

"The clock." Weston, who knew it was stuck at eleven o'clock since his first spirit circle, studied Papa.

"Oh, husband." With Camp's hand in hers, Clara shoved aside the alphabet sheet in front of her.

Then she drew their clasped hands towards her and dropped her head to rest her face on the back of his hand. Camp did not withdraw, but gazed down at Clara's brown hair collected in a knot just above the back of her neck. There was so much anguish in his eyes that Izzie could scarcely look at him herself.

"Dear husband, you are afraid you will not raise a strong son without me." Clara's voice quavered softly.

Camp waited a few ticks of the clock. "Yes."

"You will. He will be a fine man, a kind capable man, like you are."

A tear escaped his eye and disappeared into his long sideburn. Clara lifted her head a moment, kissed his hand gently, then pressed her face to his hand again. Now Clara's other hand, still held by Weston, was visibly shaking, but it didn't appear to be Clara's doing. It seemed to be Weston's. Izzie looked over at Weston's other hand held by Mrs. Mullen. It too was shaking. He was overcome by Clara's daring. Her little sister had better finish up here. This was too much. She had one man trembling, and the other crying. It was brilliant, but terribly risky. These antics could end badly. Izzie glanced over at Papa. He was swaying and looked like he was half in heaven and half in shock.

It was extraordinary that Clara didn't lose her concentration on Camp. She didn't look at Weston or his shaking hand. Without letting go of Camp's or Weston's hands, she stood up again and at that very moment, ding dong ding. The clock. *Lawk-a-mercy.* The clock chimed. Mrs. Mullen gasped. Barnes chuckled.

"Isaac, I must leave." Clara lured everyone back to her. "Clara isn't strong enough to carry me to you any longer. Come back to the Spirit Room again."

Camp looked like a poor lonely dog, longing to be patted on top of his head. Releasing the men's hands, Clara hit her forehead on the table with a stiff bump.

"Clara is exhausted," Papa finally said. "There won't be any more communications tonight."

That was her line, Izzie thought. Why had Papa taken her line? Suddenly, she felt there was a spoon stirring her mind like a big kettle of soup. Papa rocked from side to side. Everyone was looking over at Clara and swaying. The table, the windows, the walls, all swaying.

"The red rose on my pillow, Isaac." The woman's voice was clear, faraway and near at the same time.

Izzie looked around at the swaying seekers. Who spoke? It wasn't Clara. It wasn't Mrs. Mullen. Hands tingling, Izzie covered her ears as she felt herself slide from her chair towards the floor.

Nine

BILLY SPLASHED HIS WAY ACROSS THE CREEK and handed Izzie the wadded, soaked cloth. Water splattered onto the ground as she unfolded it. It was from the hem of Mamma's everyday dress, from Mamma's own homespun flax. Looking afraid, Billy pointed north along the lakeshore, "That way. There's a capsized sailboat, but no sign of her." He spun around and ran ahead to where he had just pointed. Izzie followed.

The shocking cold of wading across the freezing creek sent chills up through her legs, up into her chest and arms, then her head and neck. Drawing the cloth to her face, she breathed into it, but it wasn't Mamma that she smelled—it was the lake, its fish, its murky underwater plants.

"Show me where! Show me where!" She tried to yell to Billy, but the words stayed locked in her throat.

She arrived at a cove just behind Billy. An overturned sailboat's hull rocked and slapped in the lake's waves. It's broken mast and sail floated near the shore twenty feet beyond them. There was no sign of Mamma except that more of her dress, stuck to the rudder, drifted in the water.

Billy called out, "Mamma, are you here?"

Izzie forged into the lake toward the hull, reached into the icy water, grabbed the side of the boat and, with all her strength, hoisted the hull far enough to look underneath. Nothing. She let the boat crash back down into the water. Glancing north, she tried to see farther along the shore, but pine trees and shrubs blocked her view. She began to slosh and run through the shallow, chilling water.

She tried to call, "Mamma! Mamma!" but she could only eke out a whisper. She crawled through a tight opening in some shrubs and arrived at another small inlet. At the far end was Mamma's shape in the shallow water, face down, in her gray dress. Her long hair floated around her head like a silver fan.

"Mamma!" Again, just a faint whisper.

Heart pounding, Izzie splashed her way to the body and knelt in the water. Grabbing Mamma's dress near her shoulders, Izzie turned her mother over and propped her against some low rocks. Mamma's face was blue and white, swollen, empty.

"No, Mamma, no."

Weeping, Izzie pulled her mother to her and embraced her. "Don't be gone. Don't be gone."

Then Billy came and helped carry Mamma the short distance to the bank. They gently laid Mamma down on the oak leaves and pine needles, then both cried over her for a long, long time until all around them was quiet.

IZZIE FELT SOMEONE FIRMLY GRIP HER WRIST and lift her arm away from Mamma. She jerked her hand back from the grasp and snapped open her eyes. A tall, slender man with wavy dark hair was sitting there, right there on the bed next to her. Who was he? Next to her, Euphora lay asleep struggling to breathe. At the foot of the bed, Mrs. Purcell stood watching them. A sad sense of seeing Mamma dead and swollen lingered in her heart as she looked around at everyone in the room. Her face was wet with tears and she was hot and sweating into her chemise, her throat agonizingly sore. Then she remembered being dizzy during the spirit circle and being carried home in Sam Weston's carriage.

She was in Papa's room now. When Papa and Clara got her back to the boardinghouse, she was on fire, and they found Euphora shivering in bed. Papa and Mrs. Purcell shuffled both her and Euphora into Papa's bed, closed the door, and told Clara and Billy they couldn't enter the room.

This tall man who had awakened her smelled of lemon, mint, and something else. A chemical of some kind.

"Are you a minister? Are we going to die?" Her throat burned as she eked out the faint whisper.

"No, you both must have lucky stars about you. You are not going to die, not right now anyway and I'm not the minister, I'm Doctor MacAdams. Mrs. Purcell called for me night before last and I have been back to see you twice."

She had no recollection of his visits.

"I was going to take your pulse just now. May I have your wrist back?"

As she lifted her hand and offered it to the doctor, she tried to swallow, but the pain was so severe she stopped before fully gulping. From his blue waistcoat pocket he retrieved a watch and stared at it while he gently pressed his fingertips into the soft side of her wrist. His long brown eyebrows curled up toward the ceiling and his square chin was marked on the right with a purple scar.

Mrs. Purcell went to the washstand, picked up a towel, then sat near Euphora and placed the cloth across her forehead.

"You both are going to survive and be fine," she said.

"You're a spiritual medium, I hear," the physician said as he studied his watch. "How long have you and your sister been Spiritualists?"

"A few months." The words cut her like a knife twisting inside her ears.

He let go of Izzie's wrist and returned the watch to his pocket.

"You're much better. Your pulse has slowed a bit. Your temperature is a little lower. How does your throat feel?"

"Terrible."

"Putrid sore throat disease. You two really are very lucky. I'm leaving Mrs. Purcell with Winslow's Baby Syrup. The morphine in it will soothe your throat and help you sleep. She'll give you that as I have prescribed, but the most important thing is water. You and your sister must drink two gallons every day until you are well. And hot wet compresses on your neck. Mrs. Purcell will do that for you every half hour. She's already been doing it since you fell sick and added her own compound tincture to the cloths— capsicum, myrrh, lobelia, and I don't know what else." He glanced at Mrs. Purcell. "She's in charge of that. I want you to drink the water. I should think it will be three weeks or so."

Putrid sore throat disease. Diphtheria. They might have died. Children died of it all the time. She remembered a few winters ago one family down the street back in Homer losing two little boys.

She looked at her sister. "Is she really going to be all right?"

"She's asleep now, but she was awake earlier." Mrs. Purcell leaned over Euphora and patted Izzie's hand. "Go ahead and rest. I made a big pot of red pepper and golden seal tea. You are to drink it weak and gargle it strong. That's my own remedy and the doctor agrees to it."

"She knows far more than I do." Doctor MacAdams chuckled and stood. "I'll be back in the morning."

Bag in hand, the physician strode across the room and ducked slightly to make it through the door. As he pulled the door closed, he nodded at Mrs. Purcell and then was gone.

A FEW DAYS LATER, Izzie could swallow without excruciating pain, but she was too weak to walk across the room. She hadn't seen Papa since the night she fell sick. Mrs. Purcell told her that as soon as the physician told Papa what she and Euphora had, he took off and hadn't been back since.

The tall physician came by twice more and asked if they were drinking all of the two gallons of daily water. He took Euphora's pulse, then hers both times, but on the last visit, Izzie thought he held on to her wrist a very long time.

He said, "I hear from Mrs. Purcell you read all the time down in her library."

"Yes, sir."

"Perhaps when you are well, you can tell me what I should read." He patted the back of her hand, then stood to go.

Izzie laughed nervously. What could she possibly know about books that a physician didn't know?

FOR THE NEXT WEEK, Mrs. Purcell took care of her and Euphora like she was their own grandmother, attending to them all day long. Just when Izzie was feeling miserable and starting to long for Mamma, Mrs. Purcell would appear with another glass of water or beef broth or some red pepper, golden seal tea to drink. She'd hold a pan for them to spit into and made them gargle with different concoctions, some with salt and cayenne; some with sage, vinegar, or honey.

She'd put flannel cloths on their necks, some with her special compound, others with sweet oils and mustard seeds.

She kept their feet warm with plain hot cloths as well, and she washed them right in the bed with towels and bowls of lukewarm water. She emptied the chamber pots many times each day. After the second day of offering the Winslow's Baby Syrup, she took it away. "You might start thinking you need it even when you don't," she said. It had been wonderfully soothing and Izzie did want it again, though she didn't ask for it.

For one long week after that, whenever she wasn't drinking water or one of Mrs. Purcell's teas, Izzie lay thinking about the voice she heard before she fell off the chair. "The red rose on my pillow, Isaac." Was it delusion caused by fever? Was it the spirit of Jane Camp? Was it the beginning of lunacy? Was it like the "Susan" she heard at Mrs. Fielding's spirit circle? Would she hear more? She wrestled with these questions until she was too tired to worry any more about them. Then she would sleep. She decided one thing though, while she lay there for days and days. She would find a way to put an end to being one of the famous Benton Sisters as soon as she could.

Ten

BEFORE IZZIE FULLY RECOVERED HER STRENGTH, Papa had returned and insisted they conduct spirit circles every night except Sundays. Most often, Papa let Clara mimic a trance. She was quite an actress and even if people didn't believe her, her twirling and swooping and trembling enamored them. Afraid of hearing more voices, Izzie's throat was tight for the duration of every spirit circle, but several weeks went by and, to her great relief, she didn't hear anything odd.

Izzie found out from Mrs. Purcell that Papa was not intending to pay Doctor MacAdams for his visits. He'd said to Mrs. Purcell, "He's just a quack like all physicians. It was you that healed Isabelle and Euphora with your compresses and teas and gargles. We don't owe that quack a dang penny."

When she heard this, Izzie was angry and was ready to fight Papa for the money to pay Doctor MacAdams, but as luck would have it, that very night Papa missed the spirit circle and Izzie collected the money from the seekers herself. When Papa wasn't there, Izzie had strict orders to put the money in a box in Papa's room as soon as she got home. But this time, Izzie had enough money for Doctor MacAdams's fee and she decided that, in the morning, she would pay the physician before Papa came home from wherever he was.

At breakfast, Mrs. Purcell told Izzie she could probably find Doctor MacAdams at the Geneva Hygienic Institute. And so, with a gold dollar gripped in her fist, Izzie set off the short distance to Pulteney Park and the Hygienic Institute.

Surrounded by a painted-white wooden fence, the town green, Pulteney Park, was a square oasis kept free of the cattle that were often driven through town. At the western edge of the park, the Geneva Hygienic Institute, standing three stories high with pillars running from top to bottom, looked like a southern plantation home.

Izzie smoothed the skirt of her dress and stepped inside the tall doors. Along the walls, gas light sconces illuminated a huge hallway. At the far end of it two women in identical long white robes were talking.

Izzie went in the first door on the left marked "reception" just as Mrs. Purcell had explained. A young, fair, clean-shaven man, neatly dressed in a white shirt, fitted light trousers and a shiny black waistcoat stood near the door. He was putting on a wool coat.

"Good day, miss. I'm just going for supplies. May I help you?"

"Yes. I am here to see the physician MacAdams."

"For hydrotherapy?"

"I have a fee for him."

"I am in a hurry. You may see him yourself." He quickly turned and led Izzie past a high counter on the left, then through an empty waiting room. They approached a door with translucent glass and black painted letters reading "Dr. A.B. Smith, Director." The young man knocked.

"Come in."

The fellow opened the door and leaned into the opening.

"You have a visitor, sir, a young woman says it's about a fee."

"I'll see her." The voice lilted in a welcoming way.

The clean-shaven man pushed open the door, let Izzie in, then vanished.

Doctor MacAdams stood up from behind a spacious oak desk at one end of the room and smiled broadly. He was lanky and rather towering in his black greatcoat.

"You're well. I'm very pleased. And your sister, Euphora?"

He swung around the desk and strode toward her. His excitement seemed odd, as though there was some mistake, as though he thought she was someone else.

"Euphora is herself again." Izzie pointed at the door. "It says Dr. Smith on the door?"

"Smith. He's the director here. Gone for two months. I'm keeping the ship afloat while he's away. Please sit." He gestured eagerly toward one of two curved-back Windsor chairs.

She sat and browsed the room. Shelves, interrupted by two tall windows, lined one entire wall of the office. They were crammed with small, labeled bottles of either clear or blue glass. Along the opposite wall, bookcases supported rows and rows of thick medical books and stacks of journals. Behind the desk was an open door revealing the end of a high table covered by a pristine white sheet.

MacAdams returned to his desk chair, the noontime sun washing over his papers.

"Well, Miss Benton, tell me how I may be of assistance. You are feeling well?"

"Yes. I brought you the fee." She placed the gold coin on the desk and slid it across the smooth oak.

He left it sitting there without reaching for it. "Tell me about your recovery. Did you have any setbacks?"

"I was very tired. My father wanted me to conduct séances with my sister before my throat felt entirely well."

"Ah, yes. The Benton Sisters. You're the talk of the town. Do you really hear spirits?" MacAdams tapped two fingertips on the purple scar on his chin.

"May I ask you something?" Izzie said.

"Of course."

"When one is feverish, is it common to have delusions?"

"Delusions?"

"Voices. To hear voices."

"Fevers can create dream-like states. This happened to you?"

Izzie nodded. "I heard a woman's voice just as I was falling ill at our spirit circle."

"But not a spirit the way you usually do?" His mouth curled into a skeptical smirk.

Izzie squinted toward the sunny windows. Papa had made her and her sisters and brother swear they would never tell anyone the truth about the Benton Sisters. They were genuine mediums and that was that. Blast Papa. She'd had enough.

"We only play at being mediums. For the money. It's my father's idea, but you mustn't tell anyone."

He smiled, leaned over his desk. "We'll have a secret then." Putting his elbows on the desk, he pressed his hands together in prayer position. "People do hear and see things when they have fevers. It can be quite extreme, delirium sometimes."

"My mother heard voices all the time."

He leaned back and took a moment. "Did she ever have hysterical fits?"

"What do you mean by fits?"

"Screaming, fainting, thrashing about."

"No, not like that."

"Like what, then?"

Izzie's jaw began to quiver. Hoping the doctor wouldn't notice, she clenched her teeth a moment and grasped the two ends of her shawl. Then she sighed.

"Since I can remember, she told us she saw spirits and they talked to her."

He arched a curly brow. "Did you witness this?"

If he was shocked, he was hiding it well.

"She'd start out praying, usually holding her Bible, then sometimes—not every time—she would mumble, or sound like she was speaking with someone, but it only lasted a few minutes. She had a rocking chair and she'd rock back and forth with her eyes closed. " Izzie criss-crossed her shawl over her dress bodice. "She didn't thrash or scream."

"Mrs. Purcell told me she died a few months ago. May I ask what caused her passing?"

Opening the shawl again and grasping the corners, Izzie pulled at the wool. "She drowned…in a sailing accident. It appeared that she stole a boat from the north end of the lake one night. My brother and I found her in the water at Kashong Point." She felt tears form at the corners of her eyes, but took a deep breath and stared at the bright windows to keep from crying. "I believe the voices led her to her death."

Doctor MacAdams rose from his desk, went to the window, and looked out. "And you are afraid if you hear voices you will die like she did," he said.

"Yes."

He turned toward her, his face grave, his wavy dark hair shining in the sun.

"I'll be honest with you, Miss Benton. I am not an expert in nervous maladies, though some of our water-cure patients come to us with nervous exhaustion and other mental difficulties." He stepped toward her. "But I am a man of science. I don't believe in mediums or the tricks of Spiritualists. In all likelihood, your mother probably needed some medical care that she never got." Touching his purple chin scar, he paused for a moment.

"How will I ever know the truth about her?" Izzie asked.

"We could talk to an expert in these matters. There's a physician, Dr. George Cook, in Canandaigua. He manages Brigham Hall. It's a small hospital for the insane. Perhaps you and I could pay him a visit and you could tell him your mother's history."

"But how could he truly know about her? She's gone." Izzie stood. "Excuse me, I really must go now."

"No, please, Miss Benton, forgive me." He came close to her. "I did not mean to imply your mother was insane, merely that Dr. Cook is nearby and has a special knowledge of the human mind and might provide you with some insight or solace." He was so tall that she had to tilt her head back to look him in the eye. And there was the fragrance she remembered from her sick bed—lemon, mint, and that medicinal smell. "I apologize if I have offended you." His brown eyes were insistent.

"I must go. I have to prepare for a séance. My father and sister will be waiting."

He walked with her out to the front door of the Hygienic Institute and they stood looking out at Pulteney Park with its walkways and teeming water fountain in the center.

"I will keep your secret, Miss Benton, and I don't want you to worry about any voices you've heard. I am sure it was your fever."

She thanked him again and started off for the Spirit Room. He had to be right about the voice she had heard and the fever. He was an educated physician, a man of experience.

He just had to be. And that time she thought she heard someone say "Susan," at Mrs. Fielding's circle, someone in the room had probably spoken it even though Clara and Papa hadn't heard it. There were so many people there at that circle and so much commotion. She wouldn't think any more about it now.

Eleven

A MONTH LATER THE SPRING RAINS BEGAN. Pelted by a relentless downpour, Izzie sloshed down Seneca Street. Her boots soaking up the thin sheets of water on the wooden sidewalk and her gray-and-blue plaid dress wet up to her knees, she tilted her umbrella back slightly and glanced up at the Spirit Room windows above Mrs. Beattie's Millinery. Papa's new sign was large and impressive. The Benton Sisters. Public & Private Séances.

Clara's dramatic trances were continuing to gain popularity. Papa had been home for ten days straight and in that time had only been out in the evening once and then only for a few hours. Not only had he remained sober, but he had come home with fresh information every day for their séances. If things continued like this, perhaps it wouldn't be long before Papa and Clara wouldn't need her.

A burst of wind shoved at the umbrella. Izzie tugged it back down close over her head and ventured on. If Clara was to be the shining star of the Benton Sisters, perhaps Izzie didn't have to assist her. Euphora could do it. After all, Clara did enjoy doing the trances and getting the attention. She really was a fine little actress and she seemed to have a remarkable sense of intuition about the seekers.

At Smith & Crane Bookstore and Bindery at 33 Seneca Street, Izzie paused under the awning to shake water from her umbrella. As she entered the shop, the bell above the door jingled its welcome. She inserted her dripping umbrella into the stand and breathed in the delicious smell of ink and paper, leather and dust.

Izzie browsed at Smith & Crane whenever she could. Mr. Smith generally smiled at her and didn't seem to mind that she didn't purchase the books she read while standing sometimes for an hour in front of the bookshelves. Every once in a while, like today, she delivered or retrieved one of Mrs. Purcell's books for binding repair.

Today, on her errand for Mrs. Purcell, she was eager to finish *Madame Bovary*, a novel she had started reading in the shop when Papa had leased the Spirit Room in December. Emma Bovary had been sinking into an ugly despair and Izzie wanted to finish the book and get the anguish over with. On Izzie's last visit to Smith & Crane, Emma had begged Rodolphe for three thousand francs to help with her debts, but he had refused her. The story couldn't end well. Rodolphe, the bastard, had ruined Emma, stolen her soul.

Mr. Smith was busy with a customer, so Izzie headed along the left wall of floor-to-ceiling books, her path to the literature section. She passed religion, philosophy, history.

"Oh, Miss Benton." Mr. Smith, behind his glass counter, was looking around the shoulder of a stout man in a tan canvas coat.

"Yes."

"I am very sorry. We sold both copies of Flaubert. I have ordered it, though. I'll have it in a week or two."

Drat. Now she'd have to wait all that time. She had guessed earlier that Mr. Smith knew precisely what she was reading and now she knew for certain that he did. Thank goodness he didn't mention the scandalous title out loud.

"Thank you. Is Mrs. Purcell's book ready?"

Mr. Smith held up a finger and nodded, then returned his attention to his customer.

"Miss Benton. What luck." A man's voice came from behind her.

Doctor MacAdams, two large volumes tucked under an arm, stepped out from a break in the bookcase that ran down the center of the store and walked toward her smiling. His stovepipe hat and shoulders were rain soaked.

"Hello, Doctor MacAdams."

He took off the wet hat and smoothed back his black wavy hair. "I had been hoping to run into you. I've heard that you and your sister are still dazzling the town with your talents as mediums."

As talented hoaxes, she wanted to say, but only smiled.

"Well, you must come to a séance some time. We always welcome skeptics."

"Too much scientific training for me, I suppose." He lifted the books under his arm in her direction as though to say, "here is the wisdom of life, the real truth of existence."

She hoped he wouldn't come to a spirit circle, though. She didn't know why, but she didn't want him witnessing their Spiritualism game.

"I am famished. I had a small emergency at the Hygienic Institute and worked straight through supper this afternoon. Do you have time to join me over at the Gem Inn for tea?"

Izzie knew young women her age didn't go out publicly with men unescorted. In the world she grew up in, no one followed those kinds of rules. But in this physician's world, people did. Perhaps he wanted to talk more about her mother or Spiritualism.

He seemed to see her hesitation and grinned. "You could explain your view of immortality to me. As a Spiritualist, that is."

She'd never been to the Gem Inn on Water Street. She'd never been any place that served meals to the public and she'd never been asked to explain her view of anything.

"Yes, I have time."

IZZIE AND DOCTOR MACADAMS SETTLED THEMSELVES at a small table by the windows. A cast iron stove warmed the room. Just outside, rain drained hard off the Gem Inn's blue awning. Underneath it, waiting for the deluge to subside, a mother and daughter huddled, arms linked and hidden by the bulk of their capes and bonnets.

It was late afternoon and most people were at home or at work. The Gem's dining room was nearly empty except for a few pairs of men and two young simply dressed women nearby engrossed in earnest conversation. While Doctor MacAdams read the menu on the chalkboard, Izzie caught a word here and there from the women, "legislature," "petition," "signatures," "Garrison's views," "convention," "property rights". She wanted desperately to hear more of what the women said, to be the teapot on their table, but her eavesdropping was interrupted by a tiny old gentleman in a white apron who came to their square table and asked Doctor MacAdams what they wanted to eat. MacAdams was so tall and the man in apron so short, there seemed no more than a foot between their heights with one sitting and the other standing. After asking Izzie what she wanted and she had told him rice pudding, MacAdams repeated the "rice pudding" to the short man, then rattled off an entire roster of things he wanted to eat.

She watched him closely while he ordered. The thickness, length and curl of his dark eyebrows still astounded her. Did he brush them every morning? If he didn't, she supposed he'd look like a wild mountain man, not something his patients would likely appreciate.

While Izzie enjoyed a cup of tea and her pudding, Doctor MacAdams consumed fried oysters, boiled corned beef and cabbage, turnips, and then, chicken pie. As they ate together, they gazed off and on out the large window at the rain and chatted about the arrival of spring and muddy roads, the newest steamboat to be launched, the P.H. Field, and the terrible fire at the canal barn on Bradford Street that destroyed three buildings the previous Tuesday. He asked her about the spices in the rice pudding.

Then he wiped his long mustache several times with a napkin, picked up the white teapot and poured the tea, his hands careful and thin, filling her cup, then his.

"Do you think we should go to war to free the slaves in the south?"

"If we cannot free them otherwise." She dipped her spoon into the pudding.

"So you believe the freedom of black men is worth the lives of whites?"

"If it must be." Izzie slowly put the pudding in her mouth. It was sticky and had already cooled down.

"And if your brother Billy became a young soldier and died in battle?"

Startled, she hastily lifted the blue and white cup, a fine, almost invisible crack running from its base to the lip.

"I'd rather not give up my brother," she said and, without drinking, replaced the cup to its saucer with a clink. "Anyway, he's only thirteen. That's too young to be a soldier."

"Yes. But a war could be several years away or last a very long time. Passion for anything, the freedom of men, or women for that matter, requires a price. A high price. Don't you agree?" He shoved the empty chicken pie plate away from him.

"Most everything I know is from books, Doctor MacAdams. I know little about prices paid for idealistic causes, at least first hand."

"You mustn't underestimate what you know from books. It is from Frederick Douglass's narrative of his life that many northerners, myself included, understand the lives of slaves, and besides, your life is before you. I think you will have plenty of opportunity, for better or worse, to discover about passion and beauty and justice, and their costs. We must hope that Billy is not a cost."

The door to the Gem, just behind Izzie, opened and let in a cool draft along with the sound of rain battering the walk and a carriage slopping by. Izzie knew, and had read, the book Doctor MacAdams referred to. It was in Mrs. Purcell's library. Glancing down at the cotton napkin in her lap, she smiled to herself. Doctor MacAdams was the first man to speak to her as though she were an educated woman. He was asking her about political ideas.

"Have you heard any more voices as you did when you were ill?"

"No."

"There. I thought so. You mustn't worry." He swallowed the last sip of tea from his cup. "I must get back to a late appointment at the Hygienic Institute." He gestured toward the man in the apron. "Would you like a tour of the Institute? Except for those steamboats out there, it is the most interesting thing in Geneva."

The crow's feet spread around his cheerful eyes as he grinned at her. Why on earth did he want to take more time with her? He couldn't still be apologetic for what he implied about Mamma at his office and surely he was very busy in his hydrotherapy practice. And ... he couldn't possibly want to court her.

"Thank you, but I can't come now. I have a spirit circle soon."

"Ah, the séances. We didn't get to our immortality discussion." He raised a hand and ran two fingertips down his long sideburn from his ear until his fingertips rested on his bare chin. "Could you come next week, say, Wednesday at five in the evening?"

Izzie nodded and let a smile spill out. But Wednesday was an entire week away, a week of seven days, seven long days, each one with hours and hours between one sunrise and the next. She couldn't wait to get to the Spirit Room and tell Clara about the Gem Inn and next Wednesday.

Twelve

AT NEARLY FIVE O'CLOCK on the next Wednesday, Izzie was a little breathless and impatient as she waited for a small herd of brown cows to pass by on Main Street. When her way was clear of the cows, she crossed the street, passed through a narrow gate, and traversed Pulteney Park. A strong gust of wind swooped at her. Grabbing her bonnet, she leaned forward and forged across the square green toward the Geneva Hygienic Institute.

She hadn't told Papa where she was going, not that he paid much attention. Since he had such a scathing opinion of doctors, she knew he wouldn't approve. She hadn't told him about the Gem Inn either, and had asked Clara not to mention it.

She entered the front door. Going from bright to dim light, she was disoriented for a moment. Appearing as eerie silhouettes, a handful of men and women milled about the immense hall. Pausing to untie and remove her hat and let her eyes adjust, Izzie smelled pine wood, vinegar, and cigar smoke.

Halfway down the corridor two men stood conversing. The first man she recognized as Doctor MacAdams. The other was a hunched-over man propping himself on a cane.

Now that she could see more clearly, she walked ahead past the reception office toward them.

"The hot water bath is turning my skin red and the cold water bath is making my back hurt more than it did before I came here." The man with curvature struck the tip of his cane sharply against the floor several times.

Izzie stopped where she was and waited.

"I'll consult with Edgar first thing in the morning and we'll see about some adjustments. Be sure to get your rest tonight."

"When is Doctor Smith coming back?"

"Not for another month, I'm afraid."

"Yes. Yes. Well, I want Edgar in my room bright and early, bright and early." The man passed Izzie as he shuffled toward the stairwell. Dressed in a brown satin robe, the old gentleman grumbled under his breath, nearly spitting as he ranted to himself.

"Miss Benton." Smiling, hands deep in the pockets of his black coat, Doctor MacAdams stood looking down at her. "You are perfectly on time. I am delighted." He tilted his head toward the stairwell. "Excuse the old fellow. Very bad case of spine curvature. I'm eager to try magnets on him, but the director ordered no experimenting while he was absent."

Drawing his long hands from his pockets, Doctor MacAdams rubbed them together as though warming them.

"Shall we?"

He led her back down the hall, chattering about building dimensions, a gymnasium, private rooms, renovations. He was like a boy bragging about shooting his first rabbit.

They arrived at a long room with two sets of double doors, both wide open. It was a colossal parlor full of stuffed sofas, chairs, tables of all sizes, an emerald green rug, and a huge fireplace at one end. They stood just inside. Cigar smoke swirling around them, four men played cards at a square table. At the end of a pink sofa, a frail young woman with hair so blond it was nearly white sat alone reading a book.

Without speaking, Doctor MacAdams stepped back into the hallway. Izzie followed him to a dining room. It was vast, with high ceilings and two extraordinary, huge glass chandeliers. Tables were set with linen and sparkling silverware. Along the far wall, lush olive-green velvet draperies framed tall windows.

It was quite grand, not at all what she expected. She thought people who took the water-cure either dunked themselves in water baths, drank boat loads of water, or both. Surely they didn't need such a fancy establishment for that.

"The building used to be the Geneva Hotel," Doctor MacAdams said. "Many of the visitors today think of this as a resort because of the healing spring waters and the quiet. We use the White Spring Aqueduct." Squaring his shoulders, he gazed around the room as though checking that everything was in its proper place. He certainly was proud, even if his post was temporary.

"The White Spring Aqueduct?"

"The water you drink. The water you wash with. All the city's water comes from the White Spring. It's about a mile and a half southwest of here. The water runs into town through cast iron pipes the whole way. Used to be log pipes." He gestured toward the end of the hall. "Here, let me show you a treatment room."

He smiled again, then turned and sped off toward the west end of the building. His stride was so long that it took her two or three steps for his one just to keep up.

"How many patients are here, Doctor MacAdams?"

He paused and looked at her. "Please call me Mac. I hope we will be friends. My friends call me Mac." His eyelids fluttered a little as he said this about being friends, but then he started walking again and kept right on speaking. He hadn't really waited for her reply. But he did say "friends." Was he hinting at courtship?

"There are about ninety patients right now, but we can have up to a hundred and fifty. Each one pays ten dollars for a week of room, board, and treatment."

Lawks. Ninety people who could take time away from work to take baths and pay ten dollars for it? He certainly couldn't be trying to recruit her as a hydrotherapy patient. He already knew she didn't have ten dollars.

"Come along," he said.

Nearly at a run, she scuttled after him. Goodness, he was exuberant. But it couldn't be courtship he wanted with her, could it? After all, she was only seventeen years old and he was probably thirty-five. She wasn't educated. He was a learned man. A physician. She was poor and a humbug medium. He was a scientist. Now her curiosity really began to burn. What was it? He wouldn't have invited her here if he didn't want something from her. He was sharing this Water-Cure Institute with her for some reason. If he didn't tell her what it was soon, she would ask him. Even if he thought it rude, she'd ask. She had nothing to lose. Perhaps he wanted to experiment on her, magnets, something new, something radical. She swallowed hard.

But experiment on what ailment? She had none. Unless he was interested in her feverish delusions. Mac came to a halt again. He was saying something about soaking and water temperatures and submersion. Then a brunette woman in a simple green walking dress approached and passed them. She and Mac nodded at each other as she went by.

He paused, turned and watched her until she was some distance away.

"We have many women here seeking relief from female diseases, such as the conditions that come from irregular menses." His voice was quiet, discreet.

A tickle caught Izzie's throat and she coughed into her hand.

Mac looked at her with concern, his curly eyebrows settling low over his dark eyes.

"Is that a cough left over from your illness?"

"No. No." She covered the front of her neck with a hand. "Something scratchy, perhaps that vinegar odor, or the cigars back there."

"Forgive me. I have embarrassed you. When I am here I am so involved that I forget ordinary polite standards."

He had alluded to menses in such a casual manner. She remembered those advertisements in the newspaper. Doctor P.H. Ricord's Amie de Femme, the medicine that claimed to cure everything female as well as bring forth abortions. Perhaps that was it. He wanted to experiment on her and it was something to do with menses.

Her eyes watered as she fought off another coughing fit. She should leave now, make an excuse and go. He was up to something. There had to be some reason this man, this physician, wanted a young, poor woman under his wing. But she didn't really want to go. She wanted to know what he wanted with her. No, she wouldn't leave, not unless she sensed injury or malice.

"Are you all right, Isabelle? I do apologize."

"I'm fine. Perhaps you will tell me more sometime about the women and the water-cure."

He had called her Isabelle, not Miss Benton.

"You're curious about things, aren't you?" he asked.

"Always." She glanced down the hall, then at his face. "I prefer Izzie."

"Isabelle is a beautiful name, though." His mouth curved into the slightest of smiles.

"But Izzie suits me better, I think."

"Well, then, Izzie, you've never been to a seminary? A school of any kind?"

"No, but I've read every book I could ever get anyone to lend me. I had a friend back in Ohio whose family had a great many books. She taught me to read when I was only four, then over the years, I read everything in her house."

Leaning back, Mac laughed. "I knew you were a reader, but indeed, you are an entirely self-educated woman. I thought as much."

A woman. Mac referred to her as a woman. Even though she was old enough to be married, she still thought of herself as a girl. Women had husbands and children and they weren't forced by a father to learn how to be mediums and trick people out of their money.

"I suppose I am self-educated. I never thought of it that way. I just enjoy reading, that's all."

"Well, that's how it happens." He half-smiled. "What precisely are some of these books you've read?"

"Novels, Stowe, Bronte, Fern, Dickens, Warner, Flaubert, Austen. A little poetry." While she spoke, he kept nodding his head, hooking his index finger over his chin and hiding his purple scar. "And history and biographies. Let's see. I enjoyed Frederick Douglass's narrative of his life that you mentioned last week, and some political things, and some science."

Mac's smile fell and his eyes widened. "Science too?"

"Not really too much of that. I read a book about meteorology by someone named Wilkes."

"Did you understand it?"

"Not all of it. I had no one to ask questions of."

"Why didn't your father send you to school?"

"I don't think he wanted his daughter to know more than he did. I could know what he was willing to teach me, but no more. The romantic novels infuriated him. He said they would ruin me, make me want things I couldn't have." She felt an ache behind her eyes and looked away from him. Maybe Papa was right. There was so much she wanted.

"He told me women with too much knowledge would disrupt the proper balance of nature. Once he tore one of my friend's books from my hands, *Jane Eyre*. He ripped it from me with the most hateful look on his face, then threw it into the wood stove and watched it burn. After that, I tried not to read when he was nearby."

"What about your mother? Did she mind?"

"She thought the Bible was the only book worth reading, but she watched him burn *Jane Eyre*. The next morning after he had gone out, she gave me a dollar to buy a new copy of the book and return it to my friend. She said, 'Don't fuss about Papa.' I have no idea how she had saved that dollar."

"Hmm." Mac began to walk again, drawing her along gently by the elbow. When they arrived at the end of the hall, he opened a door as big as one in a stable. She expected to see the outdoors, but instead there was another hallway.

"This is the addition with the bathing rooms. There are four large rooms, each for different water-cure treatments." He pointed at one of them. "Come along, here's one not in use."

When they reached the bathing room, they stood together a moment in the entry and Mac waited while she looked in. The windowless room was a tall pine and white tile box smelling of fresh cut wood. It was empty except for a bar at waist level running straight across, three burning gaslights on one of the walls, and a huge water tank high above them braced by heavy wood crossbeams. The floor was white tile with a drain in the middle to carry water away.

Mac was grinning ear to ear. "This is what is called the douche bath. It uses the force of gravity. Let me show you."

He strode across the wet floor and over to a cord that ran from a spigot on the tank to a hook on the opposite wall. He untied it and gave it a strong tug. In a huge burst, water flowed in a two-inch stream from twenty feet above. It crackled, pounded, splattered and swirled off into the floor drain.

"The patient stands naked under the stream of cold water and braces himself on the bar."

Izzie could scarcely hear him over the smacking of water on tile.

"It must hurt!"

"It does hurt, but the impact is necessary to eliminate the body's morbid matter!"

She cringed as she imagined being pummeled by the water.

Mac looked up at the stream. "We usually only use this treatment at the end of a series of sweats, and hot and cold baths. Every step is designed to rid the body of impurities."

Mac walked across the wet floor toward Izzie and untied another cord. He pulled it slowly and the spigot above closed, reducing the stream to a trickle, then a few drops. The room became quiet again.

"What do you think of it?" He looked at her eagerly.

Did he want her to try it?

"I think I'd rather keep my impurities and get my peace and quiet on a canoe ride."

Running a hand through his wavy hair, Mac laughed. "You shouldn't judge something until you've tried it for yourself."

"Some things one doesn't have to try…and some things one isn't permitted to try, come to think of it." She chuckled at her own joke and Mac laughed with her, but she couldn't wait any longer. Now she was sure. He definitely wanted to experiment on her.

"Mac, why did you want me to see the Hygienic Institute? Do you want me to be part of an experiment somehow?"

Like a doused candle, Mac's smile disappeared abruptly. He took a step closer to her.

"No, Izzie, but you're right, I do want something."

"What is it, then?"

"I want." He paused, glanced aside, then down, then directly at her. The skin just under his eyes twitched slightly.

What on earth was it? She locked her jaw down.

"I want you to be my wife."

"Your wife?" Izzie stumbled back, nearly tripping on the hem of her dress.

"Yes." He pressed forward, toward her. "That moment when I saw you in the bookstore, and you were well and yourself again, I knew I wanted to marry you."

"I don't understand. You can't mean what you are saying."

"I saw something in you I had been waiting years to see in a young woman."

Izzie laughed nervously. She held her gut, feeling her face flush hot. What an idiot she had been, thinking he was going to lay magnets across her abdomen or pummel her with a jet of water. He wanted to marry her. Marry her.

She kept laughing. It was like one of those silly jokes very late at night when she was tired in bed with her sisters. One would start a giggle and they all would go on and on and not be able to stop. Then she realized that even though Mac was smiling, he wasn't laughing with her.

"Do you think I am ridiculous to tell you so soon in our friendship?"

"I'm not sure. I thought you were going to perform strange experiments on me." She wiped her temples, moist with tears of laughter. "I am relieved."

"I'm sure I could try something out on you, if you wanted me to."

"No. No." Finally she took a deep breath, straightened up, and exhaled slowly.

Mac was standing very still, very close to her. No man had ever stood so near to her, his feet almost touching the hem of her skirt.

He steadied his earth brown eyes on her. "Will you marry me, Izzie?"

She sighed. She had no idea what to say. She looked away from him to the glistening wet floor, then into his eyes to see if he was truly sincere. He wasn't even blinking, not even breathing. Not a muscle on his face, or in his entire body, flinched or shifted. He was entirely serious.

"I would like some time to think about it, Mac." She stepped back. "You haven't spoken to my father, have you?"

"No. I have to admit, I didn't expect to propose to you today. My heart was racing so fast that I couldn't slow myself down."

Racing so fast. Had his heart really been racing with the idea of her? She felt a smile rush onto her face. Oh, but there was Papa—Papa who hated physicians, Papa who couldn't earn a living wage without the Benton Sisters.

"Is a week enough for your consideration?" he asked.

"I hardly know you. I need longer. I don't even know your given name."

"Robert, and we can see each other, and get to know one another, as much as you like, at least until I go."

"Go?"

I'm afraid I don't have much time to court you and take things in a proper stride. I'm leaving soon to build my own Water-Cure Institute in Rochester. I want you to come with me. Come as my wife."

Rochester was a bustling city, much bigger than Geneva. The thought of it excited her. But could she leave the children with Papa? Could Clara handle being a medium alone? If she said no to Mac and he left, things would be simple, at least, and she could keep an eye on Papa and the children. If she said yes, she would go on to a whole new city life and be free of being a humbug medium. No more humbug.

"When will you leave?"

"A month or two."

"Well, I will see you until then, and if my father agrees, and that is a great uncertainty, I will give you my answer before you depart."

He beamed at her, his hands restless at his sides. It seemed he would reach for hers, but he didn't move.

"Mac, are you sure you didn't plan to propose to me here?" She glanced up at the tank.

He laughed loudly, the sound echoing off the bare walls.

"No, I promise you I didn't." He leaned toward her and offered her his arm. "May I walk you home?"

They left the Geneva Hygienic Institute and walked in the dusk toward Mrs. Purcell's boardinghouse. The wind had not settled down. She held the strings of her bonnet and he held the rim of his stovepipe hat the entire way. As they walked, he told her about his plans for his own Water-Cure Institute. Rochester was about fifty miles west, far enough that, if she went with him, she'd have a completely new life. His proposal in the douche room was strange, but she would consider it. There was something about this tall water-cure physician; something she wanted.

Thirteen

"IT'S LIKE ICE." Squatting at the water's edge, Clara yanked her fingers from the lake water and shook them. Along Seneca Lake's shore, trees were budding with hundreds of shades of spring green. Even if she tried, she could never count all those shades. Izzie wandered away from her along the water's edge.

The warm sun soaked into Clara's shoulders through her dress and shawl. She bent over and picked up one, two, three, four, five small gray stones and crammed them into her dress pocket. Then she walked along the mud and pebbles in Izzie's direction.

Not far out on the sparkling water, six fishermen in rowboats waited silently for something to happen. The middle of the day in the bright sunshine was the wrong time to catch fish, even stupid fish. Clara knew that. Even she, a thirteen year-old girl, knew that.

Trailing after Izzie up onto a small dock, she walked behind her sister, feet drumming on the wooden planks. When they got to the end, they sat and dangled their legs over the blue water. The water wasn't still like this very often on Seneca Lake. It always stirred and churned, churned so hard it had swallowed up Mamma. Gripping the edge of the dock tightly with both hands, she stared straight down past her shadow to the rocks and muck below.

"The lake still makes me sad." Clara stopped swinging her legs, gazed up toward the horizon. Geneva harbor to the west, hillsides of cleared pasture surrounded by narrow rows of trees to the east, three steamboats and many sailboats scattered on the water as far as she could see. She started to count the sailboats, but Izzie interrupted her at eight.

"That sailboat she took was just over there." Izzie pointed toward a row of upside down skiffs along the bank.

A tear welled at the corner of Izzie's eye. Clara was glad she wasn't the one that found Mamma. It might be the worst thing in Izzie's life, as long as she lived, finding Mamma drowned like that. She wrapped an arm over Izzie's sturdy shoulders. It always made her feel small to reach around Izzie. Even when they were old, she would always be the little sister.

A fisherman raised his oars and pulled his craft to another spot closer to shore, probably in hopes of finding a luckier spot. Fool fisherman. The oars creaked in their locks and chopped at the water, scaring a pair of mallards. The two ducks flapped their nut-brown wings and scooted off. Screening her eyes with a hand, Clara followed the birds until they were tiny spots in the sky. She glanced back at Izzie who was also squinting after the ducks. A tear rolled out of Izzie's eye and crawled down her cheek.

"Papa is better now, don't you think so, Izzie?"

"I still worry. He's slowed down drinking liquor before, but then every time he starts up again, he changes for the worse." Izzie brushed the tear away.

Izzie would never ever trust him, thought Clara. "Why don't you ever give him a chance? He is trying hard this time. It's different. He's trying to make up for Mamma being gone."

"I want to give him a chance this time, honestly I do."

Clara took the gritty stones from her pocket and tossed one into the water. It broke the surface, then was sucked down, spreading ripples upon ripples. She began counting the ripples but the way they flowed into and out of each other confused her.

"There's a special reason I am hoping Papa is stronger this time. Can you keep a secret, just for a few days?"

"What is it?"

"Can you? Between you and me only, not even Billy?"

Clara bit down on the inside of her lip. Not telling Billy was going to be hard. Could she promise that? Izzie never had secrets, though. She crossed her heart then plunked stone number two into the water.

"Clara, do you think you could ever do the séances without me, or with Euphora instead of me?"

Clara squeezed a fist over her remaining stones. She knew it, knew it, knew it. Izzie was starting to hear voices after all and wanted to become famous without her.

"Do you want to be a medium, a real one, by yourself?"

"Clara, when are you going to get that out of your mind? I've told you over and over. I am not gifted and I am not going to be gifted."

"Mrs. Fielding and Anna said you were. I know you don't want to become like Mamma, but you aren't Mamma. You're you. You could use your gift and you wouldn't be loony."

Izzie's throat looked tight, then went red. She was about to yell. Clara braced herself, but Izzie waited a long moment, then finally smiled.

"Doctor MacAdams proposed marriage to me."

"No. How could he? You haven't even courted."

"Yesterday at the Hygienic Institute."

"What did you say?" Clara ground the damp stones around in her palm.

"I have to think about it and get to know him better."

"Do you want to?"

"I believe I do."

Izzie's gray-green eyes turned clear like the lake. Clara knew that look. Izzie did want to marry him. She had that smart, clear, questioning look on her face, like when she was reading a book and she'd look up from it and stare out at nothing trying to understand what she had just read. Sometimes she'd say something about what she was reading and sometimes she'd turn the page and keep going. But why on earth did she have that clear, smart expression about Doctor MacAdams? He wasn't very handsome and he wasn't young. He just plain wasn't good enough.

"But he's old, isn't he, Iz?"

"I like that, actually."

"I mean too old. You can't marry an old doctor." Leaning all the way back, Clara lay back on the dock, the blue sky cloudless above her.

"Well, I might marry him. That's why I want to know about you and the séances."

"What does that have to do with it? You could still be part of the Benton Sisters. Lots of mediums are married. Doesn't Mrs. Fielding have a husband in New York City?"

"Mac is going to move to Rochester. I would go with him."

Clara shot up onto her feet. "Rochester? Holy rolling Moses, Izzie. That's far."

"It's not very far. There are trains, stagecoaches, packet boats on the canals."

"But it's not Geneva. We would never see you. You can't leave now."

"I'm seventeen. I have to leave sometime."

"You don't have to leave. You could marry someone here. We could find someone here. What about a young medical student from the Geneva Medical College? We could easily find one for you."

"I'm sorry, Little Plum. You'll still have Billy and Euphora with you. If anything terrible happens with Papa, I will come back and get you, all of you. I promise."

Clara thrust the fistful of rocks at the lake. Water splashed up at Izzie's dangling feet.

"How will I do the séances without you?"

"You can do them on your own with Papa's sneaky information. I've watched the seekers. You dazzle them. You are uncanny, Clara."

"I need you, though. We have to be together, like the Davenport Brothers or the Fox sisters."

"I have to make my own choices." Izzie took Clara's hand and pulled her back down next to her. "We knew this day would come."

"What if Papa refuses permission? He hates doctors."

As Izzie softly stroked the back of Clara's hand, Clara imagined all the big holes Izzie would leave in her life. There were already all the holes Mamma had left…in her rocking chair, at Mrs. Purcell's dining table, next to Papa in bed. Now there would be more and more holes, everywhere empty holes, everywhere, but worst of all, in the Spirit Room. The chair directly across from Clara at the séance table would be a sorrowful chair no matter who sat in it. Clara sighed deeply.

And besides that, whenever Papa tried to force Izzie into, or out of, anything, it was trouble. If Papa forbid the marriage, it would be muskets and cannons firing off, the War of 1812 all over again.

"Let's skip stones." Izzie rose and started back down the dock.

"I don't know how, Izzie." Scrambling up, Clara grabbed the front of her dress and bolted to catch up.

"I'll teach you."

Once down on the shore, Izzie began searching. "There are a thousand skippers here. They have to be flat like little buckwheat cakes." She shoved up her dress sleeves and knelt by the water.

Clara reached her at the shore, knelt nearby. The muck smelled like fish, frogs, stinky wet earth. Dipping her hand into the water, Izzie brought out a shiny gray stone with flecks of pink.

"Get as many like this as you can, then I'll show you."

Clara rolled up her sleeve. When she reached into the water, the cold bit her like a snapping dog, but she didn't flinch. She clenched her teeth down and started rounding up the buckwheat stones and filling her pockets, twelve in one, fourteen in the other until her dress was heavy and the wet rocks soaked through her petticoat, chilling her legs.

A few minutes later they were standing on the shore, each with a small pile of stones. Clara jammed her red, tingling hand under her armpit to warm it.

Turning her shoulder to the lake, Izzie released the stone so that it sailed perfectly low and true, like the mallards. It touched the glassy surface once, popped up magically into the air, then touched down again, then up again, four, five, six and finally it sank into the lake and was gone, leaving a trail of six sets of circles.

"See? Try it," Izzie said.

For a long time, Izzie demonstrated, instructed, guided, and encouraged her, but one after another Clara's stones plummeted into the lake. But Clara wasn't going to give up.

If Izzie could do this skipping, and she knew Billy could do it, she could too. When her heap of rocks was depleted, she found more. She kept trying. Izzie was patient like an angel, never yelling, never calling her names.

Izzie had always been in Clara's life because she was the oldest. It couldn't be any other way. Izzie always protected her, led the way, and stood up to Papa when he needed standing up to. And sometimes when he didn't.

"Izzie, if Papa disappears or hurts Billy more than a rough slap, you'll come help us? Will you promise?"

Izzie slowly lowered her eyelids as though she were deep in thought, then raised them and looked Clara straight in the eye. "Yes, Little Plum. If Papa goes wrong, I'll come and fix things."

Clara let her arms hang down and glanced around at her strewn stones. There. That one would fit her hand nicely. She picked it up. Taking her sideways position, shoulder to the water, she took a deep breath and held it. As she drew back her arm and then swung it around, she felt the rhythm, the angle, the speed, the flow she had seen on Izzie and she let go. The stone swept out over the lake into the glare of the sun and landed delicately like a miniature weightless platter on the water. But then it rose up, and dipped down, again, again, three, six, eight, nine, ten before drifting under the water's skin.

She beamed at Izzie. "There. I'm a dabster at it. You could never do ten."

Fourteen

ON SUNDAY, IZZIE WOKE EARLY and prepared for her day with Mac. Billy and Euphora were downstairs doing chores, but Clara was just waking in bed in the Blue Room. Izzie leaned over her sister. "I might be some time. It's a splendid day and I think I will go for a long, long walk on my own," she said.

Clara eyed her with a suspicious arched brow and she was right to do so. Izzie had arranged to go on a carriage ride with Mac and didn't want to explain herself. She knew she couldn't keep her plans from Clara forever, but she'd tell her later. Turning and bounding down the front stairs, Izzie set off so quickly that no one in the house had the chance to ask where she was going.

Mac was waiting for her in front of the Geneva Hygienic Institute with an open cabriolet and dapple mare. Tipping his hat slightly, he smiled at her as she approached.

"Good morning, Izzie. We have a beautiful day for our ride."

"Good morning, Mac."

He was handsome, contrary to what Clara thought, but not in an ordinary way. He was confident, finely dressed in black and gray striped trousers, stovepipe hat, leather driving gloves, a blue silk tie, black wool greatcoat, and underneath, a deep blue waistcoat. During the night, a light spring rain had fallen, leaving a sheen on everything. It was a glorious morning.

Izzie took Mac's hand and climbed onto the seat. Settling herself, she shifted and straightened the skirt of her good dress, her gray and blue plaid, and the two petticoats underneath. Mac walked around behind the cabriolet and then hoisted himself onto the seat next to her, taking the whip and reins. He moved, perhaps not gracefully, but carefully.

Izzie had only been in a carriage this fancy a handful of times back in Ohio with her friend Julianna's father and mother.

"Do you have everything you need?"

"What do I need?"

She held out her empty hands, palms up.

"Nothing." He grinned and flicked the leather reins.

As the dapple trotted ahead, Izzie felt a shiver of excitement. Not only was this her first courtship with a man, but it was a man who might soon be her fiancé.

"Would you like to visit Silver Thread Falls? It's several hours to get there. It's on the east side of the lake." His low voice carried over the din of the horse hooves clomping in the mud, the harness jangling and the rumbling of the wheels. "I'd like to take you there. We have enough daylight to get there and back."

"Yes, lovely."

They rode without speaking for some time, down along the Geneva waterfront, by shops, hotels, foundries, Long Pier with two steamboats in dock, the New York Central and Hudson River Railroad Station, a coal yard, lumber yard, and then over the canal bridge. The rented dapple was dutiful, slowing when Mac pulled the reins and speeding when he slapped her back. They passed single horseback riders and other open carriages coming from the opposite direction with men, women, children in twos, threes, fours, dressed in their Sunday clothes, fancy bonnets, capes, stovepipe hats. Izzie hoped she wouldn't see anyone she knew and, when they turned south toward Lodi, she was relieved that there weren't as many travelers.

She especially didn't want Papa to hear about her excursion. She wanted to see Mac at least a few times to find out if she was truly interested in him as a husband before they spoke to Papa about an engagement. She didn't want to fight Papa every inch of the way when, in the end, she might decide not to marry Mac.

"Are you an admirer of Elizabeth Cady Stanton? She lives just east of here, in Seneca Falls, you know."

"I have seen her name mentioned in the newspaper. My landlady, Mrs. Purcell, speaks of her once in a while, but I don't know much about her."

He looked over at her, surprised.

"You're a young woman with an intellect, an appetite for books, and you haven't come across her writings, her ideas?"

Cringing, Izzie shook her head. Now he would realize that her self-education, as he called it, was greatly lacking.

He laughed. "Well, that may be just as well for me. Mrs. Stanton and her allies are determined to get married women the rights to their own wages and every woman the right to vote. I haven't decided yet whether that's going to be a good thing for society or whether it will put us in a big fat pickle. What do you think?" He gave the horse a flick of the reins.

She buried her hands under her shawl, chilled by the breeze of the speeding carriage.

"Well, I don't see how women having more authority over their own lives in a democratic society could turn the world into a pickle. What if we could vote? What if we could attend college? How would this harm society?"

"Then you are in sympathy with Stanton. But you haven't read her addresses?"

"No, no. You are the first person who has asked me what I know and don't know, what I think about things."

"I doubt I'll be the last. You're the first young woman I've met who has educated herself as broadly as you have."

That didn't seem possible, she thought. Surely there were many others like her and surely he would have met them.

THEY DROVE SOUTH FOR SEVERAL HOURS. Mac talked a lot about his dream of building his own water-cure institution, but also asked Izzie more about her thoughts on freeing slaves and women voting like men. He told her what he'd heard about Elizabeth Blackwell, the first woman to graduate from medical school, and right in Geneva at the Geneva Medical College. Blackwell had started something called the New York Infirmary for Women and Children in New York City and he said he hoped to meet her one day. Maybe they both would.

After a long while, Mac turned the cabriolet along Mill Creek. The sound of rushing water came from ahead as he stopped the carriage. She started to climb down.

"Wait." Mac darted around the back of the carriage and escorted her out of the gig.

She'd seen men doing this her whole life, but it was the first time she'd been offered a hand down like that. In the bright sunlight, as she lowered herself, she noticed his face, the fine lines around his eyes, and his skin, a bit rough. Clara was right. He was old, but not as old as Clara claimed. He wasn't as old as Papa. A boy, even a young man, wouldn't admire her the way he did and no young man she knew—the baker's son, the neighbor boys up on Williams Street, the older boys Billy brought home from Maxwell's Nursery— none of them thought about talking to her about abolition or Mrs. Stanton's ideas about women's rights or immortality. But Mac did. He was asking her so many things.

"Let's take the path around and down to the pool at the bottom of the waterfall," Mac said.

He tossed his stovepipe hat under the seat of the cabriolet and retrieved a blanket and basket. Izzie followed him down a steep, wooded path. When they arrived at the bottom of the falls, they stood together and watched it in silence for a few moments. The silver thread of water looked like thousands of tiny glass beads cascading downward. Spray rose into a mist over the pool. The splash of it was thrilling.

Mac smiled at her. In the daylight his hair was one kind of brown, a rich color like chocolate, his mustache somewhat lighter, and his curly eyebrows darkest of all.

They stayed there a long while not speaking, only listening to the crashing water. Eventually Mac left her side and spread the picnic blanket some distance away in a clearing under a pair of oak trees.

What joy to be away from the Spirit Room, the Blue Room, Papa, the children. It was her own private holiday. She wanted to stay here forever in the sweet sunshine with the new green oak leaves above and the waterfall flooding down, and this kind man. This kind man.

She would marry him. Why not? As long as she could understand why he hadn't married sooner. That was her one question. But if he had a reasonable answer, she'd marry him and go to Rochester and start her life, her own new life. She would be free of Papa and all the hoax medium nonsense.

"Are you warm enough?" Mac put the wicker basket on the corner of the gray blanket.

"Yes. Don't you know how these dresses and petticoats pile up like quilts?" She patted her layer-covered legs, tucked under her to one side.

Laughing, he knelt down. "I can't say that I have thought about it. Are you hungry?"

She nodded and he proceeded to set a picnic out with white ceramic plates, sturdy glasses, linen napkins, then two cheeses, a loaf of bread, and a bottle of red wine.

Izzie had tasted wine once, and Papa's whiskeys a few times when he was out and she and the children were being mischievous, but she had never consumed a full glass of wine. Mac poured, then held his glass up to toast. Mimicking him, she raised hers.

"To a spring day of great beauty spent together and…" He glanced up toward the waterfall, then back at her, "…to many more moments and days and years as delightful as this one."

Then they clinked glasses and she took a small sip. She tasted the sweet grapes and, as the wine slid over her tongue and into her throat, it left a tiny soft flame, not a burning fire like whiskey.

Mac didn't need to know it was her first real glass of wine. He didn't need to know it was her first picnic with a man. He was years and years ahead of her with picnics and women and waterfalls.

"Now, are you going to tell me about immortality? I've kept your family secret about the séances. You can tell me what you really believe."

She wasn't sure she should entirely trust him yet. What if he did say something to someone in town? What if the engagement didn't work out and the gossip he generated ruined the reputation of the Benton Sisters? Papa would be unbearable.

"Seal up your lips and give no words but mum," she said. "Shakespeare."

"I should have known you could quote Shakespeare." Rolling his eyes up, Mac set his glass down on the blanket. "All right, I promise to be mum for the sake of the Benton Sisters."

"Well, I do believe that people's spirits go on after death and have enough form to speak to some of us."

"To you?"

"No. But I believe some people do have the gift. The girl, Anna, who gave my sister and me lessons. Maybe my mother. I'll never truly know about her." She took a linen napkin from him. "Do you think the Benton Sisters are awful? Humbugs for money?"

"Awful is too much. I'm not a believer in this Spiritualism trend, tables tilting, tapping, rapping. I'm not convinced about the girl or your mother either." He took a knife from the basket and cut several slices of pale, hard cheese. "I must tell you now so that there will be no misunderstanding later." He held her eyes. "If you become my wife, a Rochester physician's wife, I cannot allow you to continue as a humbug medium. My Water-Cure Institute will require respectability. There can't be any spirit rousing associated with me or my office."

He couldn't have said anything more perfect. By mandate, she would be free of the hoax once and for all. He placed some cheese and a piece of bread on a plate and offered it to her.

"I am relieved. I don't want to continue. I have fought my father since the beginning, but we rely on the income now."

"What about your father's income?"

"He hasn't had any since we arrived in Geneva, at least that we know of."

Looking pensive, Mac ate a sliver of cheese and was quiet a moment.

"I won't have much at first. I have to invest in the facility and staff, but perhaps I could send a small compensation to your father for a short period to make up for your absence. After all, if I would be whisking you away on short notice and you are indeed critical to the family wages, it only seems fair."

This was incredibly generous. "You mean like a dowry in reverse?"

"Something like that. When shall I ask him for your hand?"

"I did want to make my decision first."

He smiled. "Of course." He untied his blue silk bow-tie and took it off, then unbuttoned his collar and removed it, baring his neck. Stretching out on his side, he leaned on his elbow near her. He was so tall, his legs so long, that his boots rested on the ground beyond the blanket. His wavy hair smelled of pomade, vanilla and lemon.

She took a drink, then held the glass tightly in both hands. "Now I must ask you something, Mac."

"Anything."

"Why haven't you married before?"

Squinting, he looked toward the swirling creek. "I haven't been settled in myself. I didn't think I could be a decent husband until now." He gazed into her eyes with an intense stare. "And there's something else."

There was something then. Izzie broke from his gaze and put the glass down, preparing herself for disappointment.

"I am a horrible romantic and I have been waiting to meet the woman that would fill me with an ultimate passion, a complete devouring passion. I haven't met her until now."

Izzie's heart stopped, then raced. She was to be his ultimate passion? But that couldn't be his reason for not marrying, being an unfulfilled romantic. It couldn't be.

"Haven't you met a thousand women? I can't possibly be this one woman you have been waiting your life for."

"I have met a thousand women and more. None of them, not one, made me feel what you did when you came in from the pouring rain into that bookshop. By the time you had spoken three sentences, I knew I wanted you to be my wife."

She wanted to believe him. She sipped the wine. Perhaps it would still her trembling. But he had to have the wrong impression of her. She wasn't someone who would stand out above and beyond a thousand other women.

"I think you believe I am someone I am not."

"I am the one here who is older and wiser. You can't see what I see. I know who you are and you are beautiful and intelligent and unique."

Well, he should be wiser than she was, but even so, something was blinding him. What if they married, and the fog he was in cleared? He'd be miserable. For a moment Mac looked into her eyes without speaking. She waited, thinking he was going to ask her something, even kiss her, but he didn't.

Suddenly, the chatter of voices interrupted them. She had been holding her breath so long during their gaze that her lungs began to ache. At last she exhaled.

"Well, there goes our privacy, I'm afraid," Mac said as he sat up.

Two young couples emerged from the path. They were speaking in merry tones as they arrived in the clearing. *Rubbish and rot.* These cheerful people had stolen away her brief moment with Mac. In another minute she would have told him that she would marry him. But then, the diversion was probably for the best.

Mac kneeled, brushed breadcrumbs from his sleeves and started to pack up their picnic, folding a towel around the bread, paper around the cheese, and replacing the cork in the wine bottle.

"Let's stroll along the path that follows the creek." Mac stood and offered her a hand.

They left their things and walked toward the two couples. One of the young women, wearing a blue bonnet trimmed with white roses, a cream-colored shawl, and a green and purple dress with full crinoline, was looking intently toward Mac. How on earth did she make it down the steep path in that dress? When they got closer, the woman seemed to recognize Mac and, in that instant, the gaiety dropped from her face like a falling stone. Then just as rapidly she replaced her lost smile.

"Doctor MacAdams. How surprising to see you way down here."

"Mrs. Page, a pleasure to see you." He gestured toward Izzie. "Allow me to introduce Isabelle Benton."

Mrs. Page introduced her companions. The man at her side was her husband. She seemed nervous, stuttering a bit, but then she smiled again and said to her group, "Shall we climb back up?"

"Please. I haven't had the chance to congratulate you on your marriage." Mac looked at Mr. Page and said, "My congratulations to both of you."

The newlyweds thanked him for his sentiment and the foursome continued their walk.

For some reason, it seemed Mrs. Page didn't want to see Mac. Izzie kept wondering about this as she strolled along the greenish-brown creek.

"I met Mrs. Page at the Hygienic Institute." He leaned over and picked up a gold and white hawk feather and began to twirl it between his fingertips. "Once someone is a patient of mine, I really don't like to talk about their condition with anyone else except other physicians or family members. It's more than a courtesy in our profession." He handed the feather to Izzie. "You could see how eager she was to get away from me. Sometimes what occurs between a physician and patient is of the greatest confidence. People, especially certain women, are embarrassed when they encounter me outside the clinic."

Twirling the hawk feather between her fingers just as Mac had, Izzie recalled how Mac had told her that women at the Geneva Hygienic Institute were seeking relief from female conditions and diseases. Did he attend directly to these women regarding their menses, pregnancy, or even abortion?

He took a silver pocket watch from his waistcoat. "We better start back, I'm afraid. It's a long ride."

She wanted to hear more, much more, about Mac's medical practice, but Mac was silent as they made their way back to the gig and dapple mare. Slipping the feather, her first gift from Mac, into her skirt pocket, she knew there would be another time to learn about his life as a physician and she could wait.

On the return ride to Geneva, Izzie felt giddy with the swift pace of the carriage, with Mac and his romantic confession about his ultimate passion for her. As they clipped along, her vision seemed vaguely blurry. Was that from the wine? Then the lull of the horse's trot made her sleepy. Closing her eyes, she sensed light flashing off and on behind her eyelids as they passed under tree boughs. The day was a beautiful dream. Yes, she would marry this man. She would go to Rochester and be a physician's wife.

"I should at least meet your father before you and I see each other again," he said.

Her eyes popped open.

"He doesn't know about your interest in me yet," she said.

"Not at all?" He turned toward her, his forehead furrowing down.

"You remember I told you that first day, he doesn't like doctors. I wanted to wait."

Mac snapped the whip. The dapple picked up her pace. "Why doesn't he like us?"

"He believes you are all quacks. That's all I know."

Again, Mac snapped the whip and the dapple accelerated. "His permission will be difficult to garner, then," he said.

"Yes. I am afraid it will."

But Mac had no idea how difficult it really would be. She would have to find a way to convince Papa. Surely there had to be one.

THE NEXT DAY, on her way to the Spirit Room for an afternoon séance with Clara and some Geneva ladies, Izzie noticed Mrs. Beattie, the milliner, their Spirit Room landlady, waving wildly at her through the shop window, beckoning her to come in. When Izzie entered the shop to greet her, Mrs. Beattie told Izzie to wait a moment because she had something for her. After going to the back workroom where she made, embellished, and repaired hats, Mrs. Beattie returned with a letter in her hand and presented it to Izzie.

"It's from a very tall gentleman who asked that it be given only to you, you personally, Isabelle Benton, he said. He was very serious about it. Isn't he the one acting for Dr. Smith at the Water-Cure Institute?"

Izzie's pulse quickened. It was a folded and wax-sealed letter addressed to "Isabelle," the handwriting neat and flowing. Running her finger over her name, she realized she had not yet seen his handwriting, its sharp turns and strong slope. It suited him. Feeling Mrs. Beattie watching her, she tore herself away from the letter. Mrs. Beattie was beaming as she waited for Izzie to explain, but Izzie quietly smiled back, slipped the letter into her pocket, and thanked Mrs. Beattie for her kindness in delivering it.

"Yes. Doctor MacAdams. He's with the Geneva Hygienic Institute for a few months. You always select the loveliest of your hats to wear each day, Mrs. Beattie. These purple tulips around the brim are stunning. Are they silk?" Izzie pointed at the bonnet.

Mrs. Beattie touched her green hat. "Oh, yes." Then she took it off to show Izzie in more detail how she had changed it, taken off a nice but plain embroidered satin band, had made a wreath of purple tulips with heavy Italian silk, intertwining the closed blooms with stems of dark green. Mrs. Beattie was very proud of it and it was stunning. As Izzie cooed over the hat another minute or so, she thought all the while of the letter in her dress pocket. She was nearly frantic wanting to get away to break the seal and read it.

Claiming she had to rush to a séance upstairs, Izzie thanked Mrs. Beattie again and sped off. Hoping that the Spirit Room would be empty so that she could read the letter in peace, she pushed open the door. No was one there. The room was sun-drenched and ready for the circle. A bouquet of yellow iris on the fireplace mantle, which Sam Weston had brought to Clara a few days ago, was still fresh. Izzie strode to the windows and stood in the bright warmth.

She drew the letter from her pocket and broke the red fleur-de-lis seal with her thumb.

My Dearest Izzie,

I must speak to you at once. I will be miserable and desperate until I do. Meet me tomorrow, Tuesday, at noon at my office. Only send word if you cannot come.

Mac

She read the letter over and over. What was it? What could he want? "Miserable and desperate." "Must speak to you." How could she wait until tomorrow to find out what he wanted? Impossible. Folding the letter back up and slipping it into her pocket, she looked across the room at the clock on the mantel. Three o'clock. *Miserable and desperate.* My Goodness. He loved her, wanted her. Taking a deep, long breath, she took the letter out and read it again, and then, again.

THE MINUTES AND HOURS CRAWLED like turtles that waddled, stopped and napped, then waddled a few steps, then napped again. Everything and everyone annoyed her. They were all distractions that had to be tolerated until noon tomorrow.

When noon finally came and she walked into the front entry of the Geneva Hygienic Institute, Izzie saw a few clusters of men and women milling near the doors to the dining room. The huge hallway was filled with the smell of food cooking, a din of voices, and the clattering of dishes. Supper was being served. She imagined the room Mac had shown her with its two glass chandeliers and shining silverware, every table surrounded by hydrotherapy patients eating piles of vegetables and drinking huge pitchers of water.

But even the enticing aromas permeating the hallway didn't make her feel hungry. She was too excited, too nervous.

She opened the door to the reception area to her left just as she had done that first day she'd come to pay Mac's fee. No one was there, not even the young man who had ushered her before. Today it was cloudy, threatening rain, with only a dreary light outside, but the glass on Mac's office door was bright, gaslights burning inside. The large, illuminated translucent plate of glass in the door was like a beacon, but without the receptionist escorting her, she felt like a trespasser.

Heart fluttering, she knocked softly on the mottled glass. She heard a rustling sound. He was there. The door opened. Mac smiled and reached both hands toward her. She offered hers, a simple reflex she couldn't stop, didn't want to stop. He squeezed her hands gently, his dark brown eyes locking with hers.

"I'm glad you could come. Please sit with me."

He led her to the two Windsor chairs at his desk and turned them so that they faced each other. Once they settled into the chairs, he leaned forward.

"Have you spoken to your father yet, told him about our courtship?"

"No, I was waiting for the right moment. Why, what is it?"

He pulled his chair closer, his knees within an inch of hers, and took her hands lightly in his.

"Since Sunday, I have thought of nothing but you. I haven't slept for two nights, not a minute of sleep." His words were gaining speed like a train pulling out of the station. "Monday morning, yesterday, I was walking to my office at sunrise. I thought if I came to work, I could think of something besides you. On my way, just as the light was turning soft, the air started moving the way it does when the sun rises and strikes it. I was stirred too, like the air, and I thought, I am about to begin a new life, not just a new day, a new life, with Izzie, a perfect love, after all these years. I realized I was awake, that I had been asleep my entire life, and all of a sudden, I was awake. I have found the full, true passion I have been waiting for. And in that very moment, I knew our destinies were entwined, that we were not only a man and a woman getting acquainted, who would become man and wife, we were much more, so much more. Our union would be one of passion and devotion, but also of intellect." He paused, his chest rising and falling in his cream-colored brocade waistcoat. "Izzie, I have been alone, always alone. Only now do I believe I can be the man I was born to be with you in my life."

His words were spiraling in her head, through her heart. She felt drunk, wanted to cry, giggle, stand up, fall, jump, fly. She was breathless.

"Mac, I will marry you. I decided when we were at the falls."

He lifted her hands to his face, kissed her fingertips, first on one hand, then the other, his mustache sweetly tickling, his lips dry, his breath warm, then brought their hands down to rest on his knees.

"This is what I prayed for, Izzie."

Her heart was pounding. "I am still uncertain about my father."

"That is why I was so urgent about your coming today. You must tell him right away about our acquaintance and my intentions, because it may take time to convince him. I want to speak to him myself as soon as possible, to allay his concerns, to contend with his objections."

Everything with Mac had gone so quickly, more than quickly, a river breaking over its bank and rushing across a flat valley. She and Mac had sprinted ahead from nothing to engagement in a matter of minutes, not weeks or months. This could confound things with Papa even more. He didn't like surprises.

"I will. I will talk to him by tomorrow."

He raised her hand, pressed it against his bristly mutton chop whiskers. Bursting heat shot through her entire body, up to her head, then down to her toes. She felt the urge to embrace him, kiss him.

"There's something else," he said.

He let go of her hands, rose slowly, and walked to the window by his desk, then stared out solemnly into the gray light. *Drat*. There was something awful he hadn't told her yet, something that would stand in their way.

"What is it, Mac?"

"I want you to come with me even if your father doesn't approve, even if he doesn't accept me."

She hadn't fully considered this. She had hoped there would be a way to convince Papa, that there would be a month or two for Mac to prove himself, and of course, he could prove himself. He was remarkable. If she wanted to marry him, everything would eventually fall into place. Papa would be an obstacle, she knew that, but there would be a way to sway him.

He returned to her, knelt by her chair, put an arm around the back of it, and took her hand again. His face was close to hers, his brown eyes moist. She smelled the lemon and vanilla of his pomade.

"What we will have, what is ours to have, is too powerful, too wondrous, for anyone to prevent. I beg you. Come with me whatever he says."

She swallowed, looked into his pleading eyes. She had to be with him. Had to be. There wasn't an inkling of doubt inside her. She nodded, raised his hand to her lips and kissed his fingers as he had kissed hers.

Fifteen

WHEN IZZIE OPENED THE SPIRIT ROOM DOOR and entered, Papa was on his hands and knees straddling a narrow opening in the floor where he had dismantled two long floorboards. Dressed in suspenders and rolled up shirtsleeves, he was crouching low, working on something underneath the floor. The wallpaper that concealed the bell and the little tunnel that housed the secret cord in the wall was torn open. A saw, knife, nuts and bolts, and bits of blue and green striped wallpaper were strewn about. The rug was in a heap.

"What are you doing Papa?"

"Brilliant. It's brilliant. Don't know why I didn't come up with it 'afore. I'm runnin' this cord from the bell in the wall over to your table so you or Clara can hit either the knocker or the bell with your foot. You won't need me standin' by the wall." He gestured toward the chair that had been Clara's before, but that Izzie was using more often now that Clara was the one who went into trance. "See I already got a new foot lever in next to the other."

"Doesn't the bell need more of a pull than a push of the heel?"

"That's what's brilliant. I've got a reverse lever in here." He jumped up, shoved his spectacles back with a finger, and beckoned to her to come and look at the spot where he was tinkering.

There was a hinge piece attached to a metal rod that ran toward the table to the new foot lever. The hinge was on a pivot so that the other end of it would move opposite the direction of the push and cause a pull of the cord. That pull would ring the bell hidden in the wall.

"Papa, it's very clever. You should invent things, get patents and make new things for foundries or farms or homes, like coffee grinders or engine parts."

He was kneeling now, smiling in a relaxed way. He removed his spectacles and started polishing them with his handkerchief. He looked satisfied, even proud. Replacing his spectacles, he broke into his full out crooked-tooth grin.

"You know, I've been thinkin' that same thing. I'm goin' to look into it when I git a chance, maybe next week."

"I think you should, Papa."

"Let's test the jingle. Go sit in the chair."

This was the best she could have hoped for. He was hopeful, happy, and best of all, sober. There wouldn't be a better time than this to tell him about Mac and his proposal.

Izzie sat at the oak table, her back to him.

"Now, try it," he said.

She had to find the new foot pedal with her heel, to the right of the old one. After a little searching with her foot, she jammed it down. There was a small pop. No bell.

"Blam'd cord broke. Too much tension on it." He knelt back down again to study the damage. "It ain't bad. Needs more slack. I can fix it, yessir."

Izzie turned sideways in the chair and watched him. He wasn't daunted by the setback. Only a few months ago something that small might have set his temper off if he was drunk or hung-over or even in between. He would have yelled at whoever was nearby or stormed out and gone to one of his taverns for hours, even days.

"Papa, I have something to talk to you about."

He stood and walked to the bookshelves by the door, picked up a roll of cord, and returned to the floor opening.

"I'm all ears, daughter. It about the séances? You got some new idea?"

"No, it's about my future."

Her throat tightened as soon as the words were out. He returned to his levers and hinges in the floor and began unwinding a length of brown cord. Izzie scraped the chair around to face him, then scratched at a prickle in the crook of her elbow.

"I've had a marriage proposal, Papa."

Her heart slowed as she waited for him to digest her news. And he took his sweet time. After a long while, he stood up, stared at his cord beneath the floor, and then began measuring, pacing foot by foot, letting out new cord until he reached the bell in the wall. The inside of her left elbow began to itch so much that she had to press down on it with the palm of her hand.

Finally, his back still to her as he untied the old broken cord on the bell in the wall, he said, "Well, that was bound to come, but I haven't seen any gents callin' on you. Who is it?"

He sounded steady, not angry at all. Now she had to be careful, but how could she soften the fact that it was Mac the physician?

"It's Doctor MacAdams, the physician who looked after Euphora and me when we were sick."

He dropped his hands from his task, turned around to face her.

"You mean the water-cure quack who you paid without my say so?"

Izzie nodded, trying to hide the flash of anger that charged through her.

"And who you been sneaking behind my back courting, I guess."

"Not sneaking, Papa. I've seen him a few times. The proposal was unexpected, very surprising to me. I ran into him at the bookseller's, then we had tea at the Gem. Then he invited me to tour the Hygienic Institute and that's when he proposed. He's going to Rochester and wants me to go with him."

"Rochester. One of them racing fast fellows, in and out of town like a train, pick up a wife and go. And that's it? You ain't seen him since he proposed?"

"Once."

If he asked the circumstances of the "once" she'd have to lie about Sunday at Silver Thread Falls now or admit she lied before. And had she been sneaking? Or was it just being private, being a grown woman on her own. He'd never asked where she was before, not for years, and certainly not since last summer when they arrived in Geneva. She held her breath.

"No, Isabelle." His voice was stony.

"No, what?"

"No, you ain't marryin' him and you ain't goin' to Rochester."

"Papa, this is a chance for me to have a better life, a good chance. I may not get another proposal like this."

"No daughter of mine is marryin' a quack."

"That's exactly what I knew you would say." Anger slipped into her voice. *Rot.* She didn't want to do that. She didn't want to get him riled.

"Well, why'd you even ask me, then?"

She rose from the chair and walked to the windows to collect herself and get some fresh air. She grabbed the sash of the middle window and jerked it up a few inches, enough to get a decent grip on the frame, then she hoisted it up. It was a spectacular spring day. She inhaled the sweet, warm air, calmed herself, then walked over to Papa and stood firmly in front of him.

"Because I hoped you care enough about me to be happy for me. I hoped you'd give me your blessing when I found a good husband, one who would love me and take care of me. Isn't that what fathers want for their daughters? Isn't that what you want for me, Papa?"

Blinking rapidly, he took a moment to consider her question.

"No quacks." His voice was flat, hard.

"He's not a quack. We're the quacks, lying to people, taking their money." She strode past the table toward him as she spoke. "We're the quacks, Papa. We fool people. We take advantage of their pain, their loss." Her hands were shaking so badly she crossed her arms over her waist to still them.

"We don't kill people, Isabelle." Saliva sprayed from his mouth.

"Papa, not all doctors kill people. Why do you say that? Why?"

He was breathing hard, gripping the ball of cord with a stiff hand and arm, his neck and jaw muscles tense and quivering.

She felt he might strike her. Was he holding himself back?

"One of them quacks killed my little brother. His chin jutted, shifted.

"What little brother? You never told us you had a brother."

"I ain't got a brother. A quack killed him when he was seven years old."

Her knees weakened.

"What happened?"

"Hugh was his name. He was sick with fever. My mother brought the physician. He bled Hugh, and bled him, and bled him 'til he had no blood left."

"Why didn't you ever tell us?"

"Some things ain't for talkin' about. When my family buried him, I was only ten, but I swore on Hugh's grave I'd never trust a doctor again."

"That's why you wouldn't ever speak to a physician for Mamma's spells? Papa, it's not right. I'm sorry for you, for your brother, but you're wrong about this. Doctors are not all quacks. We might not have lost Mamma if you had let someone examine her."

"You blame me. You blame me?" He stepped close to her.

"Yes. Yes, I do blame you. You never helped her."

His hand flew up, back, then swung fast and struck hard at her face. Pain exploded in the side of her head.

She dropped swiftly to the ground to get out of his way, to give in, to protect herself. Huddling low with hands over the back of her head, she stayed still. Tears started and she began to sob. Where was he? What would he do now? Was he going to strike her again?

Then footsteps scuffled toward the door. The door creaked open, then slammed closed. Then nothing. Her tears kept streaming, dripping onto the wood floor.

After a while she stopped crying and looked up. She rose and paced around the Spirit Room holding her hand over her face. She had to get away from Papa and his hoax séances and his drunkenness and meanness no matter what she had to do.

If he would do this to her when he was sober and seemingly happy, what else would he be capable of? She despised him.

She stood by the window and looked down at the street. The sun was getting low, sending long shadows after pedestrians and carriages. Soon the evenings would be humid and balmy, soon Mac would leave for Rochester. Her eyes raw from crying, she sighed deeply. At least she finally understood the reason for Papa's hatred of doctors. Papa had lost his brother because of a physician, but he had lost Mamma too because he had never taken her to one, and maybe he would lose his daughter too if she eloped with one. She could live her life or she could live Papa's. She would go with Mac whether Papa approved or not. Tomorrow she would try to convince Papa one more time, but if it didn't work, she'd elope with Mac.

THE NEXT MORNING, out in the back yard, in Emma Purcell's long narrow vegetable and herb garden, Izzie squatted at the end of a lush row of rhubarb, the red stalks lustrous, the leaves crinkled, heart-shaped, stretching up to the sun. She was waiting for Euphora to show her little sister how to pick the plant. Rhubarb meant spring, meant the beginning of fresh vegetables and fruits, meant more to come: peas, beans, strawberries, raspberries, blueberries, potatoes, onions, carrots, parsnips, tomatoes, corn, peaches, everything to come. Izzie took a deep breath, closed her eyes for a tiny moment. *Papa, please stay sober. Please, please, stay sober and let me go.*

"Are you all right, Iz? Why is your face sore?" Euphora stood over her in her smudged apron and blue dress.

"I'm all right. I had an argument with Papa."

Euphora's eyes widened. "Was he drunk?"

"No, he wasn't. Here. Let me show you how to take the rhubarb."

Euphora squatted and placed a flat basket on the earth near them. Grasping a red-tinted stalk at its base, Izzie pulled sideways, then away from her, then sideways again. The soil loosened. The plant came free in her hand. She held it up for Euphora to see.

"You know you can't cut it because it ruins the plant for next year," Izzie said. "Mrs. Purcell says these big leaves are poison. We can only use the stalks. Try that one." Izzie pointed at the next plant in the row.

Euphora grabbed the base of the stalk with both hands and began to twist it.

"No. Don't twist. Pull sideways." Izzie demonstrated by cupping her hand in the air.

Euphora worked the stalk until it released, lifted the huge leafy plant up, and broke into a proud grin, but then her blue eyes fixed on something behind Izzie.

"Hello, Papa," Euphora said.

"Take the rhubarb to Mrs. Purcell and leave me with your sister," he said.

Euphora scrambled up and took off to the back door of the brick house with her basket nearly empty.

Izzie stood. "Morning, Papa."

She searched his face, but it was impossible to tell what he was thinking. She knew he wouldn't apologize for the slap. Even though he didn't hit her often, he never did apologize. But she did want to know if he would give her permission to marry Mac. Behind his spectacles, the whites of his eyes were white, not red, and he didn't smell like whiskey. His shirt, top button open at the neck, wasn't as wrinkled as it was the nights he slept in it. That was good too. There was a chance. A chance.

"Mrs. Purcell give you one of her poultices for that bruise on your face?" he asked.

She touched the side of her face and nodded.

"You're like me, Isabelle. You want to do everything your own way. You're stubborn as a mule. You're always wantin' to kick me like a blam'd mule, too."

Rot. He wasn't going to give her permission to marry and he was going to make a speech about it, expecting her to appreciate his rationale.

He anchored his hands on his suspenders. "Even when you were little, you came and went as you pleased. You 'bout moved in with that Julianna friend of yours with all the books. We called you home, but you only came when you pleased. You took those folks for your family and there wasn't nothin' we could do so we just let you stay with them. Your mother always fought me on it."

He took his unlit pipe from his pocket and looked into the bowl. "She wanted them to teach you what they knew. I always thought that learnin' you got yourself would come back and bite us. Hell-fire. It has been bitin' us all along."

Izzie's shoulders stiffened as she remembered the thrashings with Papa's strap when she didn't come home for too long. If he was bringing all this up now, she truly didn't have a chance.

"Yesterday I went for a long walk all the way down to that place, Kashong Point, where you found your mother in the lake. I tried talkin' to her about your marryin'. I said, Almira, if you could turn yourself into one of them voices, I'd appreciate hearin' what you have to say about Isabelle." He sniffled, scratched a sideburn with the stem of his pipe. "Waited some time. But I didn't hear any voice. I guess I didn't think I would, but I never doubted your Mamma's abilities that way. Then, I left the lake and started walkin' home. After a few miles, a thought struck me like lightnin' and I knew what you was goin' to do. Because ya see, you are like me. You was goin' to run off with him. Sure as heck. You was goin' to run off with him. That's right, ain't it?"

She nodded slightly.

He blew a puff of air out the side of his mouth. "Knew I was right." He watched her a moment.

But she didn't say anything else. She had the feeling anything she said would get her deeper in trouble with him.

"I decided if you was set on runnin' off with him, maybe I could stop it by scarin' that MacAdams away. I walked straight into that Geneva Hygienic place, barged into his fancy office."

"You saw him?"

Now, it was over. No marriage. No Rochester. No freedom from Papa and the Spiritualism hoax.

"Acted all pleased to meet me. Mr. Benton this, Mr. Benton that. Sorry for my wife's death. I nearly spit at him." Papa turned his head away and spit into the garden as though he had stored it up for Mac and still needed to expel it. "Told him to stay away from my daughter."

Izzie wanted to slap his face, slap it as hard as he had slapped her and knock him down. Holding her right hand stiff at her side, she was trying to not let it fly out.

He pressed his spectacles back against the bridge of his nose. "Don't know how he did it, but he kept me there a long time, I mean a long time, talkin'. Finally, we come to an understandin'."

"What kind of understanding?"

"Well let's say that is between us men. You don't need to know the details, but you can go and marry him, if you have to, and if you don't have to, stayin' here is fine."

She felt the fire in her slapping arm die out. He turned his back and walked toward the kitchen door, then stopped and turned again to her, poking his pipe in the air. "He ain't the best one for you as far as I'm concerned, not even almost the best one, but I can see you're goin' no matter what I say." Then he disappeared into the kitchen.

Izzie plopped down on Emma Purcell's wood bench at the end of the garden. She sighed. It was money. Mac had offered him something to fill the gap for a while, to compensate for Izzie leaving the Benton Sisters and Papa had accepted it. Papa was smart. He had realized she would go with or without his approval but then he figured out he wouldn't have to be empty-handed. How much had Mac offered him? What was enough to get Papa to change his mind? She slumped against the back of the bench. She had just been sold like a commodity, a barrel of flour or sugar on the dock, an item on a bursar's list, *Izzie Benton. Sold, a daughter. Purchased, a wife.* If only Papa could have let her go because she wanted to, without the "understanding."

Papa had nothing at all to send her into marriage with, not one stick of furniture, but Mac wanted her anyway, and not only wanted her without a dowry of any kind, but was willing to help Papa—help her family. Mac's money would, after all, be better for the children. They would have something besides Clara's séance fees and Billy's earnings from Maxwell Nurseries.

She looked up at the blue sky. She could go. She would be free. She would be with Mac, wonderful Mac. And no more being a humbug medium. No more chance of real voices creeping into false trances. Free. She closed her eyes, leaned her head back, and felt the sun on her face and breathed in the fragrance of grass and apple blossoms. A fly

buzzed by her ear. In the distance, in the harbor, a ship horn
blasted three times.

Sixteen

IZZIE PRESSED TOWARD THE TRAIN WINDOW to get the widest view she could. Red oaks, tulip trees, chestnuts, and sweet birches robust with green leaves sped by, no longer the yellowish green of early spring. Fields of wheat and rye, wide and rolling, flowed by one after the other. This morning she had been Izzie Benton. By noon she'd become Mrs. Robert MacAdams. At three, she had kissed the tear-soaked, sullen faces of Clara, Billy, and Euphora goodbye at the train depot. By this evening she would reside in Rochester, New York.

"It's my first train ride."

"I know it is, my sweet." Mac, studying a copy of the *Water-Cure Journal*, didn't look up.

Closing her eyes a moment, she let her mind drift over the day. If she re-lived it enough times, she would hold it forever in her heart, never forget it. The rotund high-voiced Reverend Hubbard Winslow had married them at the stroke of eleven in the morning in Emma Purcell's parlor. She and Mac had been surrounded by Emma, the Carter spinsters, Mrs. Beattie, the milliner, Sam Weston, Papa, her sisters and Billy.

When Izzie had glanced around the room at the wedding group, she had hoped to see Mamma somehow. It seemed wrong that Mamma wasn't there with her long silver braid and stiff upright stance. Why should Papa be there, but not Mamma? Mamma's absence was the only thing that wasn't perfect about the morning.

Even though there weren't any fresh orange blossoms to be had for her hairpiece, or a bouquet, Mrs. Beattie made her a head wreath of white silk blossoms and told her she could keep it as a gift. Mac's voice trembled slightly and his hands shook as he spoke his vows. She had never seen him be anything except confident. His jitters were surprising but endearing. After the vows, the Reverend Winslow kissed her with pudgy lips, then Mac bent over to kiss her, his mustache brushing the skin around her mouth. The minister handed the wedding certificate to Mac and then they all had sweet wine and a special wedding cake made by Emma Purcell and Euphora. It was plump with currants and raisins, flavored with nutmeg and brandy. And butter. It had more butter in it than Izzie had ever seen in Emma's kitchen.

Even though Mamma would have loved to see her in the pretty white séance dress Papa had given her after she was ill, Izzie couldn't wait to take it off and change after the wedding party. It was the last four hours she would ever wear that dress. She would shed it, then leave it behind for Clara, for Euphora—for anyone who wanted it. It would no longer be hers. At long last.

After the cake and wine, Emma Purcell, eyes misty gray, presented Izzie with the wedding quilt she and the spinsters had made with Clara and Euphora. It was a lovely quilt of pinks, greens, and blues. It was the only thing in Izzie's wedding chest.

During the party Izzie watched Papa whenever she got the chance to see if he would take wine. But he never touched it.

He looked at it many times, but never touched it. This was the best wedding gift he could have given her.

"Got some business to take care of. Write us a letter, Isabelle," he said as he put on his new straw hat. Without another gesture or word, he walked out of the house, the first one to leave the party. She had the feeling she wouldn't see Papa for some time and it gave her a sense of great relief.

STILL ENGROSSED IN READING his *Water-Cure Journal*, Mac sat close to her. She gently touched his coat sleeve.

"The train is thrilling," she said.

Letting the journal flop onto his lap, he raised his eyes to meet hers, smiled, and shifted toward her.

"See those sheep?" He pointed out the window. "That's a bit like Scotland. Fields and fields crawling with the silly things." He pressed his shoulder against hers. "I came to America with my father when I was seven. Both my mother and sister died in childbirth in Glasgow. Not long after that, my father wanted a new life in a new land. The loss of my mother and sister is how I came to be a physician."

"We've both lost our mothers, then." She took his hand and held it a quiet moment. "Tell me again about the Rochester house."

Izzie had asked three times already on the train ride, but it wasn't enough. She wanted to hear about it a hundred times.

"Again?" Mac took her hand and laced his long fingers through hers.

"Again."

"Well, let's see. It's a white frame house, two stories in the neighborhood they call Corn Hill. We're just on the edge of it, Edinburgh Street. I couldn't resist it with the street being named Edinburgh."

Izzie squeezed his hand. She'd never lived in a neighborhood that had a proper name.

"Not far, a block or two away, there's the stately brick houses, and then in another few blocks, there's some really grand homes. The kings and queens of the Erie Canal live there."

"Which direction does ours face?"

"North and it has a little porch to keep you cool in the summer. Your first task is to furnish it. It's bare except for our bed and the work table in the kitchen."

"I don't know about purchasing furniture," she said.

"We'll have a meager budget. You'll find the basic things easily. Rochester has everything there is to have."

The bed. They'd share it tonight. She clenched her teeth and felt her stomach flutter. It was their wedding night. What would it be like with him? Would she like it? Would it be pleasant? Painful? Would she become pregnant right away? Was she ready to have a child? And another? And another? To scrub, wash, clean, sew, mend, cook, heal, teach, scold?

The train conductor walked by them. "Next stop Canandaigua!"

Mamma never did cook much and never taught her, either. Suddenly she envied all that Euphora had learned from Emma Purcell about housekeeping and cooking. Would she ever have time for anything besides housekeeping, even reading a book? She leaned her head against Mac's shoulder and gazed out at a distant farmhouse. But at least she wouldn't be a hoax medium anymore. That was the important thing.

The rocking of the train and the monotony of the churning wheels began to lull her to sleep. She hummed *Jeanie with the Light Brown Hair*, the notes vibrating inside her throat and ears.

Mac began to snore softly.   Izzie picked up her satchel and found the copy of Walt Whitman's *Leaves of Grass* Mac had given to her as a wedding gift and she began to read.

I celebrate myself, and sing myself,
And what I assume you shall assume,
For every atom belonging to me
as good belongs to you.

Seventeen

WHEN IZZIE AWOKE TO THE SOUND of loudly trilling wrens outside her new house in Corn Hill, Mac was gone from the bed and the room. He wasn't gone from the house, though. Someone was clanking and rattling in the kitchen downstairs and she assumed it was Mac. That should be her, the wife, rattling around down there, cooking breakfast for him. It was her first married morning and she was failing faster than she could say Mrs. MacAdams.

Not owning a night robe, she had nothing to throw over her shimmy. Under the bed linens, she felt her bare hip. The feel of her skin brought back the long night to her. Mac had been naked just hours before, on top of her, underneath her, next to her, his curly-haired chest pressing against her bosom. A surge of warmth flooded through her.

She slid toward his side of the bed, dove into his pillow and breathed in. There he was all over again, the plain soap smell of his skin and his lovely sweat. How happy she would be if she could carry that feather pillow around all day strapped to her front, endlessly breathing him in.

His pushing inside her had hurt a little, but not much. She was surprised how playful he had been and how eager to know if she was experiencing passion as he was.

"I'd like to know what hurts you and what gives you pleasure," he'd said.

She was shocked that he spoke at all, much less about their love-making. He'd touched her gently, firmly, gently again. Once in a while, he'd ask her, "Pleasure or not?" She was so flustered at first, she kept nodding yes, but after a while she told him, "The other was nicer. Go back to that place before."

"Which? This?"

"Yes. That."

It was outrageous and yet he seemed so kind and eager to please her. And that sheath he put on himself! Explaining that it was a new invention made of India rubber, a new sort of French Male Safe, which had always been made from animal intestines, he slid it on himself. Giggling at the memory of it, she rolled over on her stomach and buried her face. *Lawks*, that was horribly embarrassing. There were going to be things about being married to a modern physician she hadn't expected or even considered in her wildest imaginings.

Dressed in a white night shirt to below his knees, Mac appeared in the door looking sleepy and disheveled with a tray in his hands.

"It's our one day honeymoon. No Niagara Falls, I'm afraid. But I made you coffee. I broke the rules and entered into your woman's sphere first thing."

"I broke the rules and let you. I heard you down there tearing things up, but I didn't rush down to stop you."

He looked around for somewhere to put the tray, but there wasn't any furniture yet except the bed and the armoire. Squatting, he balanced the tray as he sank down and laid it on the bare wood floor.

"I'm sorry, but I have to get out to the building site today. Construction on my Water-Cure Institute starts this week. Maybe in a few months we could go up to Niagara Falls."

He poured a cup of coffee and held it up. "A few basic items on loan from the neighbors across the street. You'll like them. Very kind, the Meads, a man and wife and three children."

After he poured a second cup, he brought it to her. The aroma was delicious. She started to sit up, to lean against the brass frame, but stopped when she remembered she was naked. She grasped the bed sheet and started to pull it up over her.

"Don't be modest for me, unless you want to."

"Have you no inhibitions at all?"

"I lost them long ago. It's much more interesting without them, I find."

"What about in your work? Are you polite during your examinations?" she asked.

"Oh, yes, yes," he laughed. "My Lord, of course."

This seemed the best moment to end the modesty discussion. Just now, she was afraid to know more. She'd have time to find out about Mac and, after last night, their wedding night, she had a looming sense there was a lot more to know.

As she drank her coffee, he told her how excited he was about his new water-cure establishment. Setting his cup and saucer on the floor, he stood close. The place would be small to start, nothing like Geneva, he told her. There would be private rooms for twenty-five at first, but there was plenty of acreage and plans for another wing and a gymnasium if he could get more investors. Currently, he only had one man, a Fox Holland, backing him. There would be four different bathing rooms and enough equipment to perform all the latest techniques.

A dining room and kitchen would serve mostly vegetarian meals and there would be a lovely big parlor for quiet social activities or reading, a kitchen garden, a flower garden, and paths to walk along—a true retreat from the bustle of the city.

He was nearly breathless, talking rapidly, his thin hands flying about in the air. Then all at once his hands came to rest. He picked up his coffee, then looked intently into his cup. One of the two windows opposite the bed was wide open and a slight breeze sent a cool waft of air over Izzie's naked shoulders. When she shivered, Mac noticed, and without saying anything, he walked to the window and closed it.

When he came back to the bed, he stood again at her side looking down at her. "I should tell you something about my work that I haven't told you before. You could be surprised if you hear about me in town or when we are at social occasions and I don't wish you to learn about my medical practice from people who may not appreciate my efforts."

She didn't know what was more intriguing, that he had some dimension to his work that he had held back from her or that there was the presumption of social occasions. She imagined these occasions to be different from what she had known as a girl in Homer—barn raisings, picnics at the town square, and dances accompanied by three or four fiddlers.

He sat by her. "I've lied to you, or at least held something back."

The sheet still tucked under her neck, Izzie slid down into the bed. Oh no. A rotten cruel thing was coming. He had won her heart, married her, taken her from her sisters and brother, bed her in the most delightful way, and here, on their first morning together he was going to confess something dreadful. She groaned.

"Go on then, tell me."

"Recently I have been developing an expertise, besides the water-cure, that I should have told you about."

"Are you going to try surgery like Charles Bovary and ruin some poor fellow's foot?"

He didn't laugh, or even smile. She should keep her mouth shut. That was a silly thing to say. He had a confession to make. Maybe he did want to become a surgeon.

"I mentioned a little something to you at the Falls that day. Women's physiological systems."

"Midwifery?"

"I mean the study of pregnancy, birth, female disease."

"Are you going to sell preventative pills through the mail like Madame Restelle?" She laughed nervously. "My husband is to be Monsieur Restelle?"

"No, I think not. I am writing a book for women and men about preventing conception using water-cure and other methods."

There wasn't anything truly awful about his pronouncement. It was daring really. She was to be the wife of a sexual advice physician. She sighed. She'd have to learn to get used to that.

"Something like Charles Knowlton's *The Fruits of Philosophy?*" she asked.

"How do you know about that book? Have you read it? Here I thought I plucked a young unripe peach from the tree."

"Some of it. My friend Julianna, back in Ohio, found a copy in her parents' bedchamber when I was about twelve. We took it to her basement with a candle and read and read for hours. We scarcely understood it. It was a small paperbound thing, very tattered from use. Julianna's mother came down and caught us, though, and scolded us, and we were never able to find where her parents kept it again."

Mac laughed, then a grim cast veiled his face. "Are you angry that I delayed confiding in you?"

"I wish you hadn't delayed. You won't again, will you?"

Smoothing down a sideburn, he blinked several times, then took her cup and his to the coffee tray on the floor and replenished them. He had something else to tell her. She could feel it in his silence.

"There is more." He handed her the white cup and saucer, fragrant and full of coffee. Then he sat near her. "I want to have the kind of marriage that is a sanctuary from the world…a place, a home, where there is love and quiet and rest and trust." He leaned far over toward the floor, depositing his coffee cup with a rattle, then shifted himself on the bed near her and reclined against the headboard next to her.

"Mac, if you tell me everything now on our first day, we can go ahead, man and wife, knowing the things we need to know about each other."

"Yes. That is what I hoped for." He paused, staring out across the room toward the windows.

Her hands were trembling now, jiggling her cup. Was it the coffee making her shake, or his pronouncement?

"Izzie, please don't think I am evil." He pinched back his shoulders. "I would like you to go along with my pregnancy prevention ideas as part of my study."

The cup and saucer drooped in her hands, then settled at an angle. A small splotch of coffee spilled onto their new wedding quilt, her gift from Mrs. Purcell and the others.

Mac swooped up her cup and saucer, placed them on the tray on the floor, then came back to her. *Rot.* Her beautiful quilt was stained. She glanced around the room for something to absorb the coffee, but of course there was nothing.

"I have a couple of towels in my trunk downstairs. Shall I?" He leaned forward, ready to go.

"No, it's too late. Too late." She squeezed the square with the moist stain. How could she have done this on her first morning as a wife?"

"I'm sure it can be saved." He took her hand from the quilt and held it. "You're shocked. I should have told you before we married."

"Once again, I am not sure whether you want a wife or someone to experiment on."

He was silent a moment. "My work will be important to thousands of men and women all across the country. I believe my theories and their influence will be significantly greater than any children we may or may not have over the next few years. We have many years ahead for children. I want you to be by my side in this, perhaps even help me with the book." He cracked an expectant smile.

She suddenly felt something stick in her throat. She coughed, then asked, "You don't want children?"

"Of course I want offspring, but I don't want a dozen and I don't want to see you worn out by having child after child after child. Let's see how the prevention works for a year or two."

In her whole life, there was never another notion in Izzie's mind besides the fact that marriage meant children. She never thought about trying to control when she would have them or how many she would have. Married women had children and miscarriages and that was that. But this idea that she wouldn't become pregnant right away, oddly, seemed a relief.

"What do you want me to do?"

He bent over, kissed her lips quickly, then shot up from the bed and strode toward the armoire. "To start, I want you to use a pure water douche four times a day. I believe the water alone can prevent conception, no need for the elaborate mixtures, just the water."

She chuckled. This was not how she had imagined her first morning with Mac. She should be horrified, embarrassed, but he was so enthusiastic, so dear, there was nothing to do but go along with him. She wasn't entirely sure what water douching even was.

"You mean water inside me like some kind of rinse?"

"Exactly."

"And when the winter comes and it is freezing cold, you want me to press cold water into myself four times a day?"

"Yes, they all complain of that. You could warm it on the stove if you like."

"They all?"

He opened a door on the armoire and reached for something on the upper shelf. "I have been prescribing this for over a year. We were offering it at the Geneva Hygienic Institute."

Suddenly Izzie remembered two women who were Mac's patients, the one who acknowledged Mac in the hall of the Geneva Hygienic Institute the day she had the tour and he proposed, and then there was another woman in the green and purple dress at the waterfall. That woman was so very uncomfortable and wanted to get away from them hurriedly. These two women had been his patients—his female patients—and it was likely they were experimenting with his methods.

"Was it successful?"

He brought down a small wood box with a latch on it and set it on the foot of the bed. "No one pregnant so far. I am corresponding with six women who are using the water douche according to my prescription. A few of them may come to my new Water-Cure Institute for a stay when it is ready."

"My shimmy?" She pointed at her undergarment draped across the bed's brass foot rail.

Smiling sweetly, he brought it to her and placed it on the quilt over her lap. "I'll give you instructions on the douche now, then we'll dress and go into town. We'll shop for necessaries for the kitchen and a piece or two for the parlor. You need a reading chair, my darling."

He leaned over and kissed her, his mustache bristly around her lips, his breath warm and smelling of coffee. She reached for his shoulders, letting the bed sheet fall down to her waist.

He stood upright. "Or perhaps we could postpone town for a while?"

She nodded, the warmth of a blush flooding into her face.

IZZIE SPENT THE REST OF THE MORNING embracing, kissing, and caressing Mac, his body so much longer and narrower than hers, and discovering that he knew a good deal about women's sensitivities. He had aroused her gradually, off, then on again, for what seemed like hours until she felt a crescendo of waves spread up through her back, chest, and throat, and down through her legs all the way to her toes. She released something between a sigh and a groan that rumbled on like a joyful growl. He couldn't have learned all these things from advice guides, she thought.

He rolled away from her and removed the French Male Safe made of India rubber, the second one he had used. Did he have dozens of these tucked in his trunk? She had known about the Safes because Papa used to get them by mail for five dollars a dozen and years before, on more than one occasion, Clara and Billy had opened the packages and played with them not knowing what they were.

Propping himself up on his elbows and grinning at her with crinkles around his eyes, he said, "I'll show you the water douche now."

"You want me to do it now? Wasn't your French Safe enough?"

"Yes, it should be, but the sooner we start you on the water method the sooner I can disband with the Safes, except during your most receptive times. The Safes impede my pleasure considerably."

"And when are my most receptive times?"

"Twelve days after your menstruation ends." He got up and moved back to the foot of the bed where the small box still lay.

Izzie felt her jaw slacken. Her mother had never told her any of this. If Mamma had lived even a few more months, she would have met Mac, would have known the man she married. And if Mamma had lived longer, she could have offered Izzie marital advice, mother-daughter marital advice—not something from a book or a doctor, or even a husband-doctor. Her heart ached a little at these thoughts. Still, it was hard to imagine Mamma's advice would have been as thorough as Mac's.

Maybe someday she would have a daughter and teach her everything she knew about life. Her daughter would go to school, to college, maybe be a physician like Elizabeth Blackwell, the first woman to study at Geneva Medical College.

Mac laid pieces from the polished walnut box out on the quilt. A long rubber tube with a bulb inserted in its middle stretched across the bed like a slithering snake digesting a rather large prey. Near it was a short, slender piece with a rounded tip, about the length of a pen.

"Do you really want children, Mac? I mean, eventually?"

"Of course." He pumped the bulb a few times, air hissing out the tube ends. "I had this made to my specifications, bulb and tube in one piece. I'm thinking of applying for a patent." He looked around, scratching the back of his neck. "I'll go down and get water."

After he'd left, Izzie crawled into her shimmy. The bright sun was gone from their eastern windows, but the light was clear and the sky blue outside. It was afternoon already and she was ravenous.

If Mac's prevention system worked, she wouldn't have children for a while. She sighed. She was only eighteen. There were many years ahead to have children. She could keep up the household and still have time for other things—for Rochester, neighbors, friends, books. She could go to hear lyceum lectures, concerts, maybe Jenny Lind or the Christy Minstrels, and theatre productions and exhibitions. And Mac said he might want her to help somehow with writing a book. It would all be far more exhilarating than the school she never went to.

Glancing down at the syringe, she leaned over, picked up the bulb, then squeezed it in her hand. It sucked and hissed. Mac's introduction of preventing conception did seem abrupt. Shouldn't a man and woman discuss these things in a thorough manner? The timing of having or not having children surely should be something she as the wife should have a say about. He had simply presented this experiment to her, hadn't really asked if she thought it was a good idea or not. She compressed the bulb again and held it. Hearth and home and the raising of children. That was her sphere, wasn't it? As she released the bulb, air drew back in to inflate the oval shape. Still, she had to admit she liked the idea of postponing children.

When Mac's footsteps got close on the stairs, she replaced the syringe to its spot on the quilt.

"Here we are." He appeared with a pitcher and a large bowl. "I got into my trunk." He set the bowl and pitcher on the floor and picked up the rubber tube. "There's nothing at all to this. The clamp prevents any water from getting out before you are ready. You snap it closed like this." He flipped a small metal lever on the tube between the syringe and the bulb. You need only suction and gravity. You want the water higher than you, that is, higher than your birth canal." He cleared his throat as he looked around for a high place, but they didn't even have a washstand yet. "I'll hold it up. You operate the bulb. Moderate pressure. Now stand over the bowl."

As she stood in place, he picked up one end of the tube and put it into the pitcher of water, then handed her the syringe end.

She laughed nervously. "You're quite odd."

He lowered the pitcher and tube. "Am I? I'm sorry." At first his eyes looked disappointed, but finally he smiled and laughed with her.

"All right. All right. But if you must stand there with the water pitcher, please turn away. A young woman needs a shred of modesty on her honeymoon. She held up the rounded syringe. "This goes in all the way?"

He nodded. "But not to the point of significant discomfort."

"When I know you better, I'll ask how you know all these things. Don't tell me now." She held up her palm toward his face fearing that he would begin rattling off explanations. "Look that way, toward the windows."

When he had craned his neck away from her, she spread her feet on either side of the bowl, slid the smooth shape inside her, and leaving it settled there, took the bulb, compressed it, then released it.

"I forgot to say one more thing." Mac said without looking at her.

"And that would be?"

"Hold the syringe in place, otherwise the water pressure may bring it out."

She opened the clamp and pressed the bulb closed again. The water was cool inside her, then dribbled down into the bowl.

"There, I've done it." She started to withdraw the syringe.

"Excellent. Now you must irrigate three more times."

"Three more times? What a nuisance."

"Not as much as an unwanted child."

"I thought you said you wanted children?"

"No, I mean for those in general who do not want another child, this is a minor nuisance in comparison."

"If it works," she said as she inserted the syringe again.

He started to turn toward her, but she glared at him and he looked back toward the windows.

"I believe it will work. The water will flush the zoosperm out. I don't believe there is a need for all the elements people use in douches such as alum, baking soda, vinegar, white oak bark."

As she continued to squirt chilling water into herself he named off a list that was so long she was sure he was going beyond fact: borax, metallic salts, bichloride of mercury, lactic acid, carbolic acid, pearlash.

Dripping over the bowl, she completed the fourth dousing. "Is there anything women don't put in themselves?"

She removed the syringe and sat on the bed.

Mac turned and faced her, beaming like a bright footlight. "That is precisely my point. It is all unnecessary. Water is all one needs, lots and lots of water. It is pure and gentle. These other things can irritate and damage a woman. Water is the answer to perfect health in every way. It washes away whatever one desires to wash away. I am convinced of it."

It was an interesting idea, she thought. "Mac, I think we need to go into the city and purchase a washstand so we have something to put our water on."

He stepped toward her, bent over and kissed her lips slowly, tenderly. She felt aroused all over again, then pulled away from his face and brushed her fingers down his long sideburns.

"Can we take the omnibus? I've never ridden one," she said.

"Of course."

Eighteen

SEATED IN THE CHAIR by the foot knocker and bell ringer, Clara felt downcast. Elbows on the table, she propped her chin with her palms. Sam Weston was there, but where was everyone else? They couldn't all be late. Was it because Izzie was gone? Yes, of course that was it, she thought. The seekers weren't showing up because they only wanted to see Izzie.

"It looks as though I am the only one today."

Sam Weston had his hands spread flat on the séance table as though he would join up the spirit circle right then and there. Papa stood by the mantle grinding something around in his coat pockets.

"No one sent messages to cancel. Let's wait a while." Papa looked at the clock. He sounded all right, but he was down in the mouth. It was six in the evening, a half hour after the appointed time.

Weston nodded, tapped all ten fingers on the table, and then fell still again. Papa paced to the windows, looked down at the street, then back to the mantel, then windows, mantel, windows, mantel. Nine times. He was twitching nervous. Someone had better come soon or he'd blow like a canon.

Even though Clara had been terrified for the first two or three séances without Izzie, even though her hands quivered like divining rods when she used the alphabet sheet, in the end, she had done well enough. Papa was right there behind her doing splendiferous things with three new hidden bells, tinkling them at just the right moments, and he had started something else since Izzie had gone. He'd say things like, "Silence now while Miss Clara achieves receptivity," or "please be patient while Miss Clara enters her trance."

Mr. Isaac Camp had come several times to hear his departed wife Jane and they were expecting him again this evening. Everything she tried was like magic with Camp. When he first came and was terribly sad, Izzie said he was like a lonely poet, or was it a dog? Either way, he got happier and happier each time Clara's Jane said something kind to him. And that was just her, just Clara. No Izzie. Papa said, "I'm proud of you, Little Plum." Proud. That was sweet summer cherries.

And not only that, all the seekers who had been at that circle when she tried her very first trance as Jane Camp had returned again and paid the increased price—seventy-five cents. Even cranky old Barnes, the skeptic. It was fun being Jane Camp. Clara, as Jane, could always make her husband Isaac cry, laugh, or get a sentimental look in his pale blue poet dog eyes.

Weston tapped his fingers again. The table wasn't a dang piano. Did he think it was a piano? Of course Sam Weston was there nearly every day. He was lonelier than Isaac Camp. Didn't he have any other family or friends or neighbors besides her and Papa and whoever showed up at the séances? And he stared at her too much. If he would just talk to Papa more about their business or whatever it is they did together and talk to her less, that would suit her fine.

"You look lovely in the white séance dress this evening, Miss Clara."

"Thank you, Mr. Weston."

He always said that. Every time. That or the compliment about her brown hair being so shiny and elegant or the one about her complexion being pure as milk or sometimes all the compliments at once. It was right around the time Izzie left that he started up with the flattery. He had already been bringing the flowers to her a few times each week, but then he added the honey-fuggling. She had to admit, it was nice at first. She blushed when he said these things, but now it was becoming tiresome. When he lingered at the end of the séances and she escorted him to the door, she'd try to guess. Which one would it be today, Mr. Weston? Dress, complexion, or shining hair? Two out of three times, she'd be right. Were all grown men this predictable or was it just that she knew him so well by now?

She had advised Billy, "When you get older and want to compliment a woman, make up something new each time. Otherwise you will become boring to her."

"Here's Camp," Papa said from the window.

A grin of relief spread across his face as he strode to the door. The sound of Camp's footsteps clomped up the stairs as he approached.

"Come in, Camp. Do you know about the others? No one's here."

As Papa had trained her to do when greeting seekers, Clara stood by her chair, hands folded in front of her, and smiled. Camp shoved Papa aside and planted himself like a fat tree trunk in the middle of the room.

"You liars! You worthless liars. Both of you." Camp's pale blue eyes stabbed at her like shards of ice.

"What is it, Camp?" Papa bolted to Camp's side.

"What is it? What is it? I found you out, Benton, you and your lying daughter and the other one, too."

Weston shot up like a rocket and strode toward Camp. "Now, now, Camp. Easy there."

Camp ignored Weston and looked at Papa, hate pouring out of him like a spilled barrel of poison.

"I found out how you and your daughters know so much. A certain lady told me how you get the information that you need. Then your little despicable actresses play it out."

Clara felt a kick to her stomach and sank back into her chair.

"Please, Camp, sit down. You're right about us collectin' background on folks, but my daughter is truly gifted. All the mediums need things to enhance the séances. It don't mean they aren't truly talkin' with the spirits."

"That's it, Benton. I ought to take you down to the sheriff and have you explain it to him." Grimacing, Camp turned to Clara and stabbed her with his ice-shard eyes again. "And you. I trusted you with my grieving heart. You took my dear wife's memory in vain. You lied to me. You're abhorrent. Coddling me, kissing my hand."

Warm tears streamed down her face. Her shoulders quaked.

Weston grabbed Camp's arm. "No more. Leave now or I'll kick you down those stairs."

Camp jerked his arm free. "You're already ruined, Benton. I've already told everyone I know about your hoax. I've told them down at the *Geneva Gazette*. It'll take just two days for the entire city to know you're nothing but a scoundrel."

The newspaper. They really were jiggered now, thought Clara.

"Come on now, Camp. Sit down. The spirit talk ain't gum. Let Miss Clara tell ya what her trances are, how she uses the knowledge to call forth the spirits." Papa gestured toward her.

Holy rolling Moses. Why was he offering this? She didn't want to lie right now. She wanted Camp to leave.

A mean winter storm came over Camp's face. "No, Benton. I'm through with her."

He rammed past Papa and Weston and walked out. The two men stood there, eyes locked. Then Papa left too. He didn't even look at her. All she ever did was what he wanted her to do and did it the best she could. She buried her face in her arms on the table and cried.

Weston's footsteps grew close. "Would you take my handkerchief, Miss Clara?"

Why couldn't he leave too? Why couldn't everyone get out and leave her alone? Why couldn't Izzie be here?

Clara looked up at Weston through the blur of her tears and took his red silk hankie.

"Thank you, Mr. Weston. I wish Izzie were here. She'd know what to do."

"She would, but we'll think of something, Clara. We'll think of something."

LATER THAT NIGHT, Clara woke to rustling noises.

"I'm gonna fix it. You'll see."

She bolted up. Billy was already sitting up braced against the wall and there was Papa standing by Mamma's rocking chair in the eerie, silvery moonlight. Drunk? Papa yanked off one suspender, then another, fell back into the rocker, and struggled with a boot.

"Gonna fix it. No grimy little skunk Isaac Camp is goin' ta wreck my enterprise. Ain't smart enough. You hear me, Clara?"

His boot came off and flew several feet before clunking down. He was definitely drunk. Euphora stirred. Billy lay back down and pulled his blanket over his head.

"Do you hear me, Clara?"

"Yes, Papa. You're going to fix it."

"Thass right."

He wrenched his other boot off, let it fly, then stood. The movement of the rocking chair nearly shoved him to the floor but he caught himself. Clara gripped the top of the quilt. If only Izzie were here. Papa rambled and weaved his way to the foot of Billy's bed and stood there staring at the lumpy blanket for a moment. His breathing sounded like the shushing of a fireplace bellows.

"Look at him. Coward boy hidin' from his Papa under a blanket. I ain't hit you in months. What're you skeered of? Puny jackrabbit."

Suddenly Billy threw off the blanket and was up, all the way up, standing on his bed, higher than high in his white long johns, like a swirling ghost in the moonlight.

"I ain't skeered of you, old man." He leapt from the bed.

Clara's heart stopped. *Tarnation.* He was going for Papa. But Billy landed next to Papa, not on him, then ran from the room. He slammed the door hard.

"See? Skeered, like a puny jackrabbit." Papa chuckled, swayed, sniffled, then wiped at his nose with the palm of his hand.

Clara sat still, waiting, biting the inside of her lip. What was he going to do next? She felt Euphora press against her side under the quilt. This is when Izzie would stand up to him, stare him down, yell him down, send him to bed, or at least make a good try of it. Clara put her hand on Euphora's warm back and patted her. If only she could stand up like Izzie for Euphora's sake. She waited. Euphora waited.

Finally the liquor got the better of Papa. His breathing slowed down, his shoulders sagged, his chest caved, and lastly, his eyelids drooped. He swayed another moment, then crawled onto Billy's bed and, almost instantly, began to snore. Maybe it would be just this one binge. He was upset about what Camp had done. Maybe he could fix it tomorrow when he was sober again. Papa could do almost anything. She'd help him.

She bent over and whispered into Euphora's ear. "It's all right. He's asleep. He'll be better tomorrow. I'll help him fix our reputation and get our Spiritualism business going again. I know I can do it. Go back to sleep. It's all right." She stroked Euphora's long hair until she heard her drift off.

She didn't sleep herself, though. She just listened to Papa's snoring, gravelly at times, whistling at others, and watched his tuckered out face in the moonlight. After a long while—hours probably—the silvery light seemed to vibrate and his head started to look like a big granite rock. It disturbed her so she closed her eyes. If they could get a handful of people coming back for spirit circles, she knew she could touch their hearts, amuse them, delight them and build things back up. Papa would be proud of her again and he wouldn't have to get drunk. She slid back down under the quilt and turned her back to Papa.

Where had Billy gone? He wasn't dressed. Maybe he was only down in the parlor on the sofa. He wouldn't wander undressed around town in the wee hours of the night. No, he'd be on the sofa downstairs or maybe out in the woodshed. That's what she would do, and her twin would do the same. Wouldn't he?

A FEW DAYS LATER, the *Geneva Gazette* article came out revealing that Isaac Camp had found them out. The weather turned miserable and hot that same day and all their spirit seekers just vanished. The following muggy days had been dreadful. Clara lazed around the Spirit Room with nothing to do but wait for anyone at all to come by.

Finally, after a week, the heat broke. Clara was home for the night, standing by the open window in the Blue Room. It was raining hard, pounding on the roof and windows, soaking the sill in front of her. Every once in a while thunder rumbled far off down the lake. Euphora was already asleep and Billy was out with his friends from Maxwell's Nursery. Behind his closed bedchamber door, Papa and Sam Weston were talking business.

The small news story quoting Isaac Camp was titled *Benton Spiritualists Exposed.* In it, Camp was quoted, "I found out that I was tricked on more than one occasion by Miss Clara Benton into thinking she was communicating messages from my beloved departed wife. A reliable person in Geneva, who I will not name to protect her privacy, told me that Mr. Frank Benton sought her out almost daily to gather personal knowledge of those gathering for the spirit circles and then had his daughters use that information to play humbug with the audiences. Miss Clara Benton is a full-fledged hoax."

Once in a while there were stories in the papers about Spiritualists. Often, as with Mrs. Fielding's visit, the newspaper ran notices of lectures and spirit circles. When Mrs. Fielding came to town, the *Gazette* notice said "PUBLIC RAPPING – It is announced that Mrs. Adele Fielding, a medium of considerable note, will give two public exhibitions at Linden Hall on Tuesday and Wednesday evenings."

"Of considerable note." That would have been just what Papa wanted, not "full-fledged hoax." And that little bitty article was all it took to dry up the rest of the seekers. It had slowed down after Izzie left, but now no one was coming at all, not a single sad or curious person.

Papa riled like a mad man at first when the *Gazette* came out. Billy stayed clear of him. Billy didn't even come home for a couple of days. Then Papa went sullen and silent, like the humid weather was holding him down for a while, but now, like the rain breaking the spell of heat, he was up to something with Sam Weston. She could tell by the sound of their voices through the closed door.

They'd already been in there a couple of hours. She was pretty sure they were hatching a new big idea. She crossed her fingers and hoped it had nothing to do with Spiritualism or her.

She couldn't hear much through the door, but she could hear enough to know it was about shipments on the canals and she heard the words "bank notes" a few times. She heard *Gazette* a few times, too. Reaching her hand out the open window to feel the rain, she caught some water on her fingers and brought it to her throat.

Suddenly there was a scuffling noise in Papa's room.

"You keep your skunky hands to yourself. You don't touch her. You hear me? You hear me?" Papa's voice boomed through the closed door.

"I'm sorry, Frank. It was a compliment." Weston said.

"No, it ain't a compliment. You're a goddamned son of a bitch. Now git out." Papa's other door, to the hallway, opened. "Git out!"

"I said I was sorry," Weston said from the top of the stairs.

"You don't ever bring that up agin', ever."

Papa's door slammed, but the Blue Room door to the hall was still open and Clara watched Weston in the lamplight in the hallway landing. What the *jo-fire* was it all about? As Weston swept his palms over his slick hair, Papa's hall door opened again and Weston's big hat, the wide-awake, came flying at him. Weston caught it against his chest. Then the door crashed closed again. Donning the wide-awake, Weston took a step toward the Blue Room's open door and glanced into the darkness.

Clara held still like a cat on alert, hoping he couldn't see her there by the window. He looked toward the bed where Euphora was squirming a bit and then his eyes searched around, but she was pretty sure he didn't see her standing against the curtain. Finally he snugged his hat on his head and left.

You don't touch her. Papa's words echoed in her head. Who did he mean? Was Papa courting someone Weston was also interested in? Were they fighting over a woman? Thunder drummed in the distance. She closed the window most of the way. *You don't touch her. You don't touch her.* Sliding onto the bed next to Euphora, she shoved at her sister's hip until Euphora rolled over and made more room. Clara sighed. If Papa was serious about sparking someone they'd hear about it sooner or later.

A flash of lightning illuminated the room with white light. Mamma's rocker lit up for a snap second. A single tear came to her eye. Why couldn't Mamma still be here reading her Bible and rocking in her chair with her long silver hair braid sweeping and swaying like an artist's paint brush? A thunderclap exploded just above the house. She gasped. It grumbled on and on and then faded. Euphora opened her eyes, saw Clara, then closed them again. Lulling, pelting rain pattered against the windows. It soothed Clara until she finally slept.

Nineteen

AFTER A LONG MONTH OF WAITING every single day and every single evening in the Spirit Room for absolutely no one to show up and inquire about a spirit circle, Papa finally told Clara it would be all right to spend the evenings, "just the evenings, mind you," at home. Clara figured whatever Papa was working on with Sam Weston must have been doing fine because he hadn't even come by the Spirit Room or said a word about séances.

And this evening at home was sweet summer cherries. The July light was orange and soft like a robin's belly and it seemed it would linger all night.

Reading out loud in Mrs. Purcell's front parlor window seat with Euphora, Clara couldn't remember being so happy with a book. It was *Gulliver's Travels* from Mrs. Purcell's library. Since Izzie had left, Clara had taken on being chief reader for Euphora.

In her parlor chair, Mrs. Purcell was concentrating hard on what she called her favorite embroidery of all time—a scene of a cottage by a brook with a little bridge over it. One of her lady friends who helped with making dresses for the freed slaves had loaned her a book with complicated designs in it.

"We're starting to lose our light," Mrs. Purcell said.

"A man is coming up the path." Euphora flitted from the window seat to the front door.

Clara looked up from the book and out. The man was broad in the shoulders and tall. He wore a flat summer straw hat and a light-colored summer coat. A cigar jutting from his teeth puffed out so much smoke, he looked like a steamboat trying to break a speed record.

Carefully setting her embroidery and colored threads on the chair as she stood, Mrs. Purcell walked to the front door, which Euphora had already opened. Eager to see the smoke-puffing, broad man up close, Clara joined them.

"Evening, Sheriff Swift."

Sheriff? He wasn't wearing guns, a silver star, or any kind of uniform. He took the cigar out of his mouth and held it down at his side. His eyes were blue, his face wide, big-boned like a cow's.

"Evening, Mrs. Purcell. Would Mr. Benton be at home?"

Clara swallowed. Why was the sheriff looking for Papa? Oh, *Lawky Lawks*, don't let Papa be in trouble again. Mrs. Purcell looked down at Euphora, one brow raised as if to ask whether Papa was up in his bedchamber. Euphora shook her head in a jittery "no", tousling her red hair, and Clara shook her head too.

The sheriff held his cigar up and studied it a moment. It smelled rank, like a heap of old garbage burning slowly in someone's back yard. Why did men go to all the trouble to wash and comb and shave and then get themselves stinking with stinkpot cigar smoke?

"I'll be needing to talk with him. Tell him I'll come 'round again tomorrow."

"It's not urgent, then?"

He started to bring the cigar up to his cow face again. His lips parted a little like he was about to draw on it, but then he let it fall back to his side.

"Not yet."

"Then I'll tell him you'll come by again. Would you like some herbs, sheriff? My garden is bursting. Lavender, primrose, or some sage for the headaches? Your wife might like some." Mrs. Purcell smiled at him.

She was someone's perfect grandmother. The sheriff's big-boned cow face looked confused. Was he supposed to come into the barn or stay out in the pasture, Clara wondered. And what the *jo-fire* did he mean "not yet".

Finally, he said, "No, thank you, Mrs. Purcell."

Clara suddenly felt her feet grow cold and heavy. When the sheriff in Homer started coming around asking for Papa just over a year ago, everything started to go into a long, dark rabbit hole. Papa was headed for hot water again. He was up to something with Sam Weston that the cow-faced sheriff was looking into. *Tarnation. A hundred times tarnation.*

After the sheriff said good evening and left, Mrs. Purcell and Euphora returned to the front parlor, but Clara stayed in the foyer by the open door watching him walk away. She couldn't move. Her feet were like two anchors deep in ice-cold water. Even after the sheriff had long since disappeared down the street, the smell of his cigar remained in the warm summer air. Two blackbirds in the border garden fussed and hopped about collecting something they just had to have before nightfall.

"Come on, Clara, let's read," Euphora said.

"Close the door, dear. You'll let in the mosquitoes," Mrs. Purcell said.

THE NEXT MORNING, the sheriff came right after breakfast and after Billy had gone to work at Maxwell's Nursery. Papa talked to old Cow Face privately in Mrs. Purcell's library, doors closed. They weren't in there more than two minutes when Clara, who was perching on Mrs. Purcell's footstool in the parlor, smelled the stinkpot cigar smoke. The Carter spinsters were nearby sitting on the window seat, the sunlight streaming onto their almost matching white-haired heads.

Whispering and leaning shoulder to shoulder, they were trying to hear whatever conversation drifted from the library. Clara was trying too, but there wasn't anything to hear. The longer that library door was closed, the more Clara chewed on the inside of her mouth until she made it sore. After a while, the cigar smell gave her the notion that she might vomit.

Out of the kitchen came Mrs. Purcell wiping her hands on her apron. Like a little echo of Mrs. Purcell, Euphora followed on her heel, wiping her hands on her own apron. They'd grown to be a real pair. Big E for Emma and little E for Euphora.

"Why don't you take Euphora with you to the Spirit Room this morning, Clara? I've got wonderful left-overs for supper so I won't need Euphora's help in the kitchen today." She placed a hand on Euphora's shoulder and walked her to the front door. Mrs. Purcell asked it like a question, but when Mrs. Purcell marched around like that, she didn't really mean it to be a question. "Go on now, girls. Have a nice day. Will you look at that blue sky?"

THAT AFTERNOON, Papa came by the Spirit Room and found that Clara and Euphora had drawn hopscotch lines on the floor with chalk and were tossing old coat buttons into the squares.

"Git home with Mrs. Purcell." He grabbed Euphora's arm.

He jigged and jagged Euphora like he was a wild dog trying to break a squirrel's neck. Her sweet little freckled face drained to ashen. The second he released her, she burst into tears and ran out.

"You've been up here all day doin' nothin'. You should have had two or three ladies' circles by now. You're doing somethin' to keep them away." He scuffed at the hopscotch game with his boot, smudging and ruining it. "Clean up this dang mess."

"Papa, there's no one to keep away. No one even asks about what we do anymore."

"You think you're a little angel in that white dress? Well, you ain't. You're makin' them stay away so you won't have to do anythin' but sit around and play games." Spit sprayed from his mouth. "How is this family supposed to get by? Huh? Answer me that." He jammed his spectacles back against the bridge of his nose, then strode toward her. Looming over her, whisky on his breath but hands steady on his hips, he didn't seem completely drunk, just half-shot.

"Papa. I'm doing my best. I'm doing everything you taught me. Honest." She felt her heart crumple like a piece of paper in a fist.

"If this is your best, you're worthless, worthless." He glanced around the room. "Not even that. Less than worthless. We're payin' the rent on this Spirit Room and gettin' nothin' back."

"I'm sorry, Papa." Tears bursting, Clara looked down at his dusty boots, then covered her eyes.

"Snivelin' ain't goin' ta help. If you don't git some customers by next week, we'll let the room go and you can sew your fingers off or clean some rich house on your knees all day. You ain't goin' ta sit around playin' girls' games, I'll tell you that."

Clara sobbed. "I don't know what to do, Papa."

He walked to the open door and turned back toward her a moment.

"You better figure it out."

After he disappeared, she stretched out on the floor and cried for a long while. "Worthless." He called her worthless. How the blazes was she supposed to figure anything out about anything? She couldn't get the customers back. They weren't interested in her antics anymore. Isaac Camp saw to that and besides, her spark was gone. It wasn't the same without Izzie.

THE NEXT MORNING, dressed in her white séance dress, Clara went to the Spirit Room as always, and as always, no one came by. She stood, leaning into the sunny window and looked down at the wooden sidewalk near the street door to their stairs. Perspiring slightly in the heat of the sun, she started to nibble on her thumbnail and soon had eaten it down until her thumb bled at the fingertip. Then she went on to her little finger until that nail was so short that the tender pink skin was showing. How could she get people to come back to her séances? If only she could just get the chance to dazzle again, she could make Papa see she was still his angel.

In their light summer clothes, cottons, linens, and calicos, people ducked in and out of shops. Now and then women, lucky women, went into Mrs. Beattie's downstairs and came out with hatboxes, packed, Clara imagined, with the new summer bonnets that had been on display in the window. Cooks and maids came out of the baker's across the street with packages wrapped in paper and string. Next to the baker's, the Dayton & Smith produce market had their full summer fare out on the sidewalk—flat wood crates perched on top of barrels, full of splendiferous things; strawberries, blueberries, peaches, melons, carrots, squash, onions and cucumbers. There were plenty of people about spending money and making money.

How could she get them up to the Spirit Room? She bit down on the nail of her middle finger and tore it straight across. It stung. What the *jo-fire* was she doing to herself? In her entire life, she'd never bitten her nails. Papa's face—red, angry and pinched—popped into her mind.

How was she going to get any of those people down there to come upstairs to a spirit circle? She was empty of ideas, her mind a bucket of water dumped on the ground. But something had better come to her and soon or she'd be sewing stacks of shirts or burning her hands in some fancy person's hot laundry water. She just had to win back those spirit seekers, spark or no spark.

Later, when she arrived home, everyone was there except Billy. Mrs. Purcell and Euphora were setting out bowls of fish chowder at each place and passing round a basket of brown bread.

"Does anyone know if Billy is coming for supper?" Mrs. Purcell asked.

Clara shrugged. No one else seemed to know, either. Glancing at Papa out of the corner of her eye, Clara pulled out her chair and sat next to him. He hadn't shaved for a few days. His chin was turning brown with whiskers. Was he growing his beard the way he had after Mamma died? She hoped not. It reminded her of how sad he was then. The front door clicked open and Billy shuffled in. He came around behind her and slid into his chair.

Mary-mole Carter screeched like a baby hawk and covered her mouth with her napkin. Jane's eyes got wide and alarmed.

Clara turned to see what the fuss was. Her stomach flopped. Billy's face was swollen red from his left brow all the way to his chin and his eye was half-shut, bulging and circled by black, blue, and purple. Since his hair was hanging down over his forehead, she wasn't sure he was mangled above the eye or not.

"Bless my soul. What happened?" Mary Carter said.

Billy lowered his head. "I had an accident at the tree nursery last night." He cleared his throat. "We were unloading some heavy timber fence posts off a wagon. I was on the ground and two boys in the wagon were handing the posts down to me." He raised both hands near his shoulder to demonstrate. "I lost control of one and it flew right into my face."

He was lying, she thought. Lying like a snake.

"Billy, why didn't you come to me for an ointment or poultice?" Mrs. Purcell lightly thumped the table with her palm. She stared at Papa with a worried look.

"I didn't want to bother anyone. It was late." Billy fixated on his bowl of chowder.

Papa glared back at Mrs. Purcell. "Be more careful next time, son."

"I'll make up an ointment with white lily, wormwood, sarsaparilla. Come home right away after work today and we'll apply it. No dawdling."

"Yes, ma'am."

Billy's puffy, raw face looked thunder awful. It had to hurt like the devil. What was he lying about? Her flopping stomach suddenly died flat. It was probably Papa that hit him.

"I'll bet you were in a fight," Euphora said as she took a piece of brown bread from the basket.

"I wasn't in any fight. It was a timber post." He snatched the basket away from her.

Mary and Jane Carter proceeded to tell stories of accidents they'd known about over the years in Geneva—fires, sunken canal boats, barn-raising mishaps. There was the servant girl who jumped from the third floor of the Geneva Hygienic Institute a couple of years back during a fire. Everyone thought she was saved at first, but she died later because her fractures never healed properly. Then there was the time their neighbor was knocked senseless when he was thrown from a Lewis & Colvin Stage Coach as it tipped over on a turn, but he revived. Seven times exactly throughout her stories, Jane said, "The world is a dangerous place. One has to be careful."

Finally, Mrs. Purcell said, "My own brother died in an accident with a threshing machine on a wheat farm." Tapping the end of her knife on the table and looking forlorn, she stared at Papa.

The whole supper went by and there wasn't any more from Papa, not a word the whole time and Billy never looked over at him either, not once. Clara was going to have to find out more about this supposed timber post because she was dang sure there wasn't any timber post. Here she was sitting between Billy and Papa and they weren't speaking and they weren't looking at each other. She jammed her thumbnail between her teeth and began to gently gnaw on it. She needed a moment alone with her twin. She didn't see much of him these days. He was always out, either working or in the evenings roaming with his friends. She'd surprise him and walk up to Maxwell's Nursery at the end of the day, maybe

walk him home to make sure he got the ointment on his
bruises.

AT THE END OF THE AFTERNOON, Clara slipped out of her
séance dress at the Spirit Room and into her dark blue
checker calico. She walked out of town and up along Castle
Street toward the nurseries. It was one of those sticky humid
summer days, heat peaking around five o'clock in the
afternoon. She kept thinking about Billy's bruised face.
Trying not to bite any more of her fingernails, she made her
hands into fists and buried them in her dress pockets.

As she made her way slowly along the road and got closer
to Maxwell's Nursery, and the Smith Nursery across the road,
the smell of roses grew strong. It was a syrupy smell, almost
like some kind of drink. It tickled the back of her throat and
made her sneeze several times in a row.

There were acres and acres of trees—apples, plum, pear,
peach, and shrubs of all kinds as well, laid out in rows, neat
and countable, snaking across the rolling hills. Billy probably
knew the number of rows and the number of plants in each.
There were buildings, barns, and greenhouses along narrow
roads running up and down and across the endless lines of
plants. She passed through a gate, walked around two waiting
carriages, and entered a house-like building that had a sign
over the door: Office, T.C. Maxwell & Bros.

A man in a tan greatcoat and a woman dressed in pale
yellow and full crinoline were studying a catalog at a central
counter. *Lawky Lawks*, that woman must be about to pass out
from the heat in that dress and crinoline, thought Clara.

On the other side of the counter was a fellow with curly
brown hair, beard, mustache and sideburns, all beginning to
gray. He watched his customers with friendly eyes.

"Are there any of these summer apple varieties ripe now? We'd like to see and taste the fruit on the tree," the woman said.

"There are quite a few that ripen next month, August apples, but right now there's just one called Early Harvest. It's a very nice apple. Do you want take a look? It's a bit of a ride up the hill, or you could come back in a few weeks. We'll have at least five or six varieties ripening then, Early Joe, Early Harvest, Golden Sweet, Early Strawberry, and... Sweet Dough, I think."

The couple looked at each other, but didn't speak. Then the man told the bearded fellow they'd return and thanked him. As they walked out passing her, Clara stepped forward to the counter.

"My brother, Billy Benton, works here. Do you know where I could find him now?"

The friendly-eyed man called out toward the open door behind the counter. "Joshua, do you know where young Benton is?"

A voice from an open door behind him called out, "He's right back here, sorting through some orders. I didn't want him out digging or hauling with that injury."

Billy appeared in the door. Even though his ragged, stinky black wool cap was pulled low over the hurt side of his face, the frightful swollen, purple flesh still showed. She clenced her fists inside her pockets.

"Will you be finishing soon? I've come to walk you home so Mrs. Purcell can put that ointment on your face."

"Denton's Balsam?" the man behind the counter asked.

"No, homemade with white lilies and wormwood," Clara said.

"Well, he needs something. You can go, Benton. You're lucky to have a pretty sister looking after you. You need to be more careful when doing those chores at home. Get your father or someone to help you if things are too heavy for you. And don't be cocky about your own strength. That's how boys get into trouble. You've got to learn your own strength."

Chores at home? Ah, *tarnation*. Billy was lying every which way about his smashed-up face.

He darted a hard brown-eyed "don't you dare say a thing" glance at her, then drew his cap down even lower over his brow and headed outside. "Yes, sir. Goodnight, sir."

Clara thanked the man and followed Billy out into the thick, hot, rose-smelling air. When they got outside the gate and started along the side of the road, at first they walked in silence, Billy with his hands plunged in his trouser pockets, Clara with hers in her dress. Wagons and carriages rambled by in both directions, kicking up dust. After they had walked a short distance, Billy turned right on Brook Street. As town and home got closer, her private time with him was running short. The dang silence had to be broken.

"What happened, Billy? You weren't hurt at home. Your weren't hurt with any fence post."

Billy kept on in silence, his eyes on the ground. They reached the little bridge that crossed over Castle Creek, but instead of walking onto the bridge, Billy climbed down the embankment to the stream. Squatting on a couple of large stones at the water's edge, he took off the skanky cap and dipped it into the water, sloshed it around, drained it, then set it aside. He splashed handfuls of water onto his sandy hair, then combed it back with his fingers. Clara scrambled down to the creek and perched next to him. With his hat off and his hair slicked back, she could see he'd been hiding a huge black and blue and yellow mound above his eye.

"Billy, you're swollen the size of a ham hock."

He shifted onto his knees on some flat stones, leaned toward the water, noisily sucked in air, pinched his nose closed, and shoved his whole head into the stream. He stayed under water a good long moment, letting the current swirl by. When he came up, he gulped in more air, and went down again, then up and down several more times.

When he finished dunking himself, he put his cap back on and sat back next to her.

"You know, Clara."

"I know what?"

"You know." He strung out the word "know" as if the longer he made the word sound, the more she would understand him.

And she did know. That was all he had to say. That was all he could say. It was Papa that hurt him. Papa had done something horrible and cruel beyond anything he had ever done before and then made Billy promise not to tell. She did know.

"How could he do that to you? What did he do?"

Billy scratched at the earth, picked up a pebble and tossed it into the creek.

"I might have to leave, Clara."

"What? What do you mean?" She got up and walked straight into the creek. Her feet and ankles were instantly soaked and shocked with cold. "You can't leave. You're not leaving."

"I might have to." He dug up another pebble and tossed it downstream.

Annoyed, she kicked water at him, spraying his white shirt. "Where would you go?"

He raised an arm to shield his face. "Hey!" Grabbing his wet shirt, he lifted it away from his skin. "Two of the boys from Maxwell's are going to Kansas to fight with the Free Staters, maybe find John Brown. I might join them."

"You can't do that. You're too young. You'll get killed. If you have to leave, just go and live with Izzie in Rochester. Why do you have to go off and do something dangerous?"

"I just said *might*. Nothing is for certain. But I want you to know in case one night I don't come home. I don't want to leave you and Euphora, but I've got to save my own life..." He didn't finish, but looked downstream toward the town and the lake. The water was rushing, burbling and it seemed for a moment that Billy went with the creek, all the way to Seneca Lake and beyond. A tear slipped from her eye.

He picked up another pebble and pitched it further downstream.

"I don't want you to leave." She kicked again at the flowing water, but not enough to splash him, then sloshed her way out of the stream and sat down next to him again.

Billy was frozen still a long moment, then she felt his arm rest over her shoulders. She let herself cry then and, after a while, he took his red bandana from a trouser pocket, dipped it into the water, wrung it out, and offered it to her.

"Here, wipe your eyes with this. It's nice and cool."

She took it with both hands and covered her face with it. It was soothing. How was she going to do it? Live every day without Mamma, Izzie, and now Billy, too? Everyone was leaving her. Why did they all have to leave her?

"Let's go get Mrs. Purcell's herbal concoction," he said.

She looked up from the wet bandana. Smiling down at her, his cap on, brim askew, he offered a hand. She grabbed it and hauled herself up. They walked over the Brook Street bridge, and headed for home. When she gave him back his damp bandana, he pressed it against the beat-up side of his face.

"At the Nursery, do you know the number of rows of every kind of plant and the number of plants in each one?" she asked.

"Almost, but something changes every day. Someone buys something or we plant new ones, take out sick or dying ones."

"How many Early Harvest apples?"

He looked down at the road, concentrating, smiling. "Seven rows, fifteen trees each row, one hundred and five trees."

"What about peaches?"

"What kind of peaches?"

"Billy, if you leave, who will count things with me?"

"You can count for yourself and write me letters with your findings. I'll count whatever there is to count, maybe rifles, maybe rebels, whatever they have in Kansas, I don't know, and I'll write you back.

"It wouldn't be the same in a letter."

"How many Black-eyed Susans in bloom right this minute at home?"

"Twelve plants. I don't know the blooms," she said.

"How many carriages passed us since we left Maxwell's?"

"I don't know, I was thinking about your dang bruises."

"It's just a bruise. It'll go away. Six. There were six," he said.

"I think it was only five."

He looked at her with his good eye and his chest filled up with air like he was about to argue with her, but then his shoulders came down.

"I'll only go if I really have to and you'll be all right. He won't hurt you or Euphora. He never has. It's only me and maybe Izzie he hates."

As they walked up the path to Mrs. Purcell's, past the border gardens in full bloom, she began to count the pink hollyhocks. Eleven, twelve, thirteen.

Twenty

I T WAS A WARM SEPTEMBER DAY. Out on the sparkling blue lake in the rowboat, Clara had Papa all to herself. He pulled steadily, powerfully, at the creaky oars.

In the past weeks, since the day the sheriff had come by to see him and since Billy's face had been so horribly bruised, Papa had been silent as a grave. But today, not only was he talking the hind leg off a horse, he was taking her, her and nobody else, for a row down the lake.

The days were still hot like summer, but the nights were cold and the maples, elms, and oaks were already turning sunset colors along the high bank shore. The grand houses high above them shrank away one by one like candles being snuffed out as they glided south.

"Papa, we're leaving Geneva. It's my first time out of the village since we got here last year."

"Can't be."

Sweat beaded on his temples as he cranked at the oars.

"Where would I have gone, Papa? I've been working almost every day, or at least waiting around at the Spirit Room."

He frowned. She shouldn't have mentioned the Spirit Room, but he knew she hadn't been anywhere. He was the one always gallivanting off without explanation. "Something important," for their family business he'd always say. "I'm goin' to look into somethin' lucrative up north," or "down south," or "I'm goin' ta Albany for a few days." That was all he said. Then, he'd walk out the door without a traveling bag like he was going to buy a couple of apples at the market and not reappear for days, sometimes weeks. In that first month between when Izzie left and before Isaac Camp ruined everything, he brought her small gifts—pens and paper, ribbons for her hair, tea from India. That was nice. This boat ride was nice. Since Isaac Camp blew up, he hadn't shined at her one bit, though.

"Maybe sometime I'll take you on a fancy packet boat up the Erie Canal."

Clara lost her breath. The packet boats on the canal were splendiferous, people sitting on top in the open air looking elegant and romantic.

Papa stopped rowing and removed his new brown felt hat, then tossed it down.

"Can we go up to Rochester and visit Izzie?"

"Maybe. That MacAdams husband promised me somethin' I ain't seen yet. Might be a good time to visit."

Papa wrestled himself out of his black coat, then laid the heavy garment over the seat next to him. He slipped his handkerchief out of the coat pocket, took off his wire rim spectacles and dabbed at his damp brow.

Clara knew about the money Doctor MacAdams was supposed to send Papa. Izzie had told her how Doctor MacAdams offered it to help out since he was taking away one of the famous Benton Sisters when he married her. From Izzie's letters to her, Clara also knew no money had been sent yet. Because Doctor MacAdams had more expenses than he thought he would with the new Upper Falls Water-Cure

Institute, he didn't know when he'd be able to send money to Papa.

Once Papa got his spectacles back on, he looked out across the water. He grasped the oar handles again but didn't row. The boat drifted slowly toward shore, small ripples slapping gently against its sides. The sun fell directly on Clara's face and hands, and heated the front of her dark blue, checkered dress. She felt sleepy. Closing her eyes, she listened to the water lapping, the crows bickering with each other on shore.

"Clara, you know you're my favorite little one. You're the prettiest of my three girls. Besides that, you know me best."

She opened her eyes and looked at him. Even though his back was to the sunlight, he was squinting, hiding away his gray eyes.

"Billy and Izzie're always fightin' against me." He turned his gaze from the distance and looked right at her, relaxing his eyes enough for her to see them. "But you ain't like that. That's why you're my special one."

"I never want to fight you, Papa."

"I got an idea that will help the family. You're the only one can do it. If you help me with it, I'll take you on that canal trip on a packet boat, just you and me. We'll go and see Izzie if that's what you hanker."

Papa spun one of the oars in its lock.

In the distance, ship bells clanged. Two steamboats, going in opposite directions, one into the harbor, one out, approached each other in the middle of the lake. Clara leaned sideways over the side of the rowboat and dipped her hand in, letting her fingers drift in the cool water.

Papa twirled both oars in the air. He seemed a bit nervous about this idea of his. He had borrowed the rowboat and brought her out on the lake alone to ask her something. He

always had a little bribe of some sort when he itched for
something. Sure as the sun going down at the end of the day,
she knew he wanted something now. It had to be pretty
important to him since he had gone to all the trouble to get
the boat, steal her away from the Spirit Room, and offer her
the reward of seeing Izzie.

"I ain't askin' you to do anythin' wrong or anythin' that
would hurt you. You're my sweet, sweet Clara."

"What is it, Papa?"

"There's a way we can make extra money real easy." He
hushed his voice like he was telling her a secret.

"How's that?"

Stroking his new full brown beard a couple of times, he
stared off at the horizon behind her.

"Well, I was talkin' to Sam Weston. He's mighty fond of
you. I think if you were a little older than thirteen, he'd be
interested in you for a wife."

"Oh, Papa, I'm not ready to marry."

Weston was sweet but he was much too syrupy. He was
always polite and attentive at the séances, but he wasn't
someone to marry. Did Papa want to get rid of her that way?

"I know it, Clara, but you're not too young to accept
attention from a gentleman."

"He's old as the hills."

"Isabelle took a husband older than Weston."

"But you didn't like that."

"It wasn't the man's age that bothered me. This is
different."

It was different all right. She had no interest whatsoever
in Sam Weston, whereas Izzie had been smitten with Mac
from the start.

"Does he want to spark me?"

"That's where my plan comes in. He does, but I figured out a way so that it ain't real courtin'. It's just part of our Spiritualism business." Papa blinked three times before continuing. "Weston told me he would pay us more money if he could spend a little time with you that was more private and friendly."

"He wants to pay money to be with me, but not a séance?"

"Surprised me too, but then I got to thinkin'. You're turnin' into quite a beauty, like your grandmother Elsie was. Makes sense a man might want to know you better and you *are* old enough to marry, Little Plum, even though Weston ain't right for a husband." He stroked his beard again. "But there's no harm in his gettin' to know you better and make a few bucks along the way."

Suddenly, a set of waves jigged the rowboat and made her slightly nauseous. She put a hand on her stomach.

"Papa, it sounds like prostitution."

"Where'd you hear that word?" He scowled at her.

"You just know about things. Izzie and I sometimes read about those women in books or the newspapers and talked about it."

"Well ..." He cleared his throat, then he cleared it again, and then a third time. It seemed like he was going to get riled up but all he did was sigh. "No, no, Little Plum. That's something' different."

Far across the water, the two steamboats reached each other and crossed. The smaller one behind was obscured briefly from sight, then appeared again. Pulling the oars in tight against their locks, Papa let the handles drop inside the boat. He mopped his brow again with his handkerchief.

"While we're waitin' for spirit seekers to come back, and they will soon I believe, I'm suggestin' addin' on ta what we're already doin', easy as cherry pie." He unfolded the handkerchief and, like a piece of laundry on a line, draped it over an oar. "Think how that money would help the family, Clara."

She crossed her arms. "What would I have to do?"

"Nothin'. That's the beauty of it."

"Nothing at all?"

"Honest Indian."

His forehead was sweaty again already. Reaching behind himself into the satchel he'd brought along, he plucked out a bottle of whiskey and something wrapped in a cotton napkin.

"Here, Mrs. Purcell sent these molasses muffins with us." He offered her the cotton bundle.

Clara bent over toward him, took it, and held it in her lap without opening it. "I still don't understand, Papa. Why would Sam Weston pay more money to spend his time with me?"

"Only Weston can answer that. Men do some strange things when it comes to women, Clara, especially handsome ones. You're so pretty you're gonna find out all about it, whether you like it or not."

"I don't know, Papa."

He perched the whiskey bottle on his thigh. "Winter's around the corner. All of ya need new boots." He yanked the stopper from his bottle and took a swig. "And we're behind three weeks rent with Emma Purcell."

"Papa, I thought you said you were doing well in your businesses."

"That all changed the day that Sheriff Swift came by the house. I don't have a bungtown copper left. All we got now is Billy's wages and that ain't enough for all of us."

"What happened with the Sheriff?"

As he took another gulp of whiskey and then another and wiped his beard with his shirtsleeve, Clara's heart fell dark.

"That ain't your business, Little Plum."

Papa was either in trouble with the law or tarnal close to it and if they didn't get more money somehow, they'd have to leave Mrs. Purcell's and live like they did back in Ohio, hungry half the time, or maybe worse.

"If I don't like it, can we stop the arrangement, Papa?"

"Sure we can. Sure we can. I don't want nothin' that'll hurt you or make you miserable, Sweet Plum. What do you say?"

He gave a huge crooked-tooth smile and waited.

Clara shifted her weight on the seat and braced a hand on the edge of the boat. It sounded easy enough. They did need the money. Weston wasn't really awful, just old and syrupy, and even though Papa was asking her in such a fancy way with the rowboat and all, she didn't really have a choice if it was something he wanted badly enough.

The wake from the two distant steamboats had arrived and their rowboat rocked in the little waves. Feeling a bit seasick, she held on tighter. Papa took two more swigs from his bottle waiting for her to answer. She didn't want to puke, nor did she want to be stranded in the boat with Papa if he was going to get pixilated with whiskey.

"All right, Papa. I'll try it."

"That's my girl."

He slapped his knee, leaned way over the oars toward her, and kissed her on the tip of her nose.

"It'll be easy as cherry pie. You'll see."

"Can we go home now?"

Twenty-One

SAM WESTON WAS DUE ANY MINUTE. It was five past four. Clara, already seated at the table in the Spirit Room, dressed in her lacy white séance dress, was ready for him. He was usually on time for spirit circles.

He would certainly be on time for whatever this courtship would be, thought Clara. Unless something was wrong, he'd be here shortly. Then she heard footsteps pounding up the stairs and both Papa's and Weston's voices out on the landing. While their muffled chatter went on just outside her door, she touched her hair, the coiled braids wrapped carefully around her ears, to make sure they were still properly in place. "And do somethin' fancy with your hair," Papa had ordered earlier in the morning.

The doorknob clicked and Weston came in grinning, a large package under his arm, a straw hat in his hands, and wearing a new, handsome cream-colored linen suit and maroon silk cravat. He came and sat near her, setting the bundle and hat down.

"Good afternoon, Mr. Weston."

"Hello, Clara. You look radiant. Your hair is lovely." He rested his hand on the parcel and began to tap the crisp brown paper. "Did your father have the chance to tell you we would be doing something special today?"

"Yes."

"You are such a wonderful girl. Does he ever tell you that?"

Clara felt a blush rise from her neck and flood into her face. "He doesn't tell me in just that way."

"Well, he should. Clara, you know how much I have enjoyed your spiritual trances these months." He rose, and sliding the package along the table, moved to the chair next to her. "And I have been very sorry to see your fame fade because of Mr. Camp's rumors. He's a despicable fellow."

"Papa said you've been trying to help us, praising my séances all around the village. We're grateful."

He smiled a little and nodded. "You know I've gotten so fond of you, like an uncle, really. You don't have a real blood uncle, do you?"

She felt the warmth of another blush. "No."

Clara twisted her hands together under the table. He had never spoken to her like this before. He'd been attentive with flowers and politeness and kindness, but he'd never spoken like this.

"Did your father tell you exactly what I want today?" His fingers stopped tapping on the paper.

"Not exactly. He said you would tell me, but that it would be more like courting than a spiritual reading." Clara took a deep breath, pressed back on her chair and grasped the edge of the table. "He also said I shouldn't be afraid. You'd be a gentleman." She looked down and fixated on her hands. "He said he'd be close by, right outside the door, and I should call for him if I wanted anything."

"Yes, that's right, but you won't need to call him. We'll have a nice time. You'll see." He touched her hand lightly. "I am so very fond of you, Clara."

She looked up at his face. He was smiling brightly at her, showing off his good teeth the way he always did. He seemed extra cleaned up today, even more groomed than usual with his light brown hair slicked back and parted to perfection down the middle of his head. His short beard was clipped as neatly as a shrub in front of a mansion and he smelled like cologne water. He had definitely been to the barber. What the *jo-fire* did he want?

"Come away from the table. Let's go over to that corner of the room there." He pointed to the corner near the spot where the secret bells were hidden.

This was a strange request. It was just an empty, faded blue-and-green wallpapered corner of the room, no furniture, no anything. But, it was his time with her and Papa had made the arrangements. She said she'd go along with it. He walked to the corner and turned to her.

"Clara?" He offered out the palm of his hand like he wanted her to dance.

"Is this about the spirits?" she asked.

"Not today, Clara. I'm going to show you how important you are to me. After all these months, I am going to show you." His eyes, with sagging folds of skin underneath, were moist, but not like he was going to cry. He seemed happy about his idea, whatever it was. "Your Papa agreed that I could offer my affections if I paid more than I usually do for the séances. A lot more."

Papa had said more, not *a lot* more. How much was he paying Papa? Something was wrong with this, with Weston and his watery eyes. Did he and Papa have the same idea about this courtship or whatever it was? Maybe Weston had one idea and Papa had another.

"I brought you a gift too, something just for you."

Weston left her there in the corner and retrieved the parcel from the table. Maybe this gift was how he wanted to show his fondness. He held it out to her.

"Open it. I hope it fits."

"A dress?"

He grinned at her. She took the package and reached inside the folded paper. As her hand searched its way in, the paper crumpled. She grasped a thick, soft fabric and, as she slid the item out, it cascaded toward the floor. It was a beautiful cotton summer dress, a print with indigo blue dots on white, with wide flared, short-to-the-elbow sleeves, loose bodice, and a low, off-shoulder neckline. She had seen that low neckline on girls recently in town. It made them look older, like young ladies.

"This is lovely. Is it really for me?" She pressed it to her chest.

"Yes. Yes. Clara. I wish it could be even fancier, but I think this will look nice on you. A girl like you deserves something new."

Stretching out the shoulders of the dress, she spread the garment against herself, smiled, sashayed slightly.

"Is this what you wanted to show me?"

"It is one thing, but there is another, Clara. Here, let's put that aside for a few minutes. You can try it on later." He clutched the waist of the dress and tugged it slowly toward him, but she held on. The dress floated between them. If only she could try it on now, but Weston kept smiling, easing it from her until she unfurled her fingers and let go. Then he took the dress to the table and draped it carefully over her chair.

While she waited, he removed his cream-colored linen jacket and hung it on another chair, then took off his maroon silk cravat and returned to her in his clean, white flowing shirt and vest. He faced her, stood close, then placed both his hands on her shoulders and, as if they were indeed dancing, slowly walked her all the way into the corner so that her shoulders nearly touched the walls. She could barely see around him. It didn't feel like a dance, though. Was it some kind of game?

"I have the most warmhearted feelings for you, Clara. You are very dear to me." Standing no more than two feet from her, he let his hands drop.

She let out a long sigh. There was nothing to worry about. This was Sam Weston; Sam Weston who brought her flowers all the time, who always attended her séances, and who protected her when Isaac Camp was hot as a red coal. There was nothing to worry about. He was always polite, helpful, even if a little odd sometimes. But odd was nothing. She and Izzie always laughed about him.

"All you have to do is stand where you are." He began to roll up one of his billowy sleeves to his elbow, then the other. "Do you know you are one of the prettiest girls I have ever seen, anywhere? I just want to look at you. That's all. Just look for hours and hours."

Why didn't he tell her what the game was and get it started? If he wanted to look at her all day, why do it in a dim and dusty corner? Why not go to the window and throw open a curtain? She could pose for him the way she did for the illustrator at the newspaper office when Papa had the posting bills made. Yes, maybe he would like that and she could put on the new dress with the low shoulders.

"Do you want to move over to the light? I could wear the dress."

"No. I like it here. While I'm looking at you I'm going to do something to myself you probably haven't seen a man do before. There's nothing to be afraid of. It's a harmless thing. You're thirteen or fourteen now?"

She tried to swallow, but couldn't. Her tongue locked against the top of her mouth. She nodded.

"See. That's plenty old enough." He reached for the button just below the waist of his pants and opened it.

"No." She stepped sideways along the wall, but he stopped her with a firm hand on her arm.

"Don't be afraid. I won't hurt you." He looked down at his hand, descending slowly from one button to the next, while his other hand gripped her arm. "You've seen your brother, father?"

"This isn't right, Mr. Weston. I think I should call for Papa now."

"But your Papa agreed about this. Because I admire you so much. I promised him I wouldn't hurt you. I won't even touch you, Clara. I won't touch you. I promised your father." With his fly now open all the way, he settled both hands on her shoulders, looked straight into her eyes. "Please. Please, Clara. I am so very fond of you."

"Let me talk to Papa first." Clara took his wrist and tried to dislodge his hand from her shoulder, but he tightened his grasp.

His forearm muscle bulged. "I promise I will absolutely not hurt you. Please. I would never hurt you, Clara. All you have to do is stand there." His mouth curled up at one corner. "Everything will be all right. I'll be very happy." His grip relaxed, but his hands lingered on her. "I'll tell your Papa that you were very good, and I'll give him the five dollars. You don't want to disappoint him, do you? And the family needs the money?"

Then he released her altogether. *Five dollars. Hell-fire.* What was going on? Papa wouldn't want to give that up and he'd hate her if he had to. He'd think she robbed him of the money. He'd be mad as a hornet. She tried to look around Weston's broad shoulders into the room but couldn't see much. If she really had to, she could squeeze by him, wiggle, twist, hit, maybe duck down and crawl lickety-click and low if she was afraid of being hurt. She could scream for Papa. He was out there on the landing, wasn't he? He wouldn't want her hurt, five dollars or no five dollars.

"You don't want to disappoint him." Weston carefully put his hand under Clara's chin, brought her face around so that she had to look at his watery light brown eyes. Suddenly the room seemed airless, stifling. Her undergarments now drenched in sweat, she shivered with a chill.

"I might be able to bring you another new dress in a month or two. Now just stay where you are so I can look at you. Don't move until I tell you to. Do you understand?"

"Yes."

He reached inside his new cream-colored linen trousers, inside his drawers, and retrieved his prick, just as Clara had seen Billy do a thousand times when he was going to piss, but it was big, firm-looking.

"Just stay where you are. That's perfect."

Cupping his right hand around the prick, he braced his other hand on the wall near her ear. He leaned toward her. His head was almost hanging over hers, but he was still not quite touching her. He pumped the prick slowly with his hand, back and forth, back and forth. It swelled and grew longer. *Tarnation.* How could it change like that? As his stroke quickened, the prick rose in his hand and turned red.

Don't get any closer, she thought. Not one inch. Not one. She looked away, up at the ceiling. She felt trapped, a rabbit, stuck, flailing in a snare. The room was stuffy, blazing. She was sweating, shivering, sweating.

He groaned down inside his throat. She looked away from the ceiling to his face. Mouth open, skin slack around his eyes, he locked his gaze on her like he was sighting a rifle. His warm pipe tobacco breath ate up the air between them until his used air was all that was left for her to breathe in.

"Clara, Clara, Clara."

She gritted her teeth. *Stop it*, she wanted to say. *Stop saying Clara, Clara.* Beads of sweat leaked from his temples. She stared again at the white ceiling. Stop saying it. Stop groaning out *Clara. Clara. Oh, pretty Clara.*

She could get by him. She could, like a rabbit thrashing, wriggling free. No. Don't ruin it for Papa, don't lose the money for Papa. Stand still, perfectly still. It will end. It has to end.

He pumped and moaned. This was what he wanted to do? This was what he wanted to show her?

"Clara, my beautiful Clara."

She turned her head to the side and peered over his leaning arm. At least he wasn't holding her chin again, forcing her to look at him, his face, his hard red prick. At least he let her turn her head away. She stared at an oil lamp mounted on the striped wallpaper. If she concentrated on the lamp long enough, he'd eventually finish. Then it would be over. Why was it going on so long?

Outside the door footsteps shuffled and scraped. Papa was pacing back and forth on the small landing. He was there, waiting for it to end too, waiting like she was. The frosted-glass globe on the lamp was pretty, the etching delicate. The lamp might need oil soon. She'd tell Billy. It was his job to keep the lamps filled. Now how was she going to remember to tell him? There were four lamps altogether in the Spirit Room, and there were three in the Blue Room at home, and one in Papa's room. Some of the shops in town had gaslights

now. The pacing outside the door quickened. Papa was
nervous. Her chemise was soaked with sweat. She'd have to
wash it tonight.

"Come on you old nag. Yawwh." A man outside on the
street was probably having trouble with his horse and wagon,
she thought. "Yawwh."

"Clara? Clara? Clara!"

Why the *jo-fire* was he yelling at her now?

"Yes, Mr. Weston."

"Didn't you hear me? I said that wasn't so terrible was it?"

"No. No. May I go now?"

"Would you just give me a little kiss on the cheek so I
know you aren't angry with me?"

Clara rose on her toes and kissed his cheek. His skin
smelled of shaving soap and cologne, but the tobacco smell
lingered in his cropped beard. She glanced at the lamp again.
She mustn't forget to tell Billy about the oil.

"Now let's see if that dress fits you. Try it on, then show
me. I'll wait outside with your father."

Weston stepped aside, his trousers already buttoned. She
had missed that somehow. She sprang out of the corner,
released from the snare, took a deep breath, then another.
Rushing to the windows, she pushed back one of the pale
curtains and threw open the window, letting in a warm lake
breeze. After Weston tied his cravat and put on his hat and
coat, he disappeared out the door. She eyed the dress on the
table. Two sets of footsteps and Papa's scolding voice
rumbled down the stairs, then faded away.

The dress was lovely. How strange. For standing in a
corner, no, for being jailed in a corner, but only for a short
while, she had received such a glorious gift. She quickly shed
the white séance dress and, as she draped it over one of the
straight back chairs, she noticed a wet patch on the front of

the skirt. She touched it with her fingertip. It was slimy. From him. From his prick. She'd wash it as soon as she could. It was warm out, the dress would be dry by morning. She flipped it over to hide the stain.

As she stepped into the new indigo blue and white print dress and pulled it up over her sweaty pantalettes, shimmy, and petticoat, her hands trembled. Her entire body was vibrating oddly. Struggling, hands behind her back to button the dress, she could only get at the bottom button. Because of the low-shoulder cut, she couldn't get the dress to stay up without holding it, so she perched one hand on the fabric at each shoulder. She looked down at the fabric. It really was a beauty. She wanted desperately to see herself in a mirror, but that would have to wait. How could she show the dress to Weston when it wasn't on properly? Why couldn't he go away and see it another time? Maybe they'd left. Maybe he and Papa had gone to a tavern.

It was quiet outside the door. She'd wait a few more minutes, then if Weston didn't come back, she'd go home. While she stood and waited by the fireplace, her arms grew heavy, tired from the awkward crooked position of holding the dress up.

Finally there was a knock at the door. When she said, "come in," Weston entered but not Papa.

"Miss Clara Benton, you are a sight, very beautiful." Taking off his straw hat, he approached her.

"I can't get to the buttons. Where's Papa?"

"We had a little talk. He was in a hurry to leave for a business appointment."

Double rot. She had to be alone with him again and there he was showing off his teeth, smiling ear to ear like he was trying for a blue ribbon in a contest for handsome teeth.

"Let me help you with the buttons."

She stepped back. That wasn't right, him fussing with the dress. He was Sam Weston, Papa's friend. Even if the dress was his gift to her, he shouldn't be helping her with it.

"Please. I want to see how pretty you look in it, how it fits."

She stared at him a moment, hoping he would change his mind, but when he didn't budge, she turned her back to him and faced the mantel. At first he did nothing. What the *jo-fire* was he doing behind her? He wasn't opening his buttons again, was he? Then she felt two, or maybe three, fingertips at the base of her neck. They began to inch down, a dry worm crawling along her spine. She held her breath, bit down on the inside of her lower lip. The fingertips arrived at her sweaty shimmy between her shoulder blades. Then the full warm flat of Weston's hand slid inside her chemise and came to rest on her back.

 Her back tensed up as hard as an iron skillet. Then again, there were his fingertips drifting across her skin just inside the top of her chemise. Papa couldn't have agreed to this. Why couldn't Weston just leave now? Tears began to leak from her eyes. Papa couldn't have agreed to this.

She felt a small pressure at her lower back. He secured a button and began working his way up, one button at a time. But it was taking him forever and a day. Her tears flowed now. When he finished, she let go of the dress shoulders and brushed her tears with both hands.

"Turn around then. The dress is perfect from behind."

But her face was still wet, her eyes overflowing. He'd see that she was crying.

"Come on then. Let me see. Don't be shy."

When she spun around, she was still wiping at her face with her palms. His smile vanished.

"No, no, my sweet Clara. Don't be sad. The dress is beautiful. You are beautiful. Everything is fine. I haven't hurt you now, have I?"

She shook her head, kept mopping at her eyes.

"I have an idea. Next time I come, I'll bring you a bonnet to go with the dress. Would you like that?"

A summer bonnet would be sweet. She glanced down at the indigo blue dots. Were they the color of the sea? Having never seen the sea in person, she couldn't be sure. She nodded at him.

"Good then."

Was crying and nodding all it took to get a new bonnet?

"I will talk to your father about our next time together."

While he gathered his hat and prepared to go, to finally go, she thought that she would also be talking to Papa about that next time as well. There wouldn't be one. That was all there was to it. No next time. A bonnet wasn't enough. Papa said she could call the thing off if she didn't like it and she didn't. She despised it. And not only that, there had to be a huge misunderstanding in the first place about the five dollars and Sam Weston's ideas about courting. As soon as she explained things to Papa, he'd set Weston right. There wouldn't be any more of that dusty corner, the prick, or those creepy-crawly fingers on her neck. Or anything else for that matter. Papa said she could call it off.

Weston tipped his straw hat at her from the door, winked, and left. No, sir, Mr. Weston, that's the end of that. You'll see.

CLARA TWISTED, STRETCHED, AND TUGGED until she got the new dress off. It was a perfect dress. It fit as though a seamstress had measured every inch of her body. And the blue against the white was bright and bold. Everyone would notice the dress when she wore it out, but now she wanted to go to the lake and wash her white séance dress, wash Weston's slime off it. To clean the séance dress, she'd simply swim in it.

Outside, it was hot, almost evening. People weren't rushing home. Instead of bustling, the street seemed slowed down, like a dream. People were milling around, talking or sitting on top of crates or up high on the seats of their wagons and carriages, but no one was getting anywhere.

A horse was hitched just outside her door. The mare's jet black coat, stinky with sweat, glistened in the late day sun. Clara walked to her and tentatively reached out to touch the horse's fuzzy snout. The mare snorted and jerked its big head. Clara snatched her hand away, but the horse seemed calm, its tail swishing gently at buzzing flies.

"You're not the old nag that was being yelled at before, are you?" The mare looked at her with huge round black eyes. Creeping around the side of the mare, Clara rested the side of her face on the solid warm neck and breathed in the smell of the horse's damp coat.

"I'm going swimming. I wish I could take you with me. You're hot. But don't tell anyone I'm going. I can't afford the two dollar fine if I get caught. I don't think they have fines for horses swimming so you'd be all right." She kissed the gigantic black neck. "Goodbye, then."

If she walked south of the harbor, past the Long Pier, past where Water Street ended at the bottom of the big hill, she'd mostly be out of anyone's sight. Let the Constable or that cow-face Sheriff Swift arrest her. It wouldn't matter. She was sweltering, practically dizzy. She had to wash, needed a bath, a cool bath, over her skin, toes, hair—everything all at once. She had to wash the slime away.

The town boys sometimes swam within the town limits naked after dark, after eight o'clock when there weren't any fines. But she wanted to swim right now and get rid of her sodden undergarments. She could leave them all on a branch in the hot breeze to dry while she floated on her back in the cold clean water in nothing but the white dress.

When she got to Water Street, two boys, hooting and laughing, were riding a seesaw, a big plank set on a barrel. Up one boy, then down, up the other boy, then down. The seesaw creaked and wobbled. Two other boys, waiting their turn, watched. They all ignored her, but an older boy, standing in the open doorway of a tenement building, one of those places her family might be living if it weren't for Mrs. Purcell, smiled at her, tipped his cap and said, "Lovely evening, Miss."

She crumpled the skirt of her dress where it was stained to hide Weston's spot and smiled back at him. Eyes straight ahead on her destination, she kept going. When she got to the end of the street, she walked a short while along a rubble path until she was just beneath the mansions high above on Main Street. No one was around. Nestling herself behind a huckleberry shrub, she wrenched off her boots and coaxed off her sweaty stockings. She tugged off her white dress, shimmy, petticoat, and pantalettes and dropped them all on the ground, then scrambled back into the dress. Finally she left the shrub draped with her clothing.

The rocks were cool and soothing under her feet as she made her way to the water. The rippling water slurped over her toes. What if she got caught? What if the Constable or one of his young deputies came by looking for illegal swimmers? They did that sometimes on hot days. Two dollars. Two dollars for a bath. That would be a fair part of Papa's five dollars from Weston.

Weston. A picture of him burst into her mind, with his red hard prick, his pumping hand, his slack face, his voice calling out her name, *Clara, Clara*. She covered her ears and stepped forward into the water. At first, her ankles were shocked by the cold. *Clara, Clara*. She stumbled, banged a toe on a rock. "Ouch." She caught her balance, waded in a few more steps, stumbled again, caught herself again. The water rose up to her calves, her knees, her thighs. She shivered, wrapped her arms around her waist and stared down at her dress floating around her legs. Leaning over, she stretched out her hands and dove out flat into the surface of the lake. Chilled from scalp to toe, she glided out. She swam toward the opposite shore, which was miles and miles away. His voice still echoed inside her ears. *Clara, my Clara*. If she filled her ears with water, that would shut him up.

She took a huge breath, held it in, and dove deep toward the bottom. She stroked hard. The water below was yellowish, green, full of moving shadows, shafts of light, floating specks and plants that looked like wiggling cornhusks. She stroked harder, pulled herself deeper. A school of minnows scattered into four smaller schools and darted away. Her lungs begged for air, but she kept her mouth and throat clamped tight. The beams of light and colors were so pretty, the minnows so fast, the cold water so clean.

Is this what Mamma wanted? Did she want to live under the water with her ears plugged so she couldn't hear her spirit voices? Did she want to live where no one could see whether she was naked or clothed? Mamma, is this what you wanted?

She grabbed a stalk of the billowy husk plant. It slid from her grip. She hit a pocket of icy water. Golden-eyed, and with silver sparkling scales, a fish hovered near her and stared at her. She stared back. It flitted off into the shadows.

Her lungs were about to explode. If she opened her mouth now, she could drink in the lake. The lake would quench her. She could be with Mamma, in the lake with

Mamma. Air. Air. Air. She needed to climb. Tucking, she turned herself, pointed hands up, arms up to the bright, the sky. She kicked hard.

She wasn't going to make it. It was too far. She was about to burst. She'd waited too long, swam too far down. She stroked. The water was heavy, wouldn't get out of her way. One more pull. That was two. One more. That was three. Her mouth was going to open against her will. She'd drown like Mamma. No. Mamma, don't let me. *Please.* She clenched her teeth as hard as she could. Just one more stroke, four, and five, six, seven, eight, nine, then her hands broke the surface. Her head burst out of the water. *Air.* Mouth gaping open wide, she sucked loudly. She sucked again and again. A sledge hammer beat at her chest. She was all right. Not drowned. The blue sky, sunshine, and wispy clouds were hers, hers. Her heart began to slow from its frantic pounding.

Gradually, treading became easier, breathing easier. Like a traveler on a boat she was out some distance in the lake.

On the shore, near her clothing on the shrub, there was a young man approaching the water. He was wearing a constable's hat she realized. He was a deputy. *Hell-fire.* She'd have to talk him out of the two dollar fine. He watched her as he scrambled along the rocks. Maybe he'd like a free séance, she thought.

THE CONSTABLE'S DEPUTY WAS POLITE, even shy. When she climbed out of the lake, dripping like a just-caught bass on a hook, he mentioned the fine more like a gentle threat. "You know you are breaking the village ordinance even in that dress," but then he looked her up and down and asked her if she wanted him to walk her home. When she declined his offer, he wished her a good evening without mentioning the fine again, and walked down the rubble path toward town. Her dress was clean of Weston's stain, but had turned a little yellow from the lake water. She shoveled her wet feet into her boots, rolled up her undergarments into a ball, and tucked them under her arm. As much as she could, to keep away from being seen in the clinging, dripping dress, she took alleys and footpaths up the hill to get home.

Later on, in the candle-lit kitchen, Clara held the wet séance dress across her arms, ready to hang it out on the line. As she reached the back door, lightning snapped and a giant roll of thunder boomed and rain flooded from the sky. She opened the door and stood listening to the thunder crashing and rain pelting. After a short while, the rain eased and drifted off. The trees and roof continued to spit down noisy streams. That's it, she thought. That's the end of summer. And that's the end of Sam Weston, too. She would talk to Papa in the morning about him.

She took the candle lantern with her outside and set it down on the soaked grass near the laundry line. She hoisted the dress over the line and raised a wooden pin to clip it tight.

"I brought you a gift."

"Oh!" Clara's heart hopped like a cricket. But it was only Papa. "You scared me."

"I got you these. Here." He held out something small and black, draped over his palm. "It's those lace mitts."

It was a pair of black gloves, the lace kind with open fingertips that girls and women wore when they dressed up. How did he know she wanted a pair of those?

After taking them from him, she immediately inserted a hand and tugged one on. The lace was snug and reached half way up her forearm. Bending down toward the candlelight, she admired her delicate, grown-up hand.

"They're beautiful. Thank you, Papa."

Dang. This was going to make it harder to tell him she didn't want to go on with Weston. She took a deep breath and stood up straight. If she was going to tell him, it had better be now.

"Papa, I want to stop Mr. Weston's courting arrangement. I don't like it."

"He hurt you?" Papa's voice climbed fast like he was about to rile.

"No, he didn't hit me or break anything, but he made me do something I didn't want to do and that hurt me. In a way, it did."

Papa's eyes bulged. He looked like he might explode. "He kiss you?"

"No."

"Make you embrace him?"

"No."

"Make you take any clothing off?"

"No."

That seemed to calm him. He turned his eyes down toward the candle lantern and stared at it a while. He swayed a little. He had been drinking some, maybe with Weston.

"I said if you were hurt, you could stop."

Was all the hurt Papa knew being clobbered or knocked down or getting a bone broken? Weren't there other kinds of hurt, like Mamma dying? He should know that kind of pain.

"What's hurt, Papa? What about being a prisoner to someone?"

"You're no one's prisoner. If anything, it's the other way. He's yours." He snickered quietly, stroked his dundrearies. "Think of it. In one day, for less than one hour, you got yourself a new dress from him, five dollars for the family, and some purty gloves from me. Now, what prisoner has all that?" Placing his hands on her shoulders, he smiled at her and looked straight into her eyes. "You are my Little Sweet Plum. I am prouder of you than any of my children. You did somethin' hard, somethin' brave and you're helpin' the family."

Brave, proud. She took another deep breath. He was right about the five dollars. It was a lot of money. With that kind of money, the family would be clothed, housed, fed, and maybe more. And maybe Papa would slow down his liquor again, like he did before, and lay off Billy too, and then Billy would stay home and not run off with his friends to join up with that rebel John Brown down in Kansas or wherever he was.

"Put the other mitt on."

She raised her bare hand, the one holding the other glove, and looked down at it. She had crumpled the lace glove up in her hand and hadn't realized that she was squeezing it so hard her fingers were cramped.

"I want something too, Papa," she said as she put the other glove on. "If I do keep up with Sam Weston, I want you to never hit Billy."

He chuckled. "A father has to discipline his boy, Clara. That's how it is."

"You know what I mean. You go far past discipline. You have to stop that or I won't go on with Sam. It's only fair."

"I'm the Papa here. I say what's fair." He studied her a moment. "But I want you to be happy, my little one. I'll do as you ask."

She sighed and clasped her gloved hands together.

"There's somethin' else, Little Plum. This arrangement between you and me and Weston has got to be a secret, the biggest, most fierce, kind of secret. You can't ever tell a soul about it, even your sisters. They wouldn't understand. It's private. It ain't anyone else's business anyway." He kissed the top of her head, then looked into her eyes again, candlelight glinting off his spectacles. "It's just between us."

The truth of it was that she didn't want to tell anyone. People, especially her sisters, might think something awful about her.

"All right, Papa."

Twenty-Two

AFTER THREE MONTHS IN THE NEW HOME with Mac, Izzie's furnishings were still very modest and their only pots, pans, and dishes were the ones purchased on their honeymoon day. Izzie had thought there'd be more by now—a desk, a wool rug perhaps—but Mac had his priorities and nearly every penny was going into building his Upper Falls Water-Cure Institute. Even so, he bought her a book every week and he had scraped together the money to buy her a small cherry side table, an oil lamp, and a rocking chair for the parlor. "This will be your first reading chair. It's a perfect design from the Shakers," he'd said.

Izzie had visited across the street at the Mead's home a few times. Their parlor and dining room were full to the ceilings with things she'd never seen before: a side cabinet with flowers painted on the drawers and doors, a lacquered corner cupboard, a walnut card table with ornately carved legs, a mahogany wine cooler, and there wasn't just one desk, but several.

Although the pieces were lovely and Mrs. Mead called them by specific names that sounded English or German, Izzie was still happy to write her letters to Clara at their simple pine table, the dining table she shared with Mac. Her walls were entirely bare, without wallpaper or paintings, but they were freshly painted white. There wasn't a scrap of clutter.

She'd been sewing all day and it felt good to stop a moment and lean back into the rocker. Her fingers ached from jamming the needle in and out of the calico trousers. Mac wanted two dozen American Costumes for women patients when his institute opened in the coming spring— different sizes, different materials. He'd told her that all the best water-cure establishments offered women the reform dress with short skirts, straight trousers, and a comfortable bodice to wear during treatment. He'd said, "Women should not be constricted where they shouldn't be constricted, especially the lungs and uterus. The weight of those senseless long dresses with their useless underskirts and hoops, and those preposterous corsets pressure vital organs. All that clothing ruins circulation and makes women ill. I've seen terrible things, terrible."

Izzie had been amazed. Even though she had spent nearly as much time as Clara looking at the *Godey's Lady's Book* and *Peterson's Magazine* at Mrs. Beattie's millinery shop and longing for the very garments that Mac was railing against, once he explained what dress reformers wanted to do—free the body to breathe and move in a natural state—it made utter sense. Mac told her that hydrotherapists, both men and women, were leading a movement to transform the way women dressed for improved health. That meant he wanted to go along with it and it meant she would too. "We'll join the National Dress Reform Association and go to the conventions. All the important reformers do," he'd said.

So now it seemed that not only were they to become reformers, but *important* reformers as well. Mac's ambition was swelling by the day. She'd never met anyone like him. He was electrifying and more interesting than she could ever have imagined when she met him back in Geneva. She was finishing her third American Costume, a smallish one. She didn't mind doing the seamstress work. It was one way she could aid Mac in getting his Upper Falls Water-Cure ready.

Digging the needle into the blue trousers one more time, she slackened her pace in the rocker. Having a rocking chair of her own reminded her of Mamma, even though her own chair was taller, narrower, and a lighter color wood than Mamma's. Sometimes, when she rocked gently, the rhythmic sound of wood on wood brought back a vivid memory of Mamma, holding her Bible, whispering to herself. Sometimes the whispers were the words on the page she was reading, and sometimes they were a conversation she was having with herself or her spirit voices.

Now Mamma's chair was Clara's. Izzie sighed. Poor little Clara, she thought, still stuck with Papa fabricating spirits for the innocent.

Letting the blue trousers fall into her lap, Izzie looked out the windows at the green lushness of summer. She was free of Papa's shenanigans, free of worrying that she might hear voices like Mamma did. Those few times she heard something mysterious had only come from her own fears, she had decided. The combination of fear and imagination was a potent mix. That's all it was.

Having a fever while pretending the spirits were at their séances made her conjure up things the way a child would, a child who concentrated on her own midnight terror so deeply that she saw real goblins, full-sized and horrifying, at the foot of her bed or on the ceiling. Izzie stood and took the American Costume into the dining room and set it on the table. Thank goodness that hoax spirit nonsense was over for her. Maybe Clara would be free of it soon as well. Papa was going to have to come up with something new eventually and hopefully it wouldn't be as awful as the Spiritualism idea. Summer was coming to an end. Perhaps she would take a coach or train down to Geneva and visit the children.

Izzie walked back into the parlor to the bookcase opposite the fireplace. She had her own shelf, the bottom one, below Mac's five shelves of medical books and stacks of journals. His biggest pile was the *Water-Cure Journal*, issues going back to 1851, all worn, corners tattered. She squatted down and ran her hand over the spines of her own books—red, green, brown, and black. She smelled the paper and ink. She already had nine books, each one a gift from Mac. It had always been her dream to own books. She never believed she really would.

"You're the only thing worth spending money on besides the new institute. We'll never be hungry if we have our minds and our bodies in their most perfect state," he'd said one night.

There was the book he gave her for their wedding, *Leaves of Grass*, and then one for every week they were married. He said the books celebrated their new life together and the union of their spirits. He'd given her *Madame Bovary* because that was what she was looking for in the bookshop in Geneva the day he met her by chance and invited her to tea. Even though she hadn't realized it, he'd decided that was the beginning of their courtship. And then came *Uncle Tom's Cabin* by Stowe and *Blithedale Romance* by Hawthorne and *Moby Dick* by Melville. It had been a week since that one. Would there be a new one coming today or tomorrow? She smiled to herself. What would he bring this time? Austen? Dickens? He had mentioned something about Thoreau the other day.

The front door flew open, letting in a shaft of evening sun. Mac strode through the light toward her.

"I've had the most phenomenal day. I must tell you about it." A book tucked under his arm and a colossal smile on his face, he was perspiring and short of breath. "Dr. Trall is here from New York City for a few days advising me and I have just spent the day with him. I have never been so inspired by anyone in my life."

He seemed about to lift off like a firework.

"Will you bring him to dinner?"

"Yes, but it must be vegetarian. That's what I want to tell you. He convinced me it is absolutely critical to the hygienic system. You and I must be vegetarians. Our Upper Falls Water-Cure Institute must be strictly vegetarian. He really is a genius. And no more alcohol. Temperance only." He glanced down at her long dress. "You're not wearing the American Costume."

"I want to make mine after the others, after I've tried out the different designs."

His smile turned down. Even though he was eager for her to try the reform dress, she was still preparing herself for being stared at everywhere she went. Clothing that would make her feel free to move however she wanted sounded wonderful, but she wasn't sure she wanted to pay the price of being ridiculed. She had seen women on occasion being laughed at, teased, sometimes ignored in a shop. Even she and Clara used to have their game of counting the similar bloomer costumes.

"Were there any letters for me from Clara or the others?"

Every day Mac picked up the mail at the Reynolds' Arcade and every day she asked. As always, he shook his head. As always, her heart sank a little. Then, grinning, he took the book from under his arm.

"A new book for you."

She took it in both hands and read the title. *The Science of Human Life; In Twenty-Four Lectures* by Dr. Sylvester Graham.

"It's a bit out of date, but it is definitive. There are several lectures on the effects of vegetable and animal foods on the human system. It'll guide our views on vegetarianism."

She paused a brief moment. It was not what she had expected. She opened the cover slowly and studied the list of lectures. They addressed every part of the body.

"You're disappointed I didn't bring you literature."

"A little, but if you say this is interesting, I'm sure I will find it interesting too."

He embraced her, the book in her hands pressing awkwardly between their chests.

"I had no idea that being a reformer would answer the questions I have never been able to answer before," he said into her ear.

"I'll love the book, Mac. I'm sure I will. Thank you."

ABOUT A WEEK LATER, after Mac's prodding, Izzie was ready to wear the American Costume out. She buttoned the green cotton-wool jacket and finished dressing. Her new costume was all of one forest color, jacket with wide collar, skirt four inches below the knees, and straight trousers, all matching. She hoped she would be less conspicuous if the pieces were the same color. Each time she wore the American Costume at home she liked it a little better. She had always longed to maneuver through the world more freely. Climbing on wagons, over fences and up stairs had always been frustrating and she abhorred how the yards and yards of material comprising even her meager two or three underskirts made her dreadfully slow.

Today would be her first venture outside the house in the American Costume. It was a beautiful late September morning, sunny, almost warm but not quite. It would be a pleasant walk several miles to the center of town to order her fall canning supplies and pick up the mail. She started down Edinburgh Street, then she strode along past the Church of the Immaculate Conception, and then around the curve of the oval Plymouth Park. She headed up Plymouth Avenue. The air was soft, the light shimmering and clear.

Sun-drenched golden and red leaves blazed overhead. The best thing she had discovered so far about the costume was climbing the stairs at home with both hands free. She could carry a basket of laundry under one arm and tote a pitcher of water in her other. A buggy clipping along in her direction, four girls tucked in seats around their mother, slipped ahead of her. All four girls twisted around to watch her strut along. Izzie laughed, remembering the bloomer counting game she played with Clara. Izzie didn't know then she'd be wearing something similar; that she would learn so quickly to hate the whalebone hoop once she had one.

She and Clara had both longed for a hoop, not just to be grown up and fashionable, but to have freedom from the burden of all the underskirts, to let the light frame hold up the mountains and mountains of fabric.

At the corner of Main Street, she turned right. The traffic was heavy as usual, the aroma of horse dung pungent but at least the river breezes were blowing today. Two young men, leaning against the stone wall of a building, stared at her as she approached. Here come the gaping and the whistling, she thought. She cringed, preparing. Their eyes followed her closely, then one of them, cap shoved back on his head, jabbed the other's arm and said something, his gaze still on her.

Averting her eyes, she ignored them the best she could and continued on toward the Reynolds' Arcade where she would get mail for the Upper Falls Water-Cure Institute and Mac and herself as well. She hadn't heard from Clara and the others in a month. There had to be something soon.

Inside the Arcade, light streamed in bright shafts from long glass skylights four stories above, warming and illuminating the cavernous hall. Dozens of well-dressed men and women milled about in pairs and small clusters. They were exchanging the news and gossip of the day, collecting their mail, sending telegraphs, visiting the many businesses both downstairs and up. A few of them noticed her reform dress, but no one bothered her about it.

After waiting in line a few moments at the post office, she received a handful of letters and a journal from the postal clerk. She stepped away from the window and began to shuffle through the letters. There was Clara's hand. She felt a smile burst onto her face. At last. "Mrs. Robert MacAdams" in Clara's dear hand.

She maneuvered through a dozen or so people to a spot near a shop where she was away from the stream of people. She tore open the letter. It was two weeks old already.

Dear Izzie,

Forgive me for not writing more often. I thought I might be better at writing you, but I'm not. Maybe it's because I don't have any good news. Life is awful without you here with us. There are many things I haven't written to you about before.

Not long after you left in the early summer, Isaac Camp found out about how Papa collected information about him and everyone else for the séances. Camp got fired up and told the whole town we were hoaxes. Then the seekers started disappearing. Money has been scarce and Papa has been unhappy and indulging in his liquoring ways. The sheriff came and asked some questions a while ago. Euphora and I were scared, but it didn't lead to anything. The worst of it is Papa hit Billy in the face last month. It took two weeks for the swelling to go down. Papa made Billy keep it a secret that he hit him so Billy made up a story about it. Of course, I knew he was lying. Billy told me he might have to run away to save his own life. Do you think a fourteen-year-old boy could survive on his own out in Kansas Territory with those John Brown men? That's where he says he'll go. How far away is that?

Papa thinks there's only one way to hurt somebody and that's to bring blows, but there's other ways to hurt someone. Don't you think so? I think making someone lie is a way to hurt them. It makes one a sort of prisoner like that Rapunzel in the tower.

I try to please Papa and help him, but I don't think I can do enough to keep him from being mean to Billy or slowing down his drinking. Mrs. Purcell says the Temperance people are right about liquor habits. I do wish you would come home and stand up to Papa the way you used to. He might listen to you.

Besides, we are all very lonely for you and I feel your absence most of all. Your husband can surely do without you for a few days. Please, please visit.

The only good thing I have to tell you is that Euphora is becoming a fine cook all on her own and sometimes will prepare most of the supper. Of course, Mrs. Purcell keeps a close watch over her in the kitchen, but you would be proud of her, Iz.

Your sister,

Clara

"Damn Bastard. Damn Bastard," Izzie said aloud.

She slammed the rest of the mail against the glass shop window where she was leaning. Blood surging into her neck and head, she slapped the mail again and again. People nearby turned to watch her.

A young man approached her and asked if he could help. She refused his kindness and looked away from him until he left her alone.

"Coward. Only cowards hit their sons," she said. He wouldn't have dared hit Billy like that if she had been there. She'd go and visit at once. The poor dears. Billy, Clara, Euphora putting up with drunken Papa. How could he? How could he be so terrible? And making Billy lie.

When she finally calmed to the point where she felt she could continue with her errands, she glanced around. People had returned to their conversations and business. Jaw clamped, she tucked the mail under her arm and strode through the crowd and out through the wide entrance to Main Street. She'd talk to Mac tonight about going down to Geneva. She had to see how the children were for herself.

As she marched along Main toward the grocers, she kept thinking about Billy's face and what it must have looked like swollen and wounded.

"Men wear trousers, not ladies. Haven't you noticed?"

It was one of the young fellows who had whispered about her to his friend on her way to the Arcade. Izzie felt her pulse surge again. She'd better ignore him, she decided, and stepped sideways to navigate around him.

He hopped in front of her. "I asked, haven't you noticed who wears what?" Glancing quickly around at his friend, his gray eyes like slate, like Papa's, he shoved his hands deep into his coat pockets.

She took a longer side step this time, but he was speedy as a little sheep dog, and blocked her once again.

"Let me pass."

"Let me pass," his voice mimicked in a high child-like whine.

Jaw clenched hard, Izzie looked around at the busy street full or carriages, men, women, children. It was the middle of the morning. There wasn't anything really harmful the boy could do. She took a deep breath and again, tried to get around him. Again, he jumped in front of her. Still by the wall, the friend guffawed. She clenched both fists.

"I wouldn't hit a gentleman but I'd hit a misbehaving impolite boy."

His clean-shaven face fell serious for a moment, then he smiled wide, as wide as he could, revealing a mouthful of yellow and brown teeth.

"Hit? Freddie, I told you she wasn't a lady." Gloating, he yanked down the brim of his cap.

She hauled back her right arm and thrust her fist under his ribs. He buckled.

What had she done? They'd maul her now. She scooted by the boy before he recovered. In a short distance, she turned back to face him. "I am a lady and don't you ever forget what a lady can do when she has to!"

Two older men, dressed for business, paused to observe. The bully lunged one step toward Izzie but noticed the men staring at him and stopped. He hesitated, then returned to his friend by the wall. He kept his back to Izzie and the bystanders.

"Is everything all right, Miss? Are these ruffians bothering you?"

"No, they are not bothering me. They wouldn't know how to bother me." She made her voice sound calm, but the muscles inside her neck were quivering.

The man tipped his stovepipe hat, but didn't leave. Stroking his walrus mustache, he spoke to his companion in muffled tones, meanwhile eyeing the younger men.

"Good morning, Miss." He tipped his hat again, then gestured in the direction Izzie had been walking, signaling her to go on.

She unclenched her fists. "Good morning, sir." She turned and walked along the stone sidewalk. After four or five paces, she looked back. The fancy men were still in conversation standing near the ruffians. She walked another ten or twelve paces and turned one more time. The ruffians were shuffling away.

The gentleman touched his hat one last time. She thought he winked but it was too far away to tell. She straightened her collar, tugged down at the cuffs of the green jacket, and went on to the grocers.

AT THEIR SHAKER DINING TABLE, Izzie sat with Mac in the soft lamplight.

Mac wiped his mouth and mustache with the napkin. "I don't miss eating flesh. Do you?"

Roast pork. Leg of lamb. Corned Beef. Izzie salivated as she looked down at the squash and corn stew she had invented. It was tasty but it wasn't ham. "A little."

"Are you keeping up with your four times per day water douche?"

She gritted her teeth and nodded. It was irritating how often he asked about this. It made her feel like a child. Did you wash your hands before supper? Did you?

"Mac, I received a letter from Clara today."

"Magnificent. You've been impatient to hear from her." Grinning, he leaned back in his chair. "I had a brilliant idea today. I want you to start working with me at Upper Falls now that the seamstress work is done. I think you can help me with the bookkeeping and advertising."

Izzie dropped her forkful of orange and yellow mush. "You want me to help in the business?"

"Yes. Why not? Look at Harriet Austen at Our Home in Dansville and Martha French at Mount Prospect in Binghamton. Women are very important in those institutions. Why shouldn't you be in mine?" He took a sip of water and set his glass down with a thunk. "Women patients like to know a woman is part of the institution."

"I don't know a thing about keeping accounts or advertising."

"You'll learn."

This was thrilling. She would learn about business. She would learn something besides her duties in the home.

"You really want me to be part of Upper Falls?"

"Yes. That is what I am telling you. I want you to be in charge of the kitchen there as well. Your vegetarian recipes are perfect."

"You are going to hire a cook too, though."

"We have to get the patients coming first. Perhaps by next summer. We'll be ready to move there just before opening in March. The design for our quarters on the third floor is complete. The Upper Falls kitchen will be our kitchen. You won't have to manage this home anymore."

"Oh, Mac, I'd love to work side by side with you." She pushed her chair back, stood, and throwing her arms around his shoulders, kissed his long wiry sideburn. "I'd better go visit Clara before I am too busy with everything. Papa is making the children miserable. I must go."

Mac took a moment to finish chewing and swallowing a bite of the stew, then dabbed his mouth delicately with his napkin. "You can't go now."

She withdrew her arms from his shoulders and fell back into her chair. "But there is nothing of importance happening now. You told me the funds from your investor had still not come in. It is perfect to go now." She straightened up. "When I get back, the funds will be in your hands and I can get to work on the pantries and kitchen."

"Fox Holland sent word to me this morning. The funds are to be deposited tomorrow. I'll go to the bank in the morning and get drafts for the merchants."

"Holland's been saying that for three weeks. Tomorrow. Tomorrow." She crossed her arms tight across her waist.

"There were technical snags, legal matters. It's all done now. Our credit will be good again so you can start ordering what we need for the kitchen and dining room."

"I could go to Geneva in the morning. These past three weeks, I could have gone and returned and you would never have missed me."

"I am sorry about that, really I am, but now we have lost precious time and every minute is crucial to our deadline."

"I am sure I could spend a few extra hours when I return and we would still be on schedule, Mac. You shouldn't worry so about the opening."

He banged his tight fist on the table. "None of it can wait. Your sister can wait. Your place is with me. When the kitchen is entirely ready, you can go." He grabbed the napkin from his lap, dropped it on the table, and stood, his brown eyes glaring down at her. "Izzie, I am offering you an opportunity to share in my professional life, my sphere. I thought you'd want that."

She hadn't seen him rile in the entire time she'd known him. They'd been married three months and this was the first outburst he'd had. But she was used to outbursts. She'd been raised on outbursts.

"I'm going next Wednesday, Mac. That gives me, you, and Fox Holland a week to finish the financial transactions, take delivery of the materials, and for me to make arrangements with the kitchen suppliers. And if none of that happens, I'm going anyway."

"You'll go when I say it is all right to go. We have everything at stake, Izzie. You must see that. The opening means everything to a successful beginning."

Her impulse was to stand and scream back at him, as she would have with Papa, but instead she picked up her water glass, took a sip, then another and another, then returned it to the table. The water calmed her.

"You'll see," she said. "You'll stay on schedule and I will go and make sure my brother and sisters are all right."

His shoulders came down a little. "Even if I change my mind, my word is the final word." He strode to the front of the house, then tromped upstairs to their bedchamber.

She took another bite of the sweet stew. Perhaps she had been too firm with Mac. He was under a great deal of pressure, with his credit on, then off, then on again, and then delays with builders. And he was offering to make her a partner in his medical life. He had been dreadfully worried about raising money for his institute and then when Holland nearly backed out, he was afraid he had thrown them into debt he would never be able to get out of. Still, she had to go back to Geneva soon. Wednesday. She tapped the stem of her fork on the table.

"I'm sorry, Clara."

Twenty-Three

IZZIE WAITED FOR MAC UNDER THE QUILT while he undressed at the armoire. He came naked to bed and put his nightshirt and a French Safe on top of the covers, then crawled in with her. Izzie felt a glow flood through her at the sight of the India-rubber safe, but Mac never reached for it. He was chattering on and on about Dr. Trall's genius. Finally he fell asleep after one delicious, lingering kiss. Izzie was disappointed, but she too was tired from sewing all day and fell asleep quickly.

Sometime later she woke to loud voices mumbling together, a crowd of voices. She bolted up in bed. It was a dream. The voices would subside in a second, she thought. Where was she? The Blue Room with Clara and Euphora? She stuck her hand out across the bed. Mac. He was there. She took a deep breath. She was in her home in Rochester. Leaving her hand on Mac's hip, she waited for the present to pour into her.

But the voices mumbled on. She shook her head trying to shake them off. She shook again, swatting at her ears. Maybe there was a crowd outside, a drunken mob looking for runaway slaves hidden in the neighborhood. Didn't Mrs. Mead, her neighbor, talk about the Underground Railroad every time they met? But this was Corn Hill, a quiet neighborhood, not a place for mobs.

Concentrating on the noise, she tried to listen for something specific. Her heart thumped. "My God. No!" They were here, with her. Nowhere else. Not outside. She was wide awake. Light the lamp, she thought. Light the lamp. In search of matches, she swung her arms around, hit the match holder, then heard the little sticks scattering over the floor. "Those are your voices, Mamma, not mine." Scrambling toward the floor, she landed painfully on her knees. She groped in the dark for a match and found several. Rising up on her aching knees, she lunged toward the bedside stand. Her wrist hit the oil lamp. It tipped, then crashed onto the floor, glass breaking, oil spilling, fumes reeking. She coughed.

"Izzie? What's happening?"

She felt the bottom of her sleeping gown grow wet with whale oil. "I knocked over the lamp."

"Here. Let me get a candle lit across the room. He rustled about while she knelt in the pool of oil. The voices were silent. Somewhere during the chaos, they had gone.

The light of a candle lantern illuminated Mac's narrow, tall naked shape. Leaving the candle on the straight back chair by the door, he came to her, stood in his bare feet in the thin puddle of whale oil, and took both her hands.

"Your hands are bleeding. They may have glass in them." He led her away from the breakage several steps. "Take off the gown. It's dangerous."

Raising her arms up over her head, she felt his hands take the cotton gown and lift it up and off her. Naked, hands bleeding, she stood trembling. Mac left her, went to the armoire and returned wearing his brown wool robe. He helped her into a clean shimmy.

"Let's go downstairs and turn on the gaslights. My medical bag is in the foyer."

He wrapped his arm around her waist, guided her to the chamber door, picked up the candle lantern, and led her downstairs. The house was chilly, but Mac's side against her was warm. As they descended, she began to calm. She couldn't tell him about the voices, couldn't tell anyone. They were here. They were with her. She prayed they wouldn't come again.

"It's time we got you a proper robe, a lady's robe."

She nodded.

"I heard you shout. Did you have a nightmare?"

"Yes. It was about Mamma."

THE NEXT NIGHT, LYING IN BED WITH MAC, Izzie realized he wasn't going to come close or hold her. He was immersed in his *Water-Cure Journal*. After he extinguished his oil lamp, he shifted onto his side and faced away from her.

Determined to go to Geneva as she had pronounced, in the evening, she had brought up the prospect of visiting. Once again, Mac was firm about her staying with him and working, but she was equally firm about going.

Listening to Mac's breathing deepen into sleep, she picked up *Blithedale Romance* with her bandaged hand and read. She had read the book once before and was coming to the end. The men, Coverdale, Silas, and Hollingsworth floated on the river in their small boat plunging a rake into the water looking for Zenobia's drowned body. Zenobia had killed herself for love. Such a fool, thought Izzie. But the scene in the novel reminded her of Mamma's body, swollen and blue, at the edge of Seneca Lake. She let the book drop down at the sharp stab in her heart, then pushed the thought out of her mind.

Later that night Izzie woke to a chaotic sensation. She shot up in bed, blood pulsing in her head. She had been dreaming of a dozen people arguing, all ranting at once. They were disturbed and angry, every one of them. She could feel their frustration. Then, even though she was fully awake, she realized the voices were still arguing and strident. She threw her hands over her ears.

Mac was asleep on his back. She wouldn't wake him this time. Pressing against her ears as hard as she could, she slid swiftly from bed. She grabbed Mac's robe from the armoire, raced downstairs and stumbled outside into the night.

By the time she was sitting in the moonlight on the hard brick of her front steps, the voices had disappeared. Leaves rustled on their branches in a breeze that sent a chill through her. Here and there a leaf drifted down in the silver light, then landed in the street or a yard. She wrapped her arms around her knees and buried her face. "No voices. No voices. Please." Shivering, she looked up and pulled the collar of Mac's robe tight around her neck. Tears welled in her eyes and streamed down her face. There were no lights in any of the houses on her block. It was very late. A pale-colored cat appeared at her front gate, sensed her presence, and froze, staring at her. Izzie stared back through the fog of her tears. After a little while it slinked away.

Drat. She was doomed to be like Mamma, she thought. How could she deny it one more day? She was like Mamma. Maybe she could keep the voices out somehow. She didn't have to talk to them like Mamma did. Mamma beckoned them. She'd refuse them. She was strong enough to do that.

"You might as well give up now, voices," she said, gazing up at the full moon. "I won't talk to you." She wouldn't. She'd just repeat, "No voices. No voices." She'd drown them out with her own true voice, her own anger.

She wouldn't be Mamma. She wouldn't disappear from Mac or the children she'd have someday. Time after time, Mamma abandoned her family for the world of her voices. Izzie would never do that. Mamma used to rock in her chair or wander about the house talking and listening to her spirits and when she did, she didn't know if Izzie and the others were even there. Sometimes when Izzie and the children were hungry, Mamma was off in her spirit world. They'd give up on waiting for her to cook something, split up, and go around the neighborhood begging for food. It was only luck that, when very young, Izzie had met Julianna and her parents. They always had something in the kitchen for her.

Izzie twisted the robe collar until it made her cough. She still missed Julianna. What gifts her friend had bestowed on her. Izzie wiped her eyes with her sleeve. The first time she'd seen Julianna, Izzie was only four and Papa was nowhere to be found. Mamma had been rocking so relentlessly in her chair that Izzie had begun to whine and whimper. No matter how she pleaded, Mamma wouldn't answer. The twins were just babies and they were hungry. They began to squeal, then cry for hours in their cradle, and they were no more than a few feet from Mamma.

Izzie had decided to find some milk for them and something for herself to eat. She walked a long distance to a neighborhood where the houses were large and people had horses and carriages. She knew they'd have food. She stopped at a large white house on a corner with a wide, covered porch wrapped around three sides. In a yellow dress, a beautiful young woman and her daughter who wore blue and was about seven or eight years old sat on a swinging bench. The mother was reading a story out loud. Izzie slowly tip-toed up the stairs. The woman lifted her golden brown eyes a few times and smiled at Izzie, but she didn't say anything to her.

She kept on reading. It was the first story from a book Izzie had ever heard. *Oliver Twist*. She sat on the top step and listened. It was exquisite. It was heaven.

When the woman finished reading, she asked Izzie her name and where she lived.

"I'm Isabelle Benton. I live down there." She pointed in the direction of their house. "The twins and I are very hungry."

From then on, Julianna's family took her in whenever she needed to be taken in and she always had her fill of books and food.

A screech pierced the night. Izzie flinched. Then another screech ripped through her. Then another. Then she realized it was just the cat she'd seen at her front gate.

One day, when she had her own daughter or son, she'd take care of them. She'd listen to them, feed them, and teach them. She'd never make them wander the streets and beg. She would not talk to these angry voices that had found her, not ever.

Twenty-Four

TWO MONTHS HAD PASSED since Sam Weston had pinned Clara in the corner of the Spirit Room and given her the new blue dot dress. Autumn trees had exploded into orange, red, and purple, then faded to brown. Almost every week Clara received a letter from Izzie explaining why she couldn't come visit. It was always the same. The Upper Falls Water-Cure was behind schedule. There was much to be done and Mac required her help.

Every Friday afternoon Sam Weston came to Clara at the Spirit Room with flowers, then candy when the flowers were gone for the season. Sometimes he brought a small gift—a cameo brooch, silk hair ribbons, a black neckband, paper and envelopes to write to Izzie with. A few times he brought something fancier, like the bonnet he promised and he was always cleaned up and brimming with kind words.

On each visit, he asked Clara to do something simple like wear the indigo dot dress he had given her but slip the off-shoulder neckline down lower than she normally would, or let her hair hang down, or sit up on the table just in front of him. His favorite was the corner though. He kept coming back to the corner and all this time he never actually touched her, not even her hair when it was flowing down over her shoulders.

Fridays were ghastly, but she gradually got used to them and even started to look forward to the gift that would always come. If she picked something in the room to stare at—a crack in the ceiling, the clock on the fireplace mantel, the wall sconce—she could make Sam Weston disappear, even the sound of his voice. It was like reading a story and going far off into the adventure, closing everything else out of her mind.

Papa told her that Weston paid him three dollars for each visit. He said the five dollars for the first time was more because that's just how it was. Men paid more for innocence, he'd said.

One late Friday afternoon in November, Weston came into the Spirit Room, wide brim hat in hand and bundled up in his black double-breasted greatcoat and a black woolen scarf around his neck. But there was nothing tucked under his arm or clutched in his hand. There was no gift.

Her heart sank. Was that the end of the special treats? Was it to be just the money now? Would she have to listen to him moaning and panting while he pumped his prick up hard and not get the gift? She jammed a fingernail between her teeth and started to chew on it.

Without stopping as usual at the coat tree to neatly hang his hat and coat, Weston strode right to her at the table where she sat. His mouth in a frown, the skin under his eyes sagging, he coughed at the back of his fist.

"Are you ill?" she asked.

"I'm fatigued." Drawing out the straight back chair near her, he tossed his hat on the table and sat.

Clara glanced toward the fireplace. "I got the coals burning a couple of hours ago, so the room is warm, the way you like it."

"Miss Clara, I'm afraid our dear meetings must end. What we have been doing is no longer pleasurable for me, at least not the way it was." He cleared his throat. "It's not because of you. You are more lovely than ever. It's because my desire for you is even greater now than before. Even though I doubt you could understand me, I hope you might." He reached under the table, took her hand from her lap, brought it up, and held it. "I long to embrace you as a husband embraces a wife."

Chest tightening, she swallowed hard. "Do you mean you wish to marry me?"

"No, my sweet, I have something more romantic in mind."

"But you're not married."

"No, no, you must trust that I'd be an abysmal husband. You deserve better in a marriage, much better, someone young and handsome."

As he spoke, his hand on hers grew hot and damp. She believed him. He'd be a skunk of a husband, the kind of husband who did old goat nasty things to girls. Now he was asking to bed her. She drew her hand away from his. *Jo-fire.* Papa couldn't know about this proposal. He couldn't agree to this, could he?

She braced herself. "And Papa?"

"He says you must decide for yourself. If you agree, there will be more money and I promise I will not hurt you. I never would. You know that."

Papa not only knew about this then, but there was an understanding about money. How much money was Weston proposing? She bit down on the inside of her mouth. No, she didn't want to know.

"No, sir." She shook her head. "No, sir."

"Please, Clara, I beg you. I will shrivel into a wrinkled ogre without you."

She returned her hand to her lap under the table. Let him shrivel then, she thought. Let him take his ideas of romance and good and bad husbands and go off to a dark cave in the forest and shrivel into an old ogre and let huge boulders fall in front of the cave door and seal him in forever. Weston stood, walked over to the coal fire and stared down into it. After a moment he tapped the clock affectionately, then smiled at her.

"Do you remember the day the clock started ticking during the séance? The spirit knocking was so loud that the clock started up?" He chuckled and held up a fist as though grasping something. "You were stunning that day. You had Isaac Camp under your spell, in the palm of your hand."

It had been a shining moment, a glorious moment, tricking Camp so perfectly.

"You are an enchanting girl, Clara." He coughed toward his coat sleeve.

"Camp is gone and so are the others. Sometimes I think that when Izzie left, my luck left."

"That's nonsense. You are your own luck. People and things will come to you in time. You are very young now. Don't worry about the séances. They are nothing. Women as beautiful as you have their own luck. After all, look what you've done to me. I'm a beggar at your feet." He stroked the clock's wood case. "You'll have many beggars at your feet besides me. You'll learn how to make them into your servants. You'll see."

What would she ever want with servants like him, she wondered. Not able to look at him, she turned her gaze toward the three dusk-filled windows. She felt his eyes on her. Weston and Papa were always telling her how pretty she was and it would smooth her way through life, but so far it wasn't smoothing anything. It was more like a witch's curse.

She stood staring across the table at the candlelight. "I'm sorry, Mr. Weston. I can't do what you ask."

He shuffled around toward her, stood close. Gazing into her eyes, he lifted her hand up to his mouth, kissed it with warm lips and bristly whiskers, then held it a moment. She wanted to pull it back, but left it with him. "I want you to be my paramour. The gifts will come by the wagonload if you will say yes to me. My offer stands, should you change your mind." Again, he kissed her hand, gazed so fiercely at it that it felt seared. She wanted to plunge her hand into deep, cold snow. Finally he looked up, his eyes yearning like a stray dog's. "I pray you will change your mind."

No. She would not change her mind, never *ever* change her mind and never miss their times in the corner either. Everything about this was wrong. Here was her chance to get rid of him. She lowered her eyes and he finally released her hand.

"Goodbye, my dear," he whispered.

When the door thumped closed, it was like the last note of a sad song. As she watched the door and listened to his footsteps rumbling down the stairs, she felt a wave of joy and grinned, but when the downstairs door to the street clunked shut, melancholy rushed up and through her, surprising her.

What if Weston did stay away altogether? Something tugged at her. She would miss him. Not his frigging himself, but the flowers, his admiration, his quirky devotion. At the first séance practice, there he had been, and there he had stayed, even after everyone else had gone. He had defended her. He had been a friend. She sighed deeply, walked to the window, and pressed her forehead against the chilly glass. The back of his figure, all in black, from boot to hat, walked away in the gaslight down along the other side of Seneca Street towards the harbor. When he had vanished, Clara turned around to face the empty Spirit Room, lit only by the single candle and the red coals.

Now what would happen? First there would be Papa's disappointment. He might drink too much. He might hurt Billy. She remembered Billy's wounded face, his warning that he'd leave home if he had to. It would all be her fault then. And they'd have to give up the lease on the Spirit Room and move the family to a cheaper boardinghouse or a tenement. She put a fingernail between her teeth and ripped it straight across. Her fault.

Her life wouldn't be any different than any other poor girl's. Who did she think she was? A famous medium like Mrs. Fielding or even Anna Santini? She was born a poor girl and she'd stay a poor girl. She could read and write, but she wasn't smart like Izzie, who'd found a smart husband and knew to accept his marriage offer right away.

She looked out again. Emerging from his shop across the street, the baker pulled a ring of keys from his coat and locked his door for the night. Paramour. There probably were worse things to be, but still, she wasn't going to be Sam Weston's paramour behind the locked door of the Spirit Room. She was tired of him and the secrets. She'd rather go off to the bottom of the lake like Mamma did. Maybe Mamma's spirit was waiting for her in Summerland. Maybe Mamma was lonely and wanted her to come join her.

Clara walked to the table and pushed in a straight back chair. "One." Then she slid the next chair neat and close to the table edge. "Two." Then the next and next, "three and four and five," until she had arranged all eight chairs perfectly around the oak oval.

As she walked home in the late dusk, she wondered if Billy would take her with him if he ran away, if she should ask him. But how could he roam around with rebels and John

Brown and fight against slavery with a girl along? That wouldn't do. Besides, if it came to that, she couldn't leave Euphora alone with Papa.

By the time she reached home she knew she wasn't going to wait for her mood or Papa's mood to be right. She'd tell him right away. She couldn't do what Weston wanted. She tromped up the stairs and marched straight into Papa's bedchamber. And there, in the darkish room, he sat hunched over in his spindly Windsor chair looking out the window. Outside, a couple of early stars dotted the evening sky. She walked quietly around to the front of him. Elbows propped on his knees, he was covering his face with his hands. The room smelled of his liquor and sweat, but it wasn't coming from him. That was a different smell. This was the permanent smell that had soaked into his mattress feathers.

"Papa, shall I light the lamp?"

"No, let it be." His voice was gravelly.

He lifted his head. His wire spectacles were off, and even in the dimness he looked drawn. Had he been crying? She couldn't quite see his eyes. He hadn't cried tears since Mamma died.

"You all right, Papa?"

"I ain't even a man anymore, much less a father. I can't make enough money to pay the rent. I'm asking my most precious daughter to do somethin' no father should ever ask a daughter to do, but I don't know how else to keep the family goin'. I keep runnin' into problems every time I try somethin' new. Someone or somethin' gets in my way. I don't see no other choices, Little Plum."

"Mr. Weston said it was up to me. He said you wanted me to decide."

"I do want you to decide, but I can't see no other way."

"I can't do it, Papa. I can't be Mr. Weston's paramour. I'd rather work my fingers to the bone all day and all night. I can sew shirts. I can learn to use one of those new Singer sewing machines. You can make more money on a machine."

Papa was silent, his jaw and mouth shifting around. He stared straight ahead toward the inky window. Why didn't he say something? Why didn't he say, "Yes, Clara, that's a good idea. We can make do if you do that."

"Did Weston tell you how much he was willing to pay for the first time?"

"No, it doesn't matter. I've decided."

"Fifty dollars."

She covered her mouth with a hand, staggered back a step. "No."

"Yep."

Legs weak, she walked around to the bed and sat behind him. So Papa was willing to sell her for a high price, a racehorse price, not an everyday workhorse price. That's what she was—Papa's prize racehorse. When he was happy, he had always called her Little Plum, his precious one, but these days he only called her those things if it somehow had to do with money. A tear rolled down her face.

"Why do you hate me, Papa? I've done everything you've ever asked me."

He kept his eyes on the window. "You have done. I wish I had four of you in place of the others. You know that. I don't hate you. It's the opposite."

He stood, took the chair by one of its rungs and flipped it around toward her, then sat again. Taking his spectacles from his waistcoat pocket, he put them on, ran his fingers through his hair to comb it back, then braced a hand on each knee.

"What about this? You go along with Weston for just a little while. We save most of the money he gives me, then, in a few months, we pack up the family and go to San Francisco or Colorado. I've been thinkin' I might have a chance out there. No one would be gettin' in my way, makin' black marks by my name all the time. It's new out there. Everything is growin' like weeds. There's room for fellas like me. We could all try somethin' new. Then you'd never have to do anything like this Weston thing again and there aren't near enough women out West either. There's plenty of fellas for you to pick a husband."

"But we would be a world away from Izzie."

"You can still write letters."

"Can I still decide for myself, Papa? Can I think about it a while?"

He tipped his chair back off his heels, poked his thumbs into his vest pockets. "Sure. Sure, you can, Little Plum, but you're the only one can help us now with your Mamma gone and Izzie gone. Billy's makin' nothin' wages. It's up to you."

THE NEXT MORNING, after Billy and Euphora had gone downstairs, Clara, with her stomach in a knot, knocked on Papa's bedchamber door. When he grumbled something, she entered. He was in bed, the morning sunlight shining onto his quilt-covered shape.

"Papa, I've decided. I don't need more time to think. I don't want to be Mr. Weston's paramour, even for a few months. I'm going out now to find work. I'm sorry, Papa."

He raised himself up on an elbow. "Go get your menial, finger-numbing seamstress piece work. You better start lookin' for a husband too while you're out knockin' on doors. You'll need one. If I go out West, I'm goin' alone."

Clara wrapped her arms across her waist. She felt like a tree careening, felled with one swipe of his axe.

"Would you leave us again, Papa?"

He retrieved his spectacles from his bedside table and put them on. As he watched her a moment, his scowl softened. His brown hair was sticking out in a wild mess. Clara trembled as she waited for him to answer her. In the end it didn't matter what she wanted. She would have to do whatever Papa and Weston wanted if it meant keeping Papa home, keeping the family together.

"No." He rubbed the back of his neck. "No, Little Plum. We go together or we stay here together. I didn't mean it. You and Billy and Euphora are all I've got in this world. You're all I've got left of my dear wife." He scratched the tip of one of his big ears, then tried to smooth down his hair. "Go on. Find your work. We'll be all right. I'm tired of this house anyway."

He peered around the room, his gaze lingering a moment on something. She turned to see. It was Mrs. Purcell's print of the slave traders separating a Negro man from his wife and child. "I'm tired of Emma, too. She's a strict old grandmother, givin' me the evil eye all the time. And those spinster sisters. They're always titterin' behind my back. A man don't need that." He sat up and leaned against the wood headboard. "Maybe we can build a little cabin out of town along the canal somewhere."

Trembling easing, Clara exhaled. Yes, their own place. Maybe that's what Papa needed.

"Euphora knows how to cook now since Mrs. Purcell taught her. We can take care of you, Papa, and Billy can get his strong friends from the Nursery to help build the cabin."

She longed to see Papa's crooked-tooth grin right then, to see him sparkle the way he did when there was the prospect of something new, but he didn't smile, not even a little. He took off his spectacles, returned them to the side table, then lay back down sliding the quilt up over his shoulders.

"That's right, Little Plum. Now go on and let me sleep."

Twenty-Five

CLARA KNEW SHE HAD TO GET AWAY from Sam Weston's paramour proposal and make Papa happy at the same time and nothing but money could do both. She put on her dark green dress with the white stripes and lace collar and covered up with Mamma's old black hooded cape. Then she set out in the stinging sleet of early winter to visit every tailor and dressmaker in Geneva. First she went to Mr. Finck, the tailor she and Mamma had worked for, but he said he already had too much help. Then she went to Mrs. Beattie, their Spirit Room landlady, who had the millinery shop on the street floor.

"I'm sorry, dear. I just don't need anyone right now," Mrs. Beattie had said. "You'll find something. Be sure to visit Mrs. Spencer, Miss Habernathy, and the Sullivans and tell them I sent you."

She rattled off a long list of even more names and was kind enough to write them all down for Clara, but when Clara trudged around the village and knocked on doors, no one needed her. They said, "Come back next week," or "In two weeks I might have some waistcoats for you," or "Come every Monday. Maybe I'll have some velvet bands for you to set as trim."

At the end of the second day Clara had spoken to everyone on Mrs. Beattie's list. Clara crumpled the list in her hand as she headed home. She'd never be able to get away from Sam Weston now. Dragging her feet slower and slower, she drifted to a stop at the corner of Linden Street and waited for the Price, Shimmer & Co. coal wagon to rumble by.

She thought about meeting with Weston for the money. She thought about Papa's sad gray eyes. She stayed fixed on the corner wondering what she could do. There had to be something. If only she could talk to Izzie, but she could never tell her about being a paramour, could she? For the Fridays with Sam alone, Izzie would think she was shameful and awful. Maybe she would write Izzie a letter and try to explain some of it. But if Papa found that she let his secret out, he'd be furious and there was no telling what he'd do. Glancing back toward the lake, she pondered stowing away on a steamship and disappearing for good.

Her fingers tingled with cold and her cape was soaked and heavy. She'd better get by a fire. Clara stepped down onto the dirt and stone street. When she reached Mrs. Beattie's, she looked inside. Mrs. Beattie was dusting a black velvet bonnet on display in the window and when she noticed Clara, she beckoned to her.

The doorbell jingled as Clara entered and greeted Mrs. Beattie who kept at her dusting.

"What do you think of the Chantilly lace on this one?"

"Pretty."

"It needs something else. Ostrich feathers?"

Clara felt her eyes water up, so she looked away, out at a pack of five boys running by on the street with sticks in their hands. The sleet was slower coming down now and was turning to snow.

"No one hired you?"

Clara shook her head.

"I gave it more thought. I think I could use some help in the mornings. I could only pay you a dollar a week."

Mrs. Beattie's blue eyes were a bright winter sky. Clara fell toward her, toward her golden-sun blond hair and sweet smile, and embraced her.

"Thank you. Thank you."

"Now, now. It's only a dollar a week."

Clara felt Mrs. Beattie pat her back.

"When may I start?"

"Tomorrow morning."

IT WAS A CLOUDY, COLD SATURDAY, the end of her first week with Mrs. Beattie and Clara was looking forward to being paid her first ever honest wage. She was sweeping up discarded threads and fabric bits from Mrs. Beattie's workroom floor. The room was cozy, a coal fire burning in the iron stove since dawn. The two north windows at the back of her shop faced an alley and even on a sunny day, the room was dull, but the colorful fabrics and ribbons and feathers always made the room cheerful.

On her first day at the milliner's, Mrs. Beattie had asked Clara to cut some navy blue wool for a simple cap and when she found that Clara was precise with the scissors, she lit up like a gas streetlight.

"Oh my, Clara, this is perfect."

Every day she had asked Clara to try something new. On Wednesday, when a man from out of town, who was in Geneva on business, came by wanting gifts for his wife as well as two daughters, Mrs. Beattie asked Clara to model one hat after another while she did the same. The two of them stood side by side in front of the long mirror smiling at their reflections. Mrs. Beattie lowered a wonderful brown velvet hat with two red roses onto Clara's brunette hair. Then Mrs. Beattie, who had explained that her very fair blond hair was due to her mother being Swedish, put another hat, a pale cream wool, on her own head. With the flair of an actress on stage, Mrs. Beattie tied the string under Clara's chin and made a sort of bow and curtsy.

The man must have been impressed with their presentation since he purchased three of Mrs. Beattie's most elegant hats, a blue silk, a straw with red ribbon, and a bonnet with lace, pink flowers, and wide plaid strings. Beaming like a blazing sun, Mrs. Beattie wrote up the bill. "Come back and see us when you are in Geneva again, Mr. Worth," she'd said and later she told Clara they would try her out at sales again soon.

"Clara, here is your wage." Mrs. Beattie came toward her with an outstretched hand. "I wish it could be more."

"Thank you." Into her open palm, Clara accepted the small gold dollar. She glanced at the Indian head with its feather headdress, then squeezed her hand tight over the coin. After earning three or even four dollars for one group séance, and having several séances a week when things were going like wild fire with Izzie, a dollar wage for six mornings of work seemed rather puny, but it would have to do for now. Next week she would find more work.

"What will your father want to do with the room upstairs? I need to know."

"Oh, I think we are letting it go."

"Will you ask him to come in and speak to me about it?" Mrs. Beattie's blue eyes squinted a bit.

"Do we owe you rent?" Papa hadn't said anything about this. She only knew that they owed Mrs. Purcell money, but Mrs. Purcell had been an angel and forgiven it for the time being.

"I'll talk to him about it, Clara. It's not your concern. Tell him to come by early in the week."

Clara nodded and, collecting Mamma's cape, she walked out of the shop. Out on the sidewalk the brisk air chilled her instantly. The muddy street was bustling as usual with wagons and carriages. When she had walked half way up the incline toward Main Street, she saw Papa in his low crown felt hat and greatcoat, arms tight across his chest, coming towards her.

"Papa."

"Did you get paid?" He put his hand out.

Still clutching the gold dollar in her fist, she hadn't even thought to put it in a pocket. Sighing, she dropped it into his wide-open hand. It hadn't been hers more than three and a half minutes.

His face looked empty and drained for a moment as he stared at the gold coin, the side with the "one" surrounded by a wreath. "This will carry us to about dinner time."

"I'll make more next week."

He put the coin into his coat pocket and stepped around her. Then he continued walking toward Water Street. He had left her with no "thank you, Little Plum," no "good work, daughter," no pat, no smile, no anything. She felt like one of those mud ruts on the street, flattened by a wagon wheel.

"Mrs. Beattie wants to talk to you about the Spirit Room," she called after him.

Taking long duck-like strides, he kept on down Seneca Street. Without even a sideways glance, he passed right by Mrs. Beattie's shop door, and then strutted on toward the lake, toward his taverns most likely. And with him went the dollar, her dollar, which probably wasn't going where it was owed, to Mrs. Purcell or to Mrs. Beattie for rent on the Spirit

Room, but most likely it was going to his friend, John Payne, the saloonkeeper.

Drawing up the hood of her cape, she drew the cloth as far around her face as she could. If only she could disappear altogether. Out in the harbor, a double pipe steamboat was making its way south. Someday, when she was older, she'd take a steamboat away from here. She'd go to New York City and sell bonnets and gloves and silk scarves at A.T. Stewart's store on Broadway and wear handsome dresses like Mrs. Beattie did. Someday.

AFTER CLARA STARTED WORKING for Mrs. Beattie, Papa wasn't home much. He'd come by the Blue Room on Saturday nights and collect Billy's wages and Clara's dollar and ask if she had another job yet. After five weeks and five dollars, Clara hadn't found another job. There was always an older woman, usually a mother, ahead of her that got the work. Clara would hear Papa come into his bedchamber some nights in the wee hours and some nights he didn't come in at all. A few times he came to supper, but he and Mrs. Purcell just glared at each other the whole time. That made everyone either talk too much or not talk at all. Clara wasn't sure if Papa was paying Mrs. Purcell anything for room and board or not.

One night a loud clatter, much louder than Papa's usual noises, coming from somewhere in the house, woke Clara. It was a quarter moon night, just enough to see the shape of things in the dark.

"Billy, Billy, did you hear that? Is it Papa?"

"What?"

"Wake up and git down here!" Papa called from downstairs. "We got some business. Billy. Git down here!"

Something crashed in Papa's vicinity.

Clara cringed. "He's real drunk."

Euphora grabbed her arm under the quilt.

"Aw, tarnation." Billy shoved back his blanket and sat up.

"Billy. Git down here now!"

"I've got to get out of here. He'll skin me alive. I wish this house had a back stairway."

"Maybe we should go into Mrs. Purcell's bedchamber." Clara pushed herself up in bed. It was cold, all the fires having died down hours ago.

"He sounds like he's stewed to his ears." Billy said as he rose. He picked up his trousers off the foot of the bed and began to dress in the dark. "It's none of Mrs. Purcell's business. I can get by him. He's too drunk to catch me. I can slip by him before he knows I'm there."

"What if he's faster than you think?" Euphora asked. She pressed against Clara's side.

"Clara, take Euphora into Mrs. Purcell's room if you're scared. I'm going."

Just then the doorknob clicked and a light shone in. Clara gasped and clutched at Euphora, but her little sister squirmed away under the quilt.

It was Mrs. Purcell with a candle lantern. She looked like a ghost, her white hair flowing down around her shoulders, her white cotton night robe covering her from neck to toe.

"Children, I am going to send your father away. He's in a terrible state. I don't want him home until he is sober again. Stay here, especially you, Billy. If you go down, he might act worse."

"But I should go out. That usually settles him." Billy finished buttoning his shirt, then pulled up his suspenders.

"No. I think it would be best if you stayed here with your sisters. Light every lamp you have."

She closed the door gently and it was dark again. Billy made some fumbling noises over at the pine table, then struck a match and lit the candle lantern they kept between the two beds.

"Frank Benton. You leave my house this minute! Don't come back until you are sober and reasonable!"

Clara had never heard Mrs. Purcell raise her voice before. It was low like a big brass tuba in a band. She was holding her ground at the top of the stairs. That was smart, thought Clara. It didn't seem safe to go down. Billy got the oil lamps burning on the mantel.

"Get dressed, both of you. Just in case we all might have to run for it," Billy said.

Euphora scrambled to the armoire and threw it open. Billy darted over to his bed, perched on the edge, snatched his boots up, and began to tug them on.

"Send my yella son down here! I need him at the canal!"

Billy scooted to the door, then swiveled toward Clara. "What's at the canal?"

"Don't know." Clara shrugged.

"You are not taking anyone out of this house at this forsaken hour. Now please go!" Mrs. Purcell was still at the top of the stairs.

"Billy!"

Papa sounded closer and Billy shot a nervous look at Clara.

Clara jumped from her bed and dashed the few steps to the armoire and seized the closest dress to her. Euphora was already squirming her way into her calico. Within seconds Clara was stretching up into the bodice of Mamma's old gray everyday dress. Even though she and Izzie had altered it to fit, Clara never wore it. Just seeing it hanging there every morning in the armoire reminded her of Mamma. It made her heart tear into shreds each and every time.

As her head emerged through the neck of the dress, Clara winced at the sound of shattering glass. Was it in the parlor? Euphora jerked, looked up from her buttons, her blue eyes wide with terror, then covered her mouth with both hands.

As fast as her fingers could move, Clara started buttoning up the dress.

"I'll tear up your house, piece by piece, unless my son gits his skeered ass down here."

"No, you won't. You will leave right now!"

The door opened again and Mrs. Purcell, looking like she had just seen a pack of giant rattlers, stuck her head in.

"Billy, do you think you could make it to the ground from the front porch roof outside my room?"

He nodded.

"Get Nathan Rose next door. Now."

Before Mrs. Purcell had finished speaking, Billy scurried away using Papa's bedchamber to get to the hallway. Papa couldn't see him from downstairs that way. Mrs. Purcell closed the door again, leaving Clara and Euphora alone in the Blue Room. Euphora pulled on her boots.

A pounding noise, something hitting a wall, shook the house. Clara put a bracing hand on Euphora's shoulder.

"Frank Benton, I am telling you, get out of the house! You cannot stay here while you are like this. You are a danger to your children and me and the Carters. Now, go! Billy is not coming down."

As Mrs. Purcell shouted out the last bit about Billy, her voice began to fade a little. Could she see Papa? Was he near the stairs?

"What should we do, Clara?" Euphora snuggled into Clara's side. Poor little dear was shaking like winter's last leaf in a blizzard. Wrapping her arm around her sister, Clara held Euphora's red-haired head against her shoulder.

"It'll be all right. Billy will be back in a minute with Mr. Rose."

Footsteps thumped up the first few stairs.

"Git out of the way, you old hay bag. You ain't in charge o' me and my kids."

"He's going to hurt Mrs. Purcell." Lips quivering, Euphora peered up at Clara. "We better do something."

She was right. There was no telling how long Billy would be. Clara felt like a frightened deer about to bound. She glanced around the room. She could take a fire iron out there as a weapon, but Papa might get it away from her and really hurt her or Mrs. Purcell. She bit the inside of her mouth. What could she do to hold Papa off?

"You stay away from me." Mrs. Purcell said in a growl.

Papa's footsteps were coming close on the stairs.

"Clara, please. Do something." Euphora's whole face, brow to chin, was quivering. "Please. Do what Izzie would do."

Papa could do something really horrible, something that no one could ever change. Euphora was right. She had to try. She darted to the washstand, picked up the white ceramic pitcher full of water, then flung open the door and rushed out. Papa was nearly to the top of the stairs, close to Mrs. Purcell. He was grasping the railing, veering, lurching. When he saw Clara, he stopped stunned in his tracks as though the water pitcher she held in her hands was a shotgun.

"Go back into your room," Gray eyes stern and scared, Mrs. Purcell looked intently at her.

Clara shook her head at Mrs. Purcell, then looked at Papa. "Papa?"

He was a vile mess, his greatcoat caked in mud, his hair all frazzled, his spectacles nowhere to be seen. The skin under his red eyes looked raw and he smelled like a dead fermenting squirrel. Leaning into the railing, he tilted his head and stared at her.

"Thass her dress. Take it off. It's hers." He lunged toward her.

Gripping the pitcher tight, she drew it behind her, then slung the water out at him. It flooded over him, drenching and shocking him. Faltering backward down a step, then another, he lost his grip on the railing. *Blazes.* He was going to fall. Clara dropped the pitcher. As it broke into pieces, she clambered toward him and reached for his hand to catch him. But he wove toward the railing and caught himself. Bending over, he started to plow up like a ram leading with his dripping-wet head. Clara scrambled up backwards, away from him, to the landing, to high ground.

White hair streaming down, Mrs. Purcell raised the candle lantern up high like a torch, like it had some kind of magic power to keep evil away. Papa swiped at it. She snapped it away from him and held it even higher.

"You old hay bag." He recoiled his arm again.

"Papa. Stop!" Clara flung herself between him and Mrs. Purcell. "I'll do it. I'll do what you want. Do you hear me, Papa?" She clutched his wet, grimy lapels and shook him. "I'll do it. Stop. I'll do it."

He settled his arm down reluctantly and stood still, breathing hard. His stinking whiskey breath filled the air. The three of them waited there a long moment and in case he acted up again, she kept her grip on his lapels.

"Do what, Clara?" Mrs. Purcell's soft, steady voice came from behind.

"None of your god danged business, hay bag."

Papa's chest pumped up under Clara's hold on his coat. She turned her head part way back toward Mrs. Purcell, but kept Papa in her sights. "Papa wants me to start up the séances again. That's all. I didn't want to, but I've changed my mind." She looked at him. "I've changed my mind, Papa. I've changed my mind. Do you hear me? Everything will be all right."

Mrs. Purcell lowered the lantern. "Well, it's not all right coming in here in the middle of the night threatening your children and threatening me, Frank Benton. You and I are going to talk about this tomorrow."

His eyes watering up, Papa looked at her. "You're the only one, Clara, the only one that—"

Downstairs, the front door opened. "Emma, you all right? It's Nathan. You need help?"

Nathan Rose, a coat thrown over his long johns and holding a lantern and a rifle, stood with Billy at his side.

"You coward boy. Betrayin' your own father. Too skeered to stand up to me by yourself. Had to have women protect you, didn't you?"

Clara tugged down hard on Papa's lapels, hard enough that his shoulders caved a little. "It's all right, Mr. Rose," she called downstairs. "Papa is going to bed now." She looked Papa straight in his foggy eyes. "Now Papa, leave Billy alone and go to bed." She kept the downward pressure on his coat. "We'll figure everything tomorrow."

Papa pitched his arm back. Clara ducked, then felt a swift blow on the inside of her elbows, breaking her grasp on his coat. He shoved her aside, then Mrs. Purcell aside, and stumbled off to his bedchamber. Clara glanced around. Euphora was peeking out the cracked door of the Blue Room and the Carter sisters were peering from their room as well.

What she did wasn't what Izzie would have done. Izzie would have wrestled with him even if she and Papa both careened down the stairs, even if one of them got hurt or broke a neck and died. Clara couldn't do that, wasn't brave enough or strong enough for that. At least she did something, though. At least it was over and no one was hurt. Euphora appeared at her side, wrapped her arms around Clara's waist.

"You did it, Clara." Euphora embraced her tightly, tears in her eyes.

Euphora was beaming with pride at her, but Clara's heart sank down to her stomach. Now she'd have to pay the price.

Twenty-Six

NIGHT WIND WAS BLOWING COLD OFF THE LAKE, stinging Clara's face as she stood at the street corner waiting with Papa. The closest street lamp was half a block away but cast ample gaslight for them to see. Tomorrow would be Thanksgiving Day and Euphora was at home now baking pumpkin pies with Mrs. Purcell. Clara thought if only she could be there with them in the warm kitchen, beating eggs and rolling out crusts, or for that matter, if only she could be anywhere else but here, waiting to give up her virginity to Sam Weston.

Weston had called the place they were to meet a private hotel, one with only a certain clientele. She'd never heard of such a thing. It was just down the block and across the street from where she and Papa stood. It looked like a plain wood house set between the livery stable with its expansive sliding doors and Beach's Furniture Manufacturing. She'd never even noticed the gray house before. It was probably a small inn or some kind of short stay boardinghouse.

Papa had told her what he and Weston had planned out. She and Papa were to go down to the waterfront at eight o'clock at night and before she entered the hotel on Water Street, they would look around and make sure that no one could observe her entering. If they had to, they would wait some distance away until the street was empty, then she would dart in. And indeed the street was not empty, so here they were waiting in the cold. Once she got inside, she was to ask for Miss Minnie Stewart who would escort Clara to a room where she would meet Sam Weston.

Papa blew into his cupped hands. "I need to ask ya somethin'. I want to make sure about somethin'." Crossing his arms, he tucked his hands under his armpits, then began to shuffle back and forth. He wasn't just cold. He seemed fidgety. But why? She was the one who had to go in there. He knew what was going to happen to her. She didn't know, not exactly anyway. Maybe it would hurt, and if it did, it wouldn't be hurting Papa.

Scraping his boots on the wood sidewalk, he blew at his hands again. His breath swirled into puffs in the streetlight. Watching him was turning her stomach as tight as the skin on an Indian drum.

"What is it, Papa?"

He stilled himself, cleared his throat. "Did Isabelle or your mother tell you about the menses?"

"Izzie did when it happened to her."

"Did it happen to you yet?"

"No, Papa. Izzie was fifteen. I'm still fourteen."

"Fifteen?" He raised a brow. "That's good. When are you fifteen?"

Clara waited to answer him as an older gentleman in a blue steamship uniform passed close by.

"Why is it good?" she asked.

"Because you can't bear Weston's child if you ain't got it yet."

She felt like he had socked her in her Indian-drum-tight stomach. Why the blazes was he asking her now? Why this late? Would it still have been all right if she had the menses?

Would he have called it off with Weston if she had just told him yes? What if she ended up in the family way? *Hell-fire.* Then where would she be? Where would his scheme be? If she couldn't make money for him, would he leave her and go out West?

She glanced around. Everyone had gone from the area except two men in overcoats, one with a pipe and one with a walking cane, who had been standing across the street from the gray clapboard hotel.

"Why don't those fellas hurry up out of here?" Papa jammed his hands into his coat pockets and began pacing two steps back, two steps forth, his boots scratching at the ice.

A gentleman and lady came out of the hotel's door, climbed into a cabriolet hitched nearby and drove off over the frozen dirt street. The black horse snorted as it clomped by.

"Papa, I don't want to bear a child."

"Shhh. Keep your voice down. That's what I'm sayin'. There's no worry of that if ya don't got the menses." He stretched his hand toward her. "Look, the two fellas are comin' this way. They're leavin'."

Talking and snickering, the two men strolled along the sidewalk toward them. With each step, the skinny man poked his walking stick at the wood and ice. When they got close, bringing the smell of pipe smoke with them, the walking-stick one was saying something about, "one of those temperance extremists," but then broke off and tipped his bowler hat at her and Papa.

"Evening. You're Benton, aren't you?"

"Yes, sir."

"I'm McCormick. This is Emerson." He swept his hat off and smiled at Clara. "And who is this young lady?"

"This is my fine daughter, Mr. McCormick."

"Daughter? Down here at night?" Winking at his friend, he tapped his cane twice.

Clara lowered her eyes. *Jo-fire.* Did they think she was a girl of the night, Papa's whore? She took a step back. She wanted to run, run to the black lake just around the corner, wanted to steal a sailboat like Mamma did and sail it far away.

"Clara's my daughter, gentlemen. She's a well-known medium. Has a true gift. We're on our way to a private spirit circle."

The cane tapped twice again on the crusty ice. "Ah. Yes. Yes. I've heard about you. The Amazing Miss Clara."

She didn't look up at him, kept her eyes down. Why couldn't they all just go? She wanted to be done with this moment forever, to get it over with, to do the other thing with Weston if she had to, then go home, go home to her bed in the Blue Room, to sleep the night and wake up tomorrow and celebrate Thanksgiving day and eat turkey and pumpkin pie. She bit down on the inside of her mouth until it hurt. The two men and Papa spoke a little about someone's line of canal boats going up for sale, then finally, they shuffled on.

"Good evening to you, Miss Benton." The skinny one tipped his hat again as they strolled away.

When they were out of sight, Papa glanced in every direction. "All right, Little Plum, go on. I'll be right here. I'll walk you home when you are done." He looked off into the shadows, past the end of the street lamps, away from the hotel, away from her. "I'll be right here."

Wrapping her shawl tightly over her shoulders, she crossed the street. Everything seemed still. Even the wind had died down. When she got to the hotel door, she paused, took a deep breath. In a few hours, when she left this gray building, she'd be a woman. She looked back at Papa. He waved her on with both hands. Feeling his push, even from down the street, she bit down so hard on her mouth skin that she tasted blood. She grasped the doorknob. It was bitterly cold, even through her black lace mitt. She held it without turning it. This was her chance to run. Papa was far enough away. He might not be able to catch her. But where would she go? She couldn't really steal a sailboat. It was freezing and getting late and she didn't have three cents in her pocket.

She noticed Papa was starting toward her so she opened the door and scuttled in. The small foyer was lit by a simple gaslight chandelier, had a red carpet, pretty pink and blue striped wallpaper, three tall, carved wood chairs, a grandfather clock, and an umbrella stand. To her left was a Dutch door, top open. The room behind it was brightly lit. To her right were closed double sliding doors and in front of her, a stairway with more red carpet.

"Hello, are you Clara?"

Clara flinched. Arriving behind the half door was a woman with black hair and brown eyes, wearing a royal blue taffeta dress with low neckline and lots of flounces.

"Yes."

"My name's Minnie. Minnie Stewart. He's already upstairs."

Clara squeezed a taste of blood from the wound inside her mouth and swallowed.

"Do you need anything, for during or afterward?" Minnie asked.

"No. I mean, I don't know."

Reaching down, Minnie opened the half door and came out, her blue hoop skirt rustling. She rested a hand on Clara's shoulder. "Sam told me it was your first time. If you want to, come and see me when you are done with him. Come to this door. If it is closed, knock loudly. I'll wake up if I am dozing."

Clara nodded half-heartedly.

"Yes? You'll come and see me?"

But what for, Clara wondered. To talk of womanly things? Even though she nodded again, and this time with more force, she knew she was too ashamed now, and would be even more ashamed later to talk with this Minnie woman, owner of the private hotel.

"Room sixteen. It's on the right. It's our best room. Sam wanted the best for you." She leaned toward Clara, put her mouth close to Clara's ear, and whispered, "If you bleed on the linens, don't worry, it's normal. Sam promised to pay for new ones if they're badly sullied."

Bleed? *Hell.* She felt like a knocked-over glass of water. What was this woman talking about? No one had ever said anything about bleeding. What was going to bleed? How? Why? She tried to swallow, but her throat got so taught that she couldn't.

"You look faint, dear. It's nothing to worry about. It's just something that happens to some girls the first time." She gently squeezed Clara's elbow. "You'll be fine. We all survive it. Sam's a decent man. Be glad of that." She stepped back and smiled. "Room sixteen, on the right."

As she climbed the stairs, she untied her bonnet and removed it. If it were tomorrow, this would be over and Papa would have the fifty dollars Weston had promised and be happy again. She was close to tears as she followed the door numbers along the hall. She could slip out a back door without being seen. There had to be a back door. No, she wouldn't cry. No matter what. Room twelve. She wouldn't let Sam Weston know anything that was in her heart. Fourteen. She wouldn't show him anything, wouldn't give him anything. She'd do what she had to for Papa. That was all. Sixteen.

The moment she rapped on the door, it swung open as though Sam Weston had been standing right there inside with his hand ready on the knob. Smiling ear to ear, he was dressed like a perfect gentleman in a purple silk cravat, purple satin vest with a grape vine pattern and black wool trousers. His pale brown square-cut goatee and mustache were trimmed up. He'd been at the barbershop no more than three hours ago, she guessed.

"Come in, Clara. I hope you didn't have to wait long outside for the street to clear." He took her shawl and bonnet.

The room was pretty with a big four-poster bed covered with a lacey canopy and pillows piled high, all in white. A silver tray with several decanters and different shaped glasses rested on the chest of drawers. Above that was a large mirror reflecting a good part of the room. Weston laid her shawl over the back of a pale yellow-and-blue striped sofa, put her bonnet on a chair, then poured something from a glass carafe into two glasses and brought them to her.

"Here, sherry. This will take the chill off." He offered her the small stem glass.

She took a sip. It smelled sweet, tasted warm and fruity and tingled in her throat as it slid down.

"Your coming here means everything to me. I am honored." He clinked his glass of sherry against hers.

She took another sip with him, but she wasn't honored. She was selling her virginity. That wasn't how she thought of honor. Taking another large mouthful of sherry, then another, she drained her glass.

"You are thirsty." He laughed a little, took her glass, filled it, offered it again.

"Did anyone see you come in?"

"No." She drank the second sherry down so quickly that she coughed hard.

Smiling and silent while she hacked away, Weston watched her until she was calm again. He was clean as a whistle, she thought, but he had to hate those waves in his brown hair. Why else would he always use so much greasy pomade?

While he moved about the room, removing his silk cravat, washing and drying his hands at the washstand, she took a seat on the sofa and waited. Euphora and Mrs. Purcell were probably cleaning up after putting the pies in the oven about now. Finally he returned to her and took her glass once more.

"Mr. Weston?"

"Yes, Clara."

"May we start now?"

"Clara, my sweet one, are you eager to know me?" Grinning like someone had just given him twenty-five Christmas gifts all at once, he plopped himself down on the sofa next to her.

No, *Hell-fire*, she did not want to know him. She wanted to get out of there. She knew far more about him than she wanted to already. If the fall wouldn't break her legs to bits when she hit the ground, she'd jump out the window right now. No, she was just blazing eager to get this evening over and done with.

"Yes. Eager," she said, mustering the best smile she could.

He put her sherry glass on a little side table and rested his arm on the sofa back behind her. "There's no hurry. The room is ours as long as we like. We can linger."

Clara gulped. *Linger?* Why on earth would she want to linger? He waited quietly for her answer but she said nothing. Then he removed a cufflink.

"Don't be afraid, Clara. I haven't hurt you before and I won't now."

How could he promise that when, according to Minnie downstairs, there might be blood?

After he slid the other cufflink through its slit, he dropped the pair into his waistcoat pocket. "Clara, if you don't mind, in a moment, I'd like to undress you, take off everything you have on. I've been thinking about this moment a long time. I've imagined undressing you slowly, like picking petals from a flower, until there is nothing left but the sturdy simple stem."

She looked at the window and thought about jumping again, about the pain of broken legs. When she didn't say anything about the undressing, he rose slowly and took her glass back to the chest of drawers. He poured another sherry. After returning the glass stopper to the decanter, he looked up into the mirror and caught her eye.

"Would you like that?"

Suddenly she felt like she was sinking, sinking down through the sofa, down through the carpet and floor, down to the room below and then down beneath that, and then into the earth. As he presented the glass of golden sherry to her, the room seemed turned around exactly once so that he was approaching her from the door, not the chest of drawers. She shook her head slightly as though trying to unclog her ears of water. Then he was back where he ought to be.

"May I, then?"

She took the glass from him. "What?"

"Undress you."

She gulped down half the glass. "Yes. Where do you want me, in the corner?" She pointed with her eyes to the corner between the bed and the green curtains.

He followed her eyes, then laughed. "Not this time." He unbuttoned his collar, pulled it off, laid it on top of her shawl on the sofa back, then sat near her and opened the top of his shirt, revealing curls of light brown chest hair.

"I'll start with your beautiful brown hair and work my way all the way down to your toes."

She swigged down what was left of her sherry and felt a warm flush run through her body. This was going to take all night. Papa would freeze to death out in the cold street. He'd be in a terrible wax.

Weston took her glass and set it aside. "Turn your back so I can take your hair down."

When she shifted away from him on the sofa and stared at the wood door, she was relieved not to see him. First he unbuckled her black neckband and slid it off, then she felt his fingers find the pins in her hair and remove them, then untwist her hair. Once the hair was down her back, he stroked it a few times, then brushed it forward, his hands lingering over, then pressing her bosoms. Her shoulders pinched upward, then she felt both his hands near her neck urge her shoulders back down.

"There. Lovely. Now the dress."

As he began to unbutton the back, she remembered the first time he had given her the white and indigo dot dress and had buttoned it up when she tried it on. Now here he was taking the same dress off of her. Even though it was a light summer dress and it was a winter night, Papa had insisted she wear it.

"It was a special gift from him," he'd said. "Now git out of that green stripe one and put on his and wear that black neckband he gave you too and those black mitts I gave you."

So here she sat, her back to Sam Weston on a striped satin sofa, everything on her except her undergarments—a gift from either Papa or Weston. Now, because of tonight, Papa had made new promises. "Tomorrow we'll get you one of them whalebone hoop things you been wantin' and one of those other things grown up women wear, corsets." It wouldn't be long before her entire wardrobe, even her shoes and stockings, had something to do with this paramour arrangement with Sam Weston. *Jo-fire*, the whole family would soon be wearing the clothing purchased with Weston's money.

When Weston finished with the buttons, he got up and asked her to stand and step out of the dress. After that, he laid the dress down so carefully on the back of the sofa someone would have thought he was a tailor admiring his own work. Then he moved around her and unbuttoned her red flannel petticoat. She stepped out of that too and next he lifted her shimmy over her head. All her skin above her waist was out in the chilly air now. He added the shimmy to the growing pile, then set his light brown eyes to traveling all over her, up and down, across and back again. She had that rabbit-in-a-snare feeling again, like the first time in the Spirit Room corner. With her black lace mitts still on, she crossed her arms high over her bosoms, locking a hand on each opposite shoulder.

"No. Let me look at you. Don't hide." He tried to pry her hands off, but she held tight to herself. "Please." He waited for her to let go, waited with his hands not fighting or tugging, just waiting and waiting. Then it struck her. If she kept stiff-armed like this when he wanted something else, this thing would take all *jo-fired* night and that wasn't what she wanted at all. She let her arms drop back to her sides and then he swept her hair around to her back. He stared at her chest, his eyes burning branding iron trails slowly across her skin. Stiffening up her arms again, she looked down at the soft shiny stripes on the sofa.

Suddenly, with a thud, he dropped to his knees, pulling her attention away from the blue-and-yellow satin stripes.

Then, like he was praying to Jesus Christ, our savior, he bent his head down and placed his hands on her hips at the top of her pantalettes. And there he froze. The smell of half-rotten apples wafted up, making her nauseous. That pomade. Just how much of the stuff did he use anyway? An entire tin?

Then he started whispering, repeating something over and over. She was glad she couldn't hear what he was saying. Let him keep his dang chanting to himself. Glancing around the room, she searched for something to fixate on in the moments to come. The bedposts would do. There were four of them and they were solid and dark and strong and shiny and upright. She could move her thoughts from one to the other during the evening. Start with one of the far ones, then two, three, four, as things went along. By the time she was at four, it would be over and she could go home to the house that would smell like pumpkin pie. It would be like holding her breath to a very very slow count of four.

She felt his fingers go to the button on the side of her pantalettes and release it. Bedpost number one, far left. Then she felt the cotton start to slide down her legs, and his hands with it, all the way to her ankles. Cool air hit her belly. Her stomach clenched of its own will.

"Step out of them."

Tearing herself from bedpost number one to look at the undergarment in a heap around her feet, she raised a foot, then the other as Weston, sitting back on his heels now, slid the pantalettes away. Except for boots, white stockings, and black lace gloves, she stood completely naked. He tossed the pantalettes under the sofa and began to unbutton her boots. When he had taken off each boot and each stocking and stuffed them under the sofa, he straightened up into his prayer position, eyes closed, and began to whisper once more.

What the *Hell* was he doing? He was more peculiar than she had ever imagined.

He tipped his face close to her private place. She cringed, expecting his touch, but he only took a few deep breaths. Was he smelling her, sniffing her like a dog? Was this what men and women did with one another?

"You are the stem of the flower now, perfect, lithe. Hold still," he said.

He stood up, stepped back, crossed his arms over his bunches-of-grapes vest, and began to stare at every inch of her. For a moment she watched him and his brown eyes, until she started to feel the sinking again. She looked away, searching for the bedpost, but she got trapped on the sight of the two of them in the mirror, her naked body with her two small bosoms, her young woman hips, his broad back, his billowy white shirt sleeves, his fancy satin vest. Next to him, she looked tiny, like a midget in the circus, even though she wasn't short and he wasn't especially tall.

He noticed that she was looking at them in the mirror. Turning around to face the mirror, he lodged his hands on his hips, and smiling, caught her eye there in the glass.

"You see? You are perfect, young and perfect. Nothing has touched you yet. I wish I were an artist. I'd paint your picture on a big canvas and put it in one of those ornate gold frames."

"Will it be much longer? Papa is waiting out in the cold."

His smile fell. *Dang*, she shouldn't have said that. She ruined it. She wouldn't say anything else the rest of the evening, wouldn't open her mouth, unless it was something he wanted her to say.

"Don't worry about your father. He takes care of himself. I want you to think about me right now."

She nodded. He was the one thing she was trying not to think about, trying with all her heart, all her mind, but he was strange, big, confusing. Ignoring him was harder than she had expected.

"Can you think about me?"

She nodded.

"That's better, but I wish you would smile. You've not smiled once since you've been here."

"I apologize. I'm nervous, Mr. Weston."

His grin flashed up again. "Yes. That's natural."

He reached down and opened the buttons on his trousers, then withdrew his prick. It was already large.

Stepping toward her, he embraced her tightly and picked her up. He held her in the air a moment, then carried her around to the side of the bed. Slowly he let her down onto her back, her legs dangling off the side. Her pulse began to pound. She felt like she might vomit. Taking one of her feet in a hand, he pulled her leg up and rested her ankle on his shoulder, then he did the same with the other. He grabbed her hips and slid them just off the edge of the bed toward his prick. Then she felt his hand putting his prick between her legs, the prick press into her, then plunge inside her.

Pain shot through her. It felt like he was going to bust her open from the inside out. His hands digging into the skin at her waist, he lifted her hips up and thrust himself into her again and again, each time hurting, each time bouncing her on the bed. After the third thrust, she searched for bedpost number two and pondered on it so hard that she couldn't move on to number three and four as she had planned. She stared at it, concentrated on the dark brown wood, the particular set of curves toward its top, smooth round carved shapes, shining with polish, a larger one, then a smaller one, then a third smaller one, trying to get him away, get him out of her.

When he finally withdrew, she left the bedpost, came back down into herself on the bed. She felt scorched and raw. It was over. Her body was hers again, no one in it, no one praying to it or smelling it. It was just hers.

She lay still, eyes closed, legs hanging off the side of the bed where he had left her. She listened to him shuffling about the room. Tucking her knees up against her, she rolled over and lay on her side. A blanket landed softly on her, then drifted up onto her shoulders. There was a slight rustling noise on the bed near her. She wouldn't open her eyes to see. She didn't want to see him, didn't want to see the mirror. Please, please don't ask for a smile, she begged in silence. Water splashed in the basin, then more fussing and rustling, then the door creaked opened and clicked shut. He was gone. Under the blanket she held the sore place between her legs. It was over, finally over.

In a long while, when she was sure he was gone, she opened her eyes and searched the bed for whatever had been left there. A folded piece of paper lay on the pillow. Draping the blanket around her, she sat up and opened the paper with hands still wearing black lace mitts. A gold dollar coin plopped from the folds of a note onto the white bed spread, the Indian head facing her.

My Dearest Clara,

This is for you, and only you, to do with what you please. I will not tell your father about it. It is our secret. Please tell no one about us or this gift. There will be more. Now that you are my paramour, I am the richest man in the world.
Your Devoted Lover, S.W.

CLARA DID NOT WANT to have a heart-to-heart talk with Minnie Stewart behind the Dutch door, so she slipped out as quietly as she could. The grandfather clock read ten fifteen. If Papa had really waited in the cold wind for two hours, he would be chilled deep to his bones. As she opened the door into the night, she felt ugly inside, ugly and withered, not a flower blossoming into womanhood, but a flower expired, lying on the ground all thirsty and tired and limp.

She glanced up the street. Papa was there in the shadow of the street light where she had left him, coat collar turned up around his neck, shoulders up to his ears, hands holding something at his waist. He watched her walk toward him, but when she got close, he looked down at the thing in his hands, his empty pipe. Even though he only smoked a pipe once in a while, he often had one in his coat. He clutched its bowl, twisting the mouthpiece one way, then the other.

He smelled like pipe tobacco, but not liquor. Had he really been standing there for two hours without going to one of his taverns?

"You all right?" He lifted his eyes just enough to see her face.

Even though she was as far from all right as she could get, she nodded. Lowering his eyes as soon as he saw her answer, he stared at that pipe like it was the inside of a fine watch he was set on repairing. He shivered, then started to clomp along the wooden sidewalk. She stepped in stride with him.

The whole walk home he never looked away from that pipe. It seemed he might snap it in two. Even though there were things she wanted to know like had he seen Weston, spoken to him, gotten his fifty dollars, she was glad for Papa's silence, glad for the darkness. Wrapping herself in her shawl as best she could, she longed for it to be a thick wool blanket all around her from head to toe.

She had some trouble walking right. Her feet didn't seem to connect properly to her legs and with each step she took, she felt heavy—legs heavy, arms heavy—and there was the rawness between her legs. Papa didn't ask her anything and that was just fine, because she didn't want to explain anything.

When they entered the house, there was just the one small lamp burning low in the parlor. Papa slipped his pipe into his coat pocket and when it was gone from her sight, from his crazy twisting, she relaxed her grip on her shawl. Now, finally, the evening really was over. She could go to bed and wake up and it would be tomorrow. Papa took the lamp from the parlor and carried it upstairs with them. After putting it on the upright crate by her bed where Euphora was soundly sleeping, he shuffled off, eyes fixed downward, toward his bedchamber. There was no "goodnight, Little Plum," no anything. Just as his door was nearly shut, he pulled it back open, and said, "God bless you," then closed it gently.

Clara sat for a while on the side of the bed so tired and dizzy she couldn't rise up to undress. After a long time listening to Billy and Euphora sleep, she untied her bonnet, took it off, and dropped it on the floor. Then dress, boots, shawl, and gloves still on, she lay down next to her little sister and reached over to turn off the oil lamp.

Billy lifted his head and looked at her just as she was dousing the light. "You all right, Clara? It's late."

"I'm tired out is all."

"You sure?"

She nodded, then Billy burrowed under his blanket. She wanted to rustle him and tell him what Papa made her do, but she never would. First of all, she couldn't. She was too ashamed, but second of all, Billy might go right into Papa's room and stab him with his hunting knife.

If Izzie were here, she would scream at Papa and Weston and tell them both to go to Hell forever. And if Mamma were here, none of this paramour business would have happened in the first place. Mamma never would have let Papa and Weston agree to these awful things. Why did Mamma have to die and let Papa get so peculiar and mean?

Reaching a hand into her dress pocket, she grasped the gold dollar. It was still cold from the walk home. As it warmed inside her fist, she fell asleep.

THE MORNING SUN STREAMING INTO THE KITCHEN seemed awfully bright. Clara stood at the worktable peeling potatoes with a small knife. Her tongue like a dusty farm road after months of drought, she swigged down her fourth full glass of water. Just as she had expected, she was weary but it was comforting to be following Mrs. Purcell's orders in the warm kitchen and knowing that last night was the past. It was today now and Mrs. Purcell, working at the other end of the table, was still Mrs. Purcell, round, white-haired, sweet as her own canned peaches, and Euphora leaning over the stove, sticking her nose over a pot of beans, was still Euphora, strong, eager, bright as a candle.

Ten people for dinner meant peeling twenty potatoes brought up from the cellar. The seventeen unpeeled ones sat on the table to her right in a circle surrounded by another circle with one big potato in the center. The peeled potatoes, three, were side-by-side, straight in a row. In the end, there would be four rows of five on her left. When she was finished with peeling potatoes, she would be in charge of peeling turnips. Only ten of those.

Euphora's duties were keeping the wood stove at just the right heat, getting out dishes, washing things, setting the table, stirring the beans, and scampering like a raccoon up from and down to the cellar whenever Mrs. Purcell asked for something—pickled tomatoes, canned pears, and "on second thought a few more turnips. Those young men from next door eat like horses."

Mrs. Purcell was peeling and chopping chestnuts for the turkey's stuffing. When reaching for the next shiny brown nut, her hand accidentally nudged several off the table. The nuts scattered and clacked onto the floor near Clara's feet. Clara squatted quickly to stop them from rolling. When she bent down, her private place burned. When she stood back up, with three chestnuts in hand, she felt oddly small, like she was sinking again, the floor giving way under her feet.

Mrs. Purcell took the chestnuts from her palm. "Are you all right, dear? You look peaked. Are you ill?"

To stop from sinking, from disappearing, Clara grabbed the edge of the worktable.

"Clara, are you feverish?"

"No, I'm a little tired from the late night."

"Your father should not be taking you out to conduct those spirit circles at those late hours." Mrs. Purcell flicked her knife at the air. "You are still growing, for mercy's sake. I am most unhappy with your father right now. If I didn't care so much and worry so much about you children, and your departed mother, I'd throw him out of my house." With a scowl on her face, she returned to her chestnuts.

Clara counted her potatoes one more time, then started peeling again. But suddenly Sam Weston came to mind, shoving his prick into her, looming over her. Her knees buckled a little and she felt like she was shrinking, shrinking lower than the table, a child too short to reach the surface. She seized the potato in the middle of her potato circles and held it like an anchor.

After taking a few deep breaths, she returned to herself. She shouldn't think about Weston, or picture him, or remember anything about last night. She had to toss him out of her thoughts like salt from a shaker. Three and one half potatoes done. Sixteen and one half not done.

"Mrs. Purcell, are you sure twenty potatoes is enough?"

"Yes, dear."

They peeled, cut, chopped, rinsed, stirred, mashed, and cleaned up for hours. All the while Clara asked questions of Mrs. Purcell to keep her mind away from Sam Weston. "What was the most people you ever had for Thanksgiving dinner and who were they?" and "how do you know when the turkey is done?" And of Euphora, she asked, "What's the best thing you've ever cooked with Mrs. Purcell?" and "what book shall we read next?" and on and on until there was no one else in the world but the three of them peeling, chopping, stirring, and chatting.

In all her life Clara had never smelled so many kinds of food steaming, baking, and roasting all at once. It was splendiferous, heaven on earth. They served golden-skinned roast turkey with bread and chestnut stuffing and gravy, corn bread, mashed potatoes, mashed turnips, and stewed beans. Mrs. Purcell opened three jars of her pickled tomatoes from last summer, and there were three pumpkin pies. No wine or sherry, though. Mrs. Purcell said, "I don't have a Temperance household, but I am not interested in serving any spirits to your father. I've put my few bottles away under lock and key."

A friend of Billy's from Maxwell's Nursery came to dinner. The Carter sisters wore their Sunday dresses and Mrs. Purcell also invited the widower from next door, Nathan Rose, and his two sons who both attended the Hobart Free College in town. When everyone had arrived and taken a seat, the table was as crowded as it could be, not room for one more chair, and there was enough food spread out on the table to feed half of Geneva.

After everything was ready, Clara sat and looked around the table at all the faces. Could anyone tell what she had done the night before? Mrs. Purcell said a prayer. Eating began. Talking began. It was all about the north and the south, slavery and freedom, John Brown's October raid on Harper's Ferry, and how Colonel Robert E. Lee and his men ended the raid and captured Brown, how Brown was to be executed to death down in Virginia and whether Brown was right or wrong trying to cause an uprising and using violence.

All four boys—Billy, his friend, and Nathan Rose's sons—thought Brown was right, thought he was a hero, but Mrs. Purcell said she agreed with Sarah Josepha Hale, the editor of *Godey's Lady's Book*. Sarah Hale wanted the Union to stay together and for there to be peace between northerners and southerners. "We're all going to die anyway. No need to rush it along for each other," Mrs. Purcell said.

Clara peeked at Papa every now and then. Through most of the meal he seemed to be ignoring her, but then out of nowhere, after the John Brown chatter ended, he suddenly looked straight at her, almost with surprise, as though she had just walked in and sat down.

He gazed at the boys. "Clara's never been to school a day in her life, but she is powerful smart with numbers. When she's a wife to the right husband, she'll be able to manage her household like a proper woman and a businessman all in one. My married daughter Isabelle up in Rochester reads too much, everythin' on earth. That won't help her take care of her home. No sir, it's Clara that's goin' ta be the pick of my girls. I'm bettin' my money on Clara. She's a picture too, don't you boys think so?"

Everyone stopped chewing, set their forks and knives down and looked at Clara for a moment, a long, awful moment. She started to sink down again and felt she was three years old, chin just barely level with the table.

"She's lovely, Frank. We all see that. I wish I had a daughter. I always wanted a daughter." Nathan Rose looked sideways at his two sons. "All I've got is these two plug ugly idiots."

Everyone laughed, the boys the loudest. Winking, Nathan Rose smiled at Clara and then turned to Mrs. Purcell, "Emma, this is the best roast turkey I have ever tasted."

Clara picked up her fork and knife for the first time and cut a piece of the dark meat on her plate. She ate a few bites, but that was all she could get down.

With bright blue eyes, Euphora looked over at Clara. "I wish Izzie was here, and Mamma too."

"Me too," Billy said. "When is Izzie comin' for a visit, Clara? I thought you said she was comin'?"

"I don't know, but she promised she would."

Twenty-Seven

THE MORNING AFTER THANKSGIVING, Clara was happy as a clam at high tide to get away from Papa. She left the house to go to work for the milliner before he was awake. She was so early that Mrs. Beattie told her to start the coal fire, then sit in the back workroom and wait until she had sorted through her weekly accounting. Then Mrs. Beattie promised to start her on something special.

Clara got the fire burning in the iron tailor's stove, then studied the room. The worktable was perfectly neat, everything in little boxes or wooden trays in the middle—colored threads, shears, measuring tape, buttons. Along one wall, large flat shelves held patterns and small pieces of silks, satins, velvets, wools, and black and white laces. A straw basket was half-filled with feathers, brown and black ones, long fine silvery ones, reddish ones, enough to dress a naked rooster, Clara thought.

Her favorite thing on the worktable was a bandbox. Whenever she could find a minute at work, she'd dwell on it. She drew it toward her. It was an oval shape, tall with a lid that nestled snug on top. It was covered with wallpaper of red, green, brown, and blue that showed six men in uniform pulling, and one pushing, a fire wagon along a road in front of a beautiful red brick house. The house wasn't on fire though. It was pretty and peaceful. They were on their way to a fire not in the picture. One man was blowing a horn, calling out trouble. On the fire wagon the number thirteen was painted in a circle in two places. She ran her hand over the lid. It was slightly gritty with dust.

Suddenly, there was a slap like a whip cracking. She lurched. Her hand jerked, tipping over the bandbox. It tumbled to the floor spilling snippets of colored ribbon in a mess.

"I cannot, cannot, make these accounts add up," Mrs. Beattie called out. "It's the most frustrating thing ever."

Then Mrs. Beattie was quiet again for a while, except for some hefty sighing and paper shuffling. When visiting the shop to look at hats and *Godey's Lady's Books*, Clara had heard Mrs. Beattie grumble about her accounts before. Mrs. Beattie's face would look tortured and she'd scratch her blond hair like a little monkey with an accordion player. When she was really disturbed, she'd slap or pound her ledgers. Clara picked up the bandbox and the tangled ribbons and put them on the table. She plucked at them and began to sort them by color, reds and pinks in one lump, blues and greens in another, black, white, yellow, purple in their own piles. Then she unfurled the ribbons and counted them to see which color there was the most of.

Slap. Slap. Slap. Clara's heart jumped into her throat and she vaulted from her stool. Then in a moment, when her heart settled down, she went into the shop and saw Mrs. Beattie sitting, holding her head in her hands at her small desk behind the cashier counter. Was she crying? Bookkeeping wasn't anything to cry about, was it? It was just arithmetic, numbers in a ledger.

"I can add, subtract, multiply, and divide. Papa taught us when we were little. He wouldn't send us to school, but he thought we needed to know numbers. He says both my brother Billy and I have a knack for it."

Mrs. Beattie lifted her head and swiveled around in her chair. "You can?"

Clara nodded and Mrs. Beattie grinned at her. "You never told me that." Mrs. Beattie stood up and pointed at her chair. "Here."

Clara sat and Mrs. Beattie peered over her shoulder. She showed her the list of sales in her ledger and a handful of receipts from the bank. "This column of sales should add up to my deposits and it doesn't. I check this every week."

Within a few minutes Clara found the mistake—the sale of a black cap recorded twice.

"My dear, you are a genius. If you keep my books, I'll pay you another dollar a week." She placed a hand on Clara's forearm.

A loud thump shook the wall. "Oh!" Clara rammed her hand against her throat. "What's that?"

"What on earth?" Mrs. Beattie's narrow chin jutted up. "It's in the stairwell."

Mrs. Beattie dashed out of the shop in pursuit of the noise.

Clara's heart was fluttering like a broken-winged bird trying to fly. "*Lawks*, I am jumpy today." There was another thump in the stairwell. If the noise had to do with the Spirit Room, she'd better see to it, too.

When she got out to the sidewalk, the winter cold bit at her face. The door to the stairwell was propped open with an old crate.

"You be careful with my walls. I don't want any damage. Do you hear me?" Hands on her hips, Mrs. Beattie was standing inside on the third step, looking up into the dim stairwell.

Papa, Billy, and Papa's squat saloonkeeper friend, Payne, were lugging a red sofa up the stairs. Clara stepped inside the stairwell to get out of the wind.

"We ain't hurtin' your dear walls," Papa said.

"You're moving in new furniture and you haven't told me when you're going to give me the rent, Mr. Benton."

Billy's sandy hair hung down over half his eyes, but Clara could just see he looked surprised and disgusted.

"Don't stop Benton. I'll fall over on my back. Keep moving, you bastard." Standing erect and holding the bottom of the sofa on his own, Payne looked like he was about to tumble over.

Even in the dim light the sofa shimmered like silk. It was one of those that had the arm on only one end and it was one of the loveliest pieces she had ever seen, but it had to be expensive. What the *Jo-fire* was it for? Their family didn't own any furniture like that. Even Mrs. Purcell didn't have anything like it. It couldn't be for the séances. Then Clara swallowed and took a step back out into the spider-biting cold air. It was for her and Sam Weston. That's what it was. She took another step backwards and slipped from the sidewalk onto the cobble street, then righted herself against the shoulder of the horse Papa had brought. It was certainly for her and Sam Weston. She had no doubts.

She charged back into the empty shop. The sofa upstairs, being shoved from spot to spot, grated and scraped along the floor above her. The sounds grew louder and louder until she ducked, threw her arms over her head, and ran to the workroom. She sat a moment at the table with her colored ribbons, then resumed counting them. Red and pink were by far the most popular. When she had flattened them all out, she twirled the various length pieces into pretty rolls and stacked them in tiers in the bandbox. When she was finished, she closed the lid and wiped the dust off the firemen and their wagon.

A bell jangled. Her shoulders shot up by her ears. *Lawk*, it was just the doorbell. "Calm yourself, Clara," she said.

She took a deep breath and walked out toward the hat and bonnet displays expecting a customer, but it was Mrs. Beattie returning from upstairs.

"Well, I didn't know your spirit circles were so popular again, Clara. You didn't tell me that. Your father paid me past due rent and gave me next month's too." Mrs. Beattie looked quite pleased. She strode over to her sales counter and dropped the gold coins from her hand into the slot on her cash box. "That's a fine piece of furniture. He says your customers like to socialize a little after a session and the sofa will make it more cordial." She flipped a few pages in her ledger and made a note. "Didn't you say things were still slow up there with the spirits? I don't notice people coming and going anymore."

What was she to say? That the spirit circles had slowed down to the pace of a box turtle taking a nap in his shell? That Papa wanted that red sofa for something else, something secret and miserable?

"It has been picking up a little. Papa thinks a little interest will lead to a lot of interest like it did in the beginning."

"Now tell me, dear, truly. Do you really hear the spirits? It is a hoax, isn't it?"

Oh, why did Mrs. Beattie have to ask about this now? Clara didn't want to stand here and lie all day. She liked Mrs. Beattie.

"I do sometimes hear them, not every time at every séance."

"You truly do?" Mrs. Beattie lifted a brow.

Clara ached to tell the truth. With each day that went by there was something more to lie about. It was awful wearisome. But Papa would have a fit if he knew she had told anyone in town, even Mrs. Beattie, about the hoax. It didn't matter that hardly anyone came anymore, hardly anyone believed in her as a medium. Still, she'd better not set Papa off.

She took a deep breath and nodded. Mrs. Beattie stared at her a moment, waiting for more, but Clara gave nothing else.

They spent a couple of hours poring over ledgers, receipts, bills, and the names of the businesses that Mrs. Beattie ordered things from, mostly in New York City. Twice a year Mrs. Beattie went to New York City and looked over what was new. She'd visited the famous store, A.T. Stewart's on Broadway, and described it as a castle full of beautiful things. While Mrs. Beattie spoke, Clara could see Mrs. Beattie on one of these trips, bustling around the great city, strolling along Broadway.

The milliner closed her ledgers and showed Clara how she filed away her papers, then she led Clara into the back room. Bending over the worktable, Mrs. Beattie retrieved the firemen bandbox.

"Ah, my firemen. A friend gave me this after the Crystal Palace fire in New York City." She opened the box and looked in. "Oh, look how you've organized my ribbon scraps." She looked up at Clara. "I was one of the two thousand people in the Crystal Palace when it burned to the ground in '57. Did you hear of it?"

Clara shook her head.

"No, you are too young. It was on 42nd Street and it was truly a palace." Mrs. Beattie's blue eyes drifted up, her face becoming dreamy. "All glass and iron with a huge dome, thousands of exhibitors and hundreds of sculptures, and art, and practically everything mankind has invented from all over the world. There were flags waving atop pinnacles in the breezes." Her hands waved in the air above her head. "Sun shining off the glass walls and ceiling in the daytime and at night, the whole thing glowing like a great hulking lantern." She glanced back at Clara and smiled. "Not one person was lost in the fire. The firemen got us out. That building was never supposed to burn down, it being mostly glass and iron. I wish you could have seen it. Maybe someday I'll take you to New York City on one of my fashion trips. Would you like that?"

Clara nodded and grinned. "Oh, yes."

"I've seen you admiring this bandbox. It's sweet, isn't it? These little firemen are quite noble, like soldiers in their uniforms." She patted Clara's rows of rolled-up ribbon and replaced the lid, then slid the bandbox toward Clara. "Take this as a gift, ribbons and all. I really should be paying you more than I am and it would ease my guilt if you would accept it."

"Truly?" Clara lifted the box and embraced it. "Truly?"

"Yes. And you'll keep my books?"

Clara smiled and nodded.

"Now let's get to work."

WHEN SHE HAD FINISHED WORKING with Mrs. Beattie, Clara decided to keep the bandbox in the Spirit Room so she took it upstairs. When she entered she found Papa in his shirtsleeves and suspenders, sleeping on his side like a tired old cat on the bright red silk sofa. His spectacles and boots were on the floor near his feet. As she had thought, the sofa was splendiferous. The back of it started high and curved lower and lower toward the open end where the polished wood frame ended in a curl. Papa stirred, rubbed his nose, and opened his eyes.

"That you, Little Plum? Good. Want to talk to ya. Hand me my spectacles." He sat up. "What do you think of your new sofa?" He patted the spot next to him. "Try it."

She handed him his spectacles and plunked herself down at the far end of the sofa, but not close where he had offered. She slipped off her red shawl and set the firemen bandbox in her lap.

Papa stroked the sofa's curved arm. "Purty, almost like a woman herself the way this wood swirls around."

"Why'd you get this, Papa?"

"It's for you, Little Plum."

"I don't need a sofa up here."

"Now. Now. You are goin' ta need this."

She began to feel the sinking again. She was getting smaller and smaller. Not wanting to hear what was next, she threw her hands over her ears. Her bandbox dropped to the floor, rolling onto its side, the lid cracking open part way.

"What's wrong? You got an earache?" Papa's voice was muffled. He pointed at the box on the floor. "What's that? Where'd you get money for that thing?"

He bent over and stretched a hand toward it, but she reached it first, set the lid back on properly and gripped it tight in her lap. It was hers. *Hell-fire.* He wasn't going to get his grimy hands on her bandbox.

"Mrs. Beattie gave it to me. It was a gift."

He slumped back against the sofa. "That's nice. We've got Weston comin' regular now. It'll be the same as at the hotel last week between you and him. Every Friday night. And I have to say, he's gonna pay dearly."

Clara studied the firemen as he talked. She thought it would be heavenly to be in the red brick house watching out the window at the men march by, hauling their number thirteen wagon. She could almost hear the horn that one of them was blowing.

"He even split the cost of this sofa with me. Generous man, he is. Shows how much he admires ya."

"Papa, I don't want to see Sam Weston ever again. I am getting a raise from Mrs. Beattie. I'm going to keep her accounts now. She said she'd pay me another dollar every week."

"She can't pay you what Weston can."

"Please, Papa. I hate Sam Weston. I hate him."

"My boots." He gestured for her to hand him his boots and she did.

He wrenched them on, then walked to the coat tree, put on a blue plaid wool vest she had never seen before, put on his greatcoat, took his stovepipe hat from the hook, and came back. Staring down into the empty bucket of his tall hat, he towered over her. "It's Friday nights at eight o'clock and it'll go on as many Friday nights as Sam wants it to."

"No, Papa."

"Things have to go smooth just now." He brought his gray eyes up to meet hers. "We need the money, Little Plum. You know how I get when it ain't smooth. Billy's been beggin' me for a fight. He disrespects me. You asked me not to whoop him and I'm tryin' hard for you because you're tryin' hard for me. That's our deal. You go along with Weston and your precious twin brother is safe." He put on the stovepipe hat and pulled it snug.

That hat was new, too. What a skunk, she thought, spending Weston's money on himself so hopping fast.

"Even though Billy don't deserve it," he said.

Her stomach twisted. How on earth could he say that? Papa waited a moment, watching her. Finally she lowered her

eyes to the firemen and then in a moment she heard him walk
back to the door.

"It ain't that bad. You and me are goin' ta take care of the
family and we're even goin' ta do better than most. You'll
see." He was silent a moment, then said, "You'll do good with
Mrs. Beattie's accounts. I always said you was smart with
numbers. You can keep working for her. She's a fine woman."

When he had gone, she sat on the sofa a long while
studying her bandbox, looking at the firemen and the brick
house and fingering through the rows of tidy rolled-up ribbon
scraps inside. This was going to be her secret bandbox. Sam
Weston said in his note there'd be more gifts like that gold
dollar. If he gave her any more dollars, she'd keep them in
here and hide it somewhere Papa and no one in the world
could find it. Hers. That money would be her own buried
treasure.

She gazed around the room looking for a safe spot. There.
That place under the floorboard where Papa made the
knocking contraption. She leapt up and shoved aside the
heavy chairs and table and the dusty rug. Pinching her fingers
between the floorboards, she pried up the loose one. Then she
gently set her bandbox down inside the gap and nestled it far
out of sight under the floor. That would do. No one could
see it even if they hauled the board up to fix the knocker. She
retrieved and opened the box again, reached deep into her
dress pocket where she had kept the gold coin all week, then
slipped it between the black and yellow ribbon coils. She
closed the box and kissed the lead fireman.

"You'll get me out just like you got Mrs. Beattie out of
the Crystal Palace. You'll get me out." She kissed him once
more, then tucked the bandbox as far under the floor as she
could reach.

Twenty-Eight

ON FRIDAY, PAPA LEFT CLARA AT SEVEN O'CLOCK at the Seneca Street door to the Spirit Room. He said he'd come back up later when Weston was gone and he'd walk her home, but he wouldn't wait outside the whole while this time. He'd go to Payne's tavern and come back for her.

"I don't want you walking late at night by yourself," he said.

She shuffled up the dim stairs. Before going into the Spirit Room, she stopped and sat on the landing. She could sneak away right now. Papa had gone on. Weston wasn't here yet. If she was fast she could get her dollar out of the bandbox and go. How much was the train to Rochester? She could go to Izzie's. She could just hide somewhere tonight and get an early train. Maybe she could hide right upstairs with Mrs. Beattie. She could make something up about needing to stay there.

She could say everyone was sick at home with Genesee Fever and she had to stay in good health so she could keep making her wages. Mrs. Beattie would believe that, wouldn't she? *Jo-Fire.* Yes, she would. She shot up and thrust the Spirit Room door open.

She gasped. There was the back of Sam Weston. He was looking down into the fire, a hand braced on the mantle. He turned to her, smiling. He was dressed as spiffy as an aristo in a brown-and-gold satin waistcoat with shiny brass buttons. He wore a wide dark brown bow-tie, brown wool trousers, and a clean and ironed white shirt. If his eyes weren't so tired and hollow looking, he would almost be handsome. But he wasn't. Not one smidgen.

"Clara, you look lovely. I took the liberty of starting the fire." He stepped toward her. "You look startled. Here, let me take your cape."

He came to her and, as he reached to untie her bonnet strings, his fingers grazed the underside of her chin. She bit down on the inside of her mouth.

"I'm early because I've been waiting all week for tonight. Every time I had to deal with some fool in my business, I thought about tonight and you, and then simply smiled at the idiot. You are a delightful damsel."

She despised him with every bone in her body, yet when he flattered her like that, she almost felt like she was someone grown, a beautiful lady like Mrs. Beattie.

"Isn't the sofa a fine piece? Do you like it?"

She bit down on the other side of her mouth skin so hard she nearly chewed off a chunk of flesh. Grunting with pain, she drew a hand to her jaw.

"Are you nervous again, like our first night?"

"A little."

"Sit by the fire with me for a while." He drew her by her hand into the room, then took her cape from her and hung it on the coat tree. Then he placed two of the ladder-back chairs by the fire.

A little nervous. That was the understatement of the nineteenth century. Her plan to get her hidden dollar and run was foiled. Now she was stuck. How could Papa do this to her? People didn't always understand him like she did. But now she didn't understand him either. This thing with Sam Weston couldn't possibly be anything right. Did other fathers make their daughters do these things? What would Mamma say? What would Izzie say?

She settled into one of the chairs. She was being punished for not making enough money as a Spiritualist. That's what it was. Papa had relied on her for that. She'd let him down. Now he was punishing her. Plain and simple. That's all the sense she could make of it. If she couldn't be famous like the Spiritualists Cora Hatch or the Fox Sisters or Mrs. Fielding, who traveled around and were in the newspapers, she'd have to do this horrible thing. It was her fault for not being good enough with the hoax trances.

Weston sat next to her and touched her hand. "You'll call me Sam now. I've asked you before and you haven't granted my wish. I insist."

"Sam."

"Yes. That's right." He took off his dark brown bow-tie, folded it neatly, then draped it over the top rung of his chair.

After he told her three or four times how happy he was that she had agreed to be his paramour and how ravishing she looked, he talked for a while about a canal contract that had gone his way. His bid had come in just right and he'd signed the papers that morning. She didn't understand all of it, except that he expected to make a lot of money. All the while he was talking, he kept rubbing his right knee. Eventually she became so annoyed by this, she wanted to pound his hand with a hammer to make him stop.

When he had finished his story about the canal contract, he mentioned how the room seemed warm enough. He got up and drew her by the hand over to the red sofa where he picked up a folded bed linen and offered it to her like a platter. As he leaned toward her, she smelled his over-ripe apple pomade. A swirl of memory rushed through her. That night. The undressing. Him pushing inside her, hurting her. Feeling a little dizzy, she took the folded white linen and plopped down onto the sofa.

"If you would lay this over the sofa, it will keep it clean. It is an exquisite piece and we'll enjoy it more as time goes by, if we keep it clean."

Looking up into his hollow, pale brown eyes, she rose to do as he requested. She had the oddest sensation, as though she was watching herself spread the white linen over the red silk. The shrouded sofa looked far away and ghostly, not bright and elegant.

She sat on the white linen. Kneeling at her feet, Sam unlaced her boots and slipped them off her feet. Then he took off her stockings. After that, he reached around her head searching for hairpins and began to pry them out one by one until her hair fell around her shoulders.

"I'm a fortunate man. I have you as my paramour. I'm going to make a pot of money this month. I don't pray very often, but I'd like to say a nice prayer right now. Would you pray with me, Clara?"

This surprised her. She'd never thought of Sam Weston as a church-going man. She never thought of any of Papa's friends as church-going. But it was something other than undressing so she nodded.

"Come down here on your knees by my side."

She knelt next to him facing the linen covered sofa. She'd never prayed to a sofa before. Of course she knew from Mamma that one could pray anytime, anywhere. It didn't have to be in front of an altar or a crucifix.

He closed his eyes. She closed hers, then felt his arm come around her shoulder.

"Dear Father, You have blessed me this day with Your almighty goodness, and I thank You, dear Lord. This young woman, Clara Benton, brings joyfulness to my life. I thank you, dear Lord, for her exquisiteness."

Then he was silent a moment. His breathing was full and long. Finally she opened her eyes. He was looking at her.

"I don't want to say more than that because He knows I am not in church enough to be deserving of His time, but I had to speak to Him as I am bursting with gratitude." He put his arms around her waist, pressed his body against hers, and kissed her fiercely with thin, dry lips and wiry beard and mustache. He was all teeth and bristle. The apple pomade smell was thick, mixed with a touch of whiskey and soap. She didn't pucker to kiss him in return, but let him squash her mouth down.

When he was done kissing, he settled back on his heels. "We'll have splendid times here on Fridays, Clara. Fridays will inspire me. My heart tells me that. Are you ready?"

No, she wasn't ready. She would never be ready, but she knew that the sooner he got what he wanted from her the sooner she could go home. That's what she wanted—to go home to seven whole days without Sam Weston. On her knees, she inched her way around to present her back and her dress buttons to him. He began his business of undressing her one garment at a time, starting with her indigo dot and white dress. As he had before at the hotel, he seemed to like the black mitts on her hands and the black neckband and left those on.

By the time she was naked, she had fixed her thoughts on the slats of a single ladder-back chair at the séance table. She could hear his voice, but it sounded like he was talking to someone else on the other side of the room. When he guided her up off the floor and laid her down on the sofa, she was ripped away from the distant rungs on her plain sturdy chair. Turning her head sideways, she dug her mind into the folds of white linen draping down against the back of the sofa. He was up above her pushing her legs apart. Then his prick was inside her, pushing, pulling, pushing. It didn't hurt quite as much as the first time. She wished with every part of her flesh that she could make him go completely away. She stared at the folds of white until she knew nothing but the three folds of linen near her face, a wide fold coming down from the left and two smaller folds coming down from the right.

When he was finished, she thought he would quietly leave as he did at the hotel, maybe give her another gold dollar. Shifting onto her side and drawing the lower part of the bed linen up around her, she faced the back of the sofa and her three white linen folds and listened to him putting himself back together. She waited for the sounds of the door, the latch, the hinges, but they didn't come. Instead, there was the sound of the fire iron poking at the coals, then footsteps, then one, two, three, four brisk clunks on the table, then liquid pouring.

"Wrap yourself in that linen and come sit with me."

Hell-fire. She sat up, bringing the sheet up around her shoulders. The fabric felt cool and wet near her hip. In his shirt and trousers now, he was settling himself by the fire with a whiskey. There were two different bottles of liquor out on the table and one empty glass. This wasn't fair one bit. It was over. He should leave. She'd done her duty. Now he should go. Why couldn't he just go?

She dragged herself over to the fire, her tongue running back and forth over the raw sore inside her mouth where she had chewed at herself.

"I put a dollar in the pocket of your cape." He smiled and looked her in the eye. "That's your dollar to do with as you please, not your Papa's."

"Thank you, Sam."

She glanced toward the end of the room where the bandbox was buried under the floor. She'd put it there as soon as she could. Two dollars now.

"I have something you might like." He bounced up from his chair and poured from one of the bottles. "It's Old Peach brandy. It takes a little getting used to, but you'll like it." He brought the glass to her.

She stuck a hand out from under her sheet and accepted it. It looked like whiskey, but it smelled like peach jam. She took a tiny sip. It was sugary like syrup, then it grazed the back of her throat with a gentle burn. It was heavenly. She took a bigger sip. Peaches exploded in her mouth. When she took the third sip, it was smooth all the way down, sweet and delicious. Wrapped in her white linen, she sat and listened to Sam as he told her stories about growing up in Philadelphia and his strict mother. By the second glass of Old Peach brandy, she almost forgot he was there. By the third glass the sore in her mouth, and the sore between her legs, was soothed entirely and Sam Weston was miles and miles away, clear across Seneca Lake.

Suddenly he materialized like a spirit visiting from Summerland. What was he doing? He was gesturing at the table. Then he was speaking loudly, "It's French. French."

She wasn't sure what his blurry looking figure was talking about. The French?

The next thing she knew, Papa was waking her up. She was wrapped like a package in the bed linen on the sofa. Her tongue felt fat and her stomach queasy.

"Get dressed," Papa said.

Then he left her to go and sit by the remnants of the fire. He kept his back to her while she dressed. She could only fasten the two bottom buttons on her dress, but she wasn't going to ask him for help so she put on her black cape and bonnet and went over to him.

"Here." He picked up a small bottle from the table and handed it to her. "Perfume from Sam."

That's what Sam had been saying. French Perfume. She snatched it from him and slid it underneath her cape.

In the cold fog, Papa escorted her home. Unable to walk straight, she didn't feel like herself, thudding and weaving along. Everything looked shadowy and strange in the glimmer of the gas streetlights. Thank goodness Papa was with her.

He led her to her bed in the Blue Room where she crawled, boots and all, in next to Euphora. Room spinning round her, she was just drifting off to sleep when she heard her little sister's voice. "You smell like whiskey."

Twenty-Nine

THE VOICES HAD INTRUDED ON IZZIE'S SLEEP many times during the autumn and now winter had come. Shivering was the worst part of sitting alone in the parlor night after night. Even with a wool blanket around her in her rocking chair, Izzie was cold at three and four in the morning. Sitting up in the light of a burning oil lamp was the only way she could silence the voices. She'd wake to the rattling of voices, heart pounding, slither out of bed, tiptoe downstairs, light her lamp, and after a while, settle down enough to read one of her books or the *Rochester Union and Advertiser* that Mac brought home, or sometimes one of Mac's *Water-Cure Journals*. It wouldn't be long before she'd read every word in print in the house.

The coal fire was set, black chunks piled neatly, but she dared not light it. Not only could they not afford to use the extra coal, but Mac would then certainly surmise she had been awake and downstairs during the night. She didn't want him to discover she was regularly assaulted by voices. She drew her icy hands inside the gray blanket. If only she could talk to someone, to Clara. She was at a boiling point. She'd write to Clara tonight and tell her she'd visit as soon as Mac could spare her help on the Upper Falls Water-Cure. But she had promised this too many times. Mac had always found some urgent deadline he wanted her for—receiving something, meeting someone, writing to someone, rushing to the bank, always, always, urgent and so she had not taken the rail cars down to Geneva.

She walked to the bookshelf where she kept a small stack of writing paper, pen, and pewter inkbottle. She'd tell Clara about the voices, just Clara and no one else.

"What are you doing awake down here at this hour?"

Izzie yelped, spun toward the voice. In the doorway, Mac stood lanky and sleepy in his brown robe.

"You scared me."

"I'm sorry. What is it? Are you restless?" He came to her and stood near.

Her mind raced for a second. She wanted to tell him the truth. Locking her jaw a moment, she waited for the impulse to pass. Clara. She'd tell him about her concerns for Clara again, not the many, many nights of coming down in the dark.

"Yes. I couldn't sleep. I came down to write to Clara."

"But this isn't the first night. You've been gone from bed often."

Even though he hadn't let on, he had indeed missed her in bed. She nodded.

"Are you worried about something?"

Yes, that I am a lunatic like my mother, she wanted to say as she looked away from the warmth of his brown eyes. "I am worried about Clara. You know I promised her I'd return if things were bad with Papa. I made a pact with her, Mac. I shouldn't delay any longer. I should see for myself what is going on. I've let you hold me to the work deadlines too long."

That wasn't a lie. Every night, once she turned off the damn voices and had finished worrying about herself, she'd worry about Clara and Billy and Euphora.

"It's a sense I have. Something is wrong," she said. Reaching up toward his face, she smoothed his bushy eyebrows with a forefinger. They were always messy when he woke. "Go back to bed. I'm going to write Clara and tell her I'm coming to visit."

"When?" He shifted his weight back a little.

"Next week, or the one after, I think."

"But our schedule. I need you here. We must open in three months. We've discussed this over and over. Each day is critical. Each hour is critical."

"I'm tired of hearing that. Two days, Mac. I'll go one day and come back the next. I have to see my sister."

"She hasn't mentioned any more confrontations with Billy in her recent letters. I'm sure Clara would tell you forthrightly if your father was making them miserable."

"He's always made us miserable. I need to know whether he is harming them physically." Her stomach sickened at her words.

Mac's eyes widened. "But she doesn't write that."

"No." Turning toward the shelf, Izzie picked up her writing materials. "I must go, Mac. There's nothing more to say."

"Please, dear. At least finish getting the institute's kitchen ready. The stoves and sinks are to be delivered Wednesday. The pantry supplies must be ordered, the utensils, all of that, and we need the vegetarian recipes collected." He gripped the top of her shoulder. "I can spare you then." She twisted enough to get him to release her. He reached his hand toward her again and stroked her hair.

"How long do you think all that will take?" she said.

"A couple of weeks, no more. Now come back to bed. You're chilled."

The bed would still be warm. He would be warm. She glanced longingly toward the foyer and stairs. But she couldn't. She'd fall asleep in that sweet comfort and then the voices would come mumbling again and hound her.

"I'll write to Clara first, then come up."

"Come now. You can write tomorrow by the fire." He took her arm and tried to nudge her along.

Once again, she twisted free. "No, I want to write now."

His brow furrowed. "Suit yourself, then." He turned his back and, in the dim light, his tall figure disappeared through the parlor door and his footsteps softly thudded away up the stairs.

THE NEXT NIGHT, heart thumping, Izzie bolted up in bed, covered her ears with her hands, and pressed hard. The voices had never sounded this angry before. "Listen now, listen now," a single male voice clearly rose above.

"No. I won't."

Mac stirred. *Damn.* She had wakened him. Slipping from the bed, sweat bursting at her temples, she found her robe where she left it every night on the straight back chair by the door, and descended the stairs. Using her heel to feel the edge of each step, she made he way down the pitch-dark stairwell.

"I won't listen. I won't listen. I won't listen," she whispered on her way down.

In the parlor, she groped for matches next to the oil lamp on the marble tabletop. When the lamplight broke the black, the voices faded, almost whining as they dissipated. She continued her chant. "I won't listen. No voices." In a few moments her heart slowed. She stood alone in the cold parlor, shuddering in the damp of her sweat.

Outside the front windows, the night glowed. She walked to the front door, opened it, and stepped onto the stoop, closing the door behind her to preserve whatever warmth was left inside the house. Illuminated by the light from her parlor windows, snow flurries drifted down. Goose bumps ran up her back into her neck. Across the street, at the Mead's house, something clicked, breaking the snowy silence. Then there were scuffling sounds, a door shutting, and male voices. She could just make out Mr. Mead and a Negro couple emerging onto the street. Mr. Mead handed the man something. They shook hands, then the couple walked west. *Lawk-a-mercy.*

Izzie bundled deeper into her robe. Mead was part of the Underground Railroad after all. Turning to go back inside his house, Mead stopped and appeared to look toward her windows. Although it was hard to know if he could see her on the stoop in the shadow of the door, she waved slightly. Even if he couldn't see her, perhaps he could sense her approval. He didn't respond, but gazed after his charges once more, then disappeared around the side of his house.

Suddenly her own door opened behind her and Mac stood silhouetted in the parlor light.

"What the devil are you doing out here? It is bloody freezing. You're in your night robe, for the love of God." He clutched her arm, dragged her inside, and slammed the door. "What is it?" He snapped his fingers three times in front of her eyes. "Are you awake?"

She slapped his hand away. "Of course I am awake."

"I thought you might be in a state of somnambulism."

The back of Izzie's hands prickled. "Like my mother, you mean."

He was silent a moment. "Perhaps."

She felt her face crumple up as she tried to hold back tears.

"Come, let's light the coals in the parlor."

At her rocker, he picked up the gray blanket, wrapped it around her shoulders, then eased her into the chair. Her weight set the chair rocking. Squatting at the fireplace, Mac struck a match to the kindling under the coals, then bent over and blew on the small flame. Taking the bellows from its hook, he rose and began to pump air at the fire.

"You're down here every night. How long has this been occurring?" He kept his head down and eyes on the flames.

Locking her knees, she stopped her rocker.

"A good while," she said.

"It's not occasional as I thought at first. This is why you are tired all the time now, why you are looking haggard." He puffed with the bellows, sending a spurt of orange up into the coals. "Did you think I wouldn't ever notice?"

"I didn't want to disturb you." The truth was she didn't want this moment to come, didn't want his finding her out, his interrogating her.

He shifted away from the fire and onto a wooden footstool near her. "I may be able to help you. That is, if you tell me what troubles you. In case you hadn't noticed, I am a physician."

His kindness swept into her. She wanted to tell him about the cage she lived in, but if she did, the voices would be reality, her insanity would be truth. She took a long slow breath and let go a sigh. She was tired to death, her mind, heart, body, everything worn down. She didn't want to drudge through another day pretending all was well, another night reading and shivering alone in the cold parlor. Mac fidgeted with the bellows. Izzie began to rock slowly. There was the excuse of worrying about Clara. She could talk to him about that again and it was certainly true. Where did worrying about Clara and worrying about her own lunacy start and end? These twin worries were slowly eating away at her soul like wood being devoured by a swarm of ravenous termites.

"I'm going to sit here," he said. "And wait until you are ready to tell me what troubles you, until tomorrow, or the next day. I want to help you, Isabelle."

The first waft of warmth from the fire reached her face and hands. She rocked faster as she silently rehearsed what to say to him...I've heard one voice one time...I almost thought I may have heard a voice that wasn't real, but it may have been the neighbors...I'm not like Mamma because the voices don't really talk to me. They just mumble on and on. I can shut them up anytime I want...It's just nerves.

She stilled the rocker again. The fire was beginning to comfort her. Stretching a hand toward the back of Mac's head as he sat facing the fire, she ran her fingers lightly down his wavy hair. He was a patient angel waiting for her confidence, offering his help. And he was a physician. He was the one she spoke to about Mamma in the first place. She was being a fool. If there was anyone who could help her it was Mac and here he was at her side asking if he could. He wouldn't put her in an asylum, would he?

The mantle clock chimed five times. Clenching the edge of her blanket tightly, she shoved back and began to rock and to weep quietly.

"Will you promise me something?" she asked.

"Anything."

"You won't stash me away in an asylum?"

His shoulders rose and fell as he sighed, but he still didn't turn to face her. "I promise."

She looked up at the ceiling for a moment. "I hear a crowd of voices every night. They wake me up. I come down here and light the lamp. Then they go. It's the only way I can shut them off." Her voice shook inside her throat as tears streamed down.

"When did it start?"

"September."

"That's months! Why didn't you tell me?"

"I was afraid."

"Of me?"

"Of myself. That I'm insane." Her chest began to heave, her heart flutter.

Mac turned to her, braced his hands on the rocker and brought it to a standstill. His dark eyes were serious and tender.

"You are not insane."

"What am I then? I am. I'm like Mamma. I have to admit it. Some night I'll hear the voices clearly and they'll lead me out into the black night and kill me."

Then she sobbed for what seemed like a long while. Mac stroked her hair until she finally calmed.

"What do they say?"

"Nothing. They aren't clear. It's like Corinthian Hall before a lecture when it's full of excited people. Indistinguishable voices together, high, low. Sometimes angry, but not always."

He took her hand. "Do you believe they are spirits as your mother did?"

"If they were spirits, they wouldn't torture me like this."

"We can rid you of them. The water-cure can do it. I am sure of it."

"I don't see how, Mac. This isn't a pain in my back or a disease of my liver. It's my mind that's gone awry. I'm in terrible danger."

"Even a year ago I would have given you laudanum to calm you and make you sleep, but I've changed my views. I have seen amazing cures, heard about incredible cases that have all been resolved with nothing but pure water."

His grip on her hand tightened.

"It's hard for me to believe that a bath can expunge these voices."

"Harmony. It can bring you harmony. It'll take time, undoubtedly months. I'll get advice from Russell Trall, from the Taylor brothers. I'll write them all."

"But you won't tell them the advice is for me." She wiped the tears from her face with her free hand.

"No. No, of course not. We'll make history. It'll be a groundbreaking cure. I'll take meticulous notes on the methods I use and write up the results for the *Water-Cure Journal*." He was smiling, sparkling, the way he did when he was excited about innovative ideas.

At least she would not be alone anymore whether he succeeded or not. She would not be alone with the voices.

"All right. Let's try," she said.

THE VERY NEXT MORNING AFTER IZZIE HAD CONFESSED to Mac about the voices that had been haunting her, she was with him in the back yard preparing for her first water-cure treatment. Mac held one end of a soaking wet linen sheet twisted like a rope. Izzie held the other. With aching cold hands, she rolled one way, he the opposite. Water streamed down in beads onto the dirt path that led to their kitchen garden, now hard with winter and dusted with snow.

"Don't twist too much. We want it wet, just not dripping wet." Mac pulled back, stretching the sheet tight.

According to Mac, the water-cure regimen would heal her mind. He wanted her to start right away—thirty minutes wrapped in the wet sheet every morning, and again, every evening in addition to a cool plunge bath after each session.

The idea of lying still like a mummy enshrouded in a clammy wet sheet and covered by a couple of wool blankets twice a day would be uncomfortable at the least, and dreadfully time consuming. When would she get all her daily tasks done?

"Are you sure I won't be too chilled?"

"Perhaps a little. We don't want the house to be cold when you do this. When the Upper Falls Water-Cure building is further along, you can take the treatments there, and it will be a lot simpler." Mac smiled at her. "There. That should do it."

They went into the parlor where Mac had spread out the gray blanket from her chair, and another spare one, by the coal fire on the floor. He directed her to fold the wet sheet in half length-wise with him, then they placed it on top of the blankets.

"All right then, take off all your clothing and lie down."

She gestured toward the front windows open to the morning light. "The curtains?"

While he closed the three curtains, she took off her boots and stockings, short dress, trousers, and undergarments and draped them over the back of her rocking chair. There she was, naked in the parlor, first thing in the morning. She felt silly, giggling as she sat on the cold sheet.

"Oh, it's frigid. It's dreadful. I want my nice warm clothes back." She lay down on the wet sheet, her body tensing from head to toe against the chill.

Mac took the near side of the sheet and wrapped it over the top of her, then tucked it under her from ankle to shoulder.

"That's worse. It's freezing."

"Be patient." He crouched over, grabbed the far side of the sheet and drew it back over her, tucking it under her as well.

"I can't move. I feel like a cut of beef in butcher paper."

Laughing, Mac bent over and kissed her lips. "You are my sweet little cut of beef."

She did feel trapped, but somehow it was a delicious, absurd game that meant having Mac home in the morning.

"When you commence your notes for your article about my cure, write down that it is horridly cold at first. Have you ever done this yourself?" Shivers ran along her spine as Mac draped the two blankets around her.

"No, but be patient. It only takes a moment to warm up. Your body's heat will warm the sheet." He retrieved a notebook and pen and ink from his bookshelf, then placed them on the floor and sat on a footstool near her shoulders. "I'll stay here this first time to make sure you are all right."

He took the stopper from the inkbottle, dipped his pen, and opened the book. As he scratched away on the page, he said slowly, "The patient is chilled at first."

She had the urge to smooth out his long and unruly eyebrows, but ensnared in the sheet, her hands were not free to reach for him. He continued to write without speaking. *Lawk-a-mercy*, he was right. The chill was indeed subsiding.

He looked up from his notebook. "Do you think the voices could be spirits, dead people? Isn't that what your mother believed?"

Izzie sighed. "Ever since I can remember, she called the voices she heard spirit voices. Some of them even had names. The colonel. Great Uncle Lyle. There was one she called Sister. When I was a child I believed she could talk to spirits, that she was special. Once in a while someone would call her 'witch'. I didn't like that." Izzie squirmed inside the sheet. "I knocked more than one young boy in the nose over that. I didn't think there was a name for what Mamma could do or who she was. I never heard the word medium or Spiritualist until those Fox sisters came along. Papa would read about the Fox girls in the newspapers and tell us Mamma was like them and maybe one day she'd be famous too."

"Are you comfortable yet?"

"Yes."

Mac looked at the mantle clock and made a note.

"Do you believe your mother was really some kind of medium?"

An itch prickled at the back of her neck. She tucked in her chin trying to scratch it against the wool blanket. "I did back then. But slowly, Mamma changed. She would be present with us in body, but not in mind. The children would play in a mean way sometimes, saying things to her when they were sure she couldn't hear. I would usually stop them. I told them they had to be polite to Mamma all the time, no matter what state she was in. She was our Mamma."

"Warm enough?"

Izzie nodded while Mac scribbled out a note. "But, one day, I had been sitting at the spinning wheel. It was a hot summer evening and Mamma was in her rocker staring at the wall. She and I were the only ones inside. Everyone else was outside trying to stay cool. I was spinning and spinning. It seemed like hours and Mamma simply rocked and stared at the wall the entire time. My foot grew tired on the pedal so I knew it was a long spell to just stare, even for her. She got up and walked to the kitchen worktable without even a smidgen of expression on her face.

"She didn't seem hot either, whereas I was sticky and flushed. She picked up our biggest knife and looked it up and down. I called out to her, but she didn't hear me. She touched the sharp edge of the knife with a finger. That made me nervous so I got up and walked over to her. 'Mamma? Put the knife down,' I told her. She laid her hand out flat on the table in front of her, spread her fingers open, and raised the knife up high like she was about to sling it down and chop hard. Like a meat cleaver. My heart stopped cold just as the knife started to come down. I lunged and grabbed her wrist with both my hands and steered the blade so it wedged into the table. It just missed her hand."

Jaw quivering, Izzie felt a tear roll down her temple. She turned her head toward Mac and the sound of his pen rushing furiously across the page of his notebook. "Mamma blinked at me a few times and said, 'When did you come home? Weren't you at Julianna's?' I was scared. I screamed at her, demanding she tell me what she intended to do with the knife. I plucked it out of the wood. She said, 'I ain't doin' nothing with the knife. I was getting myself a nice cool glass of water. Do you want one too?' That's when I decided she wasn't right in her mind. She wasn't a medium, a witch, a Spiritualist. She was insane."

Mac slapped his notebook closed. "You never told me that story."

"I never told anyone, ever, in my whole life. I was afraid someone might put her in an asylum and take her away from us."

Mac stroked her hair for a few moments, then began to unwrap the top blanket. "You must take the cool bath now."

She wasn't sure at all how any of this was going to rid her of her voices, but she was relieved to take Mac into her confidence. At least now she wasn't alone.

Thirty

THAT FRIDAY NIGHT AFTER WESTON LEFT CLARA at the Spirit Room, she was alone for a while. This was the part of Friday she liked. She liked how long it would be until the next Friday. She liked her gifts from Sam. This time two gold dollars. He'd said, "I didn't have time this week to properly select a gift for you. Here is an extra dollar. This does not mean my affection for you has waned." She liked the sound of the two coins clinking into her palm. On Friday evenings, she never hid her coins away in her bandbox after Weston left because she didn't know when Papa would arrive from his taverns.

A month of Fridays had gone by and Papa had been silent on each walk home. This was the fifth Friday and Clara and Papa were setting off for their boardinghouse in the snow. Clara had been waiting for him to speak to her these past weeks, maybe even ask her forgiveness for making her do the other thing with Sam. Usually they were both a little drunk as they strolled in silence up snow-plowed Seneca Street, and this night was no different. She knew Papa was ashamed of her. Maybe that's why he was stone silent. But, didn't he have to be ashamed of himself, too? No father in the history of the world ever made his daughter do the things he was making her do. Would he ever apologize?

She loved Papa more than anyone in the family loved him. Sometimes she thought she even loved him more than Mamma did, but ever since he hit Billy so hard in the face, and then made her take Sam Weston as her paramour, she felt a hardness toward him growing inside her. It was like a brick wall being raised slowly by a mason, one brick, then another, then another. It wasn't a wall yet, just a couple of rows. But if Papa didn't change things soon, the wall would be finished. She would be finished.

The snow was falling hard, whipping cold and wet into her face and she was looking forward to her warm bed.

"I'm prouder of you than you can know, Little Plum." Papa said softly.

Clara had longed for this moment so badly, she was afraid to speak. They each walked seven more strides in dreadful quiet.

Hands plunged deep in his greatcoat pockets, eyes down, Papa's footsteps crunched along the packed snow. "Some feller is goin' ta be the luckiest man on this whole earth when he marries you. You had beauty all along. Now you know how to run a millinery business and you can sew nice, too. I ain't never goin' to forget this time and how hard you been workin' for the family."

He sounded tender the way he used to, years ago, when he would put Billy on one of his knees and her on the other and bounce them both up and down. He used to call her and Billy his deuces. He'd kiss them both on the head and tuck them into bed with Izzie and little Euphora.

"Papa, I think Mrs. Beattie is suspicious of me and Sam. She was asking me a lot of questions at work this morning about whether I was alone with a man on Friday nights. She said she could hear a voice that wasn't yours and that she couldn't hear any others as she did when we had the spirit circles."

"It's none of her business who she hears in there."

"She says it isn't right for me to be alone with a grown man without your being there."

"I say what's right for my family and my daughter, not some hat-maker."

"Papa, please can we stop Sam coming on Fridays? We can't need the money so terribly much. Maybe I can get an afternoon job somewhere now that I have experience with Mrs. Beattie."

He growled like he had a stomachache, but didn't speak. Then he didn't speak the rest of the way home. That was his answer for her. A stomachache growl. That's all he had. One little bit of admiring, then a growl. That wasn't enough to stop the brick masons.

They turned up the front path to the house. A light was burning in Mrs. Purcell's bedchamber. Once inside, at the top of the stairs with Papa holding the small parlor lamp, Clara looked down the hall. Mrs. Purcell's door was ajar. That was *tarnal* strange. It was near one o'clock in the morning. Then a sliver of Mrs. Purcell in her nightdress, her white hair down and flowing, appeared in the door crack, then she closed it quietly. Had she been waiting for them to come in?

Papa didn't seem to notice or care. Inside the Blue Room, Papa wove his way over to the crate between her bed and Billy's and lit their candle lantern.

"I meant what I said about being proud." Looking right at her, he pushed his spectacles up against the bridge of his nose with his thumb.

"Please, Papa, stop him."

Face hardening, he darted a glance over at Billy in his skinny bed, then looked back at her and whispered. "We need the money. Don't ask again." He turned away from her and went to his bedchamber.

Clara stripped down to her shimmy, blew out the candle, and got into bed. She stared at the long, tall window, faintly aglow from a snowy sky. She wasn't sleepy. The house creaked and crackled. A pile of snow slid off the roof and softly thudded onto the ground outside. A while later, another pile slid down.

As the night wore on and the snow grew deeper, her heart grew sadder and sadder. Then after a long while, as dawn broke and the snow was still falling in the gray outside the window, her heart broke all the way and she began to cry quietly into her pillow. It was the first time ever that Papa had told her he was proud of her, that she was beautiful, that she would be some man's treasure of a wife, and that it didn't fill her up and make her smile inside, and make her want to take his hand and kiss his rough sideburn, make her want to run to a mirror and try to see the pretty girl that he saw. It was the first time she didn't believe him.

In the morning, Clara was awakened when Euphora tore into the Blue Room yelling, "Papa hired a sleigh and horse. We're going for a ride. Get dressed. Wake up."

In cape and bonnet, Euphora stood next to the bed looking down at Clara. Euphora's nose and chin were flushed pink from being out in the cold.

"It's two feet, maybe more. Fresh snow. Papa said everyone was doing so well lately, especially you, Clara, with your spirit circles, that we all had to celebrate. Come on, now, get up." Euphora talked rapid-fire, her arms waving about.

It did sound like a good jingle, but Clara was tired from her night with Sam and the brandy, then not sleeping and unburying such a sad thing deep inside her heart. She sat up and looked at Billy's empty bed.

"What about Billy? Will he go with us?"

"Can't say. He's downstairs. You slept through breakfast, you know. I'll get you some corn muffins and a piece of bacon. You can eat it in the sleigh." She swiveled and sped toward the door. "A winter picnic."

"What time is it? I'm supposed to be at Mrs. Beattie's."

"Oh, no, all the shops are closed because of the snow."

While Clara dressed, she heard a knock at the front door downstairs, then a woman's voice in the foyer, then Mrs. Purcell responding. Clara couldn't make out who it was. When she descended the stairs, ready with all her warmest petticoats under her woolen dress, she saw Mrs. Beattie near the front door. She was wearing a black wool bonnet with red roses and a long red cape, its hem caked with snow. She was always beautiful, but she looked especially radiant with her face all rosy.

"Did you want me to work today?" Clara asked.

"Hello, Clara." She took a handkerchief from her pocket and daubed at her nose. "No, no, dear. I am taking advantage of the snowstorm to visit with Emma. We're going to sit by the fire and not do a thing all morning except gossip and drink tea."

Tarnal strange, thought Clara. The women barely knew each other and certainly weren't friends. Clara couldn't remember Mrs. Beattie ever being at Mrs. Purcell's house since they had lived there and Mrs. Purcell had never said anything about going to Mrs. Beattie's. And the women never asked after one another either.

Mrs. Purcell's gray eyes fluttered as she took Mrs. Beattie's red cape from her and hung it by the door. "Your father and Euphora are outside waiting for you with the sleigh. The mare is that huge dapple, Duchess. You know the one. You've seen her around town."

Clara said farewell to the women, picked up Mamma's old cape, and stepped outside into the cold. Billy was on the front porch, hands tucked under his arms, black visor cap pulled down low over his forehead. Out on the street Papa was holding the dapple's reins and Euphora was standing up in the sleigh. The snow was more than knee deep.

"Clara, the plow and two work horses just went up Main!" Euphora pointed to the south. "Papa says we can follow them up that way past the Hobart Free College."

Clara looked at Billy. "You going?"

"I'm never going anywhere with him ever again."

"Come on, Bill. You can sit with me in the back."

His jaw was set hard. "No. Don't ask me. I'm never going anywhere with him again. No matter what."

His face was closed up tight like storm shutters. It would be useless to try and convince him. Whenever he closed off to Papa like this, she had always wanted to shake him out of it, get him to see Papa didn't mean what he said, get him to believe Papa couldn't help himself. But now it was different. She didn't want to change Billy's mind. She was like her twin now. She had her own storm shutters.

"I understand."

"He's up to somethin'. He doesn't go out and get a horse and sleigh for nothing."

She gazed across the perfect white blanket of snow, broken only by the furrowed path from the street to the front steps. Papa was chatting at the mare and fussing with the harness.

"You're probably right."

On the sleigh ride, Clara was cold and crabby, although it was a glorious ride for Euphora who sat in between her and

Papa up on the driver's seat. Euphora beamed like the sun, her buckteeth chattering, her laughter bursting out at her own jokes. She made up stories about the horse, about their journey. She announced they were going twenty miles to see an old Seneca Indian Chief. Papa played along, adding that the blizzard was still ongoing and they had to carry on even though they couldn't see through the blinding white, but they told the dapple mare what they needed to do and she'd get them through to the Indian village.

The more Papa and Euphora laughed, the more Clara slumped down on the seat. After a while, the wind gnawed at her so badly that she couldn't stop shivering. Finally she insisted Papa stop the sleigh and she crawled into the back and huddled down low underneath the bluster. She wanted nothing but the end of the sleigh ride to come, to get home and sit by a fire.

LATER THAT AFTERNOON, Clara napped and dreamt in Mamma's rocker by the fire in the Blue Room. Papa called to her and woke her. She was still crabby and longed to stay asleep, but she rose anyway and staggered into his bedchamber. Standing at his chest of drawers in greatcoat and wool hat, he picked up a few papers, a money clip full with bank notes, and a small pocketknife and stuffed them into his various pockets.

She plopped down in his Windsor chair by the rear window while he poured himself a whiskey and swigged it down. It was getting dark out.

"That ride was dandy." He took out his watch from his waistcoat and checked the time. "Got somethin' new for us."

Billy'd been right as rain. Papa was about to lay out whatever the sleigh ride was for. He paced over to his washstand, then studying himself in the small round mirror perched on the shelf above the basin, he picked up his comb and ran it through his hair, then his sideburns and beard. When he was satisfied, he tapped the comb on the washstand three times, then came and stood near her.

"There's a man name of Reilly. John Reilly. You know him? Came to a spirit circle long while back."

Clara pictured him, long brown hair over the back of his collar, bald at the top of his head, a hefty paunch. She nodded. Papa went and poured himself another whiskey and brought it to the bed where he sat and faced her.

"He's got that Implement Factory on Lewis Street. A real business man." He swigged from his glass. "I met him over at Minnie's the other night, you know, the place where you met Sam that time? We got to talkin'."

"What were you doing there?"

"Awh, just playin' cards downstairs with some fellas and Reilly was there and he was sayin' that young women were what pleased him most and that Minnie wasn't young and her two other gals weren't young and sometimes he had to go all the way up to Rochester to find a young enough gal for his tastes." Watching her closely, he took another swig of whiskey, then perched the glass on his knee.

Hell-fire. He was going to set her up with bald Reilly who liked young women. Trembling, she leapt from the chair and flew at him. She was about to strangle him, but instead she snatched his whiskey glass and threw it hard across the room. It shattered against the door and fell into a mess of shards on the floor.

"No, Papa. No more!"

He shot up, grabbed her wrist. "Sit down and calm down." He forced her back down into the chair. "I was hopin' you'd hear me out. You can have more money from this one."

Her skin burned under his grip. "I don't want that money, Papa. You can't make me take that money. I don't know him." She wrenched her arm from him, then started for the Blue Room.

He caught her by the arm and yanked her back. "Stay put." He plunged her down into the chair again.

Her head whacked hard against the wood and smarted. His gray eyes were bulging just the way they did with Billy. She didn't move.

He was breathing hard, giving her the evil eye, but then his eyes softened. "Please, Little Plum, don't make me behave like this with you. I ain't never been mean with you." He squatted in front of her and put his hands on the chair arms, making a kind of gate around her. "This will be easier than cherry pie. You can have half of whatever we charge Reilly. Think of it. I bet we'll get five dollars from him every time."

Tears swelled in her eyes, then flooded down her face. *Every time. Every time.* Papa hated her. He actually hated her. She wasn't good enough for him to love, only good enough to make filthy money off of.

"Sam Weston is one thing, Papa. I abhor him, but he admires me. Why do you want me to go with a man we don't even know?"

"There, there, Little Plum. It ain't so bad as that." He took a handkerchief from his waistcoat and offered it to her.

"Why do you hate me, Papa? Am I so awful?"

A sharp knock rapped at the hallway door. "Is everything all right in there?" It was Mrs. Purcell, her voice high and shaky.

Papa bounded for the door. Opening it just a peep, he lodged himself so she couldn't see in.

"I apologize for the ruckus, Emma. I had an accident and me and Clara're cleanin' it up."

"Clara, are you all right?" Mrs. Purcell asked.

Papa glared at Clara across the room.

"Yes, ma'am."

Papa nodded at Mrs. Purcell, then closed the door before she could get in another word. "She's too much of a busy body for us," he said as he headed across the room to her. "We're goin' to move out of here in a few months. I've got great plans for us, Little Plum." He patted the top of her head. She felt the urge to bite his hand like a mean old dog would, but stopped herself.

"We'll talk more about Reilly tomorrow. But you'll see. It'll be the easiest money we ever made, much easier than Sam. Go on now and tell your little sister everything is all right. You know how nervous she gets when I get loud. She's probably in there quiverin'. Now, tomorrow, I'm takin' you to the dress shop." He took a new pair of black leather gloves out of his coat pockets and put one on. "We're gettin' you a true lady's dress and one of them hoop things you been wantin'. Shoes too. Here." He pulled on the other glove, collected the hand towel from his washstand and brought it to her. "Finish wipin' your face and go tell Euphora nothin's wrong."

While she dried her tears away, he rambled on about how everything would be all right and he'd take care of things and they'd have more money and they could move out of Mrs. Purcell's. When she was finished with the towel, she flung it down at the floor, rose, and left without looking at him.

THE NEXT FEW DAYS, Papa hammered and hammered on about John Reilly. He told her the same things over and over just the way he did before she started with Sam. First, if she wouldn't go along with him, he might hurt Billy. Second, if she couldn't help the family with their needs, he'd have to leave them all and go looking for gold at Pike's Peak in Colorado, and third, she was his only hope, his pride and joy. After three days of it, Clara was worn down and agreed to meet John Reilly at the Spirit Room. She couldn't think of any other way to appease Papa.

The moment she gave in, Papa got her the new green taffeta dress he had promised, a whalebone hoop, new shiny boots with buttons, and some face paint. Mrs. Purcell didn't have a big mirror anywhere in the house for her to see herself. "They're just tools of vanity," she had told Clara. Vanity or not, she longed to see herself, so before she was to meet with Reilly, she decided she'd go into Mrs. Beattie's shop and see herself in the milliner's full-length mirror.

Just as she was rubbing a tiny bit of red paint onto her lips and getting ready to leave, Billy came into the Blue Room covered with grime from working at Maxwell's.

"What did you have to do to get that dress?" he asked.

Clara stiffened. In her hand mirror, she saw herself blush. Did he know something?

"Papa's doing well on one of his ventures. That's all."

"That can't be all. If he's doing so good, why isn't he giving things to me and Euphora? I need boots." He raised his foot backward as though he was about to get shod. There was a hole the size of a silver dollar on one of the soles. "I found a piece of Indian rubber at Maxwell's. They let me have it so I stuck it in here." He stomped his boot down. "Why is he always giving you new fancy things?"

"I don't know. Maybe he is trying to find me a good husband. Did you ever think of that?" She hated lying to Billy. It made her sick. Everything she said all day long was a lie and every lie made her feel split in two like a log under the whack of an axe. There was one real Clara inside who knew what the truth was, and another Clara—the liar, the one everyone else knew.

He squinted at her. "He's got you up to something, or he's about to, and it ain't just a husband. You can get that on your own. Watch out for him, Clara."

"I will."

Bending over the washbasin, sandy hair flopping down, Billy splashed his face with the murky water. Would there ever come a day again when she wasn't lying? She offered him a towel. Only if she got away from Papa. Only then could she stop the lying.

Papa appeared in the door of the Blue Room. "You look just like your grandmother, Elsie, a real beauty. You ready?"

"Watch out, Clara," Billy said.

Papa gave him a nasty look, so Clara led Papa out of the house quickly. It was a raw, gloomy afternoon. Papa was babbling about the house they were going to get when they moved out of Mrs. Purcell's, but she wasn't paying much attention to him.

Since it was the first time with Reilly, Papa promised to wait outside the Spirit Room. If anything went wrong, she was to call out fast and loud. Papa'd be right there in the stairwell, down at the street door, close enough to hear her, but far enough away for her and Reilly to have privacy. When she asked him what could go more wrong than what he was already making her do, he said, "Men're unpredictable sometimes. It's their nature. I've heard stories. That's all. I'm gonna be right nearby if you need me." She bit down on the inside of her mouth until it hurt. When she pressed him about what unpredictable things he'd heard, he just said, "Never mind."

She tore at a fingernail. Reilly better not be one of the unpredictable ones, she thought.

Papa waited in the street while she dashed into Mrs. Beattie's to look in the full-length mirror. Mrs. Beattie was busy flattering a fat woman who was trying on a purple velvet bonnet. Clara swept by the two women on her way to the mirror. It took her a few seconds to recognize herself. It was like the feeling she got when they first arrived in Geneva and she'd wake up in the new bed and wonder if they were in their shack in Homer or in a barn loft on the road to New York State, or in a dream. She blinked and stared. What she saw was a young grown up lady with sad brown eyes. She blinked three more times, and then Mrs. Beattie appeared behind her looking over her shoulder.

"You look ten years older. What is the occasion?" Sounding almost miffed, Mrs. Beattie was frowning, not smiling at the lovely dress as Clara had expected.

"A special séance. Papa wants me fancy. The seekers are stiff in their heels, Papa says."

"Mrs. Beattie, what about this lovely thing?" The fat woman held up one of Mrs. Beattie's most elaborate bonnets, the cherry velvet with black lace and garland of flame-colored flowers.

"I'll see you in the morning," Mrs. Beattie said to Clara, then sped toward the customer.

Papa poked his head in the shop door. "Come now. You can't be late."

Clara went up to the Spirit Room to wait for John Reilly. At precisely three-thirty, she heard a man's voice on the landing outside with Papa, then John Reilly came in alone and greeted her with only a nod. Without hesitating, he took off his coat and hat and hung them near the door. He was more or less how she remembered him, his brown hair long and thin over the back of his collar, a shiny bald spot on top of his head, his face ruddy. He was rounder in the gut than she had recalled, though. Maybe he had added to that recently. He looked a bit like Benjamin Franklin, she thought.

"I like every bit of clothing off a girl. You women wear too many things on your person." Reilly plucked his watch from his waistcoat, wound it, then settled on the red sofa. "It uses up precious time, putting all that on and taking it all off."

"Even the lace mitts?"

"Why would I want those? I don't like the feel of those. They scratch me."

Chewing at the inside of her mouth until she felt a loose piece of skin between her teeth, Clara kept silent as she climbed out of the new green taffeta dress, hung it over a chair at the table, unhooked her hoop, then lifted it over her head and set it over near Papa's secret bell ringer. Then she came back to the table and took off her shimmy, leaving her torso bare. He watched her every move, not saying anything and not showing anything on his face, either.

The room was warm enough. Papa had come down earlier and started the fire. He'd also brought in a washstand and put it near the back wall. Sam Weston's whiskey and Old Peach brandy bottles and glasses were on the shelf back there too.

She wouldn't mind one of those brandies right now. She was slightly nauseous and felt tiny as a beetle. "Do you want a drink of whiskey or brandy?"

"No, I don't take liquor. It fogs the mind. I want to know where I am and what I am doing in every moment."

She glanced longingly at the bottles thinking she could take a drink on her own, but decided Reilly would not approve so she continued undressing. When she had finished taking off her pantalettes, stockings, boots, mitts, and neckband, she stood naked and shivering by the séance table. She perched a hand lightly on one of the chairs to brace herself.

"There. You see what I mean?" Smirking, he pointed at the garb draped over every chair around the table and the whalebone hoop sitting at the side of the room. "Look at all of it. It looks like a darned dress shop." Belly laughing as he came to her, he pulled out the chair draped with her pantalettes and plopped down, legs spread wide.

"Here. Come sit on my lap."

She sidled onto one of his large thighs. Sliding an arm around her waist, he drew her against him. He didn't smell like much of anything, except a little sweat and cigar breath.

"Your father has a unique arrangement with you here. I went to a brothel in New York City once that was run by a husband and wife. Their two lovely daughters, Dinah and Alice, worked for them. That man was the only father I'd ever seen with daughters serving him like you do yours."

Brothel. The word exploded in her head. Is that what her Spirit Room was? That? That word? That kind of place? She jumped off his lap. It was. Of course it was. Before it had been a private place where Sam Weston was her paramour. Now, with Reilly, it was a brothel. She was Dinah or Alice. A whore.

"Are you feeling all right? You're perspiring and shaking. Are you ill?"

"I...I'm going to be sick." She rushed to the new washstand and vomited into the basin. Trembling and hot and cold, she stood over the bowl for a long while.

Finally, she felt something come over her back and shoulders. It was Reilly's coat.

"Come and sit on the sofa. Is it the nerves or are you with fever?" He put his wide, rough palm over her forehead as he walked her to the red sofa. "You seem cool enough."

"It's nerves, sir."

After letting her rest a while curled up in his coat on the sofa, he came over to her and touched her forehead again. "No fever. Don't fret, Miss Clara. I'm a gentleman, you know." He ran a finger over her lips. "Are you ready then? You look delicious."

Ready to die, she thought. Ready to drown in the lake like Mamma. But she sat up slowly and keeping her eyes down, nodded. He took his coat from her and hung it up again. Then he took off his suspenders and trousers and dropped them on the floor, then his collar and tie, shirt, long johns. He was fully naked, his chest hairy with black curls, his prick already hard.

He picked up his heap of clothing, dumped it on the séance table, then came back to the sofa. "Lie back."

When he lay down on top of her, she could barely breathe.

"Wait," she said.

"For what?"

"The bed linen. I have to take care the sofa isn't ruined."

Laughing, he pushed himself off her and stood. "Be quick."

She retrieved the bed linen from the cupboard underneath the whiskey and arranged it over the sofa. She glanced across the room at the mantel clock as she lay down. Three forty-three. As soon as he lowered his full weight onto her again, her lungs flattened into the sofa. She coughed for air. Then, he kissed her lips and forced his tongue inside her mouth. After that, he spit on his fingers three or four times, wiped the saliva on the tip of his prick, then with his hand, guided it inside her. She felt the first heavy thrust of him. He was an absolute tree trunk. As fast as she could, she flew away from herself and everything he was doing to her.

She imagined herself floating in the air, hovering around the room like an angel, drifting over to the window and watching the afternoon activities out on snow-covered Seneca Street. Men, women, children, dressed in scarves and hats, carrying packages, going in and out of the bakery, the bank, Mrs. Beattie's downstairs. She knew some of them and waved. She flew down to the street and joined some children throwing snowballs.

When Reilly was done, and had got up and was getting dressed, she drifted back down to herself. Then she sat up, wrapped herself in the sheet, which was wet where it had been underneath them, and watched him finish dressing. The fireplace mantel said three fifty-two. Nine minutes. That's all it was.

It was much faster than with Sam Weston, who always rambled incessantly about her beauty and repeated her name until she was sure she never wanted to hear it again. But Reilly had taken off his clothes, got into her, pushed and pumped, and was fully dressed before she had just begun to settle into her other world. Grateful for the tricks she had learned during her times with Weston, she had scarcely been aware of him after the first moment. Next time, if there was going to be a next time, she would leave herself even sooner.

"You should have a mirror in here so a man can make sure he is put together properly before going outside again. I have to go back to my office."

"I'll tell Papa." She took a deep breath. "Mr. Reilly, will you come here again? I mean, for this, for me?" Say no, please say no, she thought.

"Maybe tomorrow?"

She began to perspire and felt she might vomit again. Two men would be coming to her now. Two. Her heart sank slowly like a ship sliding below the water line for the last time. Papa had made her into a whore. If Reilly would just go away forever, if she could be unappealing to him somehow, then she would be Sam's paramour, but not a whore. Perhaps demanding money would discourage Reilly. Papa couldn't persist if Reilly wouldn't pay. Wrapped in the sheet, she stood and walked to him, faced him squarely as he was fussing with his bow-tie. She looked down at her naked feet.

"I have my own rules."

"What do you mean? You're just a young thing. You can't have any rules. Your father makes the rules."

"No, I have my own rules." She held her breath, then tried to stand straight, tried to get that look into her eyes like Izzie had when she argued with Papa. It was especially important not to blink. No blinking whatsoever. Lifting her gaze, she concentrated on his green-gray eyes.

Reilly chuckled as he finished with his tie and put his hands on his hips.

"Well, then, what are your rules, young miss?"

The room suddenly lost its air. Sweat trickled from her armpits and ran down her sides.

"You pay my father, but you pay me something else too, separately, privately."

His bright eyes darkened. Then he sauntered over to a ladder-back chair at the table, sat, and grunted as he struggled to pull a boot on. When he had both boots on, he smirked at her.

"You think you're worth more than the five dollars I already gave him? That's a dear price as it is, even if you are a stunner. I can go down to Minnie's whenever I want for less than five dollars, and besides that, you were rather lifeless in the act."

She swallowed, holding her eyes wide open and steady. She wasn't worth anything really, certainly not five dollars, certainly not more. He saw that. He stared back at her. But it might work. She might get rid of him.

"Yes, sir, I need five dollars for Papa and two dollars for myself, and the two dollars are a secret just between us. Papa can't know." Remembering Papa at the bottom of the stairwell, she kept her voice low.

Reilly clomped over to the door, snatched his coat from its hook and put it on. "You're not shy and nervous after all, are you? And why wouldn't I just tell your father about this sweet little arrangement, then?"

"Because I'll tell your wife that you came to me to speak to the spirits but that you forced yourself on me." Still willing herself not to blink, she tightened her leg muscles to hold herself fixed. "I'll say that you raped me."

Crossing his arms, then cradling his chin with a hand, he laughed harder still.

"And why should she believe a young whore like yourself?"

The room began to spin. She tasted the vomit at the back of her throat.

"Why shouldn't she?"

He watched her a moment and finally stopped his sniggering. "Ah, you're a dangerous one. Something tells me I should stay on the other side of the ocean from you." He rested his hand on the doorknob but didn't turn it. "If I come back, I'll honor your rules, but that's if I come back. I'm not saying I will."

He opened the door and was gone. She ran to the window, threw back the curtains, and waited to see him leave the building, but he didn't come out to the street right away. He was probably talking to Papa downstairs at the door. What if he told Papa about the deal she asked for? What would Papa do to her? Her stomach twisted up in a knot.

Finally, the door slammed shut downstairs and Reilly emerged onto the sidewalk. He took out his pocket watch, read it, then looked up toward her window. He tipped his hat to her in the dusky light, then headed down the snowy walk toward the lake. He would be back. He called her a stunner. He would be back. Mamma had always told her that her looks were a gift, a ticket to a better life. But they weren't. They were a curse—a horrible curse.

Two girls, probably just a year or two younger than she was, came out of the bakery across the street. While they stood in the doorway, one of them raised a small bundle and lifted back the wrapping. They tipped their noses toward whatever it was, smiled at each other, then closed the bundle back up. Suddenly, tears began to flood down Clara's face. Her chin quivered out of control.

"Papa, why are you doing this to me?"

As the two girls from the bakery climbed toward Main Street and disappeared, she cried and longed for Izzie to appear beside her, stroke her hair, and tell her everything would be all right. But instead Reilly's voice was inside her echoing the word "whore" over and over again.

She heard a knock and then Papa ask through the door if she was ready to walk home.

"I'm not ready. I'll go by myself."

"You all right?"

"I'll go by myself in a while!"

She heard nothing for a moment, then his footsteps clomp down the stairs and the door to the street creak open, then clunk shut.

Thirty-One

CLARA FELT SOMETHING JIGGLING HER SHOULDER.
"Wake up. Wake up."
"Billy?" Clara rose up on her elbow. It was pitch-dark. "What is it?"

"Meet me downstairs in the parlor. Euphora, too."

His footsteps padded softly across the room, then down the stairway. Clara rustled Euphora and told her they had to meet Billy in the parlor. They threw on their shawls and tiptoed downstairs toward the lamplight.

In the middle of the parlor, Billy stood dressed in his jacket and wool cap, his right arm in a sling, his neck swollen red on one side. A bulging full burlap sack lay at his feet. Clara's knees weakened.

"What happened?" Euphora asked.

"Shhh. Don't wake Papa. I'm leaving. Come here." His gate was gimpy and stiff as he led them to the window seat. Holding his neck and shoulders rigid, he sat down awkwardly.

"I only have a minute," he said.

Trembling, Clara sat next to Euphora who was already at Billy's side. "Papa promised me he wouldn't hurt you," Clara said.

"He was crazy drunk last night. He found me and some boys out raising Cain behind the Veazie House. We were trying to get some young gents to bring us out some beer when Papa stumbled out of nowhere and saw what we were up to. He went wild as a crazy cougar. He shoved me so hard it was like I was shot out of a sling. My neck landed on the rim of a barrel." He lifted his good arm and cupped a hand under his ear. "I thought for sure he was gonna kill me. I ran all the way to Mr. Maxwell's house up at the Nursery and he took me to a doctor."

Whimpering, Euphora took hold of his good arm. "You can't leave us, Billy. Where will you go?"

"Far away."

"Kansas, with the Free Staters?" Tears rolled off Euphora's quaking chin.

"Nah. Not since John Brown got hanged. California. That's as far as I can get from Papa." He reached under his jacket and into his waistcoat pocket. "Here, Clara." Taking her clenched hand, he curled back her shaking fingers, stuck a gold half eagle into her palm, then closed her fingers back over it. "Five dollars for you and Euphora. You save this and use it to take the rail cars to Rochester to Izzie if you need it. Never spend it. Only if you have to get away from him. That's all I can do. I can't take you with me. I want to be halfway to Buffalo by the time he wakes up."

The house creaked. Blinking rapidly, Billy glanced toward the stairs.

"It's all right, just the cold," Clara said.

"Can't you stay in Geneva, but live at someone else's boardinghouse?" Euphora tugged at Billy's jacket sleeve. He winced. He was injured all over, Clara thought.

"Can't, Euphora. He'd come and get me if he knew where I was."

"Do you still have the hole in your boot?" Clara pointed toward his right shoe. He gave a slight nod followed by a squinty look. Clara handed him back the coin. "You need boots. I have some money saved Papa doesn't know about. You can't go to California in the middle of winter with holes in your boots."

Brown eyes looking weary and scared, he took the gold piece back and tucked it into his waistcoat. "Thanks, Clara." His scared look horse-kicked Clara right in the gut.

He stood up. "I have to go now."

Clara looked over how he was dressed. Underneath his short jacket, it appeared he had on every piece of clothing he owned, two shirts, two pairs of trousers, his cotton summer waistcoat and his wool waistcoat over that and old, fraying gloves with no fingers.

"Those knitted wool gloves won't protect you from the freezing weather. Wait here a minute," Clara said.

"No. I have to go. It's getting light."

"Wait."

Clara tiptoed into the foyer. Papa's greatcoat wasn't on the rack. It was probably with him in his bedchamber since he had come in so drunk. She whispered for Billy and Euphora to wait again and then climbed the stairs as quietly as she could to Papa's door. Billy called her name in a loud whisper to get her back, but she ignored him. Grasping Papa's doorknob, she turned it as carefully as she could. The click was gentle, what she had hoped for. When she entered the room, she stood still a moment, while her eyes adapted to the dark, and listened for his sleep. His snoring was loud and the smell of whiskey thick, even with his window open.

He wouldn't wake up with that much whiskey in him, not until noon. Sometimes his coat was on a hook by the door. Sometimes, on a bad night, it was in a heap on the floor with his other clothing, but it wasn't in either place. It was one of those nights when he passed out with everything on him.

Imagining noisy pebbles beneath her feet, she took each step as slowly and tenderly as if she were a huntress wolf about to pounce. When she stood by Papa at the bed, she studied the muddle of his coat and looked for the bulge of a pocket where his new leather gloves might be. It was on the other side of him. She crept around the foot of the bed, gently slid her fingers into the tip of the coat pocket and began to inch the gloves out. It was the least Papa could do for his only son—give him a pair of dang gloves to travel with. Papa snorted. She jerked her hand back, leaving the gloves half out. She waited. After a short moment, his whiskey-soaked snoring resumed. She snatched the gloves, darted for the door, then slowed down again as she settled the latch back into place. He was still snoring evenly.

When she got downstairs, the front door was open a crack. Billy and Euphora were waiting on the front porch and Euphora was crying into Billy's shoulder. When Clara handed Billy the gloves, her eyes welled up. Her heart had that same ripping sensation she'd felt when Mamma died and again when Izzie left for Rochester.

Billy sneered at the gloves. Clara thought he was going to refuse them, but then he chuckled and stuffed them into his jacket pocket. "I'm going to the depot for the early train. The tracks should be clear. It hasn't snowed for a few days." He looked out at the street, disentangled himself from Euphora, and carefully slung his sack over his shoulder. His eyes pinched and he grunted a little as the sack landed against his back.

"Billy, don't leave right now," Clara said. "Stay a few weeks and let Mrs. Purcell heal you. Then go when you are stronger."

He looked her straight and deep in the eye. "I have to go now, Clara. You know I do."

She bit the inside of her mouth and glanced across the old crusty snow, away from him. She knew he was right.

In silence, the three of them looked out at the lavender sky for a moment. The soles of Clara's bare feet stung with cold.

"Will you write us?" Clara wrapped her shawl tight around herself.

"Not until I'm far away." He turned his shoulder toward her. "Here. Reach in my pocket." She stuck her hand in and found his red bandana. "That's yours to remember me, that day by the brook when we talked."

As she clutched the small piece of him, her tears began to flow. He kissed Euphora's forehead, then hers, then stepped mindfully down the icy stairs and along the front path. Embracing Euphora, Clara found her little sister trembling. When Billy reached the street, he waved. There wasn't enough light to see his face from that distance, but Clara knew he wasn't smiling. She and Euphora waved back, then held onto each other and watched him until he was out of sight.

"Let's make a fire." Feet still stinging, Clara led Euphora inside.

She settled her weeping sister into Mrs. Purcell's wing back chair by the fireplace in the parlor and wound a small lap blanket around her feet. Then Clara piled up the thin slivers of wood, the ones Billy had kept neatly in the brass bucket by the fireplace under the coals. She struck a match and held it to the smallest kindling until it lit. Exhausted,

Clara lay on her side on the rug by the fire. She thought about what Billy had said, that he had to get far enough away from Papa that Papa couldn't find him, that he didn't even want to write until he was so far away that Papa wouldn't come after him. He was right. And she realized then that it was true for her, too, if she had to run away. Running to Izzie wasn't good enough, wasn't far enough. If you were going to run from Papa, you had better go where he couldn't find you and drag you back.

"Will he ever come back?" Still weeping, Euphora was slumped in the chair.

"No. He'll never come back. Someday when we're older, we'll see him again, though."

She sat up, took off her shawl and wrapped it around her chilled feet. When her time came, she wouldn't go to Izzie because Papa would just hop a train or canal boat and yank her right back the same day. If she were going to run like Billy, she'd have to hide like a slave on the Underground Railroad.

About an hour later, when Mrs. Purcell came downstairs, Clara and Euphora, still in their chemises, were huddled side by side in front of the fire.

Clara looked up at Mrs. Purcell. "Billy's run off. He's gone."

Mrs. Purcell's lip curled up in a snarl. "You don't think he'll come back after a while?"

She and Euphora shook their heads.

Mrs. Purcell stood motionless in her brown-and-black plaid checker dress a moment, then went and slumped down into her wing back chair. Then they all three fell numb and quiet for a while.

"I should have done more." Mrs. Purcell looked back and forth from the fire to the daguerreotype of her husband

Richard on the side table, and kept repeating herself. "I should have done more. I should have done more."

"You can't stop anything Papa does," Clara said.

Mrs. Purcell rose up. "My Richard always said 'better late than never'. You girls must remember that. Better late than never." She turned and, walking toward the kitchen, she had an air about her like she was leading a troop of soldiers.

AFTER CLARA AND EUPHORA GOT DRESSED, and Mary and Jane Carter came down to breakfast, Clara told the old sisters about Billy. As she spoke, even adding the part about getting the gloves off of Papa while he slept, Clara noticed a lot of glances passing between Mrs. Purcell and the Carter sisters, as if they knew it was going to happen all along.

Over their breakfast of eggs and grits, they all discussed whether there was any way to get Billy to come back, but finally Mrs. Purcell said it might be for the best and the Carters both nodded. Without Billy, the dining table would be like this from now on, thought Clara, just her and Euphora and the three silver-haired ladies. Papa wasn't going to ever stay in for a meal again with these three old women evil-eyeing him. Clara sighed. That was all right. Maybe Papa would disappear for good, go searching for Billy and never come back. Or maybe Papa'd run away on his own. He had before. Then she'd be free to work for Mrs. Beattie and get another job as well, and Euphora could keep working for Mrs. Purcell and they'd stay there with the ladies.

It wouldn't be that way, though. Papa was hell-bent on moving them out of Mrs. Purcell's. He'd been talking about the little cabin up the canal a ways. That's what he was set on all right, taking her and Euphora away from the old ladies.

She reached into her dress pocket for Billy's red bandana and laid it out on his empty chair next to her. She spread it out, smoothing over the wrinkles.

"I think it would be best if we were all together when we tell your father that Billy is gone. He'll be agitated." Mrs. Purcell looked at Clara, then Euphora.

The Carter sisters bobbed in agreement. "We'll stay in until he rises. Emma, you should tell him. He gets so riled when things go wrong," Mary Carter said.

Mrs. Purcell wiped her mouth with her napkin, then set both hands firmly on the table. "Yes, I'll tell him. You young girls don't have to do that."

CLARA DIDN'T WANT TO LEAVE EUPHORA that morning to go to work at Mrs. Beattie's, but Mrs. Purcell told her she would take care of Papa if he woke up before supper. The morning at the milliner's crept slower than a heavy wagon going up a steep hill. While she took inventory of fabrics for Mrs. Beattie, Clara thought frightful things. Maybe Papa would run after Billy but take Euphora with him and then she'd never see any of them again. Maybe Papa would wallop Euphora with a pot when he heard the news or maybe he'd belt Mrs. Purcell on the chin. The noon bell up at the Presbyterian Church finally rang. Clara ran the whole way home.

As she entered the front door, she smelled onions and butter cooking, then sprinted to the kitchen. Euphora and Mrs. Purcell had three bowls set out on the worktable and were standing by the iron kettle.

"Is there coffee?"

Clara jumped. Papa was right behind her. Hair tousled, shirt and trousers rumpled, he shuffled over to the coffee pot sitting by the sink.

"It's cold by now. We can make more." Euphora flashed a scared, big blue-eyed look at Mrs. Purcell.

Papa shuffled to the cupboard, took a cup and poured himself some cold coffee. As he swigged it, he turned his back to everyone, and gazed out at the back garden. Then he started for the dining room door. When he passed Clara, with his red shot eyes and whiskey-stinking skin, she held her breath.

Suddenly Mrs. Purcell blurted out, "Billy's run away. He left this morning."

Papa stopped but didn't turn around. "When did he go?"

"Early," Mrs. Purcell said.

He took a slow sip of coffee, then looked up at the ceiling. That was *tarnal* strange. Why wasn't he throwing the cup across the room? Why wasn't he yelling? Clara felt a prickle at the back of her neck.

He took a second sip of coffee, then crooked himself around and looked straight at Clara. "He's got to get back here. He's got to help the family. He can't go runnin' off. Where'd he go?"

"How am I supposed to know?" Clara's throat tightened around her words.

Blinking and squinting, Papa looked up at the ceiling again. The Carter sisters, who must have heard the hubbub, appeared in the kitchen doorway. Everyone had their eyes on Papa waiting for him to explode. The longer it was that he didn't explode, the more petrified Clara was. Mrs. Purcell had an arm around Euphora a good distance away, but Clara was right there near him.

He stepped close to her. "Because he tells you things. Did he go to your sister's?"

"No, he said he was going to Kansas Territory, to find John Brown's men, like he always said." Clara felt Euphora staring at her.

"John Brown's executed."

"Billy said his men were still fighting for freedom. He said he was going to fight with them."

"You wouldn't lie to me about that would you? Because I can take a train right up to Isabelle in Rochester and haul him home by the collar."

"Kansas."

"Kansas," Euphora repeated.

He glanced around at everyone. "What're you all looking at? Damned females."

Striding to the back door, coffee cup in hand, he thrust the door open and staggered outside onto the crusted snow. Clara closed the door and they all scuttled to the window to watch him. In the middle of the frozen garden, he swiveled around every which way, maybe trying to decide where to go, but then he stayed put, his shoulders hunching over. His cup dropped from his hands, spilling coffee onto his shoes and turning the snow brown in a small circle. Then his shoulders began to heave and shake. Everyone, Euphora, Mrs. Purcell, the Carter sisters, all stood huddled together with Clara staring out at Papa, stooped and shuddering.

"I didn't know he'd be sad." Euphora looked up at Clara. "I thought he hated Billy."

"I don't think he hated him, dear." Mrs. Purcell pushed back a few wandering strands of Euphora's red hair. "Your father has been twisted into something mean by the liquor, but it's not hate."

After some time, Papa stood up straight and calm. He looked up toward the sky and stayed like that for a long time. Finally, his gaze still fixed upward, he sank to his knees in the coffee drenched snow. Was he talking to Mamma? To God? Clara felt a piece of her heart bend toward him like a divining rod toward water, but she didn't run out to him. She took Euphora's hand. When he finished talking to the sky, he got up, took off his spectacles, wiped them with a handkerchief, put them back on and walked away—no coat, no hat, no scarf—around the side of the house where they couldn't see him anymore.

Never come back, Clara thought. Go search for Billy but never find him and *never* come back.

BUT HE DID COME BACK. The very next night he sauntered into the Blue Room just as Clara and Euphora were going to sleep, and sat down on Billy's bed by candlelight. Her heart sinking to the bottom of a gully just at the sight of him, Clara listened to him describe all the taverns, homes, alleys, depots, and factories where he had searched for Billy. He asked everyone he could find where Billy might be.

"Kansas maybe. Kansas I'll bet. That's what everyone said," Papa told her and Euphora. "I ain't goin' that far right now. It's too dang cold, too much snow and ice. Nearly got frostbite without my gloves. You seen my gloves?"

Clara shook her head and was relieved that Euphora shook hers too.

"I'm goin' up to Isabelle's first minute this cold streak lets up. There's a good chance he's there. I'll haul him back, but I ain't goin' ta freeze myself to death over his no good antics. He ain't worth that. But I'm goin' right soon and if you two write each other any secret letters, you tell your twin brother that there's no hidin' from me." Papa stared into the candle a moment. "And tell him all will be forgiven if he comes back."

Thirty-Two

FOR THE NEXT SIXTEEN DAYS after Billy ran off, Papa kept Clara to her regular schedule with Sam Weston and got her with John Reilly whenever Reilly wanted. On the seventeenth night, Clara pushed aside the table and chairs and rolled up the rug in the Spirit Room. Kneeling down, she wedged a knife into the crack between the floorboards and wrenched up the loose board. She heaved it over, sending it clattering. Reaching underneath the floor, she found her firemen bandbox, then took three dollar coins from her dress pocket, two from John Reilly and one from Sam and placed them inside beneath the colorful ribbon remnants.

John Reilly had come back after she'd made her demands that first afternoon. Reilly had come six times total and added to her secret savings. Clara lifted the ribbons out of the box and spilled her money jingling onto the floor. Twelve dollars from Reilly and eight from Sam. Twenty. She hadn't spent a red cent of it. Papa had promised her half of Reilly's five dollar fee for each visit, but he hadn't given it to her yet. He said he had some catching up to do on expenses, but in a week or so he'd make good on his promise. He wouldn't do it, though. Maybe he'd give her some of it, but never all of it.

She felt a chill and glanced at the fireplace and clock. Seven. She'd better get the fire going now so the room would be warm when Sam arrived at eight. How much money would she need to run away? Fifty, a hundred? Maybe she could find Billy. After scooping up the gold coins and dropping them back into the box, she took each ribbon one by one and rolled them into coils. Then she set them color by color—pinks, blues, reds—in layers on top of the money. She placed the lid on the box and ran her fingertips over the troop of firemen and their wagon.

She remembered the struggling firemen and other townspeople back in Homer when Papa's gristmill had burned to the ground. As the flames reached toward the sky, he and his partners had celebrated by getting drunk and hooting at the inferno. When Clara asked Mamma why he was happy that his business had burned down, all Mamma said was "insurance," then walked away. Later that night, the Homer sheriff came looking for Papa and then it was only a few weeks before Papa disappeared and found his way to Geneva.

Seventeen days since Billy had run off. How far could he be by now? Seventeen days of the sickest heartache she'd ever known. She felt like her arm was cut off and she didn't know where it was. If she did run like him, where would she go? Could she find him and live with him? She couldn't leave Euphora behind. She'd have to take her. That meant more money to be saved. She hid the box away in the floor again and replaced the floorboard.

Suddenly, a pounding noise rammed at the door.

"Oh." Heart slamming, she covered her mouth.

"Clara, it's Mrs. Purcell. May I come in?"

Jo-fire. She took a deep breath. It was just a knock. Just Mrs. Purcell. She glanced around. *Lawks.* The rug. The furniture.

"Just a minute." Clara unrolled and spread the rug quickly, then opened the door. "I was cleaning." As proof, she held out her hands, grimy with floor dirt.

Bundled up in her cape, gloves and scarf, Mrs. Purcell was alone. She rarely went out at night in the cold unless a friend or neighbor came along. She lifted a plate covered with a white cloth towards Clara. "I brought you some supper. You're missing too many of your evening meals. Am I interrupting your preparations? I know you have a spirit circle on Fridays."

Clara stiffened. Of course there was no spirit circle. There would only be Sam. Mrs. Purcell had better be gone by the time he arrived.

"Thank you. It's not until eight o'clock. I just have to start a fire and..." She looked around. "...fix the furniture."

"I'll help you."

Mrs. Purcell came in and set the plate on the table. Together they hoisted the table and chairs into place. While Clara struck a match and lit the kindling under the coal, Mrs. Purcell made clunking sounds as she set things on the oak table. Taking down the bellows from the mantel, Clara blew at the flames. When the fire was going, she looked around. There was a plate with ham, a stewed apple, and a hunk of brown bread set tidily with silverware and a napkin. In the rear corner of the room, Mrs. Purcell was tilting back the bottle of Old Peach Brandy on the pewter tray and eyeing its label.

Clara twirled toward the fire and pumped the bellows again even though the kindling had taken nicely. She didn't want the meal. She was never hungry before one of her engagements with Sam or Reilly. She hardly ate on those days at all.

"When did you get this exquisite red piece?" Mrs. Purcell asked, stroking her hand over the silk upholstery. "I haven't been here for months. You've got all kinds of new things— the washstand, the whiskey and brandy and glasses. Do you serve your seekers potations at the séances? I didn't think that liquor and Spiritualism were compatible." She raised a brow.

Mrs. Purcell looked comfortable and grandmotherly there on the sofa in her brown jacket and skirt. It wasn't what Clara was used to—a sweet, older, rose-and-lavender smelling woman resting there, rather than Sam or Reilly jittery and eager, wanting to do the other thing with her.

"Oh, you know Papa. He takes a drink when he is being host with the seekers. It's just for him. I wish he wouldn't, but you know how he is."

Mrs. Purcell paused a moment. Could Mrs. Purcell tell absolutely everything she said was a lie? Could Mrs. Purcell hear it in her voice, see it on her face? Could Mrs. Purcell see her drinking brandy with Sam by the fire?

"Aren't you going to eat? You have lost weight this winter and you are pale as a ghost. Try the ham. Euphora and I baked it with cloves."

"Maybe later. I'll set it aside and eat after the circle." Clara covered the plate with the napkin and took it with the silverware to the shelf with the liquor. She ogled the peach brandy, imagined the delicious fruit coating her tongue and throat. A libation now would relax her before Sam came, but she couldn't take one in front of Mrs. Purcell.

"Clara, come and sit with me on the sofa." Mrs. Purcell patted the red silk. "I haven't had a chance to talk to you in a long time."

Clara nodded, then sat near her. It had better not be a long talk, though. Sam would be here soon.

"You've had to become the oldest female in the family when you weren't that at all just a year ago. Now Billy is gone. Your family is getting smaller and smaller. You and Euphora must be lonely." Mrs. Purcell tapped her hands softly on her lap.

"Yes." Clara slumped back into the sofa. "I've been trying to get Izzie to come and visit, but Doctor MacAdams always needs her for something. She wrote me she would come for certain last week.

"Did you write her about Billy?"

Clara bit the inside of her mouth. "Not yet. I don't think anything I could say would make her visit. I've given up writing to her."

"You write her and tell her about Billy. She'll come then. I know she will." Mrs. Purcell settled a warm, wrinkled hand on Clara's wrist. "With your mother passed away and Isabelle in Rochester, I feel I should have kept a better eye on you and Billy and Euphora. But I have kept my distance because your father hasn't wanted my attentions on you children and he is your rightful parent." She grasped Clara's hand. "But there are some things that only a mother or older sister, or an aunt perhaps, can offer guidance on." She cleared her throat. "I could be that for you if you want. Would you like that?"

Clara nodded.

Mrs. Purcell smiled and squeezed her hand harder. "Is there anything you would like to speak to me about, anything that you have been wrestling with?"

Yes, Clara thought. *Lawk-a-mercy, yes.* Get me away from Papa and his schemes. He is killing me. Killing me. But she couldn't betray her promise to keep it all secret, couldn't take the risk. She felt her shoulders pinch up, her jaw lock. She shook her head.

Mrs. Purcell's gray eyes grew gentle and worried. "You can confide in me, Clara. Whatever you tell me will be between us and no one else, especially your father."

Clara felt a scream rising up, tears rising up. She had to stop them. She shook her head again. "I wish Papa didn't drink as much as he does, that's all."

"Yes. We should talk about that and Mrs. Beattie has noticed some things that we could talk about, too. She thought it best if I spoke to you."

Clara sat up straight, bit the inside of her mouth again. She had to draw a curtain between her and Mrs. Purcell right away, a big heavy curtain. Papa would do something awful if she told Mrs. Purcell any of the truth.

"With Billy gone, I'm even more worried about you and Euphora than I was before. At this point I feel that I cannot keep a respectable distance." Mrs. Purcell stood up from the red sofa and paced around a little.

She was nervous about whatever it was she wanted to say, thought Clara.

Mrs. Purcell stopped pacing and looked at her. "Mrs. Beattie has told me that she sees a man, Mr. Sam Weston, come frequently to the downstairs door and that he is not followed by other men and women who might be part of a spirit circle the way she used to see people come in when you and Izzie were holding the circles together. She also told me that every Friday night, when she's upstairs in her flat, she hears only one voice, a man's voice, along with yours."

"I do private readings now. People ask questions of their spirits and I seek answers on the planchette, the board that has the alphabet and numbers on it?"

"Your father is here then?"

"Sometimes." Clara tried not to blink.

Mrs. Purcell, eyes narrowing, lips tightening, came back to the sofa and stood over her. "You shouldn't be in this room with men alone ever. Your father permits that?"

Clara shrugged her shoulders. She felt like she was being pried open with a crowbar. If she were to tell Mrs. Purcell even the tip of the truth, it would all come flooding out of her. She wouldn't be able to stop it. She was sure she would start crying and never stop, a river flooding after thirty days of rainstorms.

"Do you want me to talk to him about this?" She sat near Clara. "What if I become your séance chaperone? I could sit meekly in the background when you meet with these men alone. I'll suggest that."

Clara stared at the floor. "Papa wouldn't like that. It might distract the seekers."

"Well, I'm going to talk to him, anyway." She tapped her fingers on her knees. "There's something else."

There was more than this? This alone would rile Papa terribly. She could hear him already. "What have you been telling that old hay bag? Our life is none of her dang business!" Clara slumped deeper into the sofa back, wanting to disappear into the cushion.

"I think you should write to Isabelle and ask if you and Euphora can live with her and Doctor MacAdams. I'm not sure you are safe anymore with your father. He hurt Billy more than I realized. It's possible he could hurt you or your sister."

Clara's eyes welled up. "I have thought about that. But I am afraid he would come and get us and take us back."

"Isabelle and her husband could keep him away, I'm sure."

"Not if Papa had a mind to take us. You know how wily he is." Clara felt a tear roll down the side of her face.

Suddenly, Clara had a thought. Because Billy was gone, Papa couldn't promise to lay off him to get Clara to give in to his demands. Now he needed something else. He'd use Euphora. He'd find some way to be cruel to Euphora or he'd steal Euphora back if they were at Izzie's. He would, and that would be his trick this time to get his way.

Mrs. Purcell sidled closer, then Clara felt Mrs. Purcell's soft chin rest on top of her head and her sweet, saggy arm rest on her shoulders.

"I'm afraid you are right, dear. You know him better than any of us. I shouldn't even think any of this. It's probably against the law, but I don't care. In my soul, I believe you and Euphora are in danger. I've been thinking of another plan for a while as well. I'm going to write my cousin in New York City and ask her if you could live with her temporarily. She doesn't have much room or money, but maybe she'd take the two of you for a short time. Then, when your Papa has surmised that you aren't with Isabelle, you could go to her." She squeezed Clara's shoulders, then leaned back and looked straight at her. "It will all have to be a secret. We can't give him any way to find you for a while. We'll make it look like you've run away like Billy. We'll say you went searching for Billy." She looked into Clara's eyes. "My guess is you're considering that anyway. Then when your Papa has given up on you, I'll write you and Isabelle, and you can go directly to Rochester on the train."

"You would do all that? You'd help us get away from him?" An arrow of hope shot through her. This might be the answer. She leaned into Mrs. Purcell and embraced her.

"Yes. If you could write your cousin. Please write her."

"Very well, dear. I'll go home and do it now."

Thirty-Three

IZZIE STOOD IN THE FRONT PARLOR of her Rochester home looking out the window. Magical splendor, everything was covered with ice—rooftops, tree branches, fences, the street, all coated with glistening ice. She'd never seen anything quite like it, solid, thick ice on every pine needle, every twig, every sagging shrub, all the world glinting. There was no carriage traffic, no one going out on business, no wagons delivering milk, wood, or coal. The road was too slick for hoof or wheel.

Face covered like a bandit right up to his eyes with a black scarf, Mac had gone on foot to his Upper Falls Water-Cure. He'd told her, "I expect I'll walk, slip, and slide the three miles. There won't be any omnibuses today."

A thunderous crash erupted at the rear of the house. Izzie's heart jigged. Feet planted, she waited for more, but there was nothing. Then she dashed through the house to the back door and threw it open. Their old maple tree had lost an enormous bough to the weight of the ice. It lay on the white ground, glittering, contorted, fractured.

That tree had better not die. She loved that tree, the shade it gave her and Mac this past summer, the hours she spent leaning against its trunk when she needed a respite from gardening, and the brilliant red foliage that brightened her garden in the fall.

The biting cold nipped at her and pushed her back inside. The kitchen was a mess, the small iron kettle gummy with oatmeal, the loaf pan caked with brown bread crust, plates, cups and utensils all smeared, caked, or coated with something sticky. She ought to get to it. No more of this gazing dreamily out the window. Perhaps later when it was warmer she would venture out for a stroll, after she had cleaned, prepared for supper, and worked on the Upper Falls Water-Cure draperies.

As she poured hot water from the kettle into the stone sink, a man's voice from the backyard called out, "Run to ground!"

She looked out the kitchen window but saw nothing. Who could be in her backyard, she wondered. There was nothing but ice out there. Was it the wind playing tricks in the cold?

"Run to ground!"

She lost her breath a moment. It sounded exactly like a grown man yelling. She went to the door and went out into the yard, stepping carefully on the ice. There was no one in her yard or anywhere she could see. A freezing gust of wind charged across her yard and her maple tree threw down another branch. As it crashed to the ground, the voice shouted again, "Isabelle!"

"No. I don't hear you!" Izzie rushed back into the house and slammed the door.

But she did hear her name, and it seemed to be coming from the vicinity of the tree. She did hear it. There had to be someone near the house calling for her, she decided.

She went out back again, then walked around the house, all around the backyard, around the sides, the front yard.

There was no one. She walked around the yards of all her neighbor's houses. No one. She walked carefully up and down Edinburgh Street a couple of blocks in either direction. There wasn't a soul outside, not a wagon, a dog, nothing. She plodded slowly back to her house and sat on the front stoop hoping the man who had called out would appear and knock on her door and ask a neighborly favor.

It was just as she had feared. Mac's water-cure treatment wasn't working. Nothing was working. It was only a matter of time, maybe months, maybe years, before she'd lose full control of herself like Mamma did.

After a while of sitting on the stoop holding herself in a knotted ball, Izzie could think of nothing but telling Mac what she had just heard. She had to see him right away. Maybe there was someone he could write to that he hadn't consulted yet. Maybe there was some remedy he hadn't considered. She set out for the Upper Falls Water-Cure. Taking small choppy steps to keep from slipping, she engineered her way over the deserted icy streets all the way to North St. Paul Street. Once she passed through the two great columns at the Water-Cure entry, she strode straight to Mac's office, forged in, shut the door, then leaned back against it. Mac was sitting at his desk writing. He looked up briefly at her commotion, then back at his work.

"You must knock. I might have a potential water-cure patient with me. You know that." His eyes stayed down as he finished writing. Then he slipped his papers into a folder and looked up at her. "What is it, then? You've come all the way on foot in the cold?"

"I heard a man speak. It was either a spirit...or I am a lunatic like Mamma."

He stared at her a long while, eyes blinking off and on. Why didn't he say anything? Did he finally believe she had crossed over to lunacy? His dark eyes kept watching her.

"You mean in broad daylight? This is disturbing. Here, come sit down by the fire." He shoved his chair back, rose, and moved one of his visitor's Windsor chairs over to the fireplace where a coal fire burned, then he brought the other chair next to it and they both sat.

She rubbed her reddened hands together. She was chilled to the bone.

"I heard a man call out in our backyard. It sounded like 'run to ground'. He shouted it. Then he said my name. He clearly called out my name, Mac."

Mac slumped back into his chair, ran his palm over the top of his hair. "Surely it was one of the children playing in the neighborhood." He looked relieved.

"No, I looked everywhere. There was no one. Besides, it was an old voice, not a young voice. I know what I heard."

"A memory. Perhaps a very vivid memory? Sometimes I think I hear my mother or father saying something because I remember it so well. Does 'run to ground' bring you a memory?"

"This wasn't like that."

"But, my dear, with the blustery conditions making a ruckus, couldn't you have been mistaken? I noticed a lot of havoc with the wind blowing things around on my way here this morning."

"No. It was clear. It was a man, but there was no man."

"I don't want you to fret about this. We'll add another water-cure treatment. I have something in mind."

"I don't want any more water anything. I'm exhausted. I'm soggy. I'm getting sores on my back. I'm tired of constantly using the commode because of all the drinking. I'm sick of water, Mac. No more. I need something new."

"The sores are positive. I know they are uncomfortable, but this means the impurities are purging from your body."

"The impurities are in my mind and they are not being purged. They are growing worse."

"Please." He took her hands in his. They were warm and dry. "Please. Be patient. I am sure we will conquer this. I want you to get more rest, even if you don't sleep well."

"I'm afraid I am losing myself, my mind. I believe it would be a relief for me to see my sisters and Billy. I worry about them every minute of every day. I've delayed long enough, Mac. I'm sure it would do me well to see them."

He pushed himself up in the chair to his full, towering height. "It will destroy the continuity of your treatment. You are too fragile."

"I think it will settle me to see them, especially Clara." She steadied her eyes on his. "I'm leaving in the morning."

He was breathing deeply. "If you go and worsen, we may have to consider Brigham Hall in Canandaigua."

"You'd put me in an insane asylum?" She grasped the wooden arms of her chair. "You think I am that far gone?"

His jaw tightened as he looked away from her toward the fire.

"Look at me, husband. Tell me you would put me in an insane asylum."

His eyes came back to her. They weren't glaring with anger as they had before when he had pressed her not to go to Geneva. They were sad like a boy's eyes, a boy who had lost something precious.

"Look at you," he said. "You think you heard voices in our backyard. You walked three miles in the freezing cold with no hat and no coat or even a scarf."

She looked down at her American Costume. It was true. She had set out with no protection from the cold. Her hands were deep red and, she realized, quite painful.

"I have written Dr. Cook and described your case." His voice was quiet. "Cook wrote me in return and said that if the water-cure did not resolve your condition in a few months, and he doubted that it would, we should visit him and consider a consultation, possibly a stay."

Izzie bolted out of her chair and paced away from him to one of the grand windows. The side lawn was to be a lovely, colorful flower garden for the water-cure patients, but now it was a blank slate of snow and ice. At the perimeter of the grounds, tree limbs hung low burdened by shining ice. It would be a long time before they'd bud, before the garden could be planted.

She couldn't look at Mac in that moment. He had just proposed putting her away in an asylum, maybe for a few weeks, maybe forever. She didn't know what would happen. The ice out there would melt. That would happen, but would she be here to plant the garden outside the window?

"Mac, you've been completely confident that you could cure me, rid me of the voices. I came to believe you."

Then she felt his arm, his side softly against her. He gazed out the window with her.

"If you keep up every detail of the treatment, the wet sheets, the baths, the water consumption, along with utilizing your mental discipline, I believe I will succeed and you will be well."

Trembling, she pulled away and spun toward him. "That's it, isn't Mac? You will succeed. Not I. You. I am the one struggling, but you'll be the one to succeed. I'll make you famous. I'll be the first documented case of insanity cured

with water. Doctor Robert MacAdams will be written about,
consulted by physicians from around the world."

His bushy black eyebrows furrowed down. "You think
this?"

"I always had the sense that I was an experiment for you,
many experiments, one after another, but I didn't object
because I was interested in what you were learning, what your
mind was pursuing. But I have come to wonder whether I am
a woman to you, a wife, or simply a case study."

He took both her hands. "But, Izzie, you and I are both
experimenters in life. That is why I chose you for my wife. I
thought you were someone who wanted to explore everything
new, everything with me. I never thought I'd find a woman
with an intellect like yours. It is your very inquisitiveness that
I fell in love with."

He did love her and she believed this about both their
minds being eager for new notions and philosophies, but all
the ideas seemed to be his. Every idea had come out of him so
fast she never had a chance to discover her own sense of
things.

She withdrew her hands from his. "They are your
experiments, Mac, not mine. The preventative techniques,
the water-cure for the mind, the vegetarianism." She looked
down at her green short skirt and trousers. "You've even
dressed me in the American Costume to suit your reform
ideals."

"You told me you'd come to love the reform dress. They
are your ideals too, ideals we share, aren't they?"

She sighed. "I don't know what my ideals are. I am so
exhausted from lack of sleep I can scarcely stand here." She
turned toward the window and the white expanse. "I'd like to
lie down out there. It's pure. Maybe I'd sleep, then."

He took her shoulders and turned her toward him. "Everything I have done has been for you, for our life together."

"Not everything. There are two things I've wanted these past months besides being your wife and being by your side. One was to sleep and be free of the haunting voices. You've tried to help me with that. The other has been to see Clara and the others with my own eyes to make sure my father hasn't been harming them. You've refused me that."

"One can't do everything one wants in the moment. There are responsibilities, necessities that come first."

"That's right. Now my sisters and brother are just that. I am going tomorrow. I have to know if Papa is harming them. If I don't like what I see, I am bringing all three of them back here with me to live with us."

"Izzie, we've been over this a hundred times. If they were as miserable as you imagine, you'd know it. Clara would write you and tell you. Besides, we are in debt. Three more mouths to feed would be impossible."

Izzie cast her eyes around the huge office. "We have this entire building, the out buildings. We have room, Mac. They could even work for you. You said yourself you need many hands to run this place."

She backed away from him and his worried eyes and walked to the office door. The way home would be cold, but she could race along to keep warm.

She opened the door and looked back at him. Standing there by the big window, he had never seemed so small to her. "As long as it is running, I'll be on the early train, and be back in a few days. I'm finished with the water-cure treatments. You can enter into your case log that I was not cured, quite the opposite."

As she walked down the hall, she heard him say, "Wait, take my coat," but she kept on without looking back at him.

Thirty-Four

CLARA AND EUPHORA SAT TOGETHER on the canal wall, dangling their legs over the side. Ice on the Cayuga & Seneca Canal was a foot thick, maybe more. It was Sunday afternoon and skaters were swirling, racing, and careening in ones, twos, and threes. This was the town's favorite spot for skating, not far up from the lake, just past the Malt House. After every snowfall, a gaggle of boys shoveled it, sometimes all the way up to Marsh Creek. Papa had told them he had a surprise and that he wanted to cheer them up since Billy hadn't come back or even written yet. "Ice skating is the thing. It'll lift your spirits." Somehow he had borrowed, or maybe stolen, two pairs of ladies' ice skates. He stood below them on the ice lacing up one of Euphora's skates with his bare, chapped hands. Clara noticed that he hadn't purchased new gloves yet.

She smiled to herself at the thought of Billy's hands being warm while Papa's were practically frostbitten. Maybe Papa still believed Billy would come back and he'd get his gloves back from him. Papa was still threatening to go up to Rochester and see if he was with Izzie. "I'll drag him back by the ear," he kept saying. But Clara was pretty sure it was just talk. Papa probably knew in his gut that Billy was long gone. She missed Billy every hour of every day and the more hours that went by, the more she hated Papa for beating Billy and making him go.

Papa grabbed Euphora by the waist and hoisted her down onto the ice. She squealed as the skates slid out of control underneath her, but Papa kept a tight hold of her, waiting until she steadied. When Euphora seemed like she was going to stay upright, he guided her hands to the edge of the canal wall.

"Wait right there until Clara's ready."

Beaming up at Clara, Euphora was eager to try her first time on ice skates.

Why did Papa have to do this, Clara wondered. Why did he have to turn into the old Papa when she had finally decided to hate him forever? Why did he try to win her heart back and why was he trying to win over Euphora? Clara could hear Billy's words. "He wants somethin', sure-as-rain." Euphora was starting to inch away along the ice, using the wall to keep from falling. While Papa slipped skates onto Clara's feet, she started counting the skaters, first the girls younger than her, fourteen of those. Then girls older than her, nine of those.

"Yours're too big, but I laced them tight," he said.

"Look!" Euphora was about twenty feet away, close to the wall but standing on her own.

"Careful, Rosebud." Papa ran to her, leaving Clara perched up on the wall.

Rosebud. He hadn't called Euphora that since she was three or four. That was his red-hair-darling-girl name for her when she was little.

"Take my hand. I'll bring you along," he said.

A young arms-entwined couple glided by like two flying swans. Euphora offered her green mittened hand to Papa and he began to trot along the ice, just fast enough to get her skating. Legs stiff like a couple of fence posts, Euphora careened forward, then careened back, forward, back, forward and finally bent forward in a permanent crouch. She gripped Papa's hand in both hers and let him pull her along over the ice.

"Clara, look!" Euphora glided into the crowd with Papa.

From up on the wall, Clara glanced down at the ice three feet below her. It seemed too far to jump and land on the two skinny blades. *Dang.* Papa had left her stuck there on the wall like a piece of laundry pinned to a line. She had skated back in Ohio. She knew how to go ahead, back, and stop, but hopping down a three-foot distance onto the blades made her nervous. Out of nowhere, John Reilly skated right up to her, scraping the toes of his skates at a pitch and grinding to a halt. He was wearing his Sunday best, stovepipe hat, handsome black coat covering his round belly, red and black checked satin bow-tie, shiny leather gloves, dove gray and black striped trousers.

"Good afternoon, Miss Clara." He tipped his hat. "Do you need assistance getting down?" He looked into the mass of skaters toward Papa. "I think you have been deserted."

Tarnation. He was the last person on the entire earth she wanted to see. He offered his outstretched hands. Why did he have to be here now? Grasping his hands, she used one of her heels to shove off the wall down to the ice. When she landed, she lunged forward toward Reilly. For a tiny instant, she thought she was going to land flat on her face, but Reilly pulled her up. She came back like a seesaw and steadied herself.

"Almost lost you." He offered an elbow. "Shall we?"

She surveyed the crowd. Was anyone watching her and Reilly? Could any of them tell how she knew him? Could they see how he desired her? Would he be angry if she refused him and skated away? She sighed. She made a lot of money from his attentions. Offending him would get Papa shirty for certain. Besides that, she'd need that money someday.

"I may freeze into a snowman standing here with my arm flapping in the wind. Come, then." He grinned at her.

Giving in, she took his arm and he set off striding toward the outskirts of the crowd. All she had to do was hold on and skate enough to keep up. They passed Papa and Euphora, but Papa had his back to her and didn't notice them. While Euphora stood still balancing on Papa's hand, he was talking intently to her about something. Clara wanted to go back and listen. What was he saying to her?

Two girls skating in a pair raced full out toward Reilly, charging right for him.

"Papa, we're cold. Can we go home now?"

Jo-fire. He had daughters? The girl who spoke had thick brown eyebrows, pale white skin with large light freckles and wide green-gray eyes. She didn't know he had daughters. They both looked at Clara intently, probably wondering who she was.

"Girls, this is Clara Benton, the famous Geneva medium. You've seen her on the handbills. She's the daughter of an associate of mine, Frank Benton." He smiled at them, raised one brow, as though beckoning some response from them.

"Good afternoon, Miss Benton." They chimed perfectly, a duet. The pale one was a bit younger than Euphora. The other just a year or so younger than that.

"These are my daughters, Helen and Fannie. I'll leave you to your father, Miss Benton." Dropping her arm gently, he gestured in Papa's direction. "Is that your younger sister with him?"

"No. I don't know who that is." Swallowing hard, she tried to look at him without blinking. She didn't want him knowing anything about Euphora or her knowing anything about him.

He smirked at her. "Well, good afternoon, Miss Benton. I must be on my way." He tipped his stovepipe hat at her.

After he skated away with Helen and Fannie, Clara glided toward Papa and Euphora. Euphora was skating four or five steps in a scuffle toward Papa, then landing against him for balance. Papa would back away, then she would skate at him again, a baby learning to walk. Clara skated a circle around them three times then coasted away, weaving between the boys, girls, couples, and families. She skated up the canal to the very end of the snow-cleared area near the mouth of Marsh Creek. She paused where the creek gurgled its way under the canal ice. If the canal was completely cleared of snow, she could skate away, wherever the canal went, to the next town, and the next. She could glide as far as her legs could take her, maybe all the way to Izzie in Rochester.

"We can come back again another time. Rosebud's getting' the knack. She's quick."

Clara turned. Papa was coming toward her with Euphora skating in little choppy steps on her own behind him.

"Clara, I'm skating!"

Euphora seemed happier than she had been in a while, certainly since Billy had left. Papa stopped and Euphora clamped herself to his arm.

"I had a talk with your little sister. She's goin' ta be a medium with you, like Isabelle was. I've been thinkin'. This spirit circle business always worked best when it was the two of you. That's been our missing link since Isabelle left. You'll start teachin' Rosebud the ways tomorrow, the handwritin', trances, all of it. We'll have a new start."

"What about Euphora's job with Mrs. Purcell? That helps with our room and board and she's been learning everything about running a household."

"She'll do both, won't you Rosebud?" Papa patted her hand.

Pinching up her mouth, Euphora looked uncertain, even a little afraid, but she nodded. In that moment, Clara felt the brick wall inside her get so high she couldn't see over it anymore, couldn't see Papa on the other side. This wasn't the old sweet inventive Papa come back. This was the plain old rotten skunk Papa she and Euphora always had now. The old Papa might have taken them ice-skating, but just ice-skating and nothing else. Now, always, always, always, a rowboat picnic, a sleigh ride, an afternoon of skating, those were his ways of proposing a scheme that would pile on agony. She glared at him trying to make her eyes say, "You louse. You rat."

"Don't give me that look."

Clara looked away from him up the canal. She heard him chattering away to Euphora about how talented she would be as a medium and how much fun she'd have with her sister and how much money they would make.

Fat, wet snowflakes began to fall. Did Papa mean for Euphora to be a hoax medium or a whore like he'd made her into? She remembered Reilly's story about the husband and wife in New York City who made their two daughters into whores. Dinah and Alice were their names. *Dinah and Alice.*

She turned to Papa. "Not with the men, Papa! Not with the men!"

"Keep your voice down." He shoved a palm toward her. "What're you talkin' about?"

"Not with the men, I said."

For the first time in a long while, she felt tall, like she was looking down on Papa and he was looking up at her.

"Shut up or you'll be in more trouble than you ever dreamed of."

"I never dreamed of trouble. You gave me plenty of it. I never had to dream of it."

"You be quiet." His nostrils flared in and out.

She stared down from her imaginary height at him thinking in silence, "You rotten skunk father. You are not going to turn Euphora into a whore. You are not. I will hide her away from you so far you'll never find her. Never."

"Don't get any ideas about takin' off like Billy. Don't go scamperin' to your sister's. I'll run you to the ground. I'll find you and I'll bring you back. I'll run you to the ground, I tell you."

"No, I wouldn't do that, Papa. I understand." This was one lie she was proud of. She was going to run off all right. She was going to run far away and take Euphora where he would never ever find them.

"Skate with me, Euphora." She glided to her little sister, took her clutching hands from Papa's arm, and drew her toward the other skaters.

Papa followed behind. When she felt that Euphora was staying with her fairly well, she sped up. Tomorrow she'd make a plan with Mrs. Purcell. Tuesday they'd go to the cousin's. She glanced back toward Marsh Creek and Papa. The falling snow made him appear blurry, even farther away than he really was.

LATER THAT NIGHT, Clara found the *Geneva Gazette* in Mrs. Purcell's parlor and took it with her to the Spirit Room. Every day the newspaper printed the timetable for the N.Y.

Central Railroad. She found the notice. Eastbound left at 7:36 A.M.

She moved the furniture and rug, pulled up the secret floorboard, and retrieved her bandbox. Even though she knew exactly how much was there, nine dollars from Sam Weston and fourteen from Reilly, she counted it again and again. Papa was right. The money from Reilly was easier and Papa hadn't even given her what he had promised from Reilly. She slipped the coins back in among the ribbons, closed the bandbox carefully, and returned it to its hiding place for the last time. The next time she took it out, she wouldn't hide it away again.

ON MONDAY, when Clara and Mrs. Purcell had gone to purchase rail tickets, the station master had told them that the snow and ice was so bad on the Genesee Valley Railroad tracks that there were no trains running and he didn't know when they'd start again. He told them it would be a better bet to take a steamboat down the lake and get a train for New York City from the south. Trains were still running on the southern lines so they went down to Long Pier and got steamboat tickets for the first sailing on Tuesday morning, on the Watkins.

During the rest of Monday, Clara was jittery, her stomach in an awful twist. She had waited until the last minute to tell Euphora the details of their running away because she and Mrs. Purcell were afraid Euphora might spill the beans without meaning to. During the night as they lay in bed, Clara whispered Mrs. Purcell's plan to Euphora. They were to go to Mrs. Purcell's cousin's home in New York City. The cousin, Mrs. Agnes Hogarth, would take Euphora on as a domestic and she could live there.

There wasn't enough room or money at the Hogarth's to take a second girl, so Clara would have to work a factory job and live in a boardinghouse. But there was nothing to worry about. Mrs. Hogarth and Mrs. Purcell had it all arranged. Mrs. Hogarth knew a boardinghouse run by a woman just six blocks away and they had an acquaintance who managed an umbrella factory. Clara was promised a job there. The whole thing was a secret. Only Mrs. Purcell knew where they'd be. Even Izzie wouldn't know in case Papa pressed her to tell. Later on they would write Izzie and explain it all.

Euphora was even more afraid of Papa than Clara had realized. Euphora actually seemed eager to run away. It turned out that during the many hours Clara was at the Spirit Room, Billy had confided in Euphora, telling her some of his stories about Papa losing his temper, things even Clara never knew. Clara had expected Euphora to fight against going, but it wasn't the going that upset her sister, it was New York City, how far it was, and how big. For a good long time, Euphora whined and pleaded that they go to Izzie's. Euphora wanted Izzie taking care of things as she had done in the past. But finally, Clara made her understand Papa would be able to find them there and steal them back.

"And I don't want to leave Mrs. Purcell," Euphora said.

"I know. I wish we could live with her too, Euphora, but we just have to get away from Papa. Maybe someday, if Papa leaves, we can live here again or go to Izzie's."

Clara told Euphora they were to get up at dawn and wear as many of their clothes as they could, like Billy had done. That way they'd be warm and their bags would be light.

When the dawn finally came, they rose and moved quietly about the room, preparing to leave. With all the gifts and clothing that Clara had acquired from Papa and Sam, her possessions had grown and it wasn't so simple to throw them into a little sack, but Mrs. Purcell had realized this earlier and had given Clara her own carpetbag. To get the valise to close, Clara had to stuff her things down with all her weight. She put on her whalebone hoop, several petticoats, and her green taffeta dress over her green and white striped one. Over that she wore Mamma's cape and over that, her red shawl. Everything else was in the carpetbag—hairdressings, bracelets, combs, brooches, sewing needles, thimbles, and threads. Euphora had two shawls, two dresses, two chemises, two petticoats, two books, two wooden horses, and one hairbrush. She wanted to take Billy's checkerboard and checkers.

"It won't fit in your satchel, but if you can carry it in your other hand, take it. If we end up walking a long way, you'll have to get rid of it."

"I can carry it."

"Shhh. If you wake Papa, we're dead as two doornails."

The door latch clicked. Clara flinched. The hall door opened and there was Mrs. Purcell. She was fully dressed and carrying the small glass lamp from her bedchamber. Silently, she nodded at Clara, then vanished.

"We're meeting her in her library. Are you ready?"

Euphora darted to the table, stuffed the checkers into her satchel and grabbed the checkerboard, which clunked loudly against the table. Heart flittering, Clara tensed and spun toward Papa's door. She waited a hushed moment with Euphora. Nothing. Papa hadn't been out late enough last night to be stewed to his eyebrows. He picked one muttonhead night not to get drunk and fall into a stupor.

"Go on ahead, I want to make sure we haven't left anything." Clara shut her carpetbag with the clasp.

Euphora tiptoed out and Clara went to the chest of drawers. In the top drawer there were several nearly empty tins of Billy's pomade and a few scattered, dingy hair ribbons.

In the second drawer, there was Euphora's third toy horse, its legs broken off. How and when had that happened? In the bottom drawer there were garments they'd outgrown, a blue plaid dress that had been Izzie's, then Clara's, then Euphora's, and there were numerous pantalettes and a pair of Billy's outgrown trousers. Clara ruffled through these, but then felt something firm. She lifted Mamma's Bible out of the mess and held it to her.

Mamma was buried in Geneva and Clara was leaving her here. She might never see her grave again. Raising the Bible to her face, Clara breathed in the musty, worn smell of it. She glanced over at her bag on the bed. Could she cram it in?

She opened the valise, reached in, and found the white and indigo dot summer dress Sam had given her that first time he'd pinned her in the corner of the Spirit Room. She tugged it out and tossed it onto the bed. She wrapped the Bible in the red bandana Billy had given her and slipped it in.

At the door she put the bag down and lingered. She looked around the Blue Room one last time. She looked at the things of the life that was over now, the sky blue walls, Mamma's rocking chair brought from Ohio, the girls' big bed and Billy's skinny one, a handful of story books, the framed print of Broadway, New York City above the mantel. That seemed strange. After staring at that bustling place in the picture for so long, that's just where she was going.

She glanced at Papa's door and pictured him on the other side of it sleeping in his bed. "Goodbye, Papa."

She turned, heart still flittering, and crept slowly downstairs. Nothing ahead of her would be familiar. Nothing except her little sister.

In her blue-and-red paisley wool shawl, silver hair perfectly up and tidy in a topknot, Mrs. Purcell was waiting for her with Euphora in the study. Euphora, with the checkerboard tucked under her arm, held a small woven basket.

"Do you have everything? Tickets? My cousin's address?" Mrs. Purcell asked.

"Yes."

"If you get confused, just ask the men working on the steamboat or in the depot. Here's ten dollars." She dropped various coins into Clara's hand. "There's food in the basket and here's the letter for my cousin, Agnes." She pressed it toward Clara. "Give it to her when you arrive. I'm sorry I can't come with you down to the slip but if anyone saw us they'd know I had something to do with your leaving and it might get back to your father."

"Thank you, Mrs. Purcell. We would never be able to do this without you." Clara wished that her heart would slow down enough to be able to swallow normally.

"Nonsense. I owe it to your dear mother. My cousin is going to be a little surprised at the rush. She's expecting another letter from me giving her a date, not you and your sister on her doorstep."

Suddenly, Euphora dropped the basket and checkerboard to the floor with a thud and threw her arms around Mrs. Purcell's waist.

"There, there, darling, I'll miss you too, more than you can know." She patted Euphora. Mrs. Purcell looked pale this morning, tired, the skin over her cheekbones sagging.

"You can't get into trouble with the sheriff for this, can you?" Euphora looked up at Mrs. Purcell.

"It's not the sheriff I'm worried about. It's your father, but once the worst is over, I don't expect he'll be staying around here. He doesn't much care for me." She gently nudged Euphora away from her.

"You two better get to the pier." Her eyes moist with tears, Mrs. Purcell kissed Euphora, then Clara. Bracing Clara's shoulders, Mrs. Purcell looked intently into her eyes. "You'll be all right. Don't be afraid. My cousin and her husband will watch over you."

"I never got a chance to write Izzie about Billy running off. Will you do it for me?"

"Of course, dear."

"But you still won't tell her where we are until Papa is gone far away," Clara said.

"Only when the time is right."

Izzie not knowing their whereabouts for a while made Clara's heart kick up harder. She didn't like that part of the plan, even if Izzie didn't care about them enough to visit. She and Euphora couldn't be hidden from Papa if he could force Izzie, or even Doctor MacAdams, to tell where they were. Clara tried again to swallow, but couldn't get her tongue to shift forward and the saliva to spill down her throat. Things seemed *tarnal* slowed down, thought Clara. She should be rushing away now, but she could barely move. She took her bag in one hand and picked up the basket in the other.

"Be careful out in the cold. It's frostbite weather. The wind makes it worse."

When they stepped out the front door, the wind tore right through Clara's layers of clothing and chilled her, sending goose bumps over every inch of her body. The wind stung like a slap at her face. Her bonnet blew off her head, but the tied strings kept it from flying away.

Mrs. Purcell escorted them over the snow-crusted front path to the street, then kissed them both again. As they set off down toward Main Street, it was so blustery that they had to lean forward and take small steps just to get anywhere at all. Euphora kept repeating, "It's colder than Sam Hill. It's colder

---

than Sam Hill." At the corner of William and Main, they both looked back down the frozen white street. Mrs. Purcell waved farewell, her hand high in the air. Clara felt tears flood up.

Did they really have to do this? Wasn't there another way to stay with Mrs. Purcell in the cozy, brick house with the gardens? She tried to swallow again. This time her throat performed. It wasn't safe, though, not as long as Papa was there.

"I have to stop at the Spirit Room for my savings."

Euphora's blue eyes widened with alarm. "We'll miss the boat. Why didn't you do it yesterday?"

"I was afraid Papa might find it. We have to stay quiet so Mrs. Beattie doesn't hear us."

When they got to the Spirit Room, Clara directed Euphora with nods of her head and hand signals to clear the furniture away from the secret floorboard. They managed to pry the board out and settle it softly on the floor. Clara reached under and got out the bandbox. Then she opened it and foraged among the ribbons for her gold dollars and began dropping them into her reticule.

"Where'd you get all that?"

Clara brought a finger to her lips to hush her sister. When she had it all, she stroked the group of uniformed men hauling the fire wagon on the lid, stroked the windows on the pretty house behind them. There wasn't room for the box in her bag and Euphora was carrying all she could handle. She'd have to leave it.

"Let's go. We'll miss the steamboat," Euphora said.

As they ran out onto the street, bags in hand, Clara glanced back at Mrs. Beattie's shop window and the beautiful hats and bonnets on display. In her mind's eye, she said goodbye to beautiful Mrs. Beattie, then started down the icy sidewalk toward Long Pier.

From the foot of Long Pier, as far as Clara could see, there was a layer of ice covering Seneca Lake. It had better not be frozen hard, she thought. Everyone always said the lake rarely froze solid. She'd heard the stories about the freeze two years ago. The lake had frozen for three miles at their northern end. Steamboats were laid up and the town made a festival of it with horse racing on an ice track and ice-boat sailing. At water's edge, where it was shallow, the ice was thick, but how far out was it thick?

Shooting up thick plumes of steam through the single stovepipe into the sky, the Watkins looked ready to go. Seventy or eighty people bundled in scarves, furs and gloves stood in the wind at the end of the dock talking, but none were venturing across the wide gangplank onto the long two-story vessel. Clara scanned the crowd. She knew seven of them from spirit circles. She lowered the brim of her bonnet to hide her face.

"Why aren't they boarding?" Euphora asked.

Winding her way through the crowd toward the man in uniform at the gangway, Clara kept her eyes straight ahead.

She sidled close to the narrow young man. "We have our tickets. May we board?" She wanted to charge right past him onto the boat.

"Captain Tuthill is waiting for a wire. We might have an ice embargo."

Embargo. *Tarnation.* Everyone said the lake hardly ever froze. Everyone. Seneca Lake was too big, the currents too deep, too wild. A crash exploded at the stern of the boat. Heart flying up, Clara yelped.

"Just cargo coming off that buckboard." The narrow man tilted his head toward a wagon down the pier.

Clara caught her breath. "We have tickets for this sailing. We have to go now. It's a family emergency."

"The captain has to decide whether to go. He's concerned about the ice. He might be able to leave here, but not land at Watkins Glen. He's got to wait for the message." His gravelly voice was calm. A scar made a perfectly straight line from his left temple to somewhere in his curly, long beard. "Trust me, Miss. You don't want to be stuck in the ice in the middle of the lake. There'll be some delay either way. Go wait with the others."

For close to an hour, Clara kept her eyes on the foot of the pier watching for Papa. It was still early. It wasn't likely he'd be down here. He just wouldn't think of it. Just the same, she kept her eyes peeled. And what would they do if the boat didn't leave? Would they go home and unpack their things and leave another day? What if Papa saw them come into the house with all their carpetbags? He had already been studying her actions differently since Billy had left.

A bell clanged. Clara jumped. Euphora grabbed her hand. Then the deckhand called out for everyone to board. Clara squeezed Euphora's hand and led her across the gangway.

Once on the steamboat, they found a gigantic parlor with chairs everywhere, small tables as well as a long one in the middle of the room, and even a big rug, curtains on the windows, and a piano. They sat in Windsor chairs in front of a warm iron stove and dug into Mrs. Purcell's basket. Euphora ate several biscuits filled with strawberry jam, but Clara just held one in her lap. She had a coiled-up snake feeling in her stomach and couldn't eat.

"Are you going to tell me about where you got the money, Clara?" Euphora licked a bit of jam from her lower lip.

"Not now."

Could she ever tell Euphora where that money had come from? Probably not. It was too shameful. She'd have to come up with something, though. Clara felt a chill rush up her legs and into her back.

"We're sailing," Clara said. She gave Euphora a smile and held her hand. It was warmer than her own. "Papa won't find us now." She glanced around the room. "Look. There's a little table. Let's get out the checkers."

Across the water and ice, Geneva was fading into the distance.

BOOK II

Thirty-Five

ON THE WAY TO GENEVA, Izzie was nearly senseless with worry. Because of the ice, the train ride had taken three hours longer than scheduled. According to the conductor the trains hadn't been running at all the day before and now the engineer had to take the rails at a crawl because the brakes were nearly useless. During the trip, she wanted to scream, "Get us there now. Get me to Clara! Please."

When the train finally arrived at the Geneva depot, Izzie stepped down carefully to the slick ground. There was a carriage for hire, but she decided it was safer to walk to Mrs. Purcell's. Once the wheels of a carriage or wagon started sliding, it would be hard for a horse to maneuver even the gentle grade up to Main Street or up Castle. It was less than two miles and her valise was light. On her own two feet, she could at least be in charge of her pace.

When she had climbed up the hill and turned onto William Street, she came to a dead halt. A small crowd of twenty or so people hovered on the sidewalk at Mrs. Purcell's house. *Drat.* Was it something to do with Clara, with the children? What was it? She should have come sooner, should never have listened to Mac about delaying. She ran ahead. About half way to the crowd, her heel skidded and she started to go down, but she caught herself. She skidded again, caught herself again. She forced her legs to slow down to a brisk walk. It was like one of those nightmares, legs not moving when one needed desperately to run.

She approached the crowd. Some were neighbors from William Street, but most she only vaguely recognized from town. Wearing a red cape, Mrs. Beattie the milliner emerged and stepped toward her. Her face was drawn and pale.

"Oh, Isabelle, it is awful. I am sorry. You better talk to the sheriff." She pointed a black-gloved hand toward a tall, wide-shouldered fellow at the foot of Mrs. Purcell's front stairs. He was talking to the next-door neighbor, Nathan Rose. A sharp pain shot down the back of Izzie's neck.

"What's awful?"

"They're all gone. Your family is gone, and Emma fell on the outside stairs last night and died." Mrs. Beattie's eyes were red. Izzie could see she had been crying.

"Died?"

Mrs. Beattie nodded, tears welling up.

"Where are the children?"

Mrs. Beattie studied Izzie a brief moment. "You know Billy ran away a few weeks ago."

"No. Why didn't anyone tell me? Where are the girls?"

Mrs. Beattie shook her head. "No one knows a thing."

"But someone has to know something. Where are the Carter spinsters?"

She pointed toward the bystanders. "They say visiting their brother in Boston."

It was far more dreadful than she had feared. Without Billy around, perhaps Papa had uprooted the girls and taken them somewhere new where his hoodwinking antics would be unknown to everyone.

Mrs. Beattie embraced Izzie tightly. "You'll find them. Don't worry. I am sure they are all right."

Izzie kissed Mrs. Beattie's chilly, tear-streaked face, then shoved aside a couple of strangers to make her way to the sheriff and Nathan Rose. Clara and Euphora were not all right. Billy was not all right. They couldn't be all right. If they were, they'd be here, home, upstairs in the Blue Room.

"Where are my sisters? What happened to Mrs. Purcell?" Izzie dropped her valise at the sheriff's feet.

Teeth clenched on a cold cigar, the sheriff had been listening to Rose. Lifting a hand out of his coat pocket, the sheriff took the cigar between his two stained forefingers and looked down at her.

"Who might you be?" His breath vaporized in front of his wide face.

"That's the oldest girl, Isabelle, from Rochester," Rose told him.

"Izzie Benton MacAdams. Where are my sisters? Where is my father?"

"I'm Sheriff Swift. Would you wait inside in the parlor please? One of my deputies is looking around the house." He gestured with the cigar toward the front door. "Don't mind him."

"I have to find my sisters right away."

"I understand, but if you'll wait inside a moment, we can discuss that."

She barely heard him. She wanted to sit down, but not inside. She wanted to sit right here, on the snow and ice and give in to the flimsy feeling in her legs. She looked up at the front door, then back out across the long narrow front yard. It was all just the same as last winter, but everything was wrong, all wrong, sweet old Emma dead, her sisters and brother gone. Maybe the girls went without Papa to find

Billy. Maybe they knew where Billy was and went to join him, maybe in Kansas. Clara would do that. She'd follow her twin. There could be a letter from Clara on its way to her in Rochester right now that would explain it all. She could send a wire to Mac asking him to read Clara's letter and wire her back.

"Mrs. MacAdams?" The sheriff's big round eyes were staring down at her.

Sighing, she picked up her valise and started up the stairs to the porch. The steps were dangerously slick.

"Mrs. Purcell fell here?" Pausing half way up, Izzie turned back to Rose and Swift. Rose nodded.

"Old hay bag! Old hay bag!"

Izzie looked out at the crowd to see who was yelling. The voice rang out like it was right there, but not right there. "Old hay bag!" It sounded like Papa. But where was the voice coming from? A memory of Papa like Mac had suggested?

"Old hay bag!" The cry suddenly struck her with fear. She felt she was being chased. Legs wobbly, she was cold, alone, out in the winter with no winter clothing, no protection. Ice pressing against her skin hurt. A grueling pain gripped her back. Trying to wake herself from the horrible sensations, she blinked and reached around to touch her back. It was fine. No pain, and she was dressed warmly. She had just had a nightmare without being asleep. It was very odd, but she had no time to think about it now. She had to find her sisters.

Below her, Swift and Rose were still chatting. The neighbors, out at the street, were all babbling together, their voices sounding like the voices that woke her in the middle of the night. The voices weren't distinct and yet she could understand them. They were sorry for her—sad, worried, angry about their friend Emma dying. Each of their faces seemed close to hers even though they were far off, and each pair of eyes—gray, green, blue, tired, nervous, scared—, watched her.

She maneuvered the slippery steps and entered the house, but she wouldn't sit and wait as instructed in the parlor. She had no time for that. Dropping her valise with a thud in the foyer, she collected the front of her skirt and bounded up the stairs. When she reached the door to the Blue Room, she paused and caught her breath.

The room was the same as her last day there seven months ago, the blue walls, the lithograph of New York City above the fireplace, the two beds, the long pine table, the oil lamps, and Mamma's rocking chair, but the room was dead silent and cold.

She began to survey the way things were left, murky water in the basin, the armoire open and empty. Clara and Euphora's bed was unmade, a white and blue dot dress in a heap on top. A few strands of long red hair clung to a pillow. She picked it up and embraced it as though it were Euphora herself. A wave of anxiety shot through her, making her chest tight. She tossed the pillow back onto the bed, then brushed her hands together to shake off the lingering feeling of nervousness. Her poor dear sisters. Where were they?

There was a shuffling sound, a clunk.

"Who is it?"

No one answered. Then she remembered a deputy was searching the house. Another clunk. It sounded like he was down the hall in Mrs. Purcell's room.

The girls had packed up their clothing so their exit had been premeditated, she decided. But did it have anything to do with Papa's departure? His bedchamber door was ajar. What had he been up to these months she'd been gone? She should never have left. He had driven Billy away and done something cruel to the girls. Why hadn't she kept her promise to come back for the children? How could she have given in to Mac all these months?

She shoved Papa's door open. Papa's things were everywhere about the room, his razor, hairbrush, a pomade tin on the washstand and a quarter-full whiskey bottle and a glass near his bed. His armoire still had his clothing in it, a few shirts, a pair of summer trousers, a summer coat, and his spare suspenders. Her legs felt wobbly again. He hadn't packed up as the girls had.

"I asked you to wait downstairs, Mrs. MacAdams."

She spun toward Sheriff Swift's voice and stepped back into the Blue Room to meet him.

His unlit cigar and hat in one hand, he was nearly as tall as Mac, but much broader, and his features were exaggerated. He was a picture that a child would draw of a man.

"Will you sit at the table there with me, Mrs. MacAdams?"

"It looks as though the girls left with some thought. They took their things but my father didn't." She gestured toward the bare armoire.

"Your neighbor Rose saw the two girls go with satchels at dawn yesterday. Emma was waving at them from the porch. He also thought he heard your father having a row with Emma about two in the morning this past night." He looked at her a moment as if sizing her up in some way. "Please come and sit down with me in the other room. You must be worn out from your trip and disturbed to find your family gone. Is your husband here with you?"

She shook her head, then went to the long pine table. He sat straight across from her, his bulky hands folded neatly on the table. She shivered with cold. There hadn't been a fire anywhere in the house at all today. Mrs. Purcell's place had always hummed like an engine, fires upstairs, fire downstairs, and constant cooking in the kitchen making sweet and savory smells.

Arms crossed, she listened as his questions came. Did she know anything about Papa's canal contracts, where he did his banking, and who his business partners were. The more he questioned her, the more Izzie wondered what the *Hell-fire* he was getting at, and the more she felt the precious minutes that she could be searching for Clara and Euphora slipping away.

"All I want to know, Sheriff Swift, is where my sisters are. I don't know anything about my father's businesses. He never told us anything. Do you think they are with him?"

"I'd say not. If Emma was out there waving them off at dawn, she'd be the one to know their whereabouts, but she's gone to us. So far no one else knows a thing."

Gone to us. Izzie's saddened at the memory of Emma Purcell's kind figure in the small parlor discussing books with her.

"Well, I must find them right away." Izzie stood up. "Has your deputy discovered anything that could assist me?"

"We're more interested in your father now." Swift unclasped his hands, shoved back his chair noisily, rose and walked to the fireplace mantle where he picked up a box of matches and lit his cigar. As he sucked on the stub and puffed up a swirl of foul-smelling smoke, he glanced around the room. Then he took the cigar from his mouth and studied its ember. "I think he killed Emma. Could have been an accident, but I think he might have caused it. On top of that, I think he was in cahoots with some bank note counterfeiting a few months ago. I never could get the right evidence to haul him in on it.

Izzie slumped back into her chair. The counterfeiting was entirely possible. He was suspected of insurance fraud back in Ohio before he ran off. But killing Emma. That seemed too much for Papa. He wouldn't have a reason to harm her. After all, she was helping him raise his children in her way and Clara had written that she let them stay when they were behind with room and board.

"No, sir, I can't believe my father would kill anyone."

"Can you believe it if he was so drunk that something snapped in him? I've seen it a hundred times, these fellas beating their wives, their kids. We see it all the time."

Izzie stared at Swift a moment. Hearing him lump Papa in with other men who became violent with their families was horrible, but there was no way to deny it. Papa had harmed Billy on many occasions and maybe even the girls after she'd left. Whatever had happened, she could have stopped it if she had been there.

"I suppose that might be possible," she said.

Sheriff Swift continued with his interrogation and by the time he finished, she realized that he had very little interest in finding her two sisters, but overwhelming interest in finding Papa. After all, he thought Papa might have caused Mrs. Purcell's death as well as been involved in some kind of counterfeiting. The girls had left on their own. They had gone somewhere without Papa and that was that.

"There's not much I can do about those girls," he said, "especially if they've gone out of the area. If they were slave girls, and you were a rich plantation owner, you could hire a tracker and dogs." He smiled at her, but she did not smile back. "No, Mrs. MacAdams, you are going to have to look for them on your own. My experience is the sooner you start, the better chance you have of finding them. Talk to Mrs. Purcell's friends. They may know something. In all likelihood the girls are on their way to your home in Rochester right now. We've got to find your father, but we will ask around about your sisters and notify other sheriffs in the area. If I come across anything, I'll let you know. Leave your address with me."

After Sheriff Swift left her, Izzie sat in Mamma's rocker for a while gathering her thoughts. She caressed the chair's smooth wooden arms.

"What would your voices tell you now, Mamma? They told you to find Papa in Geneva when he ran away from us. What would they tell you about Clara and Euphora or Billy? Did the girls go after Billy?"

She could hear the deputy and Swift talking in low voices down the hall. The whole world. The girls could be anywhere in the whole world after two days of travel. Anywhere in the Northeast, anyway. Why hadn't she come sooner? Why hadn't she followed her instincts? This was her fault. She rocked the chair hard, then jammed her feet down.

The Spirit Room might tell her something. Mrs. Beattie might know something. Maybe even Sam Weston. She stood up so fast the rocker rolled hard and banged her legs. She ran downstairs, grabbed her valise without breaking her stride, and only slowed when she got to the icy front stairs. The neighbors were gone.

WHEN IZZIE ARRIVED AT THE SPIRIT ROOM, she was out of breath. The secret floorboard where Papa had built the knocker was open and the furniture all pushed aside. Had they been repairing it? There was a beautiful red silk sofa not far from the door. How had they afforded that with all the problems with the séances Clara had written her about? Everything else was much the same, except the tray with bottles in the corner. Izzie walked over to it. Peach brandy, soda water, whiskey, two short glasses, two stem glasses. Two and two? The tray was Papa's, of course, but if he was serving drinks to the seekers, why two of each kind, why not six or eight? She picked one of the stem glasses up and put her nose to it. It smelled of peaches. Suddenly feeling gloomy, she replaced the glass on the tray.

She shouldn't spend more time here. The sheriff said the sooner she searched, the better the result. The sooner, the better. The sooner, the better. She paced around the room. Everything here felt despondent, forlorn.

She considered the opening in the floor and the rod running from foot pedal to knocker. Nothing seemed unusual about it. Then she glimpsed an open bandbox on the table. Hand trembling as she fingered through the many-colored snippets of ribbon, Izzie kept thinking she would find something buried under the ribbons that would tell her where Clara had gone, but there was nothing. She turned back toward the gap in the floor. Perhaps Clara hid something under there. Izzie knelt down and searched but found nothing.

The sooner, the better she could hear the sheriff saying. She had to start asking around right away. She'd start with Mrs. Beattie downstairs.

When she got to the milliner's shop, Izzie found Mrs. Beattie's blond head just visible behind her cash register counter. The milliner looked up, saw Izzie, and rushed out to embrace her.

"Oh, Isabelle. Sheriff Swift was just here asking me questions. He said Clara and Euphora were seen yesterday morning boarding the Watkins steamship. The girls have gone south. And one of his deputies told him that Mrs. Purcell and Clara tried to buy two train tickets to New York City the day before, but held off because of the ice."

Izzie groaned. She should have come before. Long before. New York City. How on earth would she find them in New York City?

"Did Clara speak to you at all about leaving?" Izzie asked.

"No, but I know Emma had worries and was trying to think of a way to get all three of them away from your father. That was before Billy left. She was quite frustrated that she had no legal right to do anything."

"What worries?"

"I didn't know Billy or Euphora. I only knew Clara. I was concerned about some things I'd been observing."

"What things?"

"I went to Emma because Clara had been having private séances with men alone in the Spirit Room. At least, it looked and sounded that way. There was that friend of your father's, Mr. Weston. He came nearly every Friday evening. There was also another one, but I never managed to see him. I could only hear his voice if I was upstairs in my flat." She averted her eyes toward her shelves of hats, then the floor, and crossed her arms. "I thought it improper. It didn't seem right, Clara being only fourteen and those men alone with her." Her eyes came back to Izzie's. "I asked Emma if she knew about it. That's when I found out about your father's drinking habits and that he'd been so harsh with Billy."

Izzie nodded. Besides worrying about the impropriety with the single men, the two women were probably afraid that if Papa could hit Billy, he could hit the girls too. Maybe he had already been hitting them. About to explode, Izzie paced several steps away from Mrs. Beattie, then came back.

"My father wasn't there when the men were with Clara? He used to always observe and assist us. Are you sure?"

Mrs. Beattie shook her head. "I don't think so, even though Clara said he was. And Clara seemed rather in her own world lately, daydreaming, I supposed. I thought it was her age. You know how girls that age can be. But she was jittery too. Every little noise would make her jump." Mrs.

Beattie's face became flat and hard. "And there's something else, something I told Emma."

"What else could there be?"

"I told Emma that sometimes on the Fridays, I heard Mr. Weston moaning, the kind of moaning sounds my husband used to make when we were...well, being marital." Mrs. Beattie looked at the floor. "It disturbed me a great deal so I confided in Emma. I suppose it could have been something to do with the spirit antics." Mrs. Beattie's face came back up, eyes full of tears. She put her fingertips over her mouth and shook her head. "I'm sorry, Isabelle."

"You think there were conjugal relations between Mr. Weston and Clara?" Izzie felt a flood of seething anger pour into her.

Mrs. Beattie gave a faint nod.

"How can I find Sam Weston?"

"I don't know where he lives, but he was in here just an hour ago asking after Clara. He'd heard the news and seemed quite distressed. He seemed much more concerned about Clara than about your father being gone. He doesn't know anything."

Izzie gritted her teeth. "No matter the truth about Mr. Weston, he is useless if he doesn't know anything about where the girls are. I'm going after the girls."

"But how will you begin?"

"I have no idea, but I must follow them to New York City."

Thirty-Six

CLARA AND EUPHORA followed Mrs. Agnes Hogarth to the back of the house on Nineteenth Street. Clara tried not to stare at the woman's left hand as they walked. It had only two fingers and they were both twitching. When they had passed through the kitchen, Mrs. Hogarth came to a closed white door.

"We are not quite ready for you. I didn't expect you so soon, but we can get things out of here in a few days. Clara, I am not entirely sure the boardinghouse has room for you yet, but the woman who runs it knows us, expects you at some point, and is very kind."

Reaching with her good hand, Mrs. Hogarth opened the door. The room was a pantry with a very small high window that was covered with a red and blue plaid curtain.

Clara stepped back. "Euphora's to sleep in your pantry?"

"Well, it won't be a pantry when we fix it up for her. It'll be a small bedchamber. My husband is going to take out the shelves on this side." She swept her two twitching fingers toward the wall.

"Will I have a bed, then?" Euphora looked up at Mrs. Hogarth.

"Oh, yes, dear. I know it doesn't look like much, but when we take out all the jars and crocks and sacks, you can put your things on these shelves, and we'll build you a little bed right here. And that window up there opens for ventilation. There are twelve families in this house. It's the best we can do."

Euphora's freckled upper lip quivered. Clara thought she was about to cry.

"You'll like being close to the kitchen, Euphora." Clara touched her sister's shoulder.

"I won't like being away from you, though, Clara. I'll be all alone."

"No you won't, you'll have Mr. and Mrs. Hogarth and I'll visit you all the time. And it's not permanent. I told you that."

Then Euphora's face broke and she did cry. Clara let her sister sob against her shoulder.

"My cousin wrote me you needed a safe place for a while. You'll be safe here. She also told me you are quite the cook, Euphora. Maybe you can show me some of the things you've learned from Emma. I'd like to see what she taught you."

Calming a bit, Euphora stood up straight and wiped her eyes firmly with her palm.

Suddenly, dogs barked loudly outside. Clara jerked her shoulders up. Were they attacking someone? But in a quick moment she could tell they were just making a ruckus. She glanced at Mrs. Hogarth and Euphora, but they didn't seem to notice anything at all.

"Tonight you can sleep on a stack of quilts on the floor in our bedchamber. You won't be so lonely then." Mrs. Hogarth smiled for the first time since they had arrived.

She didn't have the grandmotherly warmth that Mrs. Purcell had, but she did seem kind enough.

A cold trickle seeped into Clara's stomach. In a few minutes, she would be walking out the front door, valise in hand, on her way to the lodging house Mrs. Hogarth had found for her on Thirteenth Street. Even though Mrs. Hogarth's home appeared to be a good enough place to leave Euphora, going down the street a mere six blocks felt far worse than leaving Geneva forever.

"Skunk!"

Shivers ran across the back of Clara's hands.

"Stink-pot!"

"Rat!"

"Son of a Bitch!"

Two boys, trying to outdo each other, hollered outside, setting the dogs barking mad again.

"There are tenements behind us. Those boys are always at it." She looked sternly at Euphora. "You'll get used to it, but I don't want to hear any of those words in this house."

Euphora nodded.

"Well." Mrs. Hogarth glanced around the kitchen, then back into the half-empty pantry. "I suppose you two are weary to your bones after that journey. If Euphora is going to sleep in a bundle of quilts on the floor tonight, you could just as well sleep there too, Clara. It's late. You can go to the lodging house in the morning."

The cold trickle in Clara's stomach eased, but she knew she'd feel it again in the morning.

THE NEXT DAY, as Clara steered herself along the busy, snow-crusted sidewalk down Eighth Avenue, she kept seeing Euphora's face afraid and streaming with tears. When she had said goodbye to Euphora, both their hearts broke. Euphora cried with a terrible, scared expression. Clara shook and cried watching her. Standing in the doorway behind Euphora, Mrs. Hogarth, after hesitating, put an arm awkwardly around Euphora's shoulders. With the lodging house address crumpled in her hand, Clara tore herself away and walked on. It had to be done. All of it had to be done. Leaving Euphora there was better than letting Papa push her sister at men. Head down, Clara let the brim of her bonnet hide her sadness from more strangers than she had ever seen in her life.

At the lodging house, Mrs. Hogarth's acquaintance greeted Clara cordially even though she was a little surprised to see her. She directed Clara to a room on the fourth floor that she would share with a girl named Hannah. Clara headed upstairs with her valise and when she had reached stair number seventy-five, nearly at the top, she broke a sweat and sat on a stair for a moment to wipe her brow and rest. This wasn't like her. It was no time to be ill. She heard a soft whimpering ahead. That was fitting. Crying where she'd been, crying on the way, and crying when she arrived.

She dragged herself up the final thirteen stairs and shuffled toward her room, number ten. The door was ajar. She peeked in. A weeping girl with straw blond hair, sunny and pale like Mrs. Beattie's, was lying face down on a bed.

Clara gently shouldered the door open and entered the narrow room.

"Hello," she said softly. "I'm Clara Benton, the new lodger."

The girl pushed herself up and sat on the side of the bed. Hair flowing down to her waist, she yanked the corner of her wool blanket toward her and wiped her reddened eyes. She looked to be fifteen or sixteen.

"Hannah Swenson. I heard you were coming in two or three weeks."

"I had to come sooner." Clara dropped her valise on the floor and sat on the other bed three feet away.

"Where are you from?" Hannah asked.

"Geneva."

"Switzerland?" Hannah's blue eyes grew large.

"No, up north, on Seneca Lake."

They both were silent a moment watching each other. Hannah had a wide, round forehead, a narrow pointed chin, long nose, and every tooth was as crooked as a tree branch. No one would call her handsome, but she had a sweet look about her.

"I've just been crying myself," Clara said. "I left my little sister with a stranger this morning. She's going to be a domestic."

"Are your parents dead? My parents are dead."

Clara glanced up at the sloped ceiling. It looked like a big wall tumbling over. "Yes. They're dead. My mother died over a year ago. My father passed away last month."

Sympathy filling her eyes, Hannah nodded. "I lost my job at the shirt factory a month ago and haven't been able to find another. That's why I was ..." She patted her pillow. "I'll have to leave here if I don't find something by next week."

"Where will you go?"

Hannah shrugged.

Clara stood, feverish, limbs aching, and began to unbutton her dress bodice. She wanted to sleep.

"What do you do when you want to cheer yourself up?" Clara asked.

"I walk along Broadway and look at the people parading about. I have one nice dress. It was my mother's. I wear it whenever I go."

Mrs. Beattie had described Broadway to Clara and she had stared at the lithograph in the Blue Room for many an hour. It was the one place in New York City she knew she wanted to see.

"Will you take me this afternoon after I've slept a little? I've never been so tuckered in my life."

Hannah smiled and stood. "You've never been to Broadway?"

"I just got here last night."

As Clara began to climb out of her dress, Hannah stepped toward her and helped. As soon as it was off, Hannah took it to the armoire and hung it up. Then Clara got out of the whalebone hoop and set it in the corner of the room. While Hannah watched her, Clara lay down on her new bed, sank into the straw, and wrapped herself in the blanket. Hannah started talking about the lodging house and lodgers, but within a few minutes Clara closed her eyes and was asleep.

THE WHITE WALL CAREENED TOWARD HER. She'd be crushed, buried. Heart exploding, Clara yelled, "Stop!" The wall stilled. She slowly caught her breath. It was just the dormer ceiling. She was in room ten…the lodging house. She inspected her surroundings. Hannah was gone. It was dusk. She rose and found a chamber pot under the bed, used it, then rolled herself like a sausage in her blanket and went back to sleep.

THE NEXT MORNING SHE WOKE to Hannah's voice. "Come on then. There's breakfast with the price of the room, but you can't miss it. There's no supper. It might be your only meal today if you're like me."

"I'll be along." Clara bit the inside of her mouth and thought of Euphora waking up on the Hogarth's bedchamber floor. Euphora would be lonely in that house without anyone but the old couple. She'd have to visit her little sister often. She wouldn't be like Izzie. She wouldn't promise to visit, then never do it.

"Don't dawdle, Clara. The other girls eat everything set out if you don't get there in time."

A LITTLE LATER, in the dining room at the breakfast of oatmeal and tea, there were three others besides Hannah who were somewhere under sixteen or seventeen. Then there were four older women, one with two young daughters. They were all friendly enough, asking Clara's name and whether she had employment and offering ideas, but they were quite intent on eating as Hannah had warned her. The older four seemed worn. One had a half-closed eye, one was gaunt and yellow, the third sullen, and the fourth slumped over. The younger ones had lively spirits, though, and teased each other as they shoveled down their oatmeal. Clara hadn't eaten since breakfast at Mrs. Hogarth's the day before and she ate every last bit that the others left. One by one the lodger women and girls rose and set off to go to their factory jobs or back to their rooms to do piece work. No one lingered.

Hannah waited for Clara to finish then took her back upstairs. "We'll dress up, then walk down Broadway. I'll show you your new hometown. There's all the days after this one to look for employment and besides that, the cold has broke and the sun is shining bright."

After they had taken off their everyday dresses, they helped each other with their whalebone hoops and petticoats. Clara dug into her valise and laid out her dresses on the bed—the white séance dress and Mamma's gray everyday dress. She put them next to the one she had worn to breakfast, her dark blue checker calico. She looked at them and remembered the indigo dot from Sam. It was back in Geneva, tossed out when she wanted room for Mamma's Bible.

"And there's the green-and-white stripe with lace collar in the armoire. Which one shall I wear?" Clara asked.

Hannah's eyes were huge. "You have four dresses?"

Clara glanced at the array. They weren't fancy. They weren't elegant. They weren't anything. They were simple dresses. Two of them reminded her of things she wanted to forget, Papa's séance hoax and Mamma dying. None of them was even what one would call a winter dress.

Hannah went to the armoire and brought the green-and-white stripe dress out for Clara, then she brought out a shimmering silver silk taffeta with wide, flowing sleeves and three flounces on the skirt and held it over her front. Sewn at the bosom, a single blue silk flower the size of an apple covered a few of the front buttons.

Clara reached out and caressed one of the soft flounces. "None of mine are this lovely."

"I take good care of it. It'll have to find me a husband."

"You're looking now?"

"Every day since my parents died. That's why I go over to Broadway. There's thousands of men up and down the street. You'll see."

WHEN THEY STEPPED OUTSIDE, Clara lifted her face and felt the winter sun. The ice on the stone walks was turning to glistening slush. As they walked along Thirteenth Street toward Broadway, cold water seeped into her boots making her feet clammy, but she didn't mind. Everyone was bustling, racing along the sidewalks, trying to get somewhere lickety-click. But she and Hannah had the entire day to go anywhere and nowhere.

When they reached Broadway, the sidewalks were dense with men, women, and children. Dressed fancy, dressed plain, dressed in rags, and there were Negroes of all ages and Chinese people, and a dog here and there. The air smelled like cigars, dung, and smoking fires. The street roared with the clatter of wheels on wet paving stones. Every kind of vehicle and horse imaginable was pulled up to a curb or clipping along or stuck waiting behind three others. There were delivery wagons, flat wagons, carts, closed and open carriages, single riders on horses, and omnibuses with their drivers outside on top steering two horse teams. Clara counted six omnibuses in one block. She started to count small carts, but she got dizzy searching them out and stopped.

Hannah was chattering and pointing out places she admired, but Clara barely heard her. The stream of shops was never ending, selling everything Clara could think of—carpets, clothing, wine, wallpaper, hardware, cutlery, jewelry, printing, straw goods, cabinets, toys, marble statues, tea, upholstery. And there were daguerreotype studios, bookstores, and fine art galleries with prints and paintings in their windows, and underground barrooms, and restaurants and cafes, and billiard rooms. People hustled in and out of nearly every door. Crates were being unloaded and loaded onto wagons or waiting in stacks on the sidewalk.

Clara was giddy. "How can there be so much of everything?"

"It's New York. You should see it on a warm day in spring. South of Bleecker and Houston Streets, it's the halls and theaters and hotels. I'll show you inside of a hotel. If anyone asks us what we're there for, we're to meet your uncle, Joseph Benton of Albany." Hannah cocked one brow.

Clara laughed. "Yes, my Uncle Joseph."

Just beyond Bleecker Street, Laura Keene's Theatre caught Clara's eye. The sign outside the doors announced an Irish Drama, *The Colleen Bawn* by Dion Boucicault. Tickets fifty cents.

"Who is Laura Keene?" asked Clara. "Have you seen this play?"

"A famous actress. This is her own theatre. I haven't seen it."

"Fifty cents. I want to see it as soon as I get the money. Can we go to the A.T. Stewart's store today? Mrs. Beattie, the milliner I worked for, used to go twice a year."

"That's way down, almost to City Hall Park. It's a good, long walk."

"I don't mind."

"If you've got a couple of nickels we could take the omnibus back up when we're tired. You really got to take an omnibus."

"Yes. I do have nickels." Clara was boiling over with excitement.

They passed several enormous hotels with carriages lined up outside and huge American flags flying from their rooftops. The Smithsonian, the Metropolitan, the Collamore. At Spring Street they came to the St. Nicholas Hotel.

"This is the one," Hannah said and steered Clara up the marble stairs.

Clara looked up at five stories of windows. "I wish my sister Euphora were here to see this."

As they climbed, two men took notice of them, smiled, tipped their top hats, and together said, "Good morning, ladies."

"Good morning, gentlemen," Hannah said, then turned and winked at Clara.

Once inside the hotel's entrance, Clara's jaw dropped. The ceilings were as high as the sky, the room as big as a steamboat. There were huge lit gas chandeliers of sparkling glass everywhere and more shiny upholstered sofas and chairs than Clara had seen all told in her life. Handsome young men in uniforms scurried about with luggage, small silver trays, or things tucked under their arms. Elegantly dressed women in bright colors and silks and men in fashions she'd only seen in Mrs. Beattie's magazines were standing about chatting in pairs or in small groups or sitting with newspapers and tea services.

The room smelled of pipes and perfume and roasting beef and coffee. Hundreds of voices hummed and a thousand pieces of silverware clinked on a thousand plates behind a pair of grand double doors to one side.

"Let's pretend we are looking for your Uncle Joseph in the restaurant, so we can peek in." Hannah spun and strode off toward the restaurant. Trying to catch up, Clara trailed after Hannah's lustrous silver dress.

"Hannah! Hannah!"

A girl's voice stopped Hannah. She turned to look.

"Abbie!"

Hannah and Abbie embraced as Clara caught up. They were happy to see each other, smiling and kissing and grasping each other's hands.

"This is my new friend, Clara, from the boardinghouse." Hannah turned to Clara. "Abbie lived there too until a few months ago."

Abbie had a pleasant face, freckles but not as many as Euphora, gray eyes and brown hair, nearly black. She looked to be about sixteen like Hannah. She was wearing a cape over a fashionable blue-and-black dress. Did she have a mother who left her that dress when she died like Hannah did? Perhaps she already found her husband as Hannah was hoping.

"What are you doing here?" Hannah asked.

Abbie glanced around, then leaned close to Hannah's ear. "I've just been with a gentleman upstairs." Her voice was hushed but Clara could hear.

Hannah's throat reddened and her mouth pinched. Abbie opened her reticule and held it out for Hannah to look in. Hannah drew a hand to her mouth.

"Five dollars?"

Clara suddenly was sinking down, stomach, heart, breath, shoulders, blood, hips, sinking down through the floor.

"Shhh." Abbie nodded. "Have you found employment yet?"

Hannah shook her head.

"What about you?" Abbie looked at Clara.

"I just got here two days ago."

"Well, you won't have much luck. Two, three dollars a week is all you're going to get and that ain't enough for anything except a bed and some mush in the morning. I've been trying to get Hannah to come with me to the house where I live now, but she won't budge." Abbie turned back to Hannah. "You'll better find a husband going on the town than going back to some shirt factory."

"I don't think I could do it your way, Abbie."

"Lots of girls do, Hannah. You make good friends with the other girls. You take care of yourself. You won't end up at the Five Points."

"Don't listen to her, Clara. You'll do fine. We both will."

Hannah sounded cheerful enough, but her voice was uncertain. She probably had been giving some thought to Abbie's invitation. Clara, pondering what the Five Points might be, waited patiently while they spoke about several girls from the boardinghouse. She wanted to leave, to get away from Abbie and her reticule full of five dollars. Of all the thousands of people on Broadway, why did Hannah have to know this girl? Why did Hannah have to be friends with a prostitute? Why couldn't she be friends with a milliner or a cook?

"Henry Brown! Henry Brown!"

Clara jumped nervously. She glanced around for whoever was shouting. It was one of the young men in uniform striding through the lobby.

As Abbie started to explain in awe how deluxe everything was at the hotel and that the sinks had running hot water, Clara wandered away from the two girls to the front door and looked out. The two men who had greeted them on the stairs were still there. She watched them for a few moments. Smiling and tipping their hats at every woman who was unaccompanied by a man, they would periodically nudge each other and make comments she couldn't hear.

After a while, Hannah and Abbie found her and they descended the stairs to the street.

"Do you three ladies have time for lunch with two lonely out-of-towners?"

"Not today, gentlemen," Abbie said, her skirt swirling as she twisted around. "Maybe another time."

"We'll watch for you, then."

Down on the street, Abbie wished them well and set off along Spring Street. Clara fell into stride with Hannah as they continued their walk down Broadway. As they strode along, Clara couldn't believe her eyes. There were even more grand hotels and halls and shops. Broadway seemed endless.

While they walked, Clara kept thinking how Abbie seemed happy and Hannah seemed miserable, how Abbie had made five dollars by noon, and had the rest of the day to do as she pleased and spend her money on anything she wanted, and how Hannah couldn't afford to eat anything else except the oatmeal at the boardinghouse. She wondered again what the Five Points was, but figured no matter what it was, it had to be an awful place.

When they got to A.T. Stewart's at Chamber Street, Clara looked up at the building. It was immense, the most splendiferous building she had ever seen, spanning a full block. But just now, she was too drained to be cast under its spell. Abbie, the prostitute, had left with her with a black temperament.

"They call it the Marble Palace," Hannah said.

"Would you mind if we go in another day? I'm tired and my feet are wet and cold. Can we take the omnibus back?"

Hannah smiled, her blues eyes soft and pale. Then she laughed. "The Marble Palace will be here waiting for you. And the mermaid too. She's at Ann Street, at Barnum's American Museum. I can't wait to show you the Feejee Mermaid at Barnum's. A real mermaid," Hannah said. "Twenty-five cents to go in. I've been more than once, but I don't have the twenty-five cents just now. When we get our factory jobs, we'll go to Barnum's."

Thirty-Seven

WITH MRS. BEATTIE'S PERMISSION, Izzie had slept the night in the Spirit Room on the red sofa. In the early morning, the milliner brought her a small loaf of bread and some cold bacon and told Izzie the trains were running again. Without wasting a second, Izzie bid Mrs. Beattie farewell and caught the train to New York City.

Not even taking the time to send a cable to Mrs. Fielding or Anna Santini before she left, Izzie was gambling that the Spiritualists would be at home in New York City, not traveling on tour as they had been when she first met them for the lessons. She was also gambling that they'd take her in, at least for a while. And lastly, she was hoping that if Anna Santini's gift as a Spiritualist was in some way genuine, in any way at all, she might help Izzie find Clara and Euphora. It was all she had.

On the long train ride, Izzie had plenty of time to ask herself how she would find her sisters. She had no answers. Perhaps it was foolhardy running to New York City to search for Clara and Euphora. Where would she stay if Mrs. Fielding and Anna were not at home or couldn't take her in for some reason? Then what would she do? Mac had given her ten dollars just before she left when he realized he couldn't stop her, but he only thought she was going to Geneva, not New York. Ten dollars was more than ample for anything she might need in Geneva, even bringing her brother and sisters back to Rochester. But what could ten dollars provide in New York City?

Beyond some vague notion that she could find a hotel that she could afford that night when she arrived, she didn't want to think about what she would do if Mrs. Fielding couldn't take her in. As much as possible, she let her mind drift over the snowy fields, rivers, and towns that passed by her train window. She kept her fingers crossed inside her dress pocket.

The trip took all day and it had become a bitterly cold night as Izzie found her way on foot to Mrs. Fielding's on Twenty-Fifth Street. She knew it was dangerous to walk alone with her valise in the dark looking for an address that she had no sense of, but she had asked for directions at the depot and decided to forge on anyway.

Even though it was past suppertime, the streets were dense with people, horses, omnibuses, carriages and carts. The brash street noise grated on her, but the streets were well marked and lighted with gas. She had no problem finding her way, but by the time she reached 231 West 25th Street, she was chilled to the bone, exhausted, and ravenously hungry.

There were lights shining from Mrs. Fielding's windows. Izzie's heart lifted. Someone was inside. She climbed the stairs to the door and knocked. In a short moment, the door drew back and there was Anna Santini.

Black eyes agape, Anna pressed a hand to her throat. "Oh, my, what are you doing on our doorstep? Please come in!" She stepped out onto the stoop, stretched a hand towards Izzie's valise, and took it from her.

"I need your help," Izzie said as she came inside.

Anna swiveled round to face the stairs. "Adele! Come down. You must see who is here." She turned back to Izzie. "Come and sit by the fire. You're blue."

Anna put down the valise and led Izzie into a cozy little parlor. "You've come from Rochester today? Where is your husband the physician?" Anna led Izzie to the fire, took her hands, and looked into her eyes. "You're here because of some trouble."

Izzie nodded. "My husband is in Rochester. I came from Geneva. My sisters are missing. I believe they are here in New York City."

"On their own?"

"I think so."

"Isabelle?" Wearing a blue wool night robe and cap, Mrs. Fielding rushed across the room. She embraced Izzie and kissed one side of her face, then the other. "What are you doing here, my dear?"

"I need your help. Clara and my other sister, Euphora, have disappeared. I have to find them."

"Of course we will help you," Mrs. Fielding said. "Of course, but we are leaving on a one month tour the day after tomorrow."

The need to sit overwhelmed Izzie. She stepped back and fell onto the sofa. Anna and Mrs. Fielding followed her and sat close on either side of her. Izzie untied her bonnet and removed it, settling it on her lap. Shivers were running wild down through her legs and back up.

"What is it dear?"

Izzie turned toward the husky voice. It was a smiling, short man in a blue wool night robe, a masculine version of Mrs. Fielding's. He was round with a full brown beard, crinkles at the sides of his brown eyes, and a large red wart on the bridge of his nose. Mrs. Fielding introduced her husband,

Roland, and explained to him who Izzie was and why she'd arrived. Izzie was surprised there was a Mr. Fielding. She'd always thought of Mrs. Fielding as a widow.

"Well, then. Are you hungry? You must be hungry after your journey," he said.

"Famished."

"I'm off to the kitchen, then. I'll pile you up a plate." Grinning, Roland Fielding left them.

"You must stay here. As long as you like. Mr. Fielding and Katie, our cook, will look after you and you can stay in Anna's room." Her pale red and silver hair flowing down nearly to her elbows, Mrs. Fielding looked across to Anna. "That's all right, isn't it?"

"Yes. Yes. And tomorrow we'll go over the kinds of places you might start looking." Anna squeezed Izzie's hand. "You know...it's a huge city." Her tone was gentle, but warning.

Grateful and relieved, Izzie took a deep breath. She'd have a place to stay.

While she ate the potatoes and cold roast beef brought in by Mr. Fielding, she filled Anna and Mrs. Fielding in on the past months and days. She explained about Mac's Upper Falls Water-Cure Institute and how dedicated he was to it and how it was about to open and how she couldn't expect him to leave and come to New York City. She told them of Mrs. Purcell's death and her fears about Papa's cruelty to Billy and the girls, but she did not tell them about Mrs. Beattie's suspicions, nor did she mention her wakeful nights or the voices she'd heard or the water-cure treatments Mac had been giving her. She was too tired. She knew they'd latch onto the notion of the voices as proof of her potential as a Spiritualist and that would lead to something else, something she couldn't think about. All she wanted to think about was finding Clara and Euphora and if there was the smallest chance Anna or Mrs. Fielding had genuine gifts, Izzie wanted to make use of them.

"Could I ask you to make a spirit circle for me tomorrow before you go? Can the spirits tell us where my sisters are?"

Anna put an arm around Izzie's shoulders. "I don't know, but I can try."

ON A SOFA IN MRS. FIELDING'S STUDY UPSTAIRS, Izzie restlessly slept through the night. The sofa wasn't very comfortable, too short and lumpy, and the room was a chaotic whirlwind of papers, books, and journals stacked randomly on the desk and floor. Piles of journals called *The Spiritual Clarion, Spiritual Age, Banner of Light, Spiritual Telegraph*, and *The Sunbeam* made a semi-circle on the floor around the desk chair. It was such a mess there was scarcely room to walk from one point to another. She felt the urge to read a volume or two, but she was too drained.

She hadn't expected to sleep at all, certain her voices would find her even in New York City, but her voices had left her alone. A blessing. Even so, in the morning she felt sluggish and foggy as she dragged herself downstairs to breakfast. No one was in the small dining room. Katie, the Fielding's Irish domestic, came in with some eggs and biscuits and explained in her brogue that everyone had eaten. Mrs. Fielding and Anna were upstairs packing their trunks.

Later in the parlor, Izzie drank warm coffee from a silver pot. By the third cup the fog had burned off from her mind, but now she was restless and nervous. As she paced about the room, she found paper and pen in a desk. Leaning over, she jotted down a telegram to Mac.

"At home of Spiritualist Mrs. Adele Fielding. 231 West Twenty-Fifth Street, New York City. Mrs. Purcell dead. Billy ran off. Then sisters ran off too. Papa missing. Sheriff hunting Papa. Girls probably here. Must stay to find them."

Then she sat down and fidgeted. These were precious moments. She should be out looking for Clara and Euphora, not sitting here waiting for Anna and Mrs. Fielding. Sheriff Swift's advice, *the sooner, the better,* echoed in her mind. There was frost on the windows, but the sky was blue and the sun was shining brightly. Izzie sipped the dregs of her third cup of coffee and poured herself a fourth. The fire coals glowed red. She had been pampered since arriving at this house. But what about Clara and Euphora? Did they have food and hearth?

With shaking hands, Izzie lowered her cup to its saucer and set it aside. The girls could freeze to death if they were sleeping out in doorways or alleys. Why hadn't she gone to Geneva sooner? Why? What had Papa done to them to make them do something so drastic? *Land sakes.* Had Sam Weston really done what Mrs. Beattie said he did?"

Mr. Fielding swept into the room. "Good news, Isabelle. Mr. Fielding has an acquaintance at the Children's Aid Society and he can take you there today. They know more about missing children than anyone in the city."

"Thank you." Izzie stood and approached Mrs. Fielding. "I have written a telegram for my husband."

"Roland can help you with that, too."

"May we try contacting the spirits now? Is Anna finished her packing?"

"She's coming down. Let's go into the other parlor." Mrs. Fielding strode to a pair of large mahogany doors and thrust them open.

As Izzie followed Mrs. Fielding into the next room, she remembered how Anna answered her verifying question during the spirit lessons over a year ago. Somehow Anna had known, or been told, about Clara being terrified by a white horse in their Ohio yard by moonlight. She said it was Mamma's spirit that told her or spoke through her. Whatever it was, maybe it could tell her how to find her sisters now.

Mrs. Fielding's second parlor was like their own Spirit Room in Geneva, but far more elegant. With just one shaft of brilliant sunshine cutting through a pair of slightly open maroon damask curtains, the room was dusky. The smell of lady's perfumes and men's cologne tickled Izzie's nose. A large linen-covered round table with eight simple chairs sat solidly on a huge red and navy oriental carpet in the middle of the room. Countless chairs lined two of the walls and above them hung three long rows of daguerreotypes, portraits of men and women. An armoire and matching chest of drawers painted with white and yellow flowers were the only other furniture. She wondered if there were there trick bells in the walls and knockers in the floor like Papa had put in their Spirit Room.

"I'm ready." Smiling radiantly, Anna entered wearing a shimmering white silk reform dress. The short dress, which covered her trousers, was tailored like a man's greatcoat. Very exotic, thought Izzie.

Mrs. Fielding closed the doors, then the curtains. She lit a single white candle on the table.

"Let's see who we can call on to help you, Izzie," Anna said.

"Can we call on my mother? Remember how she communicated in Geneva?"

"I'll try."

Mrs. Fielding pulled three chairs some distance from the table, making a small circle. She stood behind one of them and Anna sat in it. Then she gestured to one of the other chairs, inviting Izzie to join.

Throwing her head backward, Mrs. Fielding brushed her hands through the air over Anna's head, down her back, along her arms. She seemed to be petting Anna as she would a dog, but she never touched her, her palms drifting several inches above Anna. There was a routine to it, as though they'd done this many times before.

Anna, with a faint smile on her face, closed her eyes and began to breathe deeply. For a few more moments Mrs. Fielding kept at the petting motion and then Anna's ceaseless smile finally drifted away and her face grew distant. Mrs. Fielding finished with her air-smoothing gestures and sat in the remaining chair. Taking Anna's hand, she nodded, indicating that Izzie should pick up Anna's other hand. Mrs. Fielding's hand was small and cool while Anna's was full and warm with a slight tingle running through it.

When Mrs. Fielding closed her eyes, Izzie did the same. Anna's breathing was loud and slow. Izzie listened to carriages rattling by outside and then a series of thuds somewhere in the house, perhaps the trunks being brought downstairs. Muffled voices burbled on and off. A clock tick-tocked. More labored breathing from Anna. More carriages rattling. People talking out on the street. How long was Anna going to take to go into a trance anyway?

"Someone is here. A man. He's not familiar to me. He says he's your grandfather."

Izzie squeezed Anna's hand. "I didn't know either of my grandfathers. Which one?"

"Father's. His name is Grady?"

"Gregory."

"He worked on a dairy farm in England. He was proud of his herd."

"Yes." Izzie squirmed forward in her chair. "Papa told me that. Can he help me find Clara?"

"Ask him."

Izzie swallowed. "Grandfather, where are my sisters?"

"They are not harmed."

"Where are they?"

"Everyone is gone. Sons and daughters. Husbands and wives."

"But where?"

"Some far. Some close. Some here. Your mother is here."

"Now? Is she there with you, now? Mamma?"

"No, not here."

What on earth did that mean? Here, not here. Izzie jiggled her knee up and down a few times, but realized it was disrupting the calm of the circle and stopped.

"How can I find Clara and Euphora?"

"They are with you."

"Try to be specific, Isabelle," Mrs. Fielding said.

"He's gone." Anna's voice sounded scratchy. She held still a moment. "Izzie, ask for your mother to speak."

Izzie's hand grew clammy inside Anna's, which now felt inflamed. "Mamma, can you speak to me?"

More silence. Izzie jiggled her knee once, but stopped immediately.

"Go on, Henry. Not today." Anna sounded stern. "We don't have time for you. We want Isabelle's mother. No...Maybe later...This is urgent. Please." She squeezed Izzie's hand. "I'm sorry, Izzie. He's very annoying most of the time. I can't seem to get rid of him."

Anna resumed breathing deeply again. This time it felt like a half hour. Izzie wanted to dash out into the streets and scream out, "Clara, Euphora! I'm here! Where are you?" Maybe by some fluke, some stray chance, they'd hear her. She sighed. No, that was ridiculous. Anna did truly seem to be communicating with spirits, but the message wasn't helpful at all—a grandfather boasting about his cows and speaking broadly about the family. She had no use for that. Then there's this Henry intruding on their efforts. Maybe the spirits were really there for Anna, but it was nothing but hogwash so far. And the day was passing by. Her sisters were out there somewhere.

"In the gutter." A man's voice spoke clearly.

Izzie jerked back her hands. She glanced around. "What was that?"

There was no one else in the room. The candle on the table was flickering wildly as though catching a wind. Anna and Mrs. Fielding, eyes open now, watched her.

"What was what?" Mrs. Fielding leaned toward Izzie.

"I heard someone say 'in the gutter'. Didn't you hear it?"

Anna's dark eyes met Mrs. Fielding's, then she looked at Izzie. "That was a spirit speaking to you."

"No. No. It must have been someone outside on the street. I'm a little muddled today."

"Anna isn't having much luck. It may be that the spirits don't want to tell you where Clara and Euphora are. They have their ways." Mrs. Fielding motioned toward the ceiling. "Would you like to try to communicate with this spirit you just heard?"

"No. I truly think it was outside on the street." Izzie crossed her arms.

"Are you sure?"

"Yes. I'm sure. Perhaps I should go now to the Children's Aid Society and speak with Mr. Fielding's acquaintance. I can't sit here any longer." She bolted up and looked at Anna. "Perhaps we can try this evening."

"Maybe the planchette."

"All right."

The *dang* planchette. It was all too much like the old days at the Spirit Room. This trick and that. Giving people just the tip of the iceberg, but nothing more. A grandfather with cows. Memories of a mother. How on earth was she going to find her sisters?

"I'll get Roland. He'll take you over there. You can send your telegram to your husband on the way. I'm sorry, dear. I'm sure your sisters are surviving somehow. You'll find them. I know you will."

THAT NIGHT, after Mrs. Fielding's attempts at the planchette yielded nothing but more contradictions, Izzie asked to be excused and skipped dinner. She lay on the sofa in Mrs. Fielding's study in the dark. She missed Mac. She missed his tall, warm body, his lemony smell, and the way he looked at her with his brown eyes. She missed the way he said her name. She wanted him to be here, to hold her, to help her look for her sisters. Of course with his Water-Cure Institute nearly ready to open, he couldn't be with her, but she didn't care about that right now. She wanted him with her in the dark.

She pulled the blanket up to her chin. What she had heard from Mr. Charles Brace at the Children's Aid Society earlier in the day had discouraged and scared her. Children without homes usually ended up in trouble, he'd said. They slept in cellar doors or wagons or any covered spot. They started out as hucksters if they were cunning enough. Homeless children, along with children from poor homes, sold things to passersby on the streets—tea cakes, baked pears, candy, hot corn. "You'll see them on every corner," he'd told her.

Or they hawked things home to home—matchsticks, vegetables, scrub brushes, pins. If they got even more desperate, they'd scavenge from the docks, a bit of sugar or coffee, or things from private doorways, perhaps an umbrella, even the brass doorknob itself. Then they'd try to sell it. "That kind of thing can get them into the juvenile house of correction."

Izzie stared at the study window glowing with streetlight. Tears rolled out of her eyes and streamed down her face. Clara and Euphora couldn't end up in a juvenile house of correction. They just couldn't.

"All in all, it's harder for girls," Brace had said. "They're not as free as the boys to sleep out. Even the very young girls can end up in the brothels. It's a hard fact. I hope your sisters don't end up that way, but it's a hard fact, hard as nails. If they are lucky, they'll end up in one of our municipal orphanages, even though they aren't officially orphans. We've got an adoption program that sends orphanage children to farms in the Midwest. We ship them by train. I'm quite proud of that. But I'm sure you'll find them before that possibility comes up."

When Izzie explained that Clara and Euphora were used to working and were both industrious, he softened a bit.

"Maybe they'll both get work, but the city is teeming with thousands and thousands of immigrants looking for jobs. They're pouring off those boats every day like pounding rain. Some young women piece their living together and stay in a cheap boardinghouse. If you are going looking, I'd start with the orphanages and boardinghouses. If you go to the rotten tenements, Five Points or Corlears Hook, take a man with you, and I wouldn't worry about the brothels right away. It takes a while for good girls to make their way there."

Izzie wiped her eyes with the corner of the blanket. That voice in the morning. What had it said? "In the gutter." The tears started again. She cried hard until she was too weary to cry anymore. Starting tomorrow she would look everywhere there was to look, every orphanage, every boardinghouse, every doorway, every corner.

Thirty-Eight

CLARA LOOKED DOWN the twenty-two rows of women leaning over sewing machines, eleven on each side with an aisle down the middle.

"I've got a waiting list of twenty-nine ahead of you that can all do the work just fine." Mr. Stebbins crossed his arms over his barrel chest.

"I have training. I worked with a milliner in Geneva. She taught me the machine."

"Doesn't matter I'm afraid. I know you are here because of my friend, Mr. Hogarth, but it still doesn't matter. It wouldn't be fair if I took you ahead of the twenty-nine. I told him that plain and clear."

A seamstress nearby sneezed. Clara's shoulder jerked up.

Mr. Stebbins gave Clara a head-to-toe scan. "You're not sick are you?"

She shook her head.

"You might find outwork. Here's a place to try." Stebbins walked to his desk, dipped a pen into an inkbottle and scratched something out on a scrap of paper. "I'll put you on my list, number thirty." He opened a ledger. "What's the name again?"

"Clara Benton."

He wrote her name and "Hogarth" after it about half way down a page. "I'll tell Hogarth when your name comes up. It might be six months, a year. Maybe sooner. The girls come and go." He handed her the scrap of paper.

Hell-fire. Six months to a year. And this was a factory where she had an introduction. She looked up at the row of large filthy windows.

"Thank you, sir."

"I'm sorry I can't do more, Miss Benton. That's the way it is."

On her way back to the boardinghouse, Clara got lost. At breakfast that morning, two of the lodgers told her how to find Stebbins's factory, but warned her not to ask strangers on the street, especially men, for directions or anything else. She could be duped and raped, they told her. They'd all heard stories recently. So when Clara became disoriented, and there were men on every block who whistled and cackled at her, she walked on and on searching for streets named with numbers. She could follow those. But for a long, wearing time, she wandered only streets named with words—Bowery, Henry, Forsyth, Eldridge, Orchard, Allen—until finally, there was First Street, then Second, then Third. When she arrived at Thirteenth Street, she explored in one direction, then the other until she found her new home.

THE WOMEN AT THE BOARDINGHOUSE had explained all about work to Clara a number of times over breakfast. If she were employed in a factory on a regular basis, she could earn three or three and a half dollars a week, maybe even six dollars on a sewing machine, twice what she'd get for the outwork. Before Clara inquired with the piecework man from Mr. Stebbins's scrap of paper, she wanted to try some of the other factories. She made up her own list by asking everyone at the house the factories they knew, where they had worked in the past, where they worked now, where friends or family worked.

When Sunday came, Clara went to the Hogarths to visit Euphora. She sat with her sister on a wood bench at the worktable in the middle of the kitchen. They drank warm milk and Euphora told Clara all about the Hogarths and Clara told Euphora all about Hannah and the girls and women at her lodging house. Euphora moved about the kitchen as though she'd been born there, thought Clara. Her little sister had learned well how to handle pots and stoves, vegetables, meats, flour, things Clara knew almost nothing about.

Euphora's tiny pantry room was finished. She had a mattress and several quilts, a small chest for her personal things and a couple of hooks to hang her clothes on. A shelf held a few old books and a round blue atlas that the Hogarths had from a son who had grown and gone away. It didn't feel like a pantry at all anymore, but a cozy nest. Even though Euphora seemed a little lonely, she was safe and that was good enough for now.

DURING THE NEXT THREE WEEKS Clara and Hannah set out together every morning. They'd walk together in the cold, Hannah showing Clara the way to a factory address. Only one of them would go inside to inquire. They knew no one would hire both of them at once and they agreed it would be devastating if a foreman picked one over the other. They walked back and forth and uptown and down visiting any factory that hired females. They crisscrossed the Bowery time after time, watching the young men and women on parade there. It was different than Broadway, Hannah told her. "These are the young people who work in the shops and factories. They're more ours than them on Broadway. But I want to find my husband on Broadway, not here."

Hannah went on to describe the variety and minstrel shows and oyster shops and ice cream parlors, the balls at Tammany Hall, the dance halls, and firehouses.

"They call the young men Bowery b'hoys with an "h" after the "b" in boy. I don't know why, and the girls are gals," Hannah said.

In their odd brash dress of stripes and checkers and gaudy colors—bright reds, pinks, yellows, and green with maroon— they seemed confident, these b'hoys and gals, like the world belonged to them. The gals wore trim hats, not bonnets that hid their eyes, and they strutted up and down in bands with other gals or they hung on the arm of a swaggering b'hoy. Clara felt envious. They had work, money to spend, spirited clothing, and each other.

"Don't you want to be one of these gals, Hannah, free and roaming, not someone's wife? Don't you wish that was us parading like that?"

"It would be fun, I suppose, but not for long."

During those first weeks of trying to find work, she and Hannah asked after bookbinding and book sewing, umbrella sewing, type rubbing, straw sewing, shirt sewing, both by machine and hand. Sometimes toward the end of the day Clara got so tired and chilled that she'd cry on her way to the next factory. Hannah would lead her by the hand to a Negro woman or a child at the street corner and coax her into buying a sweet potato or baked pear or hot-corn and while they shared it, Hannah would say hopeful things. "It'll be the next one. I know it will." "It just takes time." "We can always do the outside piece work and keep each other company."

The food and Hannah's spirit warmed Clara. She'd dry her eyes, then trudge into another factory and ask another foreman for work. "Come back in April. Maybe I could use you for a month." "I don't need any more girls." "How old are you anyway? I don't take them under sixteen."

Late at night, Clara would listen to the sound of Hannah weeping quietly in bed and then Clara would whisper back to her new friend the same things Hannah had said earlier. "It just takes time. It'll be the next one."

When it was time to pay the rent at the lodging house, Clara loaned Hannah the money for another week. Then Clara visited the man Stebbins had recommended and brought home a sack of muslin strips to make shirt cuffs. Hannah sewed with her each night by candlelight.

Every day for the next week, they visited factories. At night they made a few cents on the piecework. When they were finished with the cuffs or sleeves or collars, in the dark, before they slept, they'd take turns saying the bad names they would shout at the foremen if only they could.

"Stinkpot."

"Pig."

"Booger."

"Rat."

"Swine."

"Beast."

"Shit."

Then they'd giggle until Clara was so exhausted she'd miss a turn and then they'd both fall asleep. Once they discovered the name calling, Hannah didn't cry anymore.

ON CLARA'S FOURTH SUNDAY VISIT TO EUPHORA, she saw right away that Euphora's face was sallow and her mouth tight. It was the same look Euphora would get when Papa was stewed to the ears and yelling at Billy.

"What is it, Euphora? What's wrong?" Clara stepped into the kitchen.

"Mrs. Hogarth wants to talk to us together."

"What about?"

"She wouldn't say. Only that we had to be together. Do you think she has to let me go?"

"I don't know."

Biting at a fingernail, Clara followed Euphora to the parlor. *Tarnation.* Mrs. Hogarth was going to tell them Euphora couldn't stay there? What else could it be? What would they do now? Without a job, how could Clara take care of Euphora? How the blazes could they find another domestic situation for her sister? They didn't know anyone to ask.

Mrs. Hogarth was sitting with quilting work by the coal fire. She held a red and blue patch between the two fingers on her left hand, and a needle and thread in her right.

"Girls, come in and sit down."

Euphora took a seat on a small pink sofa and sat close to her, leaning into her sister's shoulder.

"Clara, I understand our friend Mr. Stebbins couldn't take you on now at the umbrella factory. I am sorry, but he tells us you are on his waiting list. Can you make do until your name comes up?"

"I still have some savings and I have some piecework and I am asking at other factories."

"I am sorry. We hoped Mr. Stebbins could take you straight away. We wish we could help you more, but we just make our own rent and with Euphora to feed, there's not a penny left over at the end of the month."

Euphora couldn't eat all that much, Clara thought. She worked every day and evening except for these few hours on Sunday and they were only paying her seventy-five cents a week. Maybe that's all it was that Mrs. Hogarth was going to tell them. Maybe they were going to withdraw the wages. Maybe they could still keep her working just for meals and room.

"We've had sad, terrible news. We got a letter from my cousin's other boarders, the Carter sisters." Mrs. Hogarth's two fingers flicked uncontrollably. The quilt square slipped off her lap. "My cousin, Mrs. Purcell, had a deathly accident. She slipped on the ice on her porch stairs late at night and passed away. It was right after you left." Mrs. Hogarth's throat convulsed. "The Carters were in Boston at the time and the following weeks so it took a while for them to write. They say your father disappeared the night of the accident and the sheriff is still looking for him."

Clara fell back against the sofa, the air sucked right out of her. Euphora turned, blue eyes wide, and gawked at her. Clara couldn't speak.

Mrs. Hogarth's two fingers twitched like a giant spider squiggling around in her lap. "The Carters found our address among Emma's things. They also told us that Mrs. Purcell left the house and all its contents to them in her will. They don't know you two are here, do they? Emma said no one knew."

Clara shook her head.

"If your father had anything to do with Emma's death, he deserves to be hung. If he somehow traces you here, I will bring in the police right away. I mean it. The second he shows his face, either Mr. Hogarth or I will be out that back door on our way to the police."

Trembling against Euphora's shoulder, Clara slumped down, but then Euphora stiffened and sat up straight as a pine tree.

"May I still stay and work for you, Mrs. Hogarth?"

Mrs. Hogarth's bitterness melted from her eyes. "Oh, yes, dear. You may stay. Mr. Hogarth and I want you to stay, but if your father comes here, it could be very complicated. He has the right to take you away, but we have the right to call in the police. I think you should consider going to your older sister's in Rochester."

"Not yet. He would find us there for certain," Clara said.

Euphora jumped up. "May we go to the kitchen now?"

"Of course, dear." Mrs. Hogarth said, looking a little surprised.

Clara was surprised too. Euphora wasn't crying. She didn't even seem shaken. She seemed cool and distant. It wasn't like her at all. Clara was still trembling on the sofa, feeling too heavy to even get up. Had Papa anything to do with Mrs. Purcell's accident? She thought about Mrs. Purcell's white flowing hair and how brave she was holding her lantern up high the night that Papa was drunk on the stairs. She had saved her and Euphora and Billy that night. Now she was dead. Papa was gone. Where would he go? There was no way he could find them here at the Hogarth's. Maybe he would travel somewhere new and far like he'd talked about, where no one knew him. He'd want that.

"Come on, Clara." Euphora reached over, took Clara's hands and pulled her up off the sofa. "I made biscuits this morning and we have honey. Would you like me to bring you some, Mrs. Hogarth?"

"No, you girls go on."

When they got back to the kitchen, Clara sat on the bench at the table while Euphora gathered biscuits, butter, and honey and plunked them in front of Clara.

"I wish Billy were here with us. I wish he had run away to New York with us so we could be together. Do you think there's any chance he's here somewhere?" Clara asked.

"He never said anything about New York City. It was always the Freedom Fighters and Kansas. Don't worry, Clara. Papa's gone. We don't know where, but he's gone." She picked up a knife and buttered a biscuit, then dripped a golden dollop of honey onto it. "Here. Eat this. Mrs. Purcell always said tea and a buttered biscuit could fix just about anything."

The mouthful was sweet and thick, but hard to swallow. Clara didn't like not knowing where Papa was or Billy, either. She didn't like it at all.

Thirty-Nine

EET ACHING AND RAW, Izzie was dragging her way back to Mrs. Fielding's at dusk. The few times in her first week of searching for her sisters that she hadn't made it back to Mrs. Fielding's before dark, she'd had exchanges with men on the street that she didn't like. Since then she'd kept a dusk curfew. In four weeks of searching, she'd been to over a hundred boardinghouses, all the almshouses twice, and all the other charities that helped women and children two or three times each. Every child huddled in a doorway, every young girl peddling matches or hothouse radishes on the street was Euphora or Clara until she got close enough to see their faces. Her feet blistered on that first day, then bled on the second day, and bled again every day after that. At night, in the kitchen, Katie, the Fielding's cook, would prepare a lukewarm bucket of water for her to soak her feet in.

Izzie hoped her boots would hold up. She had no money for new ones. This evening she was rushing home from work because Mrs. Fielding and Anna would be arriving home from their Spiritualism tour. She longed to see them again. Having slept in Anna's room these weeks, and having lived in the Fielding home, and having read through many of the Spiritualism journals in Mrs. Fielding's study, and having

been escorted about town on numerous occasions by Roland
Fielding, she felt she knew Anna and Mrs. Fielding quite well.
They'd become friends to her while they were away. She
picked up her pace as she pictured the two women greeting
her with warm smiles.

She had been lonely. Roland Fielding had been very kind,
taking her to a few of the crowded tenement neighborhoods
the Children's Aid Society man had suggested, the Irish
neighborhoods on the west side, the Jewish and Italian
neighborhoods east of Bowery, and Five Points, but Roland
Fielding didn't want to spend much time in those places.
There were swarms of poor immigrants. He was dressed too
well and got too many stares. It made him nervous. "One of
these waifs or urchins is about to pick my pockets, Isabelle.
We best move along," he'd say when he was particularly on
edge.

Sometimes she'd go without him. She'd put on a plain
dress and go back to these neighborhoods in the mornings on
her own. She knew how to fit in. It wasn't as foreign a land to
her as it was to Roland Fielding.

Maybe there'd be another letter from Mac this evening.
She'd had a dozen letters from him begging her to come
home. He wrote that her attempts would end in vain, that
New York City was too snarled and overflowing for her to
find her sisters, even if they were there. He needed her by his
side at the Upper Falls Water-Cure Institute, which was now
open and had its first customers. He'd already sold the house
and was going to move their furniture to their quarters at the
Institute in a couple of weeks. It seemed so odd that the home
she knew with Mac was hers no more.

When she returned to him, it would be to his professional
residence, not their cozy little honeymoon home in Corn
Hill. She'd answered him right away, saying that she believed

she would certainly succeed in finding her sisters and she couldn't leave yet. Surely he would eventually understand that she had to do everything she could to retrieve Clara and Euphora. So far he had not. His letters were angry.

Something slammed her shoulder hard, jolting her. She turned. A young, nicely dressed man in stovepipe hat and black greatcoat fleeted away behind her. He didn't slow to apologize, but kept on, disappearing into the crowd.

She entered the house, then swiftly shed her shawl and bonnet. The rooms were lit. Voices emanated from the front parlor. One voice rose above. It was Anna's. Izzie hurried to the doorway.

And there was Mac. Mac. Her heart leapt. Mrs. Fielding, Anna, Roland, and tall, wonderful, Mac were all there.

"Mac."

He turned toward her, his face full of longing, and came rushing to her, knocking against the side of the sofa.

"My dear." He took up both her hands and kissed them several times.

She slid her arms around his waist and pulled him against her. She wanted to feel him against her. He was solid, warm, strong. He held her firmly in return.

"Thank goodness you're all right," he said.

"You're here."

When they separated, the others were standing nearby. Anna and Mrs. Fielding both glowed at her and took turns greeting her with kisses. Roland beamed from a few steps away.

"I told him you both must stay here with us. I won't have you going to a hotel," Mrs. Fielding took Izzie's hand.

"I'll sleep on the sofa in the study," Anna said.

"We'll only be a night or two. We'll stay wherever you like, Izzie." Mac's brow furrowed down. His beautiful, dear eyes looked worried. He had been fretting.

"You can't stay longer?" Izzie leaned toward him a little.

"I mean to take you home, my dear."

She drew back, looked at the other faces. They were all serious. She clenched her fists.

"I haven't found Clara and Euphora, yet. I can't leave. When I saw you standing there, I hoped you were here to help me."

"You know I can't."

"Now, now. You two need a long husband and wife talk, but I suggest we have dinner first. Anna and I are completely worn." Mrs. Fielding marched to the doorway. "And you, Doctor MacAdams? I'm sure you're worn from your travels as well." She turned to her husband. "Roland, will you pick something out of your wine cellar for our meal? And tell Katie we'll sit down in half an hour. Anna, come and get your trunk and move it to my study."

Adele Fielding, hoop skirt wide as a loveseat, gathered the front of it and started up the stairs. Anna scurried up just behind her and Roland headed for the kitchen.

"She's right." Mac's narrow face was gentle. "Let's sit by the fire. Tell me where you think your sisters might be. And about the voices. Tell me everything." He paused a moment, his eyes searching hers. "You're very thin. Do you feel well?"

"I am somewhat fatigued." She felt her shoulders come down, fists unclench. She sighed and led him to the sofa, then sat close to him so she could feel his shoulder. "I don't want to talk about anything, yet. I'm afraid we'll argue. I've missed you. I want a few moments." She clasped her hands waiting for him to launch into the reasons she had to go home with him.

"I understand." He plied her hands apart and held one between his.

She leaned her head against his shoulder, smelled his lemon and sweat, felt the coarseness of his wool coat against her face, heard his quiet breathing. He caressed her hand. His touch was dry and warm. Then time stopped. There was nothing but Mac and the fire.

AFTER DINNER, SITTING ON ANNA'S BED in her pantalettes and shimmy, Izzie slipped off her second stocking. As it came off, it stuck to her open blisters and stung. She cringed.

"My God, look at your feet. They're swollen and blistered." In his long johns, Mac knelt down in front of her and lifted her ankle toward him.

"I walk all day looking for the girls."

"We have to take care of this. You might get an infection and that could lead to gangrene."

"No. I'll be all right. They'll heal soon enough. That's how it works, isn't it? They'll get tougher?" She touched his long bristly sideburn. "Let's go to bed."

He let her foot drop, then rose up on his knees. He pressed her legs apart and leaned in to kiss her. His lips were warm and moist, his long mustache scratchy and sweet against her face. She felt a rush charge all the way up into her throat. After his lips lingered on hers a moment, he drew back.

"You are the most lovely woman, Izzie." His deep gaze tugged at her. "No bed, though, until we take care of your feet. I'm sure the Fieldings have some kind of ointment for this. I'll go and see."

"It can wait."

"No it can't. I'll be right back."

He put his trousers and shirt back on and left. While he was gone, Izzie put her nightdress on and waited for him. She still didn't want to talk about staying or going. She wanted to hold him, feel him naked against her. That's what she needed, not talk.

In a few moments, Mac returned with a grin on his face. "I've got some Holloway's Ointment. It will help. Why didn't you use this before?"

"I don't know. I was soaking them in water every night."

"To clean them, that's all right, but not to bring the skin back. That's one thing water isn't very good at."

"I thought water could cure everything." She laughed, trying to tease but he didn't respond.

Even though he was gentle as he rubbed the ointment onto her feet, as he touched the sores, pain shot though her. She jerked back her foot several times but he steadied it. By the time he finished, her feet were throbbing.

"I'm dead serious. You must come home with me, Izzie. This search is in vain. The girls could be anywhere by now. You look emaciated."

"I waited too long. I should have brought them to Rochester so long ago."

He sat next to her on the bed. "You couldn't have known things were as bad as they were."

"I should have known. I knew Papa was different after Mamma died."

All three of her siblings, the twins only fourteen, and Euphora only twelve, were out there somewhere all on their own. Maybe Papa was hunting them down like a bloodhound after runaway slaves. Maybe he'd already found them and taken them somewhere.

"I've missed you, Mac."

"I've missed you, too. Terribly. The Upper Falls Water-Cure is meaningless without you."

His eyes were dark as a midnight lake. She wanted to feel his skin against hers. She scooted back on the bed, drew back the quilt, and slid under. She reached an inviting hand toward him.

"Let's not talk about going back to Rochester. We're here now," she said.

As Mac undressed, the sight of his black-haired chest made her smile. He crawled under the covers with her and slid an arm over her stomach.

"Brrr. It's bloody cold out there," he said. "Are you still doing the water douche, my love?"

"No. I had no reason."

He drew back his arm. "We shouldn't then."

"Do you have one of your French Safes?"

"I'm afraid not. I'll get some tomorrow." He swung away from her and lay on his back, crooking an arm under his head.

It didn't matter, she thought. She'd longed for him every moment she was away from him. She rolled toward him, kissed his neck, his wiry sideburn. She raised herself onto his torso, her bosoms coming alive against him. She kissed his mouth.

For a brief moment his hands held her upper arms firmly as though he might push her back, but she kept kissing him, delicately, then she let her tongue search between his lips. After a moment, he pulled up her shimmy, took it off her and steered her fully on top of him. A flush of excitement exploded inside her. She pressed into him with all her weight, then slid over him. The friction of skin against skin made her dizzy. She spread her legs apart and he guided his erect member inside her.

He kissed her hard, embraced her tightly, then rolled her over onto her back and began to pump slowly inside her. She was completely open, pulling and pushing with him, her hands tight on his lower back.

Breathing deep into her belly, she was aroused beyond anything she'd felt before. Waves upon waves floated through her pelvis, her back, her legs. She moaned and moaned. And just as the waves subsided, Mac called out "Izzie, Izzie, my love."

They lay still for a while. He stayed sweetly inside her. Then he withdrew and she nestled into him. She listened to his heart beating and then, when she heard his light snore, she drifted off.

At the gray light of dawn, Izzie woke and found that Mac was sitting up in bed next to her. She reached an arm around his waist. He leaned over and kissed her head.

"We'll go tomorrow. I have train tickets. I want to visit Trall today and see his New York Hygieo-Therapeutic College on Laight Street. I'd like you to come."

"Haven't you heard a word I've said? I'm staying to look for Clara and Euphora."

"Yes, but rather, did you hear me? I said you have no idea where they are. When they can, they'll send word to Rochester, because that's where they think you are. They don't think you are here. What if they were to show up there today? You are making it all more confusing than it needs to be."

This was the most obstinate thing she'd ever heard from him. She locked her jaw and thumped herself up against the bed board next to him.

"I'm not leaving."

"Be reasonable, my love. I beg you. You are not thinking clearly. You're worried. It's clouding your mind. And you are withering away."

"I've been worried for months. If I had acted instead of stayed home and let you wrap me in a sheet like a sausage twice a day, this might not have happened."

He took her hand, but she yanked it back. She reached for her shimmy on top of the quilt, tugged it on, then crawled out of bed.

"You haven't told me about the voices yet," he said.

Shivering from the chill in the room, she plopped down in the chair by Anna's writing table, and said nothing. Mac got up and rummaged in his bag. He lifted out his brown wool robe. That color had always been handsome on him. It reminded her of their nights at home. He put it on and tied the sash around his waist.

"Do you have your robe here?" he asked.

"In the armoire."

He found it and brought it to her, then helped her into it. Why did he have to be considerate in these little things, but not be able to understand the greater things? Delicately, he took her chin in his hand and attempted to raise her face up, but she refused him. She didn't want to see him close, his bushy brow, his brown magnetic eyes, the sweet purple scar on his chin, his mussed wavy hair. She might lose her resolve.

He returned to the bed and sat. "What about the voices? Are they still disturbing you at night?"

"Why? Why do you want to know about that? So you can take me home and wrap me in the wet sheets?"

"I am only trying to care for you." He sounded calm.

Sighing, she rose from Anna's chair and stood by the desk. "A few times. They've disturbed me a few times, but not every night."

Locking his jaw, he nodded quietly. *Drat.* Why did she tell him that? Why did she tell him anything?

"That seems like an improvement. Perhaps the water-cure wasn't the right path."

She was trembling inside, but he seemed completely unruffled.

"No, I don't think it was."

"If you return with me, we can explore other remedies. Perhaps pure rest."

"Stop it." She stood. "Stop. I will only say it one more time. I am staying here to search for my sisters."

He came close to her, took her hand. "Izzie, please." She tried to back away from him, but he wouldn't release her. "You must see it is best for you at home. You must."

"No." She wriggled her hand from his and crossed her arms. "It is not best."

"You are my wife."

"Does that mean I am not a sister too?"

"It means I am first." A growl slipped into his voice.

She grabbed a book from Anna's desk and thrust it at him. He flung his arms up to shield his face. The book hit him and dropped with a thud. Watching her carefully, his face flushed, he brushed his hair back with both hands.

"Not only am I staying here, but I am going to try a trance tomorrow," she said.

As her words spewed out, they surprised her. She hadn't said such a thing to herself yet. But she was ready. If there were any possibility she could hear Mamma, or anyone on earth or in other spheres who might lead her to her sisters, she would try it. If there were truly spirits, then they could see Clara and Euphora, and if they could speak through her, she could find her sisters. And if she lost her sanity altogether, so be it. So be it.

"But why? Have you changed? Do you believe this Spiritualist nonsense now?"

"You are always experimenting with ideas, Mac. Now I must experiment with the spiritual realm. I must."

"Can't you leave it to Mrs. Fielding and Miss Santini? What if your voices become more than you can bear? You shouldn't encourage this aspect of yourself. It's dangerous. You may end up in the State Lunatic Asylum in Utica."

"I have to try." She turned from him, stepped to the window, and drew the curtain back. Snow was falling in the dull light of dawn. The deserted street was already covered in white. "Then I will know once and for all about myself, and you will too, and if I am very fortunate, I will find my sisters."

Two riders on a black horse, a man and a boy, approached from the east.

"It's perilous," Mac said.

"How?" She spun from the window and looked at him.

"The voices you hear have already made your mind vulnerable." His brown eyes were concerned, not angry.

"I want you to witness my trance. Will you?"

"I beg you not to try this. Come home with me. I'll find a treatment for you."

She remembered the wet sheet, cold, damp, and constraining around her.

"Will you witness my trance, Mac?"

He was silent. She looked out at the snow again. The riders and horse had passed below her, leaving the snow disturbed. She wouldn't look into his eyes. She might give in. She might get on the train with him and go home—their new home together.

"Yes."

Finally, she looked at him. "You won't interfere with whatever Mrs. Fielding and Anna do?"

"No, but my promise is only good for tomorrow."

She went to him then, took his hand and pressed his cool palm against the side of her face. "I was hoping you would be with me."

Forty

As Izzie and Mac waited for Mrs. Fielding and Anna in the parlor to attempt the trance, Izzie was so nervous, she felt faint.

"Will I die?"

"What do you mean?" Mac asked.

"If I let the voices in, will I lose myself completely? They'll take my soul."

"I don't know. You won't die, though. You'll still be in there." Smiling, he tapped her forehead gently as though knocking on a door.

She glanced at the parlor doors again. Anna and Mrs. Fielding had said they'd be here at noon. They were late.

"I may faint."

"I've never seen you this way. Please change your mind, Izzie."

"Don't ask me that again."

He nodded, then paced away from her through the outer parlor toward the front door. She was spinning a bit and grasped the fireplace mantel to steady herself. The house door clicked open.

"We're sorry to be late." Mrs. Fielding was suddenly at the door with Mac.

"Izzie is quite rattled. May we get it over with?"

Mac's sentiments weren't very different from her own. She desperately wanted the trance over with as well.

Beaming, Anna came in and walked directly to her and touched her hands. "It's all right. You won't be harmed."

Looking down, Izzie saw that her own hands were clasped so tightly that her fingers had turned red, her knuckles white. Mrs. Fielding was moving with purpose about the room, setting out four chairs around a small marble-top table, closing the maroon damask curtains, and lastly lighting a candle. When done with her tasks, she joined Izzie and the others by the fire.

"You are awfully pale, my dear," Mrs. Fielding said. "Anna is telling you the truth. You won't be harmed. If you hear or see anything you don't want to hear or see, you just ask the spirit to leave. They are usually respectful."

"They aren't, though," Izzie said.

"What do you mean?"

"I've only told Mac this." Izzie glanced at Mac, then looked back at Mrs. Fielding. "I hear voices, many voices, at night, in the dark. I tell them to leave and they don't unless I have light."

Mrs. Fielding's mouth dropped a bit as she exchanged looks with Anna. "You're clairaudient. Then, we must teach you how to listen and how to not listen."

"You can do that?" Mac crossed his arms.

Nostrils flaring, Mrs. Fielding threw back her head and looked up to Mac's face looming down. "It is a skill all mediums must learn. Izzie has a gift, but she has much to learn." She swept her arm toward the daguerreotypes on the wall. "Your wife is about to join the famed Spiritualists of our time. Mr. Fishbough. Mrs. Eliza Farnham. Mrs. Emma Hardinge. Miss Cora Scott. Mrs. Edgeworth from your own Rochester. Our dear friend Mrs. Kellogg." Blue eyes aglow, she looked directly at Izzie. "And soon, after a little training, I suspect we'll be taking Isabelle down to one of the daguerreotype studios on Broadway so that we can add her portrait.

"I only want to find my sisters, Mrs. Fielding."

Mrs. Fielding shot another look at Anna. "Yes. Yes. One step at a time. I'm sorry, dear. I do get carried away."

Mac's jaw stiffened. "She may be a Spiritualist, or she may be playing with delusion. You'll promise me that we will stop your exercise if she seems endangered."

"Of course, but there is no danger. You'll see her talent for yourself. It has been obvious to me since we met in Geneva."

Izzie swallowed. She was ready to go on, ready to listen to her voices. She was at the top of a high river ledge, ready to jump into the flowing water. Now or never. She had to jump now or she would back away. She had to find her sisters.

Izzie felt Anna's arm slide around the back of her waist and start to steer her toward the chairs. Lowering his voice to a snarly whisper, Mac continued to speak to Mrs. Fielding. Izzie heard snippets. "Delusion." "Fragile." "Fear."

"Breathe in slowly, breathe out slowly, in slowly, out slowly." Like lapping waves at the edge of a lake, Anna's voice soothed her. Anna took Izzie's hand and began to stroke it.

Izzie directed her thoughts to the pictures on the wall, the women in their broad, hoop dresses and men in their cravats and black coats. Somehow they comforted her. There were so many who had all done what she was about to do, who had all done in earnest what she and Clara had done in jest. Mrs. Fielding brought an alphabet, paper, ink, and pen to the table.

"If a spirit comes to you, I'll ask the questions." Sitting next to her, Mrs. Fielding took Izzie's other hand. "You are the medium. That means you are the vessel or instrument for one of us to speak to the spirits. I'll ask about Clara and Euphora and where they are."

Still breathing deeply and slowly with Anna's guidance, Izzie nodded. Mac took the seat across from her.

She smiled at him. "I'll be fine."

Blinking rapidly, he scratched at the purple scar on his chin. "I'll be patient but not too patient."

"Close your eyes, Isabelle," Mrs. Fielding said. "Allow your breathing to relax now. Clear your mind and listen for a voice."

The sensation of both her hands being held and caressed pacified her. Gradually, peacefulness descended over her like light snow. Izzie concentrated on the snow, but not the snow here on West Twenty-Fifth Street. She saw the snow covering a great wide empty field like she had seen from the train window. Empty. White. She moved over the snow field, not trudging in the sinking depths of it but floating above it, flying over the field, over partly frozen rivers, to another white field, and another.

"Can you tell us where Clara and Euphora are?" It was Mrs. Fielding's voice, far away, across several of the snow-covered fields.

"I've drowned. I'm dead. My steam ship has gone down. It's called the *Hungarian*. About a mile off the shore of Nova Scotia." A man's distant voice spoke to Mrs. Fielding.

"Clara and Euphora. They're sisters of the one you speak through. Are they in Summerland with you?"

"I'm not in Summerland. It's foul and cold here. Tell my brother I've drowned."

"What's his name?"

"John Child."

"I'll try. Is there anyone else there who can speak about the Benton sisters?"

"I'll leave you. Tell my brother."

It was quiet then. Izzie lay on the snow and looked up at the blue sky. A few small clouds drifted by. Someone was gently lifting her right hand, putting a pen in it.

"Keep your eyes closed and write. Let the pen do as it wishes."

Izzie felt the familiar sensation of her hand sliding over paper line after line. Her other hand began to move as well in a similar way, but without a pen. Then she felt a pen in her left hand as well and paper underneath. Both her hands glided on and on, letters, words, flowing, leading to other words and to others.

When the words stopped, her hands froze in place.

"Can you hear me, Izzie? Izzie?"

It was Mac calling her back from the snowfields. She floated toward his voice, then opened her eyes. He was next to her, kneeling beside her, his arm around her shoulders, his forehead pressing against her temple. "Izzie, please."

She inhaled. The smell of lavender filled her nostrils.

"Do you smell the lavender?" she asked.

"Yes," Anna said. "It's the woman who was writing through you."

Izzie looked at the table in front of her. There were two stacks of paper. She reached out and flipped through them. There were eight or ten sheets in each pile filled with large script.

"What is all this?"

"You wrote two different letters, one with each hand," said Anna.

"What do they say?"

"They're from two different spirits." Mrs. Fielding, eyes bulging, looked nearly wild. "The left-handed one is in another language."

"I don't know any other languages."

Anna stood next to her with an enormous grin. "Are you all right?"

"She must rest." Mac bolted up from his knees. "Come my dear. I think you should lie down. We can talk about all this later."

"Was there anything about my sisters?"

The three of them were silent, trading sharp glances back and forth.

"Nothing that we could see or hear, but you have proved you are a great medium." Mrs. Fielding grasped her hand.

"But how can I be great if I can't use my gifts to find my sisters?"

"There are many things the spirits cannot tell us about our own lives, Isabelle."

"Izzie is right." Mac glared down at Mrs. Fielding. "None of this is useful to her or anyone else. No more trances." He snatched up one of stacks of paper and tossed it out into the room, pages flying out and landing on the sofa, chairs, and rug. "It may not be dangerous for you and Anna, but it is dangerous for Izzie."

"You're wrong, Doctor MacAdams," Anna said. "She is gifted and can be of true service. She must develop her talents."

Everyone was pulling hard at her. She'd done what she had to do. There was no clue to help her find Clara and Euphora. All these weeks she'd been marching about the freezing streets of New York City with raw, blistered feet, never finding a hint of the girls. Now it seemed there was no hope at all.

"I'm cold and very tired," she said.

"Yes, come over to the fire." Mac reached for her hand, then looked at Mrs. Fielding. "Leave us, please."

"We'll go over the letters with you later, Isabelle." Mrs. Fielding kissed Izzie's forehead.

"That was beautiful, Izzie. I'm extremely happy." Anna kissed her as well and left with Mrs. Fielding.

Worn out, Izzie shuffled over to the sofa near the fireplace and plopped herself down, but she couldn't feel the fire's warmth. Fatigued and chilled from head to toe as though she'd walked ten miles through foot-deep snow, she longed desperately to lie down and sleep.

"I'm afraid I'll lose you forever if you stay here with Mrs. Fielding."

"Do you mean I'll lose my mind or my devotion to you?"

He winced. "I'm not sure. Before the trance, you said you might die. Now I'm the one who is afraid."

"I don't know what all that was." She flicked a hand toward the marble table where she had written the trance letters.

Mac leaned over, reached under the sofa, and rose up with one of the paper sheets he'd thrown across the room. He read to himself, then handed it to her.

She stuck her palm out, refusing it. She didn't want to see it yet. She wasn't ready.

Mac looked across the room toward the portraits of the Spiritualists. "Do you want to be on that wall?"

"Oh, Mac, I don't know. I want to find Clara and Euphora."

"I'm going to see Trall at his hydropathic college. Come with me."

She shook her head. "I have to lie down. I'm cold."

"Tomorrow morning we'll go home. It's best. The girls will either write you or come there on their own. You'll want to be waiting. Maybe they're there now or there's a letter sitting at the post office."

The picture of Clara and Euphora standing at the front door of the enormous Upper Falls Water-Cure, and the door answered by strangers, made Izzie feel woeful. She clutched a silk pillow, spread out, and tucked the soft square under her head. Mac took a lap blanket from a nearby chair and covered her, then left her. She heard papers rustle here and there about the room. Finally, from the door, he said, "I'll see you at dinner and help you pack your things." She didn't answer him. She was too tired. She knew she wasn't leaving though.

IT WAS EVENING AND DUSKY in Mrs. Fielding's spirit parlor when Izzie woke on the sofa. Outside, the sound of rattling carriages was muffled by snow on the street. The fire was still burning strong. Someone must have had added coal to it while she slept. There were voices in the front parlor. In turn, she heard Anna, Mrs. Fielding, Mac, and Roland. Their conversation was heated, but she couldn't understand what they were saying. No doubt it was about her. Propping herself up, she became slightly dizzy. All she wanted was to go straight up to bed and sleep through the night. She certainly didn't want be part of the argument going on in the next room and she didn't want to fight with Mac about going back to Rochester.

She just wanted to stay in New York City and find her sisters. No matter what she had to do. If she had to go into a trance every day until she got some sort of impression of their whereabouts, she would. She'd survived her first trance. She was still here, not lost. She was tired, but she was the same as she had been in the morning. She still had her mind, all her senses. Mrs. Fielding and Anna would help her understand about talking to the spirits.

She made her way to the stack of papers she'd written, where Mac had left them on the table. Gathering the pile up, she returned to the fire and lit a tall glass lamp. She took a deep breath and began to read. The first page was scrawled in a colossal rolling script. The handwriting was huge but it was hers.

Dear Izzie,

Don't be afraid. You are gifted beyond most others. You must accept this truth and your powers. You must learn and become a great medium. You will bring forth the most astounding physical manifestations. You will travel to London, Paris, Rome, Berlin, and all over America. You will help people understand life and death and find peace and consolation. Your mother struggled, but you will not. You have strength that she didn't have.

You will be reunited with your sisters one day. You must embrace your spiritual gift. If you deny it, you will suffer in every way, perhaps even illness. If you embrace the gift, you will flourish. There are many of us who dwell in the spirit country who will guide you. Listen to the celestial voices. We speak in divine poems.

The pages shook in Izzie's trembling hands. There was no signature. Had she written this letter to herself or was it truly from a spirit? It seemed like something Mrs. Fielding would write, but everyone witnessed her and told her she'd written the two letters, one with each hand.

She looked at the next sheet of paper. It was in a different hand, rather wobbly, and in another language, possibly French by the look of the accents. She didn't know French, but had seen it in Julianna's family library. But how could it be?

"Nonsense! That's nonsense. You are all in cahoots to take her from me." Mac's voice bellowed from the next room.

"No one is taking me from you, Mac," she said to herself out loud.

She was simply going to find her sisters. When she found them, she'd go home to him. Why couldn't he understand that?

She clutched the letter in her fist. Why couldn't the blasted letter tell her how she'd find Clara and Euphora? Why couldn't the spirits have told her, "Go now to the corner of Bleecker Street and Fifth Avenue or wait in front of Trinity Church." If the spirits were able to see and know everything, why couldn't they just tell her what she needed?

She took the English letter telling her what an astounding Spiritualist she would become, tossed it into the fire, and watched it flame up. She held the other letter in her lap.

The double doors clicked and swung open and Mac led the others into the room. They were like a posse charging in.

"Come, Izzie. We're leaving right now."

As the foursome rushed in, she stood up waiting for their attack. They surrounded her. Mac was red in the face, his jaw tight, shoulders square and stiff. Mrs. Fielding, small and erect next to him, looked oddly calm. Anna was without her usual smile and Roland looked worried.

Mac tugged on her elbow. "Please come."

"I'm staying. I *will* find my sisters. I won't leave them here."

"You are welcome to stay with us as long as you want, Isabelle." Mrs. Fielding said.

"Is this a coven? What's going on here? She's my wife. I am demanding she come home with me."

His brown eyes flashed from one face to the next as though he expected one of them to break ranks and side with him.

"I think we should leave the MacAdams to confer," Roland said to Mrs. Fielding and Anna.

Mac threw up his arms. "No, don't bother yourselves. I'm going." He peered down at her. "Are you coming?"

Izzie's felt a pit in her chest. She shook her head.

"You're in danger here. You may have a mental illness. You know that. You've known it all along. I can find a remedy for you. This house is itself a delusion. It is the worst environment for you." Mac's face had a gloom and apprehension she had never seen before, his bushy black brow furrowed down, his eyes flitting.

"You are no longer welcome here, Doctor MacAdams. We ask that skeptics at least respect what goes on here. You have crossed over to condemnation." Like an angry queen railing against an impudent subject, Mrs. Fielding threw her head back, flared her nostrils, and stretched herself to her fullest height.

Mac's eyes moistened. Was he going to cry? He stared at Izzie a long pleading moment. "Please."

She longed to fall into his arms, to rush upstairs and grab her valise. She wanted to ride the train home with him, lean into his shoulder, watch forests and towns pass by the windows. She wanted to sleep by his side tonight, every night, work by his side during the day. She wanted him—tall, lanky, dark-haired, inquisitive, passionate Mac.

But she needed more time to look for her sisters. She knew they were here in New York City. She knew it. She shook her head and looked away from him. She couldn't bear another glimpse of him tortured like that.

Without another word, he slipped away from the group. As she watched him disappear out the parlor doors, she felt the world ending. Mrs. Fielding began to speak about having tea and sitting together by the fire. Izzie couldn't bear any of it. She dashed after Mac up to Anna's room.

Shoving his things into his carpetbag, he gazed up at her as she arrived in the doorway, but he said nothing. She came into the room and fell into the Windsor chair by the window where they had started the day.

"Where will you stay tonight?" she asked.

"What does it matter to you?"

"Mac, I love you. I will come home to you when I have found the girls."

"I don't think you will." He bunched up a shirt and stuffed it into the bag. "You are either going to become a celebrity medium or find yourself in an asylum. Neither one includes a life with your husband."

"I want to be your wife."

"Wives don't do what you are doing." He pressed the bag closed and latched it, then picked it up along with his medical bag. He stared at her a silent moment, then walked out.

This time, she didn't follow. She listened to his footsteps vanish down the stairs and then, the front door close. At the window, she watched him go, a tall, narrow figure in stovepipe hat and black coat, a bag in each hand. He gradually disappeared in the eerie lamp-lighted snow.

Forty-One

CLARA SAT ON THE EDGE OF HER BED going over her list of factories. After three more weeks of inquiring and three more weeks of loaning Hannah the money for boarding, all but two factories were crossed off.

"You still haven't seen Stewart's, The Marble Palace, yet. Let's go today." Her long straw-blond hair hanging nearly to her waist, Hannah stood smiling at the open armoire. She grasped her fine silver dress hanging inside and drew it out.

"But we don't have employment yet, Hannah. Shouldn't we go out looking again?"

"We need to think about something else besides all those beastly foremen. It's just for one day." Hannah raised the shimmery fabric up to her face and covered all but her blue eyes.

Clara looked out their window. It was a sunny, blue-sky morning. Broadway would be bustling. It would be like a holiday. Clara nodded at her friend and Hannah let out a little chirp.

Clara had already decided to look for more outwork and give up on the factories, for now anyway. She was going to tell Hannah today, but she also had to tell her something much worse—that she couldn't loan her any more money. Just thinking about how to tell her the loans were done made her stomach feel like a bucket of mud, but she had to be sparing with the rest of her savings. She had no choice. The two of them going to Broadway would soften her news. She jammed a thumbnail between her teeth and chewed at it.

They dressed up for Broadway and then bustled down the stairs and out. It was one of those March days that promised spring would come soon. It had rained the night before, not snowed, and melted the last frozen patches on the streets. Hannah suggested taking the omnibus all the way downtown so that they wouldn't get distracted or tired this time.

"That's two more nickels. We can't," Clara said.

"All right, but let's get there straight away."

They made their way over to Broadway and strode along the stone walk. She and Hannah were rushing, determined, just like all the other New Yorkers. It hadn't taken very long to get used to the city—the noise, the commotion, the haste, the smells.

As they walked, Hannah described the one time she had gone to the Bowery Theater with some of the older girls from the boardinghouse. The songs were lewd. The comedy was lewd. The acting was silly. The men and women jeered and shouted from every seat. They threw things at the stage. She adored it and hoped to go back someday, maybe with Clara. With half an ear, Clara listened but she also had her mind on how Hannah would react to her news about the money. Would Hannah be her friend by the end of this day? Would she cry or yell or call her by some of the names they used for the factory foremen? *Rat, swine, sod.*

As soon as Clara saw the tall trees and wide open acreage of The Park where City Hall was in the distance, she knew they were close to The Marble Palace.

"I want to show you the shawl room," Hannah said.

"A room just for shawls?"

Clara's pulse kicked up. When they reached A.T. Stewart's, the women pouring in and out of the front doors looked like a fashion parade, like they were stepping out of the pages of *Godey's Lady's Book*. Wide skirts flared—blue, green, orange—sashes swept, shiny boots and delicate shoes danced. Parasols swung and tapped. Hats of silk floated.

"I wish my sisters could be here to see this."

Hannah smiled and linked her arm through Clara's.

"Act like you have what they have, know what they know."

Clara laughed. "How do we do that?"

"Watch the ladies and the girls. You pretend all this is just here for you and no one else." Hannah lifted her small chin up and started up the stairs.

Inside it was even bigger than the St. Nicholas Hotel.

"Jo-fire," Clara gasped.

"See?"

Clara thought nothing could be bigger than the St. Nicholas Hotel, but this was. It was truly a palace. She gazed up and down. Five stories high. More finely dressed people than she could ever count, maybe a thousand, maybe more, milled about, hovering over goods, climbing and descending a grand staircase, carrying packages, chatting. Young men darted about or stood with customers displaying wares. Two men carrying a rolled-up carpet bustled after a woman dressed in blue plaid taffeta and a paisley silk shawl swooping nearly to the floor.

"Lawks." Clara spun slowly around. "Lawks."

There were miles of counters and tables filled to the brim with delicious objects of every sort—lace, embroidery, cloaks, blankets, towels, bed linen, damask, silks. Daylight streamed in through fifteen enormous plate glass windows and a dome high above. Ornate chandeliers were lit with gas even though plenty of sunlight was streaming in. Not only were there landscape paintings in frames hung all over the walls, but the ceiling itself was painted with pictures just like at the St. Nicholas Hotel. Gorgeous brocades drifted in the air, suspended from the rotunda like giant flags.

With Hannah still on her arm, Clara began to wander. They entered a room with nothing but hosiery and gloves laid out on mahogany counters.

"Look at these." Clara picked up a pair of leather gloves lined with fur, slipped a hand into one of them. "Splendiferous."

Hannah took another pair and tried one on as well. Grinning brightly with her crooked teeth, she held out her left hand. Clara extended her gloved right hand next to it.

"A pair," Hannah said.

The back of a man just outside the room caught Clara's eye. His shoulders hung low like Papa's. The brown hair was his, too. Was it Papa? She couldn't see his face, but she could tell he was wearing spectacles. It did look like him. Heart banging, Clara tore off the fur glove and threw it down on the table. Then she grabbed the tips of Hannah's glove, ripped it off her, and threw it down as well.

"Let's go over here." Clara steered her friend over to two mannequins in fancy chemises by a marble table piled neatly with stockings. Picking up a pair of ladies silk, she pretended to examine them.

"I think my father is out there," she whispered.

"Your father is dead, isn't he? You mean a spirit?" Hannah sounded alarmed.

"Shhh. No. No. My father is alive. I ran away from him."

Hannah craned her head around to look toward the door.

"I have to leave," Clara said. "He can't see me."

"Are you sure it's him?"

"I think so."

"I swan, Clara. Why didn't you tell me this?"

"Never mind right now. I have to leave. Walk over there and tell me if there's a man in a black greatcoat, brown hair, no hat, spectacles, dusty boots."

Hannah slipped her arm out of Clara's and snuck away. In a moment, she was back.

"There's a man like that walking away just now with two others." She pointed toward the interior of the store.

"Let's go." Clara took Hannah's hand and scurried with her to the hallway. She wanted to steal a rapid glance at the man, but couldn't risk being seen, so she turned her face down and away as they left the store.

When they had descended the front stairs, Clara led them south along Broadway. She needed to get as much distance from this man who might be Papa as she could and as fast as she could. Hannah followed willingly, weaving and sprinting ahead of men in pairs, around crates, in front of moving carriages at the cross streets. A driver near Trinity Church had to dodge them and screamed out, "Idiots. Get out of my way!"

They finally reached the Battery. Hannah had brought her by here once when they were asking around for employment. People strolled the walks, streamed out of Castle Garden, and generally milled about. Steamships and huge three mast sailing vessels were anchored in the distance and barges and other smaller craft were tied along the walls of the park. The river air was dank. Feeling hidden enough in the commotion, Clara slowed her pace and, just behind some shipping crates near the water, found a spot to pause. Still arm in arm, they stood in silence a long while watching a stream of large rowboats full of people head out to board one of the great sailing ships.

"Why did you run away from him?" Hannah's voice was soft.

Clara steadied her gaze on one of the rowboats, six people embarking on a journey to somewhere far away. If that was Papa at Stewart's, New York City hadn't been far enough. Maybe she needed to get a hold of Euphora straight away and find a way onto one of these ships.

"Clara?"

"He drank too much liquor and beat my twin brother, Billy. He was so harsh he made Billy run away before I did."

"Did he beat you too, then?"

Clara shook her head. She didn't want to explain about Weston and Reilly and Papa's plans for Euphora. She couldn't, not yet.

"I was miserable, that's all, always worried he would hurt me or Euphora."

"Why didn't you go to your older sister in Rochester?"

"I was afraid he'd find me there. My plan is to wait at least six months before we go there."

"He won't find you here. There's too many people. The city's too big. It just can't happen, even if he is here. And maybe that wasn't even him in the store."

"You don't think so?"

Clara turned toward Hannah who was shaking her head.

Hannah squeezed Clara's arm. "Nah, it just can't happen. It's too crowded here."

"Maybe he tracked Euphora to Mrs. Purcell's cousin. Maybe that's why he's here. Maybe I should go and get her right this minute."

"He would have found her by now if he knew about the cousin."

That did seem sensible. It had been seven weeks since they'd been gone and no one had heard anything about him at the Hogarth's. Clara sighed. Perhaps Hannah was right. Perhaps the bustle of New York could hide her, but she'd have to be watchful all the time when she was out. She'd have to scan every man's face on every block of every street. It was exhausting just to think of it. Hannah withdrew her arm and walked a few steps away.

"I want to tell you something too," Hannah said. She paused while a woman and two boys passed them. "I made a decision." Clearing her throat, her pointy chin rising up, she wrapped herself tighter inside her black wool shawl. Her mouth twitched a bit.

Blazes, what was it? Clara held her breath.

"I went to visit Abbie last evening when you were sewin' downstairs with some of the girls. You remember her, don't you? She's the friend we saw at the St. Nicholas Hotel that first day."

Clara had not forgotten who Abbie was, with her five dollars and lovely dress.

"I can't owe you or anyone else more money. I can never repay it. It's too much. You need your money or what's left of it. There's only a tiny little breath or two between me and the Five Points or Corlears Hook…or the Almshouse."

Clara couldn't stand to think of her friend in one of those places. She had heard about the Five Points and Corlears Hook at their boardinghouse at night when the women told stories in their rooms. Five Points was a terrible, poor, slum of a place at Anthony, Cross, and Orange Streets, where there were overcrowded tenements and diseases and criminals and murders every single week. Corlears Hook was over on the east side along Walnut Street near the coal dumps and shipyards and the Brooklyn ferry. They said there were more brothels in Corlears Hook than all the other kinds of shops and businesses put together. Both places were full of prostitutes who sold themselves cheaply and got sick and sometimes were injured by their customers.

She couldn't let Hannah end up there. She just couldn't, and she wouldn't let herself either.

"Abbie says her madam is looking for a girl or two," Hannah said. "I'm going to see the madam this afternoon. That's why I wanted to dress up today, the true reason." She let out a big breath.

Clara desperately wanted to sit. She looked around but there was nothing nearby to perch on.

"You'll live there if the madam takes you?"

"Abbie says she's a fair woman."

The rowboat Clara had been watching arrived at a barge that was docked beside the tall ship. The six passengers began to disembark the little boat and climb a stairway up onto the ship.

At least now she wouldn't have to tell Hannah about the end of her loans. But Hannah was leaving her. This was worse.

"If the madam takes me, I'll pay my debt to you soon and take care of myself and we can still be friends, Clara."

"Why wouldn't she take you?"

"It's a fancy place. For the aristos." Hannah smiled slightly. "I might not be fancy enough for the aristos. Abbie says the madam only takes the pretty ones."

"You're fancy enough and pretty enough for anyone."

"Do you think I'm shameful?"

Clara bit the inside of her mouth. "I want to come with you."

"You mean walk me there?"

"Not just that. Maybe the madam will take both of us. We can stay together."

Hannah grinned, but then her eyes grew worried. "What if the madam only wants you? She'll be sure to take you over me. You're much prettier than I am."

"That's just not so, but I'll tell her we come as a pair and that's that."

"Are you sure?"

Clara gazed out at the barge. Her six people had all climbed the stairs to the ship and were gone from sight. She nodded at Hannah, then took her arm again. They walked back through the park, back up Broadway, then west over to 75 Green Street, the address Abbie had given to Hannah.

CLARA AND HANNAH WERE USHERED into the parlor house by a Negro man with a wild beard and equally wild hair. He introduced himself as James and, as he escorted them into the madam's office, Clara glimpsed fine furniture, oriental rugs, and a piano in a parlor to their right. He told them to sit and left them. Afternoon sun poured onto the madam's oak desk, which was tidy and clear except for a stack of ledgers. Hannah was quiet so Clara decided not to speak, either. Looking around the room, Clara became entranced with a large painting of a ship thrashing at sea. The ship was rocking so violently that it made her queasy so she looked down at her hands in her lap.

"My name is Mary Johnson. How did you girls hear about my parlor house?" The madam, in her plain brown dress, was a giant, at least six feet tall. She spoke in a low voice as she crossed the room and swung around behind her desk. Clara was surprised, expecting the madam to be more dazzling, but this woman had a simple, kind look.

Hannah sat up alertly. "My friend Abbie told us, ma'am."

"How old are you both? What are your names?" Mary Johnson retrieved a tiny cigar from a drawer, then took her seat.

Lawks, she couldn't mean to smoke it, thought Clara.

"I'm seventeen. I'm Hannah."

"I'm sixteen. Clara."

If Hannah was going to lie about her age, she'd better too.

Lighting a match, the madam put the slender cigar into her mouth and sucked the flame into the rolled tobacco. Then she blew out a stream of smoke that formed a smelly cloud in front of her face. She leaned back in her chair.

Clara raised a fist to her mouth and coughed. She had never seen a woman smoke. Mary Johnson gave her a wise-looking half smile.

"You both look younger than that." She took another draw on the cigar. "Do either of you have any experience as girls on the town?"

Clara froze. If she explained her qualifications, Hannah might lose respect for her. She'd better let Hannah answer first.

"No, ma'am. I haven't been with a man yet in that way, for pay or not."

"Why do you want this kind of work?"

"It's the money, ma'am. I can't find anything but seamstress piece work and I've got debts now." Hannah glanced at Clara. "I know all about men, though." Her voice cracked, but she kept on. "I worked as a barmaid in a tavern last year in Pennsylvania. I heard everything there was to hear coming out of 'em."

Clara didn't know about Hannah's being a barmaid. She wasn't entirely sure it was true, but Hannah sounded convincing. Her friend sure as blazes had courage.

"There's a big difference between hearing them talk and screwing them, one after another on a daily basis." Mary Johnson put the wet end of the cigar into her mouth and inhaled again. She looked at the two of them, studying. "What about you, Clara?"

If she wanted to be in Mary Johnson's brothel, and get Hannah in with her, she'd better put her experience forward. She'd been told her entire life that she was pretty, but that might not be enough.

"I do have experience of a sort." Clara swallowed slowly. "Not here in New York City, back home in Geneva."

"Who did you work with there?"

Clara hesitated, glancing up at the ship careening in the storm. Her scalp tingled. "I worked for my father. I only had two clients, but it was steady, over a number of months."

The urge to cry rushed up from her gut, but she concentrated hard on keeping the tears back. She felt Hannah's eyes on her, but couldn't look over at her.

"Well, that's a new one on me. I've known mothers who have groomed their daughters to be courtesans, but never a father." Mary Johnson took a moment to stub out her cigar. "How did you start at such a young age? You're not sixteen. I know sixteen."

"First it was one man who was fond of me and asked for me. Papa told me every day that our family needed the money. Besides that, Papa's a drinker. Sometimes he'd hit my twin brother, Billy, and hurt him badly. It got so I was afraid he'd kill Billy someday." She bit the inside of her mouth. "I tried not to go with the man, but Papa said that if I didn't bring the money in, he'd be so worried that he knew he'd lose control of himself and take it out on Billy. So I did what my Papa asked me. Then he made me keep it a secret. After a while he brought this other fellow who paid even more." She looked down at her hands in her lap, still feeling Hannah's eyes on her. "So I just went on and kept quiet."

It felt good to let the ugly secret out into the air. But as she did, something stirred in her belly, a terrifying anger. It made her want to jump up, pound the desk and scream, throw something heavy through the sunny window. But she held steady. Mary Johnson and Hannah were both looking intently at her. She locked her hands tightly onto the carved wooden arms of her chair and waited for the flood inside to pass.

Finally she turned toward Hannah. Her eyes now moist with tears, Hannah looked away toward Mary Johnson. If Hannah turned cold on her, it would be impossible to keep from crying.

"Are you two good friends?"

"Yes, ma'am." Hannah's voice was clear as she returned to her alert posture. "We only met this winter, but we're like sisters. The first time we spoke we were like sisters."

Sighing quietly and relaxing her grip on the chair arms, Clara settled back slightly.

"Hannah, do you have any more dresses as nice as this?" Mary Johnson gestured toward Hannah.

"No, ma'am, just this one."

Mary Johnson sat back, then selected a ledger from the stack and pulled it out. She tapped her fingers on it a moment.

"Well, then, I'll bring you on together. Friends take care of each other in the life of prostitution." Mary Johnson looked at Clara. "If Hannah has a hard time when she starts out, then Clara, you can let her cry on your shoulder or whatever it is she needs."

Hannah tittered nervously and grinned. Clara wasn't sure they should be happy, but they had succeeded. They'd be together and they'd make a living wage and they'd be far enough from the Five Points and Corlears Hook.

Mary Johnson opened the ledger. "We're putting your bodies to work and those bodies will need care. I've got a regular physician for the house, but I'll go over all that sort of thing with you later."

Clara gripped the chair arms again. If the physician was regular, someone in the house was in need of attention more often than not.

Mary Johnson dipped her pen into an inkwell and began to write. "You can come in tomorrow to talk to the girls if you like, but I want you in two weeks. I charge you ten dollars a week, plus one dollar bed money per night."

Eyes wide, Hannah gasped. Mary Johnson put the pen down firmly.

"I set the prices with the men, usually five to eight dollars, but you collect the money. It's yours except what you owe me. You'll find that's more than fair for a house of this caliber. And there's no streetwalking unless it's slow and you have my permission. My house has an excellent reputation and I don't want you wrecking it. When I do give you permission, your arrangements are up to you, but you'll still owe the bed money every night you have a gent."

She continued writing, her hand solid and steady. "But most nights there's usually plenty of sporting gents in the parlor to go around. I provide a clean, safe place with good locks on the front and back doors. The men only get in if they have an introduction and then we lock the doors up as soon as all the girls are taken. There's a stocked liquor cabinet and the customers pay for that as they use it. They buy the bottles and you can drink what they offer if you like." She finished with her ledger and looked up. "My girls don't take opium. Ever. If a gentleman offers you an opium smoke, you refuse. If I find out you are taking the opium, you are out on the street. Agreed?"

Clara nodded.

Hannah watched her, then nodded as well. "Is it slow now? Will we have to street walk now?"

"To be honest, it is a little slow. There are too many girls out there. They're everywhere—dance halls, concert halls, theaters, hotels, Broadway, Bowery. It'll pick up when the weather turns. That's when I want you, in a couple of weeks. Spring fever comes and there are plenty of men. The girls will teach you everything you need to know. Some things work for some, and not others. You have to find your own style." She returned the pen to its stand and leaned back into her chair. "If you get in good with the girls, they might introduce you to someone they don't like to get you started." She looked at Clara, her expression businesslike. "With your face and figure, you'll have it easy, but Hannah, you'll have to develop something interesting about you. Don't worry, we'll help you with that, too. It's not always the looks they want. For instance, your virginity. I can negotiate that for you. I'll get you the best price anyone could and you and I will share it. Your debts, unless they're huge, will be gone the first day." She closed the ledger. "I make them pay like it's a bar of gold."

Clara thought about Sam Weston at Minnie Stewart's house in Geneva and how he had paid Papa fifty dollars, but then also gave her another dollar that Papa never knew about. Mary Johnson stood and walked around the desk.

"Come back two weeks from today." Mary Johnson extended her hand to both of them and led them to the front door. "Think about new names, made-up fancy names for yourselves. Girls don't use their given names, usually."

They went out into the cool sunny afternoon. Clara didn't want to do the work, which she knew too well. Talking to Mary Johnson had brought Papa and Reilly and Weston back to her when she had traveled so far to escape them. But now she would be able to survive on her own. And she had her friend Hannah. Like sisters. As they headed away from the brick row house down Green Street, she took Hannah's hand.

"We're wantons now," Hannah said. "We'll be drinking champagne and going to theater matinees and shopping at Stewart's by next month."

"I suppose we will." Clara stopped and waited for Hannah to look at her. "But what price will we pay for that, Hannah?"

"Come on now, Clara, we'll make the best of it. We'll be the most desired girls in New York City." Hannah leaned a shoulder into Clara as they resumed their walk.

At least this time she'd have someone to talk to, she thought. It wouldn't be a secret from everyone. "Let's walk back to Broadway and look at the spring fashions."

They turned east onto Broome Street, into the warmth of the spring sunshine.

Forty-Two

THE FIRST NIGHT AT THE PARLOR HOUSE, Mary Johnson came to Clara's tiny room with a short yellow silk dress with matching pantalettes and a broad white sash. She spread it out on the bed. It was a girl's dress, not a lady's.

"I can't wear that. It's for a little girl."

"It'll make you look more like a child. I need a young one right now. My last young one left me to be the mistress of one of our regular gentlemen."

"That's what they want? Little girls?"

"Some of them do, I'm afraid. I thought you'd understand from what you told me about your father and those two men."

"I never thought there were others who—"

"You've got plenty more to learn," Mary Johnson interrupted. "I'm afraid your eyes are about to be opened to things about men and women you could never imagine. I won't keep you in the girl's dresses forever." Mary Johnson stepped toward the door, her head nearly reaching the top of the frame. "I've no doubt you'll be stunning in something elegant, but once I grow you into a lady, I can't take you back to being a girl again. You and Hannah come to the rear parlor at nine o'clock. We'll open the doors and let the men in around nine-thirty. All you have to do is talk to them or bring them a drink if they are empty-handed until one of them picks you out and brings you up here to your room." She started away but then hesitated. "And get the girls to explain the champagne and throne game to you and ask Abbie to show you and Hannah the douche before you go downstairs. Lettie makes up the acid solution for you girls. If it hurts you, tell her to change it, and don't waste your hard earned money on Madame Restelle's Female Monthly Pills. They don't do a damn thing for you. Do you have your menses yet?"

Clara shook her head.

"Good. Do the douche anyway. There's no telling when you'll start."

When she had gone, Clara glanced down at the spread out dress. The yellow silk was pretty. A couple of years ago she would have been in love with this dress, would have put it on and twirled round and round. Now she despised it. She would sooner use it to mop the floor than wear it.

At dinner that night, Clara and Hannah met all the girls and began to learn about the house. One girl, named Adeline, was absent. She was at Madame Restelle's down on Chambers Street getting an abortion. They expected Adeline back in a few days. Hers was the room across the hall from Clara's. If there were no complications, Mary Johnson brought back girls who had abortions. They always went to Madame Restelle's or sometimes Mrs. Byrnes's or Madame Costello's, but nowhere else. As Clara absorbed all this, she locked eyes with Hannah across the long kitchen table, silently expressing her shock and worry.

Most of the girls had come to eat dinner wearing their shimmys and pantalettes, their corsets on but open and loose, and their hair down. Some had shawls thrown over their underwear. A few had on robes. A short Negro woman with one half-closed, drooping eye and one ordinary eye brought bowl after bowl of steaming food. One of the girls explained that she was Lettie, who ran the kitchen, and was married to big James with the rambunctious hair and beard and the couple had bought their freedom from slavery and been working for Mary Johnson for ten years. If there was ever any trouble, either with the house or with the sporting men, big James and Mary Johnson usually fixed whatever it was.

Stretching across the table and grasping at whatever bowl or platter they wanted, the girls introduced themselves. They had the most splendiferous names, thought Clara. There were three Duchesses, two Princesses, and one who called herself Satin Rose. Delighted that neither Clara nor Hannah had any ideas for their new names yet, the girls set to work. First they considered Hannah. Abbie said her name should have something to do with her beautiful blond hair so they called out names like Cinderella, Princess Star, Stella White. In the end, they agreed Katrina Diamond fit the best. Hannah beamed and looked happy as a clam at high tide.

"Katrina Diamond," Clara said, smiling at her friend.

One of the girls, who went by Carlotta Leone and said she liked her name because it meant "lion," somehow got it into her head that Clara should be French like the famous young ballerina, Emma Livry. "A French beauty," she said. The girls laughed hard about this and started yelling out French sounding names, Babette, Antionette, Suzette, Juliette. They settled on Lizette.

"Do you like the sea?" Carlotta asked.

"I've never been to the sea."

"Never seen it?"

Clara shook her head.

"Then we will call you Lizette LaMer with the "m" capitalized for effect on your calling card. It means "the sea" in French."

The girls all clapped. "Katrina and Lizette," they called out.

This was truly a strange world, eating dinner in your underwear, making up names for each other. As Clara ate her biscuits and boiled chicken, she listened to the girls fume about how the Negro servant, Phoebe Ann Holmes, at the brothel across the street, lost her bastard child in court to the father because he had an honest job as a porter for the City Express Company. She was a friend of Lettie's and they were all irate about it.

Then she stopped listening. She put her fork down and took a deep breath. She wasn't Clara anymore. There was no more Clara, no more Benton. No more of Papa in her name. She was Lizette—someone new, someone she didn't even know yet. Lizette. She rolled the name over in her mind. It sounded free and saucy, like someone who could come and go as she pleased, someone who could never be owned or understood, someone beautiful, unpredictable, turbulent, like the sea. Lizette LaMer. She drew the letters lightly with the end of her fork on the table.

At nine o'clock in the evening, in the rear parlor, Clara huddled with Hannah and Abbie. She felt ridiculous in the child's yellow dress and a flower wreath on her head. Some of the other young women were scattered about the room wearing dainty shoes and fancy low-cut dresses with big hoops. Every dress was a different brilliant color—greens, blues, reds, purples, with stripes and flounces and bows. Their faces painted with rouge and eyes drawn with dark lines, the young women were mostly pretty. There were blonds, brunettes, and redheads with jewels, flowers and ribbons decorating their hair. They were adorned with gold necklaces and bracelets and red, white, and blue glass earrings glinting in the chandelier light.

It seemed she was at the wrong party. Her party had to be elsewhere, next door perhaps, with little rich boys and girls running around throwing pillows at each other and playing tag. What was she doing here with the Duchesses and Princesses?

The room was filled with velvet sofas, divans, chairs, ottomans, lounges, small tables with marble tops, several enormous mirrors with gilt frames, oil paintings of rivers and mountains and one thundering large painting of a nude woman reclining on a sofa. There were glasses and plates, bottles of wine and liquor, fruit, plump meat pies, and small cakes sitting on a fancy lace tablecloth.

Piano music and the high quivery notes of a girl singing drifted in from the other side of the double doors.

Dreams of the radiant hills and sunlit streams,
Dreams of the bright and blue unclouded skies.
Sleep, for thy mother watches by thy side.

"Out there is where the sporting men gather," Abbie said. "The front parlor. They're greeted and entertained. Four or five of the seasoned girls set the mood and look tantalizing while Mary Johnson does her business."

Abbie turned around and took a few steps closer to the mirror that hung near them. First she rubbed at her face paint trying to even it out, then stuck her index finger in her mouth and, with her wet fingertip, smoothed out her eyebrows.

She looked at Clara and Hannah in the mirror. "Mary Johnson is making sure she knows the men. If she doesn't, she's getting to know them right now. Now's when she tells them if there's anything special going on, like you two, Lizette and Katrina." Satisfied with her appearance, Abbie rejoined them. "Then she goes to her office and one by one the new gents—or anyone wanting a virgin—go in and she lays out her terms. After that, the men can stay as long as they like until the morning."

Hannah's mouth was pinched up like a little walnut. Clara knew her anguish, remembering her own first night at Minnie Stewart's with Sam Weston.

"Hannah, it will be over soon. There will be a tomorrow. I promise," Clara said.

Hannah smiled but she sure wasn't happy.

Then Abbie explained the throne game—how there was a huge, very gaudy, gilded, red-cushioned chair near the fireplace, and how it was close to the nice warm fire and seemed inviting, but none of the men wanted to sit in it. If they did they'd have to buy a round of champagne for everyone. It was the girls' mission to get someone to sit there without them thinking about it. Then they could all have champagne and the night would go a lot better.

"Champagne makes everyone laugh and, unless a gent offers you a drink, you can't take one yourself unless one of us wins the game with our gent," Abbie said.

One of the double doors opened. Carlotta Leone, dressed in red and black silk, swept in first. Clara swallowed. Cigar smoke wafted in and turned Clara's stomach to mud. She counted the men. Twenty-two. That was more than the nineteen girls in the house at the moment. How would that work out? At least there wouldn't be streetwalking tonight.

"The first night is the hardest. You'll both do all right. Don't worry. If one of them tries to hurt you, and I don't mean *pretend* to hurt you, I mean truly hurt you, scream like bloody hell." Abbie spoke through the side of her mouth as she smiled radiantly at the men fanning out into the room. "Mary Johnson or James from the kitchen will come and check on you if they hear you. The most important thing, the thing that makes you popular, is you got to act like you love them. You tell them they're your favorite gent of all the gents that come here. Here comes that sewing machine fella."

The man approached Hannah. "Good evening. Are you Katrina?"

What the blazes did Abbie mean about the *sewing machine* fella? He was around fifty, Clara guessed. His bushy beard was grayish. His dark eyebrows swept out toward his temples like little wings.

"I am pleased to meet you. I'm Isaac Singer." He bowed slightly.

Clara pictured Mrs. Beattie's sewing machine. It was called Singer and so was almost every sewing machine in the whole world.

"Would you like to come with me and get a drink? I have an awful thirst." Mr. Singer offered Hannah his arm and led her away saying, "Excuse us ladies."

In her mother's silver dress, Hannah looked back over her shoulder with sweet, scared blue eyes at her and Abbie. Clara wanted to run at her and grab her back from this sewing machine fella's arm, but Hannah was like a leaf falling onto a rushing stream, speeding away with the water.

"He's got enough money for the virgins, I'll tell you that," said Abbie. "They say he has three wives, three families, three different homes. One of them is a mansion on Fifth Avenue."

Three grinning men, one old and slender, one red-haired and handsome but a little puffy looking, and one swarthy with big round eyes, approached before Clara could ask anything more. She wasn't sure she liked Hannah going off with a bigamist, but there was nothing she could do. The three men were all dressed handsomely in satin waistcoats, silk ties, trim coats and trousers, and polished boots.

The old one said, "Hello, Abbie. How have you been? This is my friend Freddie."

While Abbie offered her hand to Freddie, the redhead leaned toward Clara's ear.

"You're mine tonight, sweet Lizette."

He sounded like a Brit. He stood back, looked into her eyes, and gave her a half smile.

Blazes and *jo-fire*, what was she supposed to say? Was she supposed to say how happy she was? How charmed she was? How lucky she was? She was supposed to be a little girl. Did she have to speak like one too? She glanced quickly at Abbie for some hint, but Abbie was involved with the old man and Freddie.

Then out of nowhere, she heard herself say, "Merci." *Tarnation*, where'd she get that? Some book Izzie read to her when she was little, probably.

"Ah, then you are French? That's smashing. Mary didn't tell me you were a genuine French girl."

Now what had she done. She laughed. "No, Monsieur. I am not from France. My mother was." She smiled, hoping he would drop this line of conversation.

"I love Paris. Women there are very interesting. A beautiful city. I trust your French mother taught you some French ways?"

Holy rolling Moses. What on earth did he mean by that? Clara speedily recounted all she knew about France. Napoleon. Bread. Wine. Joan of Arc.

"She showed me how to bake bread."

He seemed confused a moment, then laughed. "Of course, ma petite."

His red dundrearies were long, thick and curly, reaching down to his chin. Leaning toward her again, he whispered, "Come, Lizette, sit on my lap."

Clara glanced around, spotting the empty throne close by. Why not? She could try. She stepped back away from the others and walked over to the tall, red chair. She didn't want to be too obvious, so she lightly touched the arm and gave the redhead a piece of a smile, but not too much, as he approached.

"You haven't told me your name, sir."

That might distract him.

"John."

As John eagerly fell into the chair, spread his legs out, and reached for her to sit, just as Reilly had done his first time at the Spirit Room, someone called out, "There, John's in the throne." The room broke into applause, cheers, and laughter. "Hooray, Lizette!"

As though burned, John hopped up from the chair faster than a darting rabbit. But it was too late. Clara giggled. He stretched his arms out wide toward everyone. "Enjoy your champagne, les femmes et les hommes."

A sound popped and there was more cheering. At the large round table, Mary Johnson started pouring the champagne into wide shallow-bowl glasses. After she poured two, she handed the bottle to Carlotta, then picked up the glasses she had filled, and with a huge smile, brought them to her and John at the throne to more cheers.

"On your first night, Lizette. You'll be very popular, I'm sure." She kissed Clara on both cheeks, then drifted away into the party.

"Let's start again, shall we?" John sat in the chair and took a sip of the bubbling pale drink. He patted his left thigh.

Clara sat on John's leg, wrapped her right arm around the back of his shoulders and sipped the champagne with her left hand. The fizz was delightful. She smelled John's cologne water as he began to talk about how he had come to New York five years ago without a penny to his name, how he had landed a job at the Metropolitan Bank, how he was already doing well enough to build himself a new house uptown. As he spoke, and Clara sipped the champagne, nodding now and then as though she were interested in him, it all seemed familiar. There was Weston and his peach brandy. There was Reilly and his plain water, talking endlessly about themselves. All the same.

He paused and looking into the fire, he swigged down his champagne. "Little Lizette, what games do you play with your friends?"

Did he really think she was a little girl? It had been so long since she played with Euphora, or Billy, or even Izzie. Her séances had been like games, though. Guessing games. Guessing what people wanted to hear.

"I like guessing games."

And so they went on drinking champagne and talking as adult and child for a long while, he, asking about her favorite this or that, she making things up or recalling them from her childhood. After a while, Clara noticed that seven of the girls and seven of the men were gone. Hannah was gone. Abbie was gone. The others were lounging in pairs and small groups. One foursome was singing a sailor song by the piano. The extra three men must have left because there were just twelve girls, including herself, and twelve gents remaining.

John's nose and cheeks had gone crimson from the champagne. Permanently grinning ear to ear now, he was thoroughly pixilated.

"I'm a bit merry. Aren't you? Let's go up."

Clara stood and wavered a moment. The room was fuzzy, voices muffled and distant. She headed for her room on the second floor. He followed closely. She'd never had Reilly or Weston for an entire night. Would he stay until morning? Would she have to do the other thing with him over and over? She counted the handrails on the banister as they climbed the steps. Sixty-two.

When she opened the door to her room, he said, "Ah, yes, Matilda's room."

As she walked over to her armoire and opened it, she wondered what had happened to Matilda. Did she not come back after an abortion? John sat on the bed and watched her. Grabbing the bow on the sash at her back, she pulled it around to her stomach and untied it. She thought of Hannah with her Mr. Sewing Machine. He'd better be kind to her. The bigamist.

"It'll be a thunderstorm and you're scared, see." John stood and took off his jacket, then unbuttoned his waistcoat. "I'm in bed asleep." He fell back onto the bed. "Come and get the boots, would you, Lizette? S'il vous plait?" He laughed loud and long.

Tarnation, he was going to split his sides laughing that hard, she thought as she tugged off one of his boots, then the other.

"You're in another room. You're trembling. You're crying. The thunder is booming. I'm here sleeping in my long johns." He patted the bedspread. "You come in through the door. You say, 'Can I get in bed with you, Mr. Forsythe? I'm afraid of the thunder and lightning.' But I don't hear ye, see. I'm too asleep." He raised his hands as in prayer and rested them against the side of his face, closed his eyes, then guffawed.

Jo-fire, he had an entire theatrical play in mind.

"You stand close to the bed. 'Mr. Forsythe, please. Please. Please. I'm scared.' I wake then, ye see." He took off his waistcoat and laid it on the bed. "Go on, undress down to your chemise, everything off but the chemise."

As Clara followed his directions and he finished undressing, he explained the rest of it. He would wake. He'd say, "Of course you can come in to bed. I'll protect you." She was to crawl under the blanket with him and huddle up close to him, as close as she could and pressing and wriggling too. When his prick got hard, she'd touch it and ask him what it was. "That's how I'll protect you. If I put it inside you, you'll be safe until the storm passes, as safe as can be." Then she would pull up her chemise, take the prick in her two dear little hands and guide it between her legs and inside her. While he pushed into her, she'd say, "I'm safe now. I'm safe now. The storm can't hurt me. Thank you, Mr. Forsythe," again and again until he was done.

In the end, Clara only had to act out the play once. She didn't like it because she had to keep talking and it was hard to drift away from herself. John fell asleep when he was done, his chest rising and falling with a slight snoring sound. While she listened to the songs from those who had stayed downstairs drinking, she used the douche with Lettie's special mixture of vinegar and alum and carbolic acid the way Abbie had showed her and Hannah earlier in the evening. She liked the cool water rinsing him away into the pewter bowl below her, but it did sting a little. Then she went back to bed next to John Forsythe and fell asleep.

Later, a rapping on her door woke her. The very first light of day had broken. John and his clothes were gone.

Hannah peeked in. "Yours is gone."

"Yes."

"Mine too."

Hannah tiptoed in. "Can I crawl in with you?"

Clara threw back the blanket and linen and Hannah slipped in with her. "How was it? Are you all right?"

"I'm all right, a bit sore." Hannah lay down on her side, her back to Clara. "It was a mess, though. Blood all over the linens. He left and dear Lettie came and changed the bed. I couldn't sleep."

Clara drew the blanket up over their shoulders, then rolled up against Hannah and put an arm around her waist. "Did it hurt much?"

Clara felt Hannah's body convulse and then Hannah began to cry.

"Bastards," Clara said.

"Swine," Hannah answered.

"Pig."

"Stinkpots."

"Rat face."

Hannah finally giggled.

"Skunk."

"Beast."

They kept at the name-calling for a while until there was a long pause between each slur, and the sun had risen and the room was light. Clara noticed several bank notes on the bedside table. It was Saturday. She would use a dollar to cheer up Hannah. She'd take her to see the matinee of *The Colleen Bawn* at Laura Keene's Theatre.

THE PLAY WAS ABOUT A YOUNG BEAUTIFUL WOMAN, a "Colleen", named Eily who was secretly married to an upper class man who was in financial trouble. Clara was a bundle of tension through the entire play, but entranced with the actors, especially Laura Keene. To Clara's horror, the man's servant devised a plan to take Eily out in a rowboat and drown her in Lake Killarney to get her out of the way so that his master could marry his wealthy cousin and be saved from ruin.

As she waited for the drowning to take place, Clara was overtaken by her memories of Mamma and was so sad that she was considering leaving, but then a shot boomed out on stage. Rattled, she flew up and stood.

"Sit down." Several voices hissed at her.

Hannah was tugging at her dress to settle back into her seat. The evil servant had been shot, Clara realized, and Eily had been saved. Eily did not have to drown. Her pulse slowing, Clara sat and took Hannah's hand. At the end of the play, the secretly married couple openly announced their marriage and love and Laura Keene, who played the wealthy cousin, saved the day by taking care of the money that was needed.

When Clara and Hannah went back outside, the sun was still shining. Not wanting to return too soon to the parlor house, they took a long walk down Broadway and sat in City Hall Park until it was dusk. Clara talked about Billy, how he counted everything, how handsome he was, how he never let Papa get the best of him, how she missed him. Then, finally, she knew they had to go back and sit with the hairdresser. She dreaded putting the little girl's dress back on.

"It'll be easier tonight, Hannah. You'll see."

"Promise?" Hannah tried a smile.

"Yes. I do. Come to my room again when your gent is gone."

"All right."

As they walked across the park's green lawn, Clara put her arm around Hannah's waist. "We won't be at Mary Johnson's forever. Neither of us will. You'll see. I want to be an actress like Laura Keene. Do you think I could?"

"You'd be just as fine as Miss Keene and you could have your own theatre, too."

"You could help me with the plays or selling tickets or the costumes."

Hannah grinned and slipped her arm around Clara's shoulder. "I'd like that."

As they headed back to Green Street, arms entwined, Clara quietly pictured herself taking a bow to a room full of applauding people and she felt her heart grow warm.

Forty-Three

"**I**T'S IN THAT GIBBERISH LANGUAGE that looks like French again." At the small marble table in Mrs. Fielding's spirit parlor, Izzie shuffled through six pages of trance writing.

"Your letters are in tongues. The spirits sometimes speak languages that we don't know," Anna said.

Izzie's left-handed letters always came out this way. They weren't written in French as she had originally thought. Roland had taken her first foreign looking letter to a friend who was a language scholar at Columbia College. He described it as gibberish although he said there were a few French words sprinkled throughout it.

Roland had also looked into the account from the spirit in Izzie's first trance, the voice that said he was John Child's brother and that he had died on the sunken ship, the *Hungarian*. To Izzie's and everyone's amazement, there had been a passenger named Child on the *Hungarian* and it had gone down that very night of the trance just off of Nova Scotia. Roland tried to find John Child but, ultimately, had no idea how to go about it.

After Izzie's first trance, Mrs. Fielding brought Izzie into every spirit circle she held at the house and took her out to others as well. Izzie went into trance easily and sometimes spoke what she heard and sometimes wrote it. Occasionally, she said something that seemed so accurate that the seekers were sure they were communicating with loved ones in Summerland. Most of the time she couldn't even remember what she had said and was surprised when she came out of the trance and the seekers were gasping with joy or crying miserably.

There were no physical manifestations at Mrs. Fielding's spirit circles on Twenty-Fifth Street. When Mrs. Fielding and Anna went on tour they used rapping or knocking because people expected it, but in her home, it was not invited or permitted. Still, they did not confide in Izzie exactly how they made the rapping occur when they were on tour. They simply said they had ways of encouraging it. They both declared they fervently believed in genuine manifestations and swore that some mediums were capable of allowing spirits to perform in our tangible world. Over the years they had witnessed many spirit circles with perfect and true manifestations.

"Izzie, while you are here, you will surely have the opportunity to experience the rapture of divine presence," Mrs. Fielding said.

Izzie wasn't much interested in the rapture of divine presence unless it could help her find her sisters. Since she had begun her own trances, it was only on a rare night that voices would interrupt her sleep. The voices were more content to wait for the daily activity of trance and letter-writing and planchette communication. It didn't matter whether Izzie was acting as the medium or someone else was. It now seemed her voices had suddenly become very polite and were pleased to wait to be spoken to rather than intruding. Mrs. Fielding told her that each Spiritualist developed in her own unique way and she wasn't surprised at all that, as Izzie took more command of her gifts, the spirits were happier.

Izzie flipped the papers over to the blank sides. "Let's start again."

"I have to go to bed, Izzie. I'm depleted." Anna stood up.

"Just once more. I'm not tired yet. I can handle one more trance. I'm sure of it."

"We've been working until past midnight every single night for weeks." Anna placed a hand on Izzie's shoulder. "Nothing about your sisters has come out of it."

"Does that mean it won't the next time or the next?"

"No, but I can't really get clear communication if I am exhausted. Adele has been disappointed with my trances lately."

"Did she say so?"

"No, but I know her. She is fussing over you, Izzie, and talking all the time about you and not saying a word to me. I haven't even heard or seen a spirit in a week." Anna took her hand away. "I'm so very tired."

"Anna, I don't want to take attention away from your trances. I only sit at Mrs. Fielding's circles because she wants me to and because there might be a new medium she's invited who I can ask about my sisters."

"But, you are gifted. You have wonderful transcendent powers. Don't you care about using your gifts for those who seek solace?"

"I can only think about Clara and Euphora. By now they could be dead or in some unbearable situation. Why haven't they written to me in Rochester? Something has gone wrong, something unimaginable." Izzie broke into tears. "And why hasn't Billy written to me? Where are they all?"

Anna came back to her and kissed her forehead. "I'm going to bed. We'll try again tomorrow night."

THE NEXT DAY, the sun was shining. The snow and ice had lingered through the cold days of March and April, but now even the last few small pockets of slush clinging to the walks in the northern shadows of buildings had melted. Izzie walked all day looking for her sisters. She had been around to all the orphanages and charitable societies three times. This day alone, she'd gone to fifteen boardinghouses that took single women. Her knuckles sore from knocking on doors, she decided it had come time to visit the parlor and assignation houses. Roland had told her about sporting guides, pamphlets, that listed all the houses. She'd ask him to get her one.

She arrived home at Mrs. Fielding's from her daily search just in time for the late afternoon spirit circle. It was a circle of eight. A medium from Boston, a Mr. Dexter Dana, was there with four of his New York friends. Izzie was impatient to ask for a spirit communication. Everyone at the table could ask for a message, medium or not. Mrs. Fielding's rules were that Anna and Izzie always waited until all the guests asked first. If there didn't seem to be much occurring for the seekers, and people wanted to take more time because they were still interested in the possibilities of any communication at all, then Anna and Izzie, and even Mrs. Fielding could ask, especially if there were guest mediums.

So far, in all of Mrs. Fielding's séances, no one had been able to tell Izzie anything at all that would help her in her search. A few times Mrs. Fielding made coherent sentences on her planchette, but they were about Izzie's gifts, not her sisters. Twice Anna felt the presence of Izzie's mother, but didn't receive any specific message. Another time a guest medium seemed to have words from her farmer grandfather, Gregory Benton, back in England. His communication was about his dairy cows and farm.

All of this teased at Izzie. It made her desperate for more, her own trances, Anna's, Mrs. Fielding's, anything from anyone who called themselves a medium or Spiritualist. Maybe one of these times she'd get the information she longed for. Maybe from Mr. Dana tonight. She eyed him. He was young, fair, with long locks of yellow hair covering his ears, clean-shaven, and spectacles resting on a small nose.

Dexter Dana sat on Mrs. Fielding's right. Since there were four mediums altogether, the other seekers were spread between them. Spreading her hands on the table, Mrs. Fielding directed them to be silent a moment, then said, "When one of you feels the urge, ask if there is a spirit here who wishes to speak to you."

They fell quiet. Seconds ticked by. Minutes. No one asked for a spirit. Izzie watched Mr. Dana. Eyes closed, he swayed slightly from left to right, like he was listening to music. He looked ready to go into trance.

"Is there a spirit present who will communicate with me?" Izzie asked.

Mrs. Fielding grimaced at her and Izzie knew she would have scolded her if it wouldn't have disrupted the circle. Izzie's knee bounced nervously under the table.

"Flowers of spring, flowers anew," Mr. Dana sang and swayed. He had a tenor's voice. Izzie sank back in her chair, both knees bouncing now. *Rubbish.* He was going to sing. The singing mediums never offered anything specific. Mrs. Fielding hadn't mentioned he was a singing medium.

The earth brings life
The angels soar
Glad song of love and joy
Heaven is open to all
Oh, Heaven is open to all

When he was finished he became still, opened his blue eyes, and grinned at Izzie. She smiled back emptily. Worthless, she thought. Completely worthless.

The rest of the séance was mundane, lots of slips of paper with names of living and deceased, another song about mothers and their mothers, and Anna went into a short trance in which she described a beautiful forest. People thought it was lovely, but no one drew meaning from it.

Izzie was too irked to even try a trance. Mrs. Fielding kept looking over at her, expecting her to try, but Izzie was simply too irritated. After Mr. Dana sang to her, it was hard to even hold still. She wanted to turn the table upside down and get rid of everyone. She could run upstairs pretending to be ill, a pain in her side perhaps, or a fit of coughing. Anna was watching her closely, too. She and Mrs. Fielding could watch her all they wanted. She wasn't going to go into trance with these people.

AT SUPPER, MRS. FIELDING WOULDN'T LOOK AT IZZIE. She seemed to be ignoring her, but afterward when Izzie was sitting on the sofa in Mrs. Fielding's study, taking off her boots, there was a knock on the door.

"Come in."

Eyes narrowed, nostrils flaring, Mrs. Fielding stood in the doorway in her robe. "You know the rules at the table," she said.

"I'm sorry. I won't do it again."

Mrs. Fielding stepped into the room. "And you didn't even try to go into trance. You're restlessness was a distraction to everyone in the circle. You know it takes solemn concentration by all."

"I'll be better next time."

"You will."

"I feel I will never find my sisters."

"You may or you may not. I know this is dreadful for you, but you are a true medium now." Mrs. Fielding sat down next to Izzie and put an arm around her shoulders. "You must adhere to the highest standards of grace and kindness. It is a privilege to communicate with the spirits, not a penance."

Izzie nodded, hoping the lecture would be short.

Mrs. Fielding walked to the door, her red and silver hair flowing down over her shoulders, then turned back to Izzie. "The Grand Circle of mediums is next Saturday. I expect you to be a perfect apprentice. I've told you all along. People rarely hear exactly what they want from the spirits."

"I only want to know this one thing. This one thing."

Mrs. Fielding sighed. "We are not meant to know everything about our own lives. We must discover our own destinies." She shut the door and was gone.

"What good is any of it? Rapture. Trance. Transcendent powers. *Rot.*" Izzie yanked a boot off and threw it hard at the bookcase. It crashed into a handful of books, dislodging them, then fell with a thud onto the wood floor.

THE ROCKAWAY JOUNCED hard over a rut in the wet street. Roland Fielding grunted. Rain was pouring down and, even in late morning, it was as dark as dusk. Izzie was beside herself with excitement. She was on her way, with Anna, Roland Fielding, and Mrs. Fielding, to Anna Coan's home. They were to attend the Grand Circle of mediums there and she was absolutely sure that today she would finally receive a spirit communication that would lead her to her sisters.

All week, Mrs. Fielding and Anna had been in a twitter, reminiscing and chatting incessantly about previous Grand Circles. The grand spiritual circles were gatherings of some of the most renowned mediums from the Northeast—Boston, Hartford, Bridgeport, Philadelphia, Albany, and of course, New York City. For days they'd been talking about circles they'd been part of, or witnessed, with some of the mediums who would be there today—Mrs. Pettis, Mrs. Guile, Miss Jordan, Miss Cole, George Redman, and Katy Fox, one of the famous Fox sisters. Katy Fox was a young woman of twenty-three now, no longer the young girl who, with her sister, made spirit rapping into a national sensation. There were to be all types of mediums at this event—rapping, singing, testing, healing, writing, tipping, manifesting, and even a painting medium.

The more Izzie listened to all the stories of songs and tables tipping and visions, the more nervous and thrilled she became. She would certainly get the information about her sisters from talents like these. She hadn't slept one wink this past night.

"Remember what I told you, Isabelle," Mrs. Fielding, sitting across from her, looked deadly serious. "Communications are rarely as complete as people want them to be. Also, you may not get a turn to ask for a communication. There will be forty or fifty people there. You must be patient and gracious."

Izzie nodded at Mrs. Fielding and looked out at a sea of black umbrellas along Fifth Avenue. Always on the lookout for Clara or Euphora, she rarely took her eyes off the pedestrians on the street when riding an omnibus or carriage. Since they hid everyone from her, the umbrellas were a terrible nuisance. Izzie scratched at the crook of her elbow through her dress sleeve. She would have to find a way to take a turn with the circle. She had to, no matter how many seekers there were.

"The color is lovely on you. It's bringing out the green in your eyes." Mrs. Fielding reached out and patted the green taffeta of Izzie's new dress, a gift from the Fieldings especially for the Grand Circle.

"Someday you'll sit in the inner circle, Isabelle. It won't be long." Mrs. Fielding smiled, then beamed at Anna. "This is only Anna's second time at a grand inner circle."

Sitting in the center circle didn't mean half as much to Izzie as speaking to a spirit who could help her. Izzie felt Anna's weight against her shoulder. Anna was silent and serene, breathing evenly and deeply. She was already preparing for trance, thought Izzie.

When they arrived at Ada Coan's parlor, the expansive room was half full already. There weren't very many men. Mostly there were women everywhere, in hoops and colorful dresses, with hair in ringlets and curls. There were no furnishings except a piano, a very large round mahogany table with at least a dozen chairs around it, and then two more rings of chairs around those. The special mediums were to sit at the table and the seekers in the outer circles, but other mediums, like Mrs. Fielding, would sit in the outer circles as well. Izzie's heart fluttered with anticipation.

Mrs. Fielding and Roland introduced Izzie to at least twenty women, including the famous Katy Fox, while Anna quietly slipped away and took a chair at the table. Izzie kept glancing over at Anna's shining, jet-black hair parted perfectly in the middle, her burgundy and black dress, her smooth olive skin, her scant mustache. Anna spoke to no one, but smiled radiantly at all who sat at the mahogany table. The women Izzie met were all ages, some young like her, but some older, with lined faces and wizened brows. Some had soft, feathery voices, some squeaky voices, some had fixed, sharp eyes, others, luminous vacant eyes. They all exuded warmth and cheer. The men wore beards and had a gentle, educated air about them. Everyone asked Izzie what kind of a medium she was. She'd say, "I'm only in training." But, then, rather loudly, Mrs. Fielding would go on about Izzie's marvelous gifts and how she could hear the spirits as well as write in trance with both hands. She'd say, "By this time next year, she'll be in the Grand Circle." And Roland would chirp in, "Yes. Yes. She's completely remarkable. She's my Adele's second protégé. Anna, over there at the table, is her first, you know."

By now, in the month or so since her first trance, Izzie had heard these claims so many times that she had started to accept them in an odd way. They didn't seem to be her own desires. It was as though she had read the same page in a book over and over until she had memorized it and it was part of her, like her skin or hair. Their claims were just facts that she had learned.

Izzie wondered what her mother would have thought of this gathering. If Mamma had decided to be a Spiritualist and had teachers, would she be sitting at the grand table of mediums? Or would she still have been at the mercy of her voices and ended up dead too soon because of them?

After what seemed like hours, the doors were closed and everyone settled into their seats. A dozen or so women and one man, Mr. George Redman, sat around the table. Mrs. Fielding had chosen seats positioned so that they could see Anna's face. The curtains were partially drawn, leaving the room cloaked in dull light. Everyone grew silent. Rain pelted against the glass windows and distant thunder rumbled out over the Hudson River somewhere. After a few moments of stillness, a woman with a profusion of auburn ringlets cascading onto her shoulders rose from the second circle and stepped over to a piano. She took a seat and began to play.

Everyone sang with her, their voices strong, carrying the melody vigorously.

'Twas a calm, still night,
And the moon's pale light
Shone soft o'er hill and vale;
When friends mute with grief
Stood around the deathbed
Of my poor lost Lily Dale...

Izzie's throat tightened. She edged forward in her chair. She'd only heard the song once before and struggled to keep up with the fifty or so singers. When they went on to the third verse, she nearly sprang up and screamed, "Start the circle now. Now!"

Finally the song ended and silence befell the room. After a short quiet moment, one of the older mediums at the grand table said, "Is any spirit here who will communicate with me?"

The room was somber. No one responded. No raps. No cedar pencils scratching on paper. No song. The next medium asked the same question. Again, nothing. The mediums at the table began to dart glances at each other and stirred in their chairs. Next was Anna. She asked for a spirit. Mrs. Fielding twisted her hands in her lap. Roland cleared his throat. Please, thought Izzie. Please talk to us, spirits. Nothing from Anna. Muffled whispers erupted among the observers in the outer circles. The mediums fidgeted. One after another, each of the mediums asked for a spirit and nothing happened, nothing whatsoever, except the pounding of rain on the windows and the cobblestones outside on the street. Hair ringlets bobbing, the women at the grand table blinked, fussed, cringed, and sighed, looking from one to the other. Mr. Redman was restless as well.

"We must join hands," said a round, pale-faced woman.

"Yes, and we are in the wrong order. Let's all stand, and then settle again where it feels harmonious," said one with thin lips and huge eyes.

Getting up and bumping into one another as they shifted right or left or stayed in place, the mediums appeared to be playing a confused game of musical chairs. *Lawk-a-mercy.* Weren't these the most gifted mediums in the country? And there wasn't one spirit who could communicate or rap a single yes or no?

The pianist with auburn hair got up and went back to the piano and started the same song all over again. Izzie let out a huge sigh. She had been holding her breath for some time. When the first verse was over, the pianist looked over at the table. The mediums were organized now, their hands joined on the table. The pianist stopped and, just as the room fell back to silence, there was a rap on the table, then under the table, then two on a wall.

Smiles broke out. Mrs. Fielding nudged Izzie and whispered, "Here we go."

Eyes closed, Anna shot up out of her chair like a rocket. Shaking all over, she vibrated and swayed, arms stiff and jerking about. She kept this up for a few moments, then simmered to a sort of rigid jiggle.

"Who do you wish to speak to? Who?" Anna asked. Her voice trilled like a tiny bell.

Mrs. Fielding took Izzie's hand in one of hers and one of Roland's in the other. With eyes closed, Anna swayed away from the table, nearly careening into a man's lap behind her. People nearby gasped and thrusted out their arms to break her fall but she recovered her balance. Then, wandering blind around the mediums at the table, she touched a head or shoulder, then gently groped for the next. When she had touched everyone at the table, she drifted, eyes still shut, from person to person in the first outer circle, touching a forehead, an ear, or a neck on each person. Teeth clamped tight, Izzie impatiently waited for her to come around to her. Pick no one but me, no one but me, she thought.

Anna left her palm on Roland's forehead a long moment, then standing in front of him, set both hands on his temples. She stayed there longer than she had with anyone else. It was Roland. Roland? Suddenly, Anna's hands came off his head like he was on fire. Roland snickered quietly and looked relieved. Anna barely grazed the top of Mrs. Fielding's reddish hair, then stepped in front of Izzie. Izzie swallowed and grasped the edges of her chair. Anna was less jittery now. Placing a palm over Izzie's forehead, the way she had with Roland, she leaned back a little, stretching away as far as her arm would let her.

"Is this the one?" Her voice trilled again.

A rain-filled wind gust slapped at the windows. Izzie's heart raced. It is me, she thought. *Me. Lawks.* Anna couldn't play-act that wind beating on the windows. Clutching Izzie's upper arms, Anna coaxed her up, then took her hand and led her, with eyes closed, slowly through the outer circles back to the grand table. They strolled around the backs of the mediums once, then twice, then a third time. Why was Anna doing this circling? Why wouldn't she start speaking for a spirit as she had done so many times before?

When they started around the fourth time without any rapping or singing or movement of any kind, Izzie's heart began to deflate. Not even the Grand Circle could bring her a communication. She followed Anna round and round past the heads full of coils and ribbons. The mediums across the table watched her and Anna closely. On the fifth circuit around the table, just before they reached the painting medium, another huge rain-filled gust of wind slammed against the windows. The painting medium snatched up a piece of charcoal. Izzie halted and forced Anna to stop with her. The medium's hand holding the charcoal floated over the paper in front of her. It swirled and swept in the air. The medium next to her, a young woman with a pink silk shawl, got up and left her seat. Anna, now with eyes open, directed Izzie to sit next to the painting medium, then took her own chair a few seats away.

The room was as silent as three in the morning. Izzie was about to burst. The painting medium was one of the older women. She had a long narrow face, long slender nose, big round hazel eyes and thin, skin-pocked, wrinkled hands.

"Place your fingertips on the corner of the paper," she said without looking up at Izzie.

Izzie reached for the paper with a shaky hand and let her fingers rest on a corner. Then the painting medium's hand rose up a foot or so, then dropped down to the paper. She stroked rapidly with the charcoal creating little scratching lines, lengthy swooping lines, then swathes of shadow. Izzie was breathless. It was the sea. A ship with great swollen masts appeared, then storm clouds, then violent waves crashing against the bow. The ship wasn't sinking, but it was endangered.

It was astounding, exhilarating, horrifying. But what did it mean? What did it have to do with her or her sisters? She hoped it wasn't the *Hungarian* again.

After some time passed, and the details of the drawing had been filled in, the painting medium put down the charcoal and leaned back in her chair.

"What is it? What does it mean?" Izzie asked her.

"You must find the meaning. I saw it in brilliant color, a deep blue and green ocean, and iridescent white caps on the waves. The ship was brown, but glowing like a silver light."

But this wasn't enough, thought Izzie. Izzie looked around at the faces, their blue, gray, hazel, and brown eyes all on her. Taking a deep breath, she grasped the hand of the medium one side of her and also the hand of the medium on the other side of her, completing the Grand Circle.

"Is there a spirit who will communicate with me?" Izzie asked.

She waited. She would probably feel the urge to take up a pencil in a moment. The others waited. Thunder rumbled. Someone in the room hacked a sickly cough. A long moment went by. She knew she couldn't trance write herself. She wasn't relaxed enough. Her mind was in chaos. Her shoulders were pinched tight. She could barely breathe. She had enough experience with Mrs. Fielding and Anna to know this was not welcoming to the spirits.

"An old woman is here."

Izzie swung around. The voice came from the first outer ring. It was Ada Coan, their hostess, standing at her chair. Her face was empty, eyes open and raised blankly up toward the ceiling.

"What old woman?"

She was quiet a second. "Friend."

Izzie shot up out of her chair and scrambled over to Ada, knocking into knees, stepping on feet. There were yelps and grunts as she made her way. When she reached Ada, she stared at her, trying to collect her thoughts. She glanced over at Mrs. Fielding who was sitting about seven people away. Raising her brow, Mrs. Fielding mouthed the word "test" and nodded. She was right. Whatever Izzie was about to learn would be more meaningful if she tested first.

"What is her name?" Izzie asked.

"Emily."

Izzie thought for a moment. "Emma?"

"Yes."

"How did she pass over?"

"Slipped...on ice."

Izzie clutched at her throat, remembering the slick stairs at Emma Purcell's house in Geneva. That was evidence enough. It was Mrs. Purcell.

"What is the drawing of the ship for?"

Silence. Then, "Clara's house."

"Clara lives on a ship?"

"No."

"Clara travels on a ship?"

"No. Mary."

"Who is Mary?"

"Friend."

"Where is Clara?"

"Mary."

"Who is Mary?"

Silence. The longer Ada didn't answer, the more Izzie wanted to shake her, shake all of them. A ship. Someone named Mary. How on earth was any of this supposed to lead her to Clara and Euphora?

Finally, she yelled. "Who is Mary?"

Ada's eyes lowered. Her shoulders fell and she appeared to be out of the trance. She looked at Izzie. "She's gone. I saw Emma."

Izzie nodded. She began to shiver all over. "Emma, speak to me through someone else. Tell me more." She gestured toward the mahogany table. "Speak through any of them. Please. I beg you." Tears flowed from her eyes. The mediums stared at her, but no one moved. "What use are you? What use are your gifts? What is everyone here for?" She surveyed the guests. "You can't even tell me where my sisters are."

Anna and Mrs. Fielding were suddenly on either side of her. They took her arms and led her toward the door. Thunder boomed overhead. She cringed, then twisted around. "What use are you? You're all hoaxes!"

Roland blocked her as she tried to free herself and plow back into the room.

"What good are any of you?" Writhing, she tried to break free of Anna and Mrs. Fielding. They held her wrists, tugging and coercing her out of the room.

It took all three of them to get her out into the foyer and get the doors closed. When Izzie faced the doors blocking her out, she pounded them.

"Izzie. Izzie." The voices of Roland, Anna, and Mrs. Fielding scolded and beckoned her.

Slowly, Izzie caught her breath and looked up at her friends. Roland's mouth was hanging open. Anna had tears in her eyes, but Mrs. Fielding had fire in hers.

"You have humiliated me." Mrs. Fielding's head was tilted back, her face quivering. "Those are the most revered mediums in the country. You will never, *ever*, sit at one of my spirit circles again. Do you hear me?"

"Come now, let's get a hack. We'll discuss this later. Come. Come." Roland nudged and poked them all as though he was herding them like sheep out the front door, through a blast of soaking rain, and into their hack.

No one spoke on the way back to Twenty-Fifth Street. Izzie pressed her forehead against the cold damp window, trying to see under the umbrellas that marched along the sidewalk.

Forty-Four

AS THE ORCHESTRA TUNED THEIR INSTRUMENTS, Clara worried about whether the dance lessons she'd had from the girls at the parlor house the past four days were enough. It was her first dress-ball and it was by far the grandest of the season, or of many seasons, according to Mary Johnson.

While three or four men at a time chatted with her and wrote their names on her dance card, Clara tried to count the women and men at Castle Hastings, but there were three different parlors and far too many people coming and going. And men were still arriving. So far she'd counted one hundred and two women and eighty-five men. In addition to that, there were six madams plus the Empress Kate, whose home it was, greeting the gentlemen at the door. There were sixteen men in the orchestra, seventeen men and women in serving uniforms, two men taking invitations, and two taking coats.

If Billy were here, he would challenge her on her count of all these people. She was sure she was right, though. But then, she didn't really want him here seeing her as a courtesan. She was glad he couldn't see her, glad Mamma couldn't see her, glad Izzie couldn't see her. Two more women she hadn't noticed swept into the ballroom. That was one hundred and four women.

Mary Johnson and the other madams were hostesses and shared in the arrangements along with the Empress, and each madam brought her girls, but it was the Empress's home and she was in command of the evening.

Earlier in the week Mary Johnson had prepared Clara and the girls with not only dance lessons, but a long lecture in which she had explained that the men would all be upper crust, fancy and fast, New York's finest. She'd been like a schoolteacher presenting the day's lessons, standing in her parlor with the girls all sitting around.

"The most celebrated courtesans from the Empress Kate's house will be there—Mary Queen of Scots, Marchioness D'Orsay, Princess Jenny, the Jewess. And Julia Brown's girls will be there too. I want you to watch them. Some of you are as accomplished as they are, but you can always improve yourselves. Watch them closely. What they eat and drink. How they move through a room. How they use their eyes, their hands, their faces. If you are near them in conversation, listen to what they say and when they say it. If they are silent, try to understand why they are choosing to be so. And don't forget that your gentleman of the moment is your favorite. He is, as always, exceptional.

"This is a special opportunity for our new girls, Katrina, Lizette, and Duchess Elena. You may all drink the wine and champagne, but only very little. Take the smallest sips to make the gentlemen feel they are not drinking alone. You may enjoy yourselves, but you are working and you must stay alert." She paused for a moment and looked around at all the girls carefully. "If anyone embarrasses me by their behavior at the ball, then I assure you, tomorrow you will be streetwalking." Her eyes drifted from face to face, letting this comment sink in. "This is not an idle threat. It is a fact. I want you to make me proud. This is your chance to shine in front of the very best. If you do well, we will gain new clients. We will all do well."

Later that day, Mary Johnson called Clara to her office and told her the best news of all. Lizette LaMer would be permitted to enter womanhood at the ball. She could wear a lady's dress. Clara could be a young lady from now on. Since Clara could not yet afford a dress that would be suitable for an affair such as this, Mary Johnson would loan her one from a half dozen dresses she kept in her quarters for such occasions. Clara chose a blue and white silk and lace with four flounces on the skirt and wide ribbons flowing down from the waist.

On the afternoon of the ball, Clara's new hairdresser came by the house and fixed her hair in perfect shiny coils at the back of her head and laced a string of imitation pearls through them like a heavenly vine. When she was ready, she stood in front of the mirror in her room and studied herself— dress shimmering, hair exquisite, lips painted to perfection, arms bare, and bosoms round and firm revealed by the low cut of the dress for anyone to see. She stared a long while at herself. She was Lizette. Lizette LaMer.

Hannah was stunning with her hair done by the same new hairdresser and she also wore a borrowed dress. Mary Johnson said her silver wasn't quite provocative enough and loaned her a gold and blue satin. Then, at nine o'clock in the evening, five hacks arrived at their door on Green Street and carried all twenty-one girls and Mary Johnson off to Castle Hastings, home of Empress Kate and her girls.

Now, at eleven, the orchestra struck its first note. It was a waltz. Clara was relieved. That was the one they'd practiced the most.

"Lizette, I'm the first one on your card. Jim Fisk."

Fisk, a roundish fellow with an extra chin, took her gloved hand and led her into the center of the floor. He was confident in his stride and she fell into his lead. They spun round. They glided across the room among the other twirling couples. The music was bright as sunlight. As she swept near the doors, she noticed Hannah wasn't dancing, but instead was standing to the side with a girl Clara didn't know.

When it was time for the next dance, another man appeared. He was tall with a mustache so long it hung two inches below his chin. He stepped on her foot, but she claimed fault as she'd been taught to do. As they reeled around, she noticed Hannah still wasn't dancing. The third dance was another waltz. Two men came to her and checked her card. One of them was number three, the other four. Number three wore a red rose in his lapel. He was dark-complexioned like Carlotta Leone and could have been her brother. He was a better dancer than number two and tried to find out about her. Did she ever go to school? Where did she grow up? Did she have sisters as beautiful as she was? Clara was Lizette more than ever. Lizette did go to school and Lizette's mother also taught her to read French, though she couldn't speak it. She grew up right here in New York just above Washington Square. She had no sisters. Number three never said a thing about himself. He seemed enchanted with her every word and they were all lies.

When the music stopped, he stared into her eyes without speaking. Then he said, "I want you to come with me upstairs when the dancing is over."

Clara nodded. He was the first to ask, so she had to agree. Going upstairs was part of the evening. First there would be dancing, then around one o'clock in the morning, any of the men could take a girl upstairs to one of the boudoirs, dressing rooms, or small parlors and have their pleasure if they liked. About an hour later, everyone would return to the parlors where tables would now be set with crystal and silver and a fine French supper. Then about three o'clock in the morning, the rooms would be swept clear of the dishes, tables and chairs and dancing would resume until daylight. The sporting men could also take girls back to their respective parlor houses or hotels or wherever they liked.

When the orchestra stopped for the break, Clara's partner left her and she looked around for Hannah. She wanted to see how her friend was fairing so she began to search the crowded rooms for the large gold-and-blue bell of Hannah's dress. Dead in the middle of one of the busiest parlors, she spotted Hannah. She set off toward her, but before she had gone more than a step or two, she realized Empress Kate and her courtesan Princess Jenny were heading straight for her with great welcoming smiles on their faces.

"Has someone invited you upstairs?" Empress Kate asked.

"Yes, ma'am." Clara curtsied. She didn't know why she did it. Empress Kate wasn't a real Empress, after all.

"What is your name, dear?"

"Cl ... Lizette LaMer, ma'am."

"Not royalty?" Empress Kate snickered, looking at her courtesan companion and winking.

The Empress extended her hand to Lizette. She was handsome, had probably been a beauty when she was young, but she had a hard look about her. Clara held her breath.

"I am pleased to meet you, Lizette. This is Princess Jenny. You are with Mary Johnson?"

"Yes, ma'am."

"I've had a number of compliments about you already tonight and the evening has only just begun." Empress Kate's diamond tiara glinted under the chandelier gaslight. Clara wondered if they were glass diamonds on the tiara or real ones. "I want you to keep me in mind if you ever decide to leave Mary Johnson's, not that you would, of course. She has an excellent house. But you are always welcome to visit me and discuss your future."

Sporting gent number three, perspiring and smiling, popped into their group next to the Empress. Clara sank down but kept her smile on. It was time to go upstairs with him.

"Ah, Mr. Livingston. You're here for Lizette?" Her wrist laden with bracelets, she reached over and touched his sleeve. "I won't keep you." She gazed at Clara. "Remember what I've said. Now, enjoy yourselves."

"Thank you, we will," said Mr. Livingston.

Empress Kate and Princess Jenny turned away. "And where was the other one?" the Empress said quietly to the Princess.

"Ready?" Mr. Livingston took a blue silk handkerchief from his coat pocket and wiped his brow, then, as he was replacing it, stared at Clara's bust. Suddenly he lowered his damp forehead onto her bosom and left it there a moment. *Hell-fire*, what was he doing? And why was he perspiring in the first place? She hadn't seen him dancing. It wasn't a hot night and the tall windows were thrown open to the cool night air. Two gentlemen passed by, observed Livingston resting his head on her bust and laughed with each other. This was horribly damned embarrassing. What a stinkpot this muttonhead was.

While she waited for him to raise his head, she looked about the room again for Hannah, but she was gone now. Had someone chosen her friend to go upstairs?

Finally, Livingston stood erect and said, "I can tell already, I'll have no self-control with you. You are divine."

He glanced over his shoulder at the room emptying. "The rooms will all be taken. Let's get along." He put an arm around her waist and led her brusquely toward the grand staircase out in the foyer.

As they started up the stairs, a familiar belly laugh broke above the blended voices. A chill ran up her neck and over her scalp. Reilly. It sounded like John Reilly.

"Just a minute." She pressed backward against Livingston's arm to force him to stop. From the height of several stairs, she searched the shapes and faces. It was Reilly. He was here. *Here.* She absolutely couldn't be seen by him. He'd tell Papa if he knew Papa's whereabouts.

"What is it, Lizette? Did you forget something?"

"Yes. Yes." That was her escape. She could hardly speak.

"Shall I go on and find us a room?"

"Please. I'll only be a minute."

"I'll get a room, then meet you at the top of these stairs." He wagged a finger at her. "Don't dawdle."

"Yes. No. I'll be right there."

She descended the few stairs, turning her face away from Reilly's direction and went back into the ballroom. There were no longer guests in the room, only staff carrying in tables and chairs. Clara approached one of them.

"I need air. I'm a bit faint. Is there a back entrance this way?" She gestured toward the big door where the staff was pouring in with the furniture.

The young man pointed and said, "Go half way through that room, turn right, then left, down the hall until you come to the upstairs kitchen. That'll take you to the alley."

Too afraid to look back, Clara rushed against the stream of staff people through a drawing room and followed the directions. She kept mumbling, "Excuse me. I need air. Excuse me, I need air," to everyone who seemed surprised by her presence in the rear quarters of the house. Finally she arrived at the service entrance. There was a long line of delivery wagons and horses waiting along the alley.

She couldn't stay at the ball now. She couldn't risk being seen by Reilly. Had he seen her already and not greeted her? If she went back in, and Reilly saw her, he might tell Papa and then Papa might find her and Euphora. But if she left the ball, Mary Johnson would boot her out of the house. And what about Hannah? She bit down on to the inside of her mouth. *Hell-fire.*

She had to go. She'd figure the rest out tomorrow.

IT WAS EERIE BEING ALONE at Mary Johnson's. Clara was the only one in the parlor house except for James and Lettie downstairs. At one in the morning there would usually be cackles of laughter, the smell of whiskey and cigar smoke, male voices booming and groaning intermittently, sometimes there'd be singing downstairs. Clara had undressed and gone to bed, but lay sleepless. Had she done the right thing? Would Mary Johnson really throw her out? Would Hannah go with her if she did? Clara doubted Empress Kate would take her in after insulting one of her guests. And Empress Kate probably wouldn't take Hannah into her house anyway. Clara bit the skin inside her mouth. If Reilly had seen her, it was possible he could tell Papa. She sat straight up in bed. But maybe Reilly didn't know where Papa was. That was possible, too. Papa had left Geneva after Mrs. Purcell died. Maybe she had a chance. Yes. She had a good chance.

Papa hadn't been good friends with Reilly the way he had with Sam Weston. But then, what if Reilly told Sam Weston and Sam Weston told Papa? She lay back down, then after a few minutes, sat up again picturing Reilly and Weston talking, then lay back down. Did Reilly know Weston? She couldn't remember.

After fretting for hours about Papa and Mary Johnson and Hannah and Reilly, Clara began to drift toward sleep but then heard the girls coming in downstairs. It was after dawn. They were giggling and chattering in high, excited voices. As they came up the stairs, they were finishing up stories about the gents from the ball, then saying goodnight to each other and going off to their rooms.

Her doorknob clicked. She sat up.

"Hannah?"

She could just make out Mary Johnson's figure in the dark. In silence, Mary Johnson lit the wall sconce, then came and stood at the foot of the bed. *Damn.* Mary Johnson was *jo-fire* going to boot her out of the house. She could feel it.

"For Christ's sake, Clara, I told you what would happen if you embarrassed me." She slammed the door, then came and stood close. "Mr. Livingston was furious. He insulted Empress Kate in front of a half dozen people and stormed out. No one cares much for Mr. Livingston, but it doesn't matter. If anything like that happens again, Empress Kate will cut me and my house out of her parties."

"I'm sorry."

"I told Kate you were taken ill." She paused, waiting, but Clara said nothing. "Well, were you? People said they saw you run out the back saying you needed air."

Clara turned and dangled her legs off the side of the bed. It would be easy to say she was ill, just the way it was easy to tell Mr. Livingston that she had forgotten something. Mary Johnson was angry, but so far Clara had told her the truth about everything except her age. She had told her about Papa and Weston and Reilly that first day at the interview. And she had told Mary Johnson about Mrs. Purcell dying, and about how some people, including the sheriff, thought Papa might have killed Mrs. Purcell, and how Papa had disappeared, and how she had Euphora hidden away at Mrs. Hogarth's. Everything.

"I saw one of the men, one of them that Papa had me do the other thing with, back in Geneva. Mr. Reilly. I was afraid he'd see me, then somehow Papa would find out I was here. I got the all-overs and had to rush out."

"What could your father do to you now? You're free of him."

"If he finds me, he'll make me go with him." A shiver ran down her back. She wrapped her arms around herself. "He'll make me tell him where Euphora is and he'll sell her to men, like he did me."

Mary Johnson sat down on the bed close to her. She smelled like cigars and flowery perfume. "How can he force you to go with him if you don't want to?"

"He's my father."

"But you left him. Why would you have to go with him now?"

"He'd take me. I don't know. He has ways of making me do things."

Mary Johnson sat there a while, her big shoulders slumping, her jaw shifting slowly, eyes squinting. She seemed like she might cry, like she was remembering something sad, but it was too long ago to cry over anymore. Then she drew in a long breath, squared her shoulders, and sighed.

"I'm not throwing you out. This time. We're going to tell everyone you were deathly ill. If you pull one more blunder like that. Just one. You're out. I don't care how pretty you are." Mary Johnson rose up tall as a tree and set her iron-brown eyes on Clara. "If your father ends up finding you here at the house, you call for me."

Clara hopped off the bed and started to reach out to embrace Mary Johnson, but she caught herself. No one embraced the madam.

"Thank you."

Mary Johnson lingered a half moment glancing around the room from spot to spot. Clara waited, sure she was about to say something else, maybe tell her a story about herself or another girl, but she didn't. Finally Mary Johnson left and Clara ran to find Hannah.

Forty-Five

IZZIE SKIMMED OVER the morning's trance letter. There was something about the universe, something about the seasons, higher purposes of humanity, something funny about a cat. As usual, there was nothing that could help her find her sisters. Her letters were becoming philosophical. They were interesting to Anna and Mrs. Fielding and Roland, but not to her.

She picked up the papers. "Thank you for guiding me again, Anna. You are a dear friend."

"I love seeing what comes of these communications."

"They aren't enough, though. They aren't helping me find my sisters. Do you think Mrs. Fielding will ever let me back into her spirit circles?" Izzie asked.

Anna winced. "Not anytime soon, I'm afraid."

They walked together into the social parlor. Anna was right. Izzie had been a fool to embarrass her mentor that way. The morning after the Grand Circle, when Mrs. Fielding had calmed down, she told Izzie she was still fond of her, that Izzie was welcome in her home and could continue to look for her sisters, but she was absolutely not welcome in her spirit circles.

At least she wouldn't be thrown out onto the street, which she probably deserved. If Izzie stayed, Mrs. Fielding said she would expect Izzie to assist her in setting up furniture, starting the fire, keeping their supplies in order, and writing correspondence. But finally, she'd said, "My reputation is severely compromised and I cannot be publicly associated with you in the Spiritualist community. I will not waver on this."

Anna was chattering on about Izzie's description of the gray cat in her trance letter and how often animals appeared in communications while she led Izzie out to the front foyer. Anna began looking through the morning mail.

There was a knock at the front door and Izzie strode over to answer it. It was an errand boy, short and tired looking with circles under his eyes. He held out a large, flat package addressed to Mrs. Isabelle MacAdams. Izzie took it from him, brought it to the table where Anna stood, and set it down.

"What is it?" Anna grinned.

Izzie untied the brown string and unfolded the wrapping. It was the charcoal drawing of the ship in the storm done by the painting medium at the Grand Circle. Her heart pinched a little remembering that awful day—that day she had lost so much hope.

She read the note. "I thought you would like to have this. Yours truly, Mrs. Kendall, Boston, Massachusetts." Izzie immediately folded the paper back over the drawing and tied the string.

"There's a letter from Mac here." Anna waved an envelope at Izzie.

Mac. Her first letter since he'd gone away angry. She couldn't face reading it just then. She took it from Anna and slid it into her dress pocket.

"I'll read it later. I am going out now. I'm going searching at a few assignation houses today. Tell Mrs. Fielding I'll be back to set up for the circle tonight, would you?"

Izzie had several addresses that were all the way down near City Hall Park. By the time she got down there, her legs felt heavy and she decided to sit on a bench in the park for a while before visiting the houses.

She found a spot in the sun and settled down. In the flowerbeds, yellow and white narcissus were in bloom. She thought about Mrs. Purcell and her gardens and wondered who was tending them this spring. Three girls tossed peanuts at a cluster of pigeons nearby. The sun was sweet and warm on her face. Tilting her head back and closing her eyes a moment, she soaked it in.

The three little girls screeched in unison, causing the pigeons to gurgle and flutter up and away. Suddenly she remembered Mac's letter and pulled it from her pocket.

My Dearest Izzie,

Good news! You received a letter from your brother Billy and I took the liberty of reading it. He has found employment on a merchant ship, a clipper, and has sailed for China to bring back tea and silk and Chinese laborers. The letter was sent from San Francisco. He asked after Clara and Euphora. It seems he believes they are still in Geneva. His letter reveals no knowledge of anything that occurred since he ran away, so we can presume there has been no correspondence with either sister.

The Upper Falls Water-Cure is attracting more customers and patients every day. Last week the Rochester Advertiser and Union carried a story about me and the new establishment. People have begun to come by in their carriages to visit. I give them tours of the building and the treatment rooms, but am only able to ask them to imagine what the gardens and walkways will be like when they are planted later. The first few patients have been quite satisfied and promise to return. As I write this, a few are down the hall with two aides getting pummeled by the douche bath.

I am proud, of course, but I miss you terribly. I had hoped we would share this moment, that it would be our moment, not just mine.

More importantly, I wish to tell you that I have taken it upon myself to understand what I can of Spiritualism so that I might understand your predicament better, my dear. I have called upon a number of well-regarded citizens in the community, Isaac and Mary Post, Mr. G.B. Stebbins, and a Mrs. Edgeworth, among others. They all believe that the voices that disturbed so many of your nights were spirits and that you must be a very powerful medium because the spirits were calling you as opposed to your calling them. Mr. Stebbins told me that the voices were a natural demonstration of your gift and that every medium must learn to exploit her or his gift in their own unique way.

In truthfulness, I cannot say I believe all this as irrefutable fact. I do, however, believe these are fine people and they have given me much to consider late at night when I have longed for you.

I want you to come home to me. I want you to be my wife again. If you wish to practice Spiritualism, I will accept it. If you wish to have children, I will welcome them into my heart. Anything you want to do will be acceptable to me just as long as you are my wife here by my side. And should your sisters or brother appear here on our doorstep, they are welcome too. I have had many long, lonely hours to think all this through. I would give you anything in the world if you will only come home.

I await your answer to my plea.

Your devoted husband,
Mac

Yes. Yes was the answer that she heard inside herself. She ran her fingers over his handwriting on the letter. She imagined him sitting at his big oak desk in his office writing to her. She saw him pacing the halls of the Upper Falls Water-Cure, training the aides in the water techniques, meeting the inquisitive visitors and giving them tours. She saw him alone at night in their quarters on the third floor. She held the letter to her nose and remembered his lemon smell, his thick wavy hair, the rough feel of his long bushy sideburns on her face. She thought of the way he touched his scar when he was nervous, the way his dense eyebrows rose when he delighted in something new, and the time he sat with his back to her in front of the fire when she was afraid to tell him about the voices. And what a relief to know of Billy. China. *Lawks.* Such an adventure for a young man.

Two of the little squealing girls chased the third past Izzie. Izzie rose and gazed after them tearing through the park. She felt it strongly in that moment. She wanted to go home to Mac. She wanted to be with him. She strode toward the park entrance. It was time to go home. It was past time. It was spring. She could plant flowers as well as the vegetable gardens for the kitchen. It wasn't too late. And she could wait for Clara and Euphora there, with him. She would wait with him, work with him, and love him.

EARLY THE NEXT MORNING, Anna and the Fieldings escorted Izzie to the Hudson River Railroad depot on Thirty-first Street and Eleventh. Several train engines, ready for departure spewed and hissed, sending steam into the air.

"You'll find your sisters one day. I am sure of it." Roland kissed Izzie's hand.

Mrs. Fielding looked Izzie in the eye and clasped her shoulders. "I still believe you will be a great medium, Isabelle.

When you learn to be disciplined, your greatness will shine forth. The spirits are your champions." She kissed Izzie on the forehead.

Then Anna held Izzie close for a long moment and whispered in her ear, "I will miss you more than you know. We will be friends forever."

"I'll write you ... but not trance letters," Izzie laughed.

She felt Anna's body jiggle in laughter. With carpetbag in one hand and her rolled up ship drawing in the other, Izzie boarded the train. When she took a seat, she watched her three friends wave farewell to her as the train pulled away, their eyes full of sadness. Her heart was heavy as well. She was leaving her first true friends and deserting her sisters all at once.

As the train forged along the rails through towns, past green farms and spring forests budding with young pale green leaves, her grief would sometimes let go of her a little as she started to look ahead to her new life with Mac, a second beginning with him. During the day-long journey, she lurched back and forth between feeling miserable about giving up on finding her sisters and leaving Anna and the Fieldings and then feeling excited about returning to Mac. By the time she arrived at the New York Central Station at Mill Street in Rochester, she was tired out. She hired a hack and told the driver to take her to the new Upper Falls Water-Cure on North St. Paul Street.

As the cab jostled onto North St. Paul in the dark, she breathed in the smell of the Genesee River and wondered if Mac had received the wire telling him she was on the way home. Roland had promised to send it right after her train departed New York City.

When she was standing at the front door with her carpetbag, she considered ringing the bell, but then decided if this was to be her home, she shouldn't ring to enter. She pushed one of the double doors open and stepped inside.

A young man in transit, dressed in a short black jacket and gray trousers, stopped upon seeing her and smiled. "Good evening, ma'am. Are we expecting you? Do you have a reservation?"

"I'm Mrs. MacAdams. Is my husband here?"

"Oh, Mrs. MacAdams. I apologize. Yes. Yes. Please come in." He took her bag and the drawing from her hands. "He's dining with Governor Morgan. Follow me." He set off down the hall.

The neat man quickly clipped away from her carrying her things. The governor? Mac was dining with the Governor of New York?

The young man, sensing that Izzie wasn't following, skidded and came back toward her. "Please. This way." He gestured with his free hand. The sound of forks clinking against dishware and the smell of bread and cooked tomatoes sent rumbles through her empty stomach. The Governor. Would Mac want to see her now?

"I can wait in his office." Izzie turned around and headed for Mac's office in the opposite direction.

The young man's footsteps scuffled behind her. When he had followed her into the office, he set down the carpetbag and drawing. "I'll tell him you are here."

"I can wait until he is finished with the Governor, if he likes. I'll be content here by the fire or I can go up to our quarters."

After he left, Izzie glanced around at Mac's world, his desk full of papers, correspondence, and journals. He had a bookcase with glass doors full of his medical and other books, and several framed pictures she had never seen before. There was a print of a horse perched on the fireplace mantel.

Alongside it was a drawing of the Upper Falls Water-Cure building rendered with additions and gardens that didn't exist yet, and hanging on the southerly wall was a sketch depicting a couple looking over Rochester's thundering, swirling Lower Falls. She walked over to the desk and touched the back of his chair. She imagined Mac sitting there every day, swiveling to greet patients and aides, reading, writing, ruminating as he stared at his fire. She stroked the smooth wood on the chair arm, then sat.

"Izzie!" Mac rushed through the door and across the room to her.

"Mac!" She jumped up from the desk and fell into his embrace.

He felt solid and warm.

"I got the telegram an hour ago. Thank goodness you are here." He was grinning ear to ear.

"What about the Governor? Must you go back to him now?"

He untied her bonnet, removed it, and dropped it on the desk, then ran his hand gently over her hair. "I'll see him in the morning. He's here for several days. It's you I want to see now." He took her shoulders in his hands and kissed her on the mouth.

Bursting inside, she clasped her hands around the back of his neck and pushed herself against him. His lips were dry and sweet. His mustache tickled the edges of her mouth.

In a moment, she tore herself away. She wanted to see him, his long narrow face, the dear scar on his chin, his brown eyes smiling at her.

"Will you show me our new home upstairs?"

"There's something else I want to show you first." He offered her his hand and led her out into the hallway.

Even the hallway was lovely with its dark wood and pretty brown and navy blue rugs leading down the center of the building. It was comfortable, like a large home. He probably wanted to show her the dining room with guests enjoying their meal, or the treatment rooms or the gymnasium, which had not been completed when she left.

She stopped at the tall double doors of the small parlor across the hall from his office and peered in. Two women dressed in American Costumes were sitting on a red sofa with cups and saucers in their laps.

She whispered, "Are those the American Costumes I made?"

Mac nodded. "This way." He tugged at her hand and drew her along.

"What are you going to show me? The treatment rooms?"

"No. I have a surprise for you." He stopped at a closed door just across from the staircase. "Here." He pointed to gold lettering on the wood.

She read the words. "Mrs. Isabelle MacAdams, Spiritualist."

"Mac, I'm still not sure I want to practice Spiritualism."

"It's your room to do with as you please." He turned the knob and shoved the door open. "You can have spirit circles in here or read literature, anything you want."

She stepped onto a crimson-and-black carpet. A gas chandelier lit the room and a fire crackled in a small fireplace. There was her rocking chair from the Corn Hill house and her marble-top side table and the lamp she had read and sewed by day and night. At the other end of the room, a small round table covered with a white cloth and surrounded by six ladder-back chairs stood in front of three wood bookcases with glass doors like the ones in Mac's office. She walked over to the one that had books in it. They were her books.

"I know you'll fill at least three bookcases eventually, so I had them built for you."

She opened the glass cabinet door and reached in. She took out *Leaves of Grass*, Mac's wedding present to her, and held it to her chest. She ran her fingertips over the other spines—red, green, brown, Flaubert, Fern, Melville, Stowe, Graham.

"They're here, all here."

"I want you to be happy here, to lead whatever life you want to lead."

"You'd allow me to practice Spiritualism in your Water-Cure Institute if I chose to?"

He nodded. "I've learned a great deal while you've been away. I knew if you were ever to return to me and stay with me, I had to change my mind about many things."

She looked around the room. It felt familiar, as though it had always been her room, as though she had arranged every item in it for herself years before.

Arms crossed over his chest, Mac stood grinning in the middle of the room. "The windows face east. You'll have sun in the mornings."

"I have a drawing of a ship. I'll have it framed and put it over the mantel."

"Perfect. Now, let me show you our home upstairs. I left Billy's letter in our sitting room there for you."

Forty-Six

AS THE COURTESAN HEROINE, blinded and scarred by the vitriol her madam had thrown at her face, was about to die lonely and broken, gloom settled into Clara's heart. She read aloud slower and slower, trying to stop the inevitable conclusion of George Thompson's book, *The Gay Girls of New York*. Her back ached against the metal rails of the bed's headboard. Hannah and Abbie, in their chemises, sat with their backs against the wall and their legs underneath hers.

Ever since Abbie had learned that Clara could read, she had brought her one novel after another filled with courtesans and madams and treachery. The books—written mostly by Ned Buntline, George Thompson, and George Foster—were tattered, read over and over again by the girls at the parlor house. Even though Clara was getting tired of the stories, she loved the long, lovely afternoons lying about with her friends.

A summer thunderstorm had been rumbling off and on all morning. Raindrops spattered and pinged against Clara's windows. She didn't want the heroine, Hannah Sherwood, with the same first name as her dearest friend, to die. *Hellfire*, there were too many prostitutes dying in this story altogether.

"I'm not going to read anymore." She snapped the book shut with a thwack.

"What do you mean? We're almost at the end." Abbie's sweet eyes were moist, about to fill with full-fledged tears in honor of what would certainly be a tragic ending.

Clara slapped the novel's yellow cover. "She's going to die. She's going to die. Do you want her to die?"

Hannah's eyebrows came down, making her long forehead even longer. Clara knew the look. She was angry too.

"I know what you mean, Clara. I'm soured on it myself," Abbie said. "Why aren't all the sporting men dying? It's only the girls that die. That author Thompson's a rat bastard. That's what I say. I think he likes killing them off for his own satisfaction. But you can't just stop reading before the story is over."

"Abbie, this novel is about us. The women are supposedly like us—seductresses and she-devils trying to get every little thing we can out of the men, then falling into despair. Then we die because we're fallen and fallen women have to die, or at least be entirely miserable. I'm sick of it. No more reading."

Clara dropped the book on the nightstand where some bank notes and a single glass with a few drops of whiskey remained from her last customer, Colonel Woodruff of the United States Army. He wasn't a Colonel, though. She didn't know what he was. First he said he was from Philadelphia, then later he was from Richmond, then a bit after that, he was from Providence. He knew Cornelius Vanderbilt. He knew Queen Victoria. He knew Henry Beecher. But when she started asking him questions about all these people and places, he'd clear his throat, thick with the whiskey, glance up at her ceiling, and suddenly he was from Boston and not in the army any longer at all. Upon his command, she had to snap his leather riding crop across his back until his skin was red and just about to bleed. Only then did he get aroused and ask her to hold off. It was good that he stopped her because she had begun to get lost in the sound of the cracking, his flesh stinging, his whimpering.

"Well, it's not fair, Clara, you can read and I can't. I want to hear the ending." Huffing and crossing her arms over her ribs, Abbie, who had just turned sixteen, was acting more like eleven.

Hannah dug her elbow into Abbie's upper arm. "We'll make up our own ending. Abbie, you start. What do you want to happen to Hannah Sherwood the Brave?"

Abbie's freckled face brightened. "All right."

A bolt of lightning cracked. Clara cringed. Cannonball thunder boomed and rolled out over the river.

"Well then?" Hannah smiled at both of them.

Abbie lifted a finger to her mouth and thought for a short moment. "She marries the nice one."

Hannah croaked like a frog. "No. No. She gets rich like the great madams Julia Brown or Empress Kate and doesn't marry at all."

"What about love?" Abbie asked.

"I like Hannah's ending. She becomes a great madam, generous and independent."

"But what about love?" Abbie asked again.

"All right then, she can keep a man as she likes, but no marriage. And she can have whoever she wants." Hannah smiled at Abbie with a look that dared her to think of something better.

Abbie slumped. "It doesn't happen that way."

"It doesn't happen the story's way either," Clara said.

Hannah looked down at her hands in her lap. "Once you're fallen, can you get back up?"

"Up where?" Clara asked.

"You know, respectable."

"Some do," Abbie said. "You've got to lie about your past and start over somewhere new. Some gals go home to their families. Last year, one of Mary Johnson's girls married and moved off."

Clara felt Hannah's mood suddenly plummeting. "Come on. Let's get dressed up and go to a matinee. Let's go to Laura Keene's Theater again."

"In this rain? Besides we've seen *The Colleen Bawn*," Hannah said.

"I don't mind. I've seen it twice." Abbie jumped up off the bed. "I like it when Myles na-Coppalen saves Eily from being murdered on the lake."

"Well then, let's take umbrellas or get a hack." Hannah sat up.

Hannah and Abbie scrambled away to dress. With the door to Clara's room left open, the smells of sausage and coffee drifted in and made her mouth water. She picked up *The Gay Girls of New York*, went to the window, then shoved it open. The storm was torrential, almost deafening. A gust of wind blew rain right at her, spraying her face with cold water. She grasped the book flat in one hand, and then threw it as though she was skipping a stone, so that it sailed flat, pages closed, into the rain. It flew out, then descended out of sight, pummeled by the downpour. She leaned out over the windowsill and looked below. The yellow book had landed in a long, deep puddle in the alley.

A LITTLE LATER IN THE KITCHEN, Clara and Hannah found Lettie, hands coated with flour, kneading dough on the worktable. She and Hannah greeted Lettie, then Hannah filled the kettle with water and set it on top of the stove.

"Lizette." Abbie burst into the kitchen and rushed toward Clara. "There's a man at the front door. He says he's your father."

The words slammed at Clara like the morning's thunder. She looked over at Hannah, locking eyes a moment. Then she glanced over at the back door. She could go. She could run. They could tell him she didn't live here.

"Did you tell him I live here?"

"No, but he said he's seen you come in here before," Abbie said.

"Damn. I'm jiggered. How did he find me?" Clara considered the back door again, but changed her mind. "I'm going to talk to him." She tilted her head back, looked straight up at the ceiling and took a deep, long breath, then she looked at Hannah. "I'm going to tell him to go away."

"Do you want us to come with you?" Hannah said.

"No. I have to do it myself, but could you tell Mary Johnson he's here?"

"Mary Johnson ain't in now, miss," Lettie said.

Struggling to swallow, Clara looked at her friends. "Don't let him take me out of here. Let me talk to him, but stay close."

"We didn't let him inside. He's out on the stoop," Abbie said. "We told him it was the madam's rules."

As she walked to the front door with Hannah, Abbie and Lettie trailing some distance behind, Clara felt like vomiting. If Papa had seen her entering Mary Johnson's, he had to know she was a courtesan. She breathed hard to keep from puking.

When she opened the door, there he was. Drenched by the rain, he was a pitiful, wet dog sight. She covered her mouth with a hand. He was pale and sunken looking, his gray eyes dull. His long soaking wet beard hung all the way past his neck. It had turned mostly gray since winter. His spectacles were cracked straight across on one side. Rain streamed off his dingy stovepipe hat, but when he saw her, he took it off and let the rain stream down on his head.

"Little Plum, it's you. I've looked all over for ya all these months." He half-smiled.

"Hello, Papa."

"The girl said only the madam can allow men in, but seein' that I'm your Papa and it's rainin' so fierce, you can let me in, can't ya?"

"No, Papa."

Eyes widening, he swayed back a little. "Now, Little Plum. I need to talk to ya. I been searchin' high and low." He stood up straight. "I got some things I want to say to you, daughter."

"You can say them here." A wave of nausea swept through her. She placed a hand on her belly.

"Please. I have some apologizing to do. Is there some place inside here?"

She didn't expect apologizing. In his waterlogged coat, fidgeting with his hat, he waited for her answer. He didn't seem at all like he was liquored and the girls would be nearby. He could have his say and she could have hers. She knew she was never going back to him and she was never going to tell him where Euphora was. Nothing he could do or say would change her mind.

"Please. I've looked for ya every day since you left last winter. Let me speak my mind, then I'll go if that's how you want it."

Clara drew back the door and stepped aside, letting him enter the foyer. Hannah, Lettie, Abbie, and now Carlotta too, were standing just inside.

"These are my friends, Papa." She gestured toward Mary Johnson's office. "I'm going to take Papa in there so we can talk in private."

"We're going to wait for you in the parlor here, Lizette," Hannah said.

It was odd that she called her Lizette just then, since Hannah was the only one in the house who always called her Clara. It seemed like Hannah was reminding her that she wasn't Clara Benton any more.

"Lizette? That's what they call ya? That's nice."

He didn't seem surprised at all that she had another name. Did he know that courtesans took special names? She took him into the office and slid the doors together leaving them open a foot or so to let the girls and Lettie hear if Papa got riled. She thought of letting him sit down, but didn't want him comfortable enough to stay long so she stood with him in the middle of the room. He looked around at the furnishings, then put his dripping hat down on the oak desk.

"Yessir. I had one time findin' you."

"How did you find me?"

"Oh...John Reilly said he saw you at a fancy affair and I asked a lot of questions until I came here."

"How did you happen to see John Reilly?"

"I still have a little business with him. I see him here in New York. I live here now, over at the Five Points." He leaned back against the edge of Mary Johnson's desk.

Even though the rims of his eyes were burning red, he was sober. Definitely sober.

"Where's Euphora? She here with you?"

"That's what you think? You think I would have Euphora working with me in a parlor house?"

He raised a palm toward her. "Don't get shirty, now. I figured ya would be with her no matter what."

"She's not here." Her hands were trembling, but she didn't want him to see so she clasped them tightly in front of her.

"Where is she then? With Isabelle? She's all right?"

His brow pinched down and his gray eyes had worry in them. He waited. Clara didn't answer.

"Tell me," he said.

"She's fine. Someplace safe."

Papa took a moment thinking, his face twitching a bit. Then, he just nodded.

"I heard Isabelle was here looking for ya too," he said. "Left her husband and came here to find ya."

Another swell of nausea flooded through her. Izzie was in New York City looking for her? Izzie was right here?

"Did she find ya?" he asked. "I didn't go lookin' for her. Thought she might send me to the sheriff. You know how she is."

"Is she still here?"

"Don't know. Don't know about Billy's whereabouts either. You?"

"Nothing."

He scratched at an ear. "You look the purtiest I ever seen ya. Can't believe something comin' from me can be as handsome as you. Always said it was your grandma Elsie ya took after." He pushed himself away from the desk and walked toward her.

When she jumped backward, he stopped. Hearing about being pretty didn't make her shine the way it did once. In fact, it didn't do a thing inside her. She'd heard about her beauty so many times, it didn't mean anything anymore, from anyone, not even Papa.

"I made mistakes with all my children, Clara. Most of all with you. Even more than Billy. Billy could stick up for himself." He took off his spectacles and searched his pockets for a handkerchief. That was Papa. Looking in every pocket for some dirty old handkerchief, then wiping his smudgy spectacles while he gathered his thoughts. "That was the sin of it. I always loved ya best."

He found his handkerchief and rubbed at his spectacles. His face seemed churned up, like he was about to cry. He put his glasses back on and looked into her eyes. Her shivering and shaking and nausea started to settle. He was actually sorry for what he'd done, she thought. He really was. It was in his voice, his eyes.

"And I had to find ya and tell ya. I'm sorry, Little Plum. I shouldn't have set you up with Reilly and Weston. That wasn't right." He reached out and tried to take her hand, but Clara kept her hands clasped tight. "Can you ever forgive me, daughter?"

She wanted to say no. She wanted to hate him. She wanted to say yes. She wanted him to be her Papa, the Papa from so long ago. She didn't answer him, except with the tears that began to roll down her face.

"What happened with Mrs. Purcell?" she asked. "Did you kill her?"

"Oh, no, no, Clara. That was an accident. Terrible. The front stairs were covered with ice. She fell. I got scared, so I ran. I knew the sheriff was after me anyway. Remember how he came to the house? He wasn't goin' ta listen to me. I had ta run."

She watched him talk, trying to see if he was lying, but she couldn't tell.

"Were you there? Were you drunk?"

"Nah. I was out lookin' for you and Euphora half the night in the bitter cold. I was worried sick about you."

Had he? Had he really been worried and looking for her and Euphora since that night?

"You've got to believe me, Little Plum. Please…I want to make it all up to ya."

She kept her eyes on the windows and the rain outside. She didn't want to look at him just then. He was making her sorrowful and confused.

"Please, Little Plum. I got an idea for us, you and me and Euphora."

There was something about his voice then, something as familiar as the hard rain and as normal as waking up in the morning and going to sleep at night. He was about to cast his spell, to entice with an adventure.

She spun toward him. "No! No ideas."

"I'm goin' ta take you and your sister to Pike's Peak. In Colorado." He broke into a grin. "There's gold all over the mountain. I've got friends that'll help me get started. We'll get a stake. We'll find you a handsome, rich husband. Everything'll be new. Look here." He pulled some paper stubs from an inside coat pocket. "I already got the train tickets. We just need a little more of dough for a stake. You probably already got that in a tin box upstairs."

"Damn it, Papa! Damn it! No!"

He grabbed her wrist and yanked her arm up between them. "Don't ya dare talk to me like that. I'm your Papa. I came here to make things right."

"I won't go with you, Papa." Trembling flooded through again, but she stared right into his sad stone-gray eyes.

His grip tightened. It burned. She felt her wrist might break in two.

"Tell me where Euphora is."

The doors crashed open. Mary Johnson, pointing a small derringer pistol right at Papa, and with a crowd behind her, marched in. Hannah, Abbie, Lettie, Carlotta, and Mr. Singer, Hannah's bigamist, were all there, staring right at Papa.

"Mr. Benton, these are my witnesses in case something happens with this gun I'm holding." Her voice and hand were steady.

Papa dropped Clara's wrist and stepped back. *Hell-fire*, was Mary Johnson really going to shoot him?

"Wait," Clara said.

"Mary Johnson kept her eyes on Papa. "You have two choices, Mr. Benton."

"You must be the madam." Papa smirked, looking at her right down the barrel of the little four-barrel gun and ignoring the others. "This is my daughter. I got rights to my daughter, not you." Papa took one half-step toward her.

"I said you have two choices. You can leave now and never come to my house again. Because if you do, I'll shoot you down as an intruder. Or you can stay a few more minutes and leave with the police who will take you back to the sheriff in Geneva. I understand he's looking for you."

Papa looked away from the gun at Clara. "I meant what I said. Come with me. Please, Little Plum. You're my sweet luck."

"No, Papa."

"Come on. We'll get Euphora, find the gold, and have an easy life, not like here. This life will ruin you, your good looks, your sugar plum spirit."

Clara shook her head. Papa quickly glanced around at everyone watching him, then grabbed his soaked hat off of Mary Johnson's desk and shoved his way through the group.

As he left through the front door, the sound of the rain pouring down burst in.

Mary Johnson let the gun down. "All right everyone. That's over now. Get back to what you were doing."

Clara ran to the office windows. Head bent against the rain, Papa crossed the street and walked briskly to the north. Two policemen, with Lettie's husband James, were on their way toward the parlor house from the south. Papa was getting away. He snaked his path through passers-by on the sidewalk until he was out of sight. She sighed. Good. Now go find your gold, Papa. She hadn't told him where Euphora was and if he came back, she still wouldn't tell him. Mary Johnson's voice drifted in. She was at the front door telling the policemen that the man had left and no one was hurt.

Papa had his train tickets. The gold would draw him like a magnet. Clara looked down the street where he had disappeared. He wouldn't be back. She'd never see him again, maybe never in her life. She was no use to him now that she couldn't make money for him or give him Euphora.

"We heard everything," Hannah said. "He said Izzie was looking for you. Will you write her husband now and find her?"

"Yes. Yes." Clara embraced Hannah and rested her face a moment on Hannah's shoulder.

"We still have time for breakfast and the matinee," Hannah said.

Taking Hannah's arm, Clara walked with her to the kitchen. Abbie, Carlotta, and a few of the other girls were prattling on wildly about Mary Johnson and the pistol. The room smelled of sausage and coffee as before, but now also baking bread and cinnamon. The girls circled Clara and began asking a hundred questions. Was she scared? Was she sad? Did she know Mary Johnson had a gun? Where did her father go? Would he come back?

Meanwhile Lettie set out coffee and tea and cinnamon rolls and sausages on the big table. Even though she wasn't hungry, Clara stayed with the girls in the kitchen a long while talking. Eventually Hannah suggested that they lie around in the rear parlor and forget the hack and the theater because the rain was so dreadful. They drifted into the parlor and sprawled and lounged, some girls dressed, some in shimmys and robes, and they continued asking Clara about her father and mother and Billy and Izzie and Euphora and Sam Weston and John Reilly and Mrs. Purcell and Mrs. Beattie. The afternoon passed with Clara sitting snuggly on a sofa between Abbie and Hannah. Clara patted her friends' knees and, in turn, they patted hers as she told stories and more stories about spirit circles and burning gristmills and her mother's voices and her brother's bruises and then how her father got her to screw Weston and Reilly for money and how she longed for her sister Izzie to come back and save her from it all, but finally how Mrs. Purcell helped her run away.

Then, after some time, the light grew dim and Mary Johnson came in and clapped her hands sharply. "Time to get dressed for the evening, girls. Get upstairs now."

Forty-Seven

"IZZIE!" MAC'S VOICE BOOMED OUT from down the
hall.

Alarmed, she shot up from her rocker, dropping the
new issue of the *Banner of Light*.

"Izzie, Izzie. It's a letter from Clara. In today's post. A
letter from Clara!" Arriving at her door with envelope in
hand, he skidded to a stop.

Breathless, Izzie tore it from him. It was in Clara's tidy
hand. The return address said "Clara Benton, 75 Green
Street, New York, New York."

"New York City, Mac. I was right." With shaking hands,
she tore open the flap of the envelope, slipped the paper out,
and unfolded it. She read aloud.

June 15, 1860

Dear Izzie,

*I have not written you before this because I was hiding from
Papa and was afraid he would find me and Euphora too. I
couldn't take the chance that, if you knew where we were, he
would find us by pressing you for our whereabouts. He found me
anyway, though I still refused to tell him where Euphora is*

living. I believe Papa has now gone to Pike's Peak in Colorado in search of gold. Euphora is living not far from me and is a domestic for Mrs. Purcell's cousin, Mrs. Hogarth. I see her most Sundays. I assume you have heard about Mrs. Purcell's terrible death and that the Geneva Sheriff suspects Papa. We are doing the best we can on our own here and at last we are free of Papa.

Papa told me you were here in New York City looking for us. I suppose I am glad you didn't find me. You will be ashamed of me when you learn how I have made my way, but there were things I had to do. I will tell you about them someday.

Please write to us. Have you had any news of Billy?

Your sister,

Clara

Izzie let her hands fall. "What did Papa do to them, Mac? What horrible thing could he have done to them that made them hide like this?"

Mac took Izzie by the arm, settled her in a chair at her table, and sat next to her.

Izzie glanced over the letter again. "What did he do? *My God.* She sounds so old and distant. How can she think I would be ashamed of her? My own sister... 'At last we are free of Papa?'... I didn't protect them, Mac. I didn't protect them."

"She's safe. They're both safe. You finally know."

"I'm going to go there and bring them back."

Mac leaned back in his chair, his brown eyes steady on her. She gritted her teeth. Was he going to prevent or discourage her again? He pulled his watch from his waistcoat and studied it.

"Excuse me, Doctor MacAdams." Mac's aide stood in the doorway. "Mrs. Monroe is waiting in your office for her consultation."

"Tell her I'll be right along." He returned his gold watch to his waistcoat. "You can make the next train. I'll wire the Fieldings. You'll bring both girls back here right away."

Izzie threw her arms around his neck and kissed him. "I'll have my sisters again."

He smiled. "They can have the room at the back on the third floor. Now, go pack your bag. I'll take you to the depot."

"What about Mrs. Monroe?"

"I'll take care of her. Go get your things."

THE TRAIN SEEMED TO CRAWL. The time between each town was like a long day. Every time the engineer slowed the train, Izzie asked the conductor if something was wrong. What had Papa done to them? What could he have done? But it was over now, whatever it was. She'd get the girls and bring them home with her. Finally. It had been an entire year since she got married in Geneva and left. They'd be more grown, perhaps a lot more grown after surviving on their own in New York City.

The brakes squealed against the tracks. Another blasted stop. What had he done to them? The longer the ride took, the more furious she became.

But the girls would be safe with her now. She imagined Clara and Euphora home with her at the Upper Falls Water-Cure. They could help her in the gardens, with the vegetables, in the kitchen. Euphora could do some cooking for the patients. She imagined the girls teasing and confiding in each other in the little room Mac had in mind for them, but most of all she imagined them safe from Papa, together under the same roof and not on the streets of New York City or in an orphanage or on an Orphan Train heading out West. When Izzie had been searching for them, she imagined them for too long in the grim places she had looked.

Now finally she could replace those pictures with new, gentle ones of her sisters at the Upper Falls Water-Cure.

That evening, when she arrived in New York City, she hired an open carriage and set right off for 75 Green Street. The air was thick and hot and smelling of horse dung. Even though it was nearly nine o'clock, the streets were still busy, and being June, it was just dark.

As her hack arrived at 75 Green, two men were entering the door. Piano music poured out, then cut off as the men disappeared inside and the door closed.

A fancy party? That seemed odd for a boardinghouse. Izzie fumbled for coins in her reticule to pay the driver.

"Are you a new girl here?" The driver, standing on the sidewalk now, reached for the coins, then offered her a hand to help her down.

"You mean work here?"

"Yeah, for Mary Johnson. Girls say she's one of the good madams."

Izzie landed on the stone walk, her knees buckling. She caught herself with the help of the driver's firm grip. "It's a parlor house?"

"Sure, lady. Where did you think you was goin'?"

"I thought it was a boardinghouse. This is 75 Green Street? You're sure?"

He nodded. "You want me to take you somewhere else?"

Izzie stood for a moment looking at the door and the bright light shining from the windows. *Clara was in there.* She was there, just a few feet away. The sweaty crook of Izzie's elbow prickled. Was she a prostitute for this Mary Johnson?

A gentleman in a stovepipe hat trotted up the steps and knocked briskly on the door. Once again, the black door swung open. A brunette woman in a bright blue dress opened it. "Hello, Mr. Anderson. Lovely to see you." The piano music, laughter, and loud voices poured out. Then the heavy door clunked shut. Cigar smoke wafted down to her. She'd come back in the morning when the sporting gents were all gone.

"Yes," she said to the driver. "231 West Twenty-Fifth Street. The name is Fielding."

The driver climbed back onto his seat, snapped his whip, and the gig set off. Izzie stiffened against the jostle of the seat. Could it be? Clara, a prostitute? Maybe not, maybe she was a maid. One of the carriage wheels hit a rut in the stone street and wrenched the vehicle. Izzie's neck jerked. Of course, Clara could be a prostitute. In the months that Izzie had searched for her sisters, she saw what often became of girls who had no family.

It was all her fault. She should have taken the girls from Papa long before. She should never have left them with him with Mamma gone.

The street was vibrant with people, omnibuses and carriages. They passed a lamplighter climbing down his ladder. With each block the horse trotted along, Izzie felt Clara getting farther away from her.

"No! Turn around. I want to go back."

The driver cranked around. "What's that?"

"Go back."

He hauled back on the reins and steered the horse to the side of the street. He twisted around on his seat. "Now you say you want to go back to the parlor house?"

"Yes. Please."

"You sure, ma'am?"

"Yes. Yes, I'm sure. Please take me back there."

WHEN SHE ARRIVED AT MARY JOHNSON'S, the brunette woman in blue answered the door. The woman's smile dropped as soon as she saw Izzie.

"Yes?"

"My sister is here. I have to see her." Izzie held her breath.

"What's her name?"

"Clara Benton."

"Lizette. We call her Lizette. She's working right now."

Izzie stepped inside. "I've been looking for her for months. I must see her. Please."

"Come with me."

Valise in hand, Izzie followed the woman across a large foyer and past a parlor where a pianist was playing *Jeanie with the Light Brown Hair*. Izzie peered in. A blond woman with a wreath of white and pink flowers on her head stood by the piano singing, "Never more to find her where the bright waters flow." At least eight men stood around holding cigars and glasses of whiskey and wine, listening to her. Others stood aside with several women.

"This way."

Her guide sounded impatient. Izzie caught up with her and followed her downstairs into a large kitchen. A tall Negro man with narrow shoulders and a Negro woman stood at a sink washing dishes.

"It's the only room the girls don't use in the evenings. I'm Carlotta, by the way." She pointed toward the couple. "That's James and Lettie."

"I'm Izzie MacAdams. Please, tell Clara it's Izzie." Izzie settled her bag on the floor.

"This is Lizette's sister," Carlotta called over to James and Lettie.

They both grinned and said hello.

Izzie looked at Carlotta. "You're sure this Lizette is my sister Clara?"

"You're the one from Rochester?" the man James asked.

"Yes."

"She told us about you. That's her."

"Wait here." Carlotta darted away through the swinging door.

James walked to Izzie and handed her a glass of water. "I see the likeness. Can we get you some tea or somethin' to eat?"

"No thank you."

Several pots on top of the stove steamed and rattled, making it unbearably hot in the room.

"Your sister'll be glad to see you." He grinned at her a long moment, with big teeth, some broken, some missing, then left to take up his work with Lettie again.

"Jus' make yourself comfortable. It might take a minute or two for her to take leave of the gentlemen," Lettie said.

Izzie felt a stab in her chest. She clunked the glass down on the table. The gentlemen. Her little sister was out there, a prostitute at a party. She lived in a parlor house. *Rubbish and rot.* Izzie wrapped her arms tight around her waist and began to pace back and forth along the length of the table. Her skin grew sticky with perspiration. The crooks of her elbows itched. She took up the water glass from the table and gulped it down. Clara was going to walk through that door any second. If she could get her to gather up her things right away, they could go get Euphora and all leave in the morning. Izzie couldn't wait to show her the Upper Falls Water-Cure and the gardens. It would be heaven for Clara after this. Heaven.

Several moments passed. What was taking so long? Wasn't she just upstairs? Izzie stared at the kitchen door. The piano and singer were still at it.

Drink to me only with thine eyes
and I will pledge with mine.

She paced back and forth. *Ridiculous.* Clara was just a room or two away. Why couldn't she just run to her and grab her hand and drag her away? In another minute, that's just what she would do.

The white door swung open.

"Clara!"

"Izzie!" Clara's face opened into a huge smile.

Izzie immediately sensed her sister was older, so much older. She rushed to Clara, threw her arms around her and kissed her. "I've looked all over the city for you. I tried and tried to find you." Izzie pulled away from the embrace to see her sister.

Clara's dress was dazzling, red-and-white satin, her hair beautifully decorated with flowers and small jewel-like baubles. Izzie took a deep breath. This wasn't the Clara she remembered, but it was Clara—dear Clara.

"How long were you here?" Clara bit down on her lower lip.

"Nearly five months. I stayed at the Fieldings on Twenty-Fifth Street. I walked the streets all day from the day after you left Geneva until a few weeks ago."

Clara stared at her at long moment, looking almost as if she didn't believe what she had just heard, then as she seemed to understand, her eyes filled with tears. "You were here that long? Oh, Holy rolling Moses, Izzie. How on earth did you do that? Was Mac with you?"

Izzie shook her head. "He couldn't be here. I tried séances and trance writing to get clues of your whereabouts. I roamed all the neighborhoods asking strangers. I went to orphanages and boardinghouses and even some of the brothels."

Clara looked like a thousand years had passed and a thousand more were passing just as she stood there.

"I wish you had found me," Clara said.

"Oh, Clara, I wish I had too. Where's Euphora? Is she all right?

"She's with Mrs. Purcell's cousin and husband now, uptown a little. She's lonely, but safe. What about Billy? Have you heard from him?" Clara asked, voice shaky and tears now fully streaming down her face.

"Yes. I had one letter." Izzie took it from her dress pocket and offered it to Clara. "San Francisco. He's on a merchant ship to China."

Clara grabbed the letter and pressed it to her. "Will he ever come back?"

"I don't know. Why didn't you write me? Why? I never would have told Papa anything about you."

Sniffling, Clara wiped a palm against her cheek to dry her tears. "I was afraid he'd find me and Euphora if he had even the slightest idea of where we were."

"What did he do to you?"

Clara's jaw stiffened and she diverted her eyes from Izzie, then looked over Izzie's shoulder toward James and Lettie. "I'll explain it to you later."

Feeling overwhelmed at the reunion and the sense she had that Clara had changed profoundly, Izzie covered her face with her hands. She had failed her sisters, failed them. She looked up again. Clara was waiting for her. She had to get Clara out of here right away.

Izzie collected herself and drew her shoulders back. "Can we go get Euphora now?"

Clara's eyes darted away. "I've already been chosen for the night. By a gentleman, one of our best gentlemen."

"But you don't have to do that now. I'm here to take you home."

"Home?" Clara's brown eyes came back to Izzie.

"To Rochester. You and Euphora will come home with me and live with me and Mac."

Clara smiled softly. "Oh, Izzie."

"We can go right now. Mac wired the Fieldings. We can get Euphora and stay with the Fieldings tonight, then take a train in the morning." Izzie reached for Clara's hands.

Clara paused, a curtain coming over her face. "I'm not sure, Izzie. My home is here now."

"Your home?"

"Mary Johnson, our madam, has taken care of me. She protected me when Papa came. I have friends. It's home."

"You want to stay?"

Eyes down, but standing straighter, Clara slowly nodded.

The white door swung partially open and Carlotta poked her head into the room. "Clara, Mary Johnson wants to know if you are coming back. Mr. Ferguson is anxious. He's getting impatient."

"I'm coming."

Carlotta slid out of sight and the door closed. Izzie felt like she was about to explode.

"No. You can't go back in there. Tell her you are leaving with me now, as soon as you gather your things," Izzie said.

"I have to go with this gentleman. I don't want to do anything to anger Mary Johnson's gents. Can you stay at the Fieldings and come back in the morning first thing?"

"What are you saying? No, Clara. Come with me now."

"We'll go in the morning and see Euphora." Clara's voice was steady and her tears had stopped.

"Clara, do you understand? I've come to take you home to Rochester."

"I can't decide that right now."

"Decide? Whether to be a courtesan or come to Rochester with me?"

Clara's face crumpled as though Izzie had hit her, then her expression grew blank. She turned her gaze across the kitchen. "James, will you find a hack on Broadway and take my sister to where she is staying?" She looked back at Izzie. "You have money?"

"I'm sorry, Clara. I'm sorry I didn't visit last year when you asked me. I tried to come. Mac wouldn't allow me. His new Water-Cure Institute was consuming him and I...I was haunted by voices. He thought I needed these special daily water-cure methods to treat my sensitive condition and that I was too fragile to go."

Clara took her in her arms and held her a long moment. "It's all right, Izzie. We'll have a long talk tomorrow. I'll tell you about Papa and you'll tell me about your demons. We have each other again. That's all that matters."

"It's not all that matters. You must come to Rochester with me."

Clara withdrew her embrace and stepped toward the door. "Come early."

In her red and white satin gown and fancy hair, Clara pressed a hand against the swinging door and disappeared.

WHEN IZZIE ARRIVED AT THE FIELDINGS at the late hour, the house was lit up. They had received Mac's telegram and they were waiting for her. It was good to see Anna and Mrs. Fielding and Roland. Even though Izzie had let Mrs. Fielding down at the Grand Circle, she felt welcomed by her. All three of her friends fussed over her, leading her right away to the kitchen, and offering her cold potato soup and a cool glass of water. They immediately asked her about Clara and Euphora.

There didn't seem to be any point in hiding what she had found, not after everything she had been through with them over the winter and spring. She told them she had just seen Clara and that Clara was a prostitute in a fancy parlor house and that Euphora was a domestic in a home not far from the Fielding's. They weren't surprised by Clara's situation, but they were surprised that she wasn't eager to leave straight away with Izzie—that she wasn't with her right this moment.

Izzie was to sleep on the sofa in Mrs. Fielding's study as she had in the winter and spring. She and Anna stayed up well into the night talking. Izzie asked Anna over and over again why Clara or anyone would choose to stay a prostitute.

"If a woman can live well and come and go as she pleases, and have everything she wants, she is free in a way, isn't she?" Anna asked.

"But how can you call that freedom?" Izzie clenched both her fists in her lap.

"It's work. It's independence." Anna sat on the sofa with her feet tucked under her next to Izzie.

"Submitting to the desires of different men every night is independence?"

"For most women, it is survival I think, but for others, if it is lucrative, it may be more. A sort of freedom."

Izzie pondered this. She pictured Clara in the satin dress with the low neckline, her brown hair luminous, and the other young women she saw, all dressed elegantly, all laughing and chatting and singing as though at a ball. Maybe Clara did enjoy that life, but did she enjoy it so much that she wouldn't choose to live with her and Mac?

When Anna had kissed Izzie goodnight and gone off, Izzie lay awake recalling every detail of her search for Clara. She remembered the children on the street scavenging, selling things out of their carts, sleeping in doorways and boxes. She remembered the women she'd seen in the Five Points and Corlears Hook who sold themselves cheaply. Those women were barely surviving. That wasn't independence.

Air flowed through the open window and finally cooled her and then, when the moon rose, it glowed against the buildings across the street. A crashing noise somewhere set off a chain of dogs barking and howling. The dogs carried on a long time, then faded off. As the first light of morning broke, carriages began to rattle by and Izzie drifted into sleep.

"There's Hannah."

"What?" Izzie sat up on the sofa and looked for the man who had spoken to her. "Roland?"

"There's Hannah."

"What's that?" Izzie waited for the door to open, someone to show themselves. She listened and waited, but that was the end of it.

It had been quite a while since she'd heard voices outside of a trance. She wasn't afraid of them anymore. She had learned from Anna and Mrs. Fielding to concentrate, to open other ears inside her, to hear them better or if need be, to cover those ears to silence them. Sometimes she'd hear a word or two and try to understand the message or pick up pen and paper and trance write. But this morning she didn't want to stop and listen for messages. She wanted to see Clara and Euphora.

IN THE BRIGHT SUMMER MORNING at Mary Johnson's, the house was no longer exuding frivolity. It was dead quiet. Clara, dressed plainly and without face paint, answered the door herself. Izzie's heart burst with joy at the sight of her. It was truly Clara—an older Clara—but truly Clara. Izzie stepped inside and embraced her sister.

"My little Clara, what have you been through?"

She took Clara's hands and they looked at each other a moment.

"Did you ever walk along Broadway when you were here?" Clara asked.

"Often."

"Let's stroll down to the Battery while it's still cool. I like it when the street is waking up. We can look at the ships."

"What about Euphora?"

"Afterward. I have things to tell you I don't want her to hear."

"But the trains. We'll be late to leave. Can you tell me later?"

"Let me have a day or two with you before you go."

Izzie yanked at Clara's hands. "A day or two! Clara, you must come with me. I insist. I demand it."

"I can't go with you." Clara slid her hands out of Izzie's grip.

"Why?"

"Walk with me."

"Please, Clara. I've come to take you home."

"We have so much to tell each other."

Clara seemed entirely resolute standing there on the stoop. She wasn't going to change her mind. A shuffling sound on the stairway behind her drew Izzie around. A gentleman in a gray suit had just come downstairs and was approaching them.

"Good morning, Lizette."

He paused a moment and put on his stovepipe hat, then proceeded toward the front door, winking at Izzie as he passed her. Clara smiled briefly at him. Had he been her visitor last night? Clara's gaze did not follow him as he left, but remained fixed on Izzie.

Then Izzie walked with Clara south along Broadway, and once they passed Houston Street, they strolled by the Metropolitan Hotel, Henry Wood's Marble Hall, Taylor's Saloon, and the theaters and galleries and furniture stores. It was familiar. Izzie had walked along Broadway many times looking for Clara and Euphora. As they walked along, Clara pointed out her favorite places—Wallack's Theater, Barnum's American Museum, the Lyceum Theater.

"But most of all I love Stewart's and wandering from department to department. My friend Hannah and I can spend an entire afternoon there."

"Hannah?"

"My dearest friend. She's been with me since I first arrived here."

Izzie wondered if the voice that had awoken her during the night had been referring to Clara's friend. It seemed a strong coincidence.

Clara began to babble on again about Stewart's, how elaborate it was, how the young shop men darted around trying to assist you, how the light showered down through the Rotunda, how the wealthy men and women pored over coats, furs, rugs, linens, dresses, perfumes. Her voice rose and fell as she described finery after finery.

Izzie wanted to hear about Papa, about Euphora, about the parlor house, even about this Hannah, but she let Clara prattle on. It was reassuring to see Clara no matter what she wanted to speak about. Izzie knew Clara was avoiding the difficult things they had to discuss and that she needed a little time to get the courage to reveal what happened.

"Here it is. Chambers Street. The Marble Palace. A.T. Stewart's. Look, they've just opened. Shall I show you? You've never been in?"

"I can't shop now. I have to know what happened to you. Please."

Looking a little sheepish as though Izzie had caught her in a trick, Clara agreed and they went on to the Castle Garden, then strolled along the Bay Harbor. It was already growing hot and humid. They had to detour around a cluster of men who were hoisting large crates onto a tall ship.

"Are you a real Spiritualist now, Iz?"

"I suppose I am."

"What is it like? What happens? Do you really hear voices like Mamma did?"

"I don't think I am like Mamma. I'll never know, of course."

"I always knew you had a gift."

"When I hear the voices, I still keep a sense of where I am. I don't think Mamma did. When I was in Rochester, I started hearing them and I tried as hard as I could not to, but I was miserable and exhausted when I fought to shut them out. Mac tried to cure me with a water-cure method, but it was Mrs. Fielding and Anna who helped me."

"Do you hold séances like we used to?"

"It's not the same as our antics. I practiced Spiritualism with Mrs. Fielding and Anna for a while when I was trying to find you. I'd beg the spirits for information about where you were but they never gave me anything to go on. Then when I went home, Mac introduced me to some Spiritualists in Rochester. I sit with them and we take turns with trances. I don't know if I will hold my own séances or not. People have started asking me to. If you would come home with me, I could teach you what I know and we could work together again as genuine mediums. Not as hoaxes."

"It's not for me. I want to become an actress like Laura Keene. She has her own theater on Broadway, near Houston Street. Have you seen it?"

A pair of Bowery b'hoys, one in green and yellow plaid pants and coat, the other in wide blue and cream stripes, strode by, looking them up and down. "Morning, ladies," the one in plaid said. They stood about eight feet away and lit smelly cigars.

"Maybe Euphora would like to learn from you," Clara said.

"I'd rather you."

It was Clara she had to get to Rochester. Izzie believed Euphora would come without hesitation.

The b'hoys sauntered away.

"I'm sorry, Iz."

"Please, Clara, tell me about Billy and Papa and Mrs. Purcell. Tell me everything."

Clara arched her back as though Izzie had poked her, then was silent a moment. A ship crew, calling out commands to each other, worked at raising sails on a ship close by. At the bow, seagulls squawked and swirled where a deck hand dumped the contents of several barrels into the water. The walk was busy with travelers, ship hands, dock men, servants.

"Can anyone hear us?" Clara's brown eyes flitted around.

"No one is paying attention to us. Those two Bowery b'hoys are gone. Let's walk over there." Izzie pointed to a path that led away from the harbor activity.

When they reached the end of the path, Clara grasped the railing and faced out toward the water, toward Governor's Island. Her mouth and eyes twitched as she began to speak.

"After you left…do you remember I wrote you about Isaac Camp and how he ruined my reputation as a medium?"

Izzie nodded.

"Then our money dried up and Papa was drinking all the time. He was surly with the three of us, but most of all with Billy. I wrote you how he hit him badly and threatened him. He was cruel, Iz, and Euphora was scared all the time." Clara stopped a moment and looked like she was about to cry.

Izzie felt like she was going to explode and she hadn't even heard anything new from Clara yet. She took a deep breath. It was going to be more awful than anything she imagined. It was going to be horrible. She rested a hand on Clara's shoulder and looked out at the water with her.

"It broke my heart to see Billy tortured like that. I kept thinking I could fix it. I could protect him. I could make Papa stop if I did everything he told me to. He promised me if I did certain things for him, for the family, and kept secrets, he wouldn't hurt Billy."

Izzie lost her breath. "Damn him. I would have torn his face off. What did he have you do?"

Clara tilted her head down, then turned her eyes out to the water again. Izzie remembered the night she told Mac about the voices and how he sat with his back to her. Somehow he had known sitting like that would make it easier for her to confide in him.

"By the end of the summer we owed Mrs. Purcell money. Things kept getting worse between her and Papa, too. After Papa hurt Billy so badly that last time in the winter, Billy ran away. Mrs. Purcell became fearsome worried for me and I was fearsome worried for Euphora. She wrote her cousin, Mrs. Hogarth, and asked if she could take us secretly in for a while. Then the very night after we left, Mrs. Purcell fell and died on her icy front steps."

"I arrived later that day at the house. I was worried and I finally came for you."

"You did?"

"That's why I came to New York City. The sheriff found out you had tried to buy rail tickets for New York City. Do you think Papa killed her?"

"When Papa found me and came to the parlor house, he told me it was an accident because of the ice. He said he wasn't even there. Do you think he could have pushed her?"

"I don't know." Izzie grasped the iron railing. "Poor, sweet Mrs. Purcell. Do you think he could have?"

Clara winced and nodded, then turned one more time to stare out at Governor's Island. She began to tell the rest of her story of Papa and the Spirit Room. First, there was the strange courtship with Sam Weston. Stuttering a little, Clara told about Weston's strange frigging himself near her and her disbelief that Papa understood what Sam was doing, her disbelief that Papa not only had agreed to it, but took money for it. Clara had trouble finding the words to describe everything, but Izzie understood. Clara spoke of gifts from Sam and Papa, perfume and jewelry and clothing, that made it all seem better than it was. She explained how Papa used threats to hurt Billy to keep her silent and agreeable.

While Clara spoke, Izzie imagined tracking Papa down at Pike's Peak and finding some way of ruining him. Then Clara began to cry as she told about Minnie's parlor house and losing her virginity to Sam and then becoming Sam's paramour.

"Why didn't you refuse Sam, refuse Papa?"

Clara cried harder. "I tried at first but I couldn't. I was confused. I was afraid."

"You could have gotten on a train and come to me anytime."

"I thought I was protecting Billy. I was so afraid." She was silent for a few moments. "Then I got used to it, I suppose." Her sobbing subsided. "I got used to the attention, the money and the gifts. They treated me like I was beautiful, a glorious young lady. I got used to it."

"Is that how it is now at the parlor house?"

"I am always chosen right away so I never worry about money. And I have my friend, Hannah. We stick together."

There was that name again. This time it stabbed a little. This Hannah had become the sister Izzie had not been.

"Does Euphora know any of this?"

"No. I have managed to keep it from her."

Clara went on with her story. Izzie couldn't believe there was more, but Clara told of the second man, John Reilly. Clara had begun to extort money from him on her own so that she could leave one day. She said after several times with him, she had to admit to herself that she was not just a paramour to one man, but a prostitute. Izzie heard the word stick in Clara's throat.

Clara went on. "Mrs. Purcell and Mrs. Beattie had seemed suspicious of my routine in the Spirit Room and asked about it. Then Mrs. Purcell finally came forward and offered to help me and Euphora. Then Billy ran away. After that, Papa told me the family needed more money and he wanted to teach Euphora to be a medium and join me in the Spirit Room. But that's not what he wanted to teach Euphora. He wanted to make her into a whore like he did me. Sweet little Euphora with her joyful way. I couldn't let him crush that. I had to get her away from him."

Boiling over, Izzie paced away from Clara. "How could he do it? How could he?"

"You mean how could I?" Clara's face was as pale as chalk.

"No! I mean him. Him." Izzie strode back to Clara and embraced her. "I should have come home to you. I'm sorry." Izzie felt Clara's forehead burrow into her shoulder and her back shake as she cried. "It's over now. We'll go get Euphora and go to Rochester."

"Where were you?" Clara swatted Izzie's shoulder. "Where were you? You said you would come and take care of us." She swatted again and again.

Izzie let Clara pummel her, let the ache in her arm build, but she didn't let go of her sister. Finally Clara pulled away. Her face was soaked with tears, her eyes red and full of misery. Izzie's heart shriveled.

"I'm sorry. I'm sorry. I know I failed you. I should have been with you. Let me make it up to you. Let me take you and Euphora home now. Please. You can't want to stay here and live as a prostitute."

A gaggle of seagulls swooped by on their way to a squawking swarm of birds by the ship. Clara withdrew a red bandana from her pocket and wiped her eyes.

"I threw him out, Izzie. I threw Papa out when he came to get me at Mary Johnson's. She helped me, but I stood up to him, the way you always did. I'm free of him now."

Clara finished her story. There was the steamboat escape and the threat of the ice embargo. Euphora's domestic situation. Finding Hannah. The disappointing search for factory work. Being afraid every moment that Papa would find her and then finally how Mary Johnson held a gun to him. The path Clara took to becoming a prostitute once she was in New York City on her own was a story Izzie had heard before while she searched for Clara.

But what Papa had done to her beforehand wasn't like anything she had heard. Izzie knew Papa, though. She believed every word. She was so outraged and furious that she was trembling. She wanted to find Papa and get him tossed in jail for the rest of his life. More than that, though, she wanted Clara to come with her back to Rochester.

"I'll stay another day or two. I want to know everything that has happened to you," Izzie said.

"And you have to tell me about your voices and Mac and everything that has happened to you."

"Can we get a hack and go directly to Euphora? I can't wait another minute."

IZZIE WAITED IMPATIENTLY while Clara dug into her paisley reticule for the proper coins to pay the hack driver in front of the Hogarth's home. Her purse was brimming with silver and gold. *Lawks*, no wonder she didn't want to go to Rochester.

"We need to celebrate. I want to show you and Euphora the new park. I've never taken Euphora. Maybe Mrs. Hogarth will give her a few hours off. There's a free concert at four-thirty." She dropped some coins into the driver's hand and said to him, "Will you wait for us to take us up to Central Park? We'll be a few minutes."

It had only been a year or so since Izzie had seen Clara, but her sister seemed leagues older, with her reticule full of money and her ability to give orders to the hack driver.

"The servant's entrance is around the back." Clara pointed toward an alley.

They entered a courtyard. Six or seven yelling youngsters chased a single speeding, shirtless boy. A pair of mongrels was wrenching a rag from each other's jaws.

"Don't forget. She thinks I am a seamstress at a factory with my friend Hannah. Please don't say a word about the parlor house."

Clara led Izzie up some rickety wood steps to an open door. And there was Euphora chopping carrots. Dear

Euphora, a year taller, and dressed in a full-length white apron and maid's cap, her red hair tucked sloppily inside it.

"Euphora!"

Euphora's beautiful freckled face fell into cold blank shock for a short moment. Then she burst like a fire dowsed with kerosene, her bucktooth smile exploding.

"Izzie!" Dropping her knife, Euphora leapt toward Izzie, throwing herself into Izzie's arms. "Izzie!"

Buckling with the weight of Euphora coming at her, Izzie grabbed her sister tightly, recovered her balance, then lifted Euphora off her feet. She twirled Euphora around, delighting in her little sister's squeals as she spun her. After several twirls, Izzie got dizzy. She released Euphora and careened toward Clara who caught and steadied her.

"You're here. Clara, she's here." Euphora's eyes glowed.

"I know and now I want to take you both up to Central Park for the concert. I will ask Mrs. Hogarth. She has to agree." Clara strode off.

Izzie was so excited that she picked up Euphora again and twirled her around one more time. "You're coming home with me. You're coming home."

Euphora settled back on her feet. "Rochester? When?"

"Yes. A few days."

Euphora grinned from ear to ear. "To live with you?"

Izzie nodded. "We'll go and speak to Mrs. Hogarth right now."

Forty-Eight

WHILE SNARLS OF CARRIAGES AND WAGONS slowed them down as they rode up Fifth Avenue in the hired coupe, Clara worried. How was she going to tell Euphora she wasn't going to Rochester? And for that matter, how was she going to get Izzie to leave her in New York City in the first place? Clara sat with both sisters on one seat, facing forward with Euphora crammed in the middle.

Izzie took a letter from her pocket and handed it to Euphora, saying it was from Billy and that he had gone to China on a ship. Euphora's face crumpled at the news, then she read the letter out loud and it made all of them weep. He was so far away. The notion they might not see him again fell over the three of them like a big heavy blanket.

But after a few minutes of riding along in silence, sweet Euphora couldn't help herself. She was tickled silly about going home with Izzie and started asking about the Upper Falls Water-Cure where she would live with Izzie and Mac. Clara didn't mention just then that she wasn't going, but smiled and changed the subject when Euphora tried to get her talking about their new life with Izzie. Izzie didn't say anything either, but kept glancing over Euphora's head at her and giving her a pleading smile. She and Izzie were sure-as-

rain going to have a real bull and cow about her staying at
Mary Johnson's.

Passing through the gate at Fifth Avenue and 59th Street,
they headed for the Promenade, where the concerts took place
at the band shell. Their coupe joined a parade of every
possible shape, size, color, and model of carriage there could
be in the world—cabriolets, runabouts, phaetons, landaus,
bretts. They were mostly open rigs, long and curvy, short and
square, fast and trim, some with owners driving, some with
servants driving. The horses were elegant, mostly in pairs, and
the ladies and gentlemen were dressed like royalty. Clara fell
quiet for a while watching them all and wondering how she
was going to get her sisters to understand about her staying.

Izzie and Euphora were jabbering like they were full of a
pot of coffee each. Euphora listed off all the new dishes she
had learned how to cook since Mrs. Purcell's. Izzie talked
about Central Park, how she had learned about it from the
Fieldings while she stayed with them, how it was being built
section by section.

"See these little saplings." Izzie pointed at some spindly
trees lining the road. "Elm. Maple. Locust. They are desperate
for water. Roland Fielding says if they make it through the
heat of summer, they'll be grand someday."

Everywhere stones were piled high, compost heaped,
holes and ditches dug. Some areas were torn up with holes
and mounds of dirt everywhere. Sweaty men were slinging
pickaxes, swigging from jugs, hoisting shovels, and loading
and unloading horse-drawn carts. Some spots were grown in
and as pretty and splendid as Clara had ever seen.

After believing for so many months that Izzie didn't care
anymore about her and Euphora, Clara was still finding it
hard to believe Izzie had really gone away from her husband
and had been looking for them all over New York City. Now

finally here they were together, riding in a carriage on a hot summer day in Central Park.

A crimson runabout with two stunningly dressed women sitting beneath their pink parasols sped around and passed them. Clara wasn't sure, but thought they were courtesans from Empress Kate's house.

"Do you and Mac have a carriage, Izzie?" Euphora asked.

"No, but next year we will get one if things go well. We use a livery stable down the street."

Clara looked away again at the carriage parade. If Izzie had come to Geneva when she said she would last fall, Izzie could have taken her and Euphora and Billy to Rochester then—and she would have gone with Izzie lickety-click. But now it was too late. She had Hannah and Mary Johnson and Abbie and Carlotta and the others. She couldn't very well leave them. Maybe Mrs. Purcell wouldn't even be dead if Izzie had come back. And Billy wouldn't have had to run away. She'd still have Billy.

They neared the band shell. Spreading out along the wide boulevard and on the grassy lawns, the crowd was dense. Children darted about. Women and men milled and chatted or sat in long rows dotted with parasols and stovepipe hats on twenty-foot benches. Nursemaids in white with youngsters in strollers congregated in twos and threes. The open carriages were parked with their passengers at the edge of the crowd offering a fine vantage for the concert. Clara guessed there were a thousand or two who had come for the music. Later on, when the music was playing, maybe she would try to count the audience.

Once they had climbed out of their coupe, Clara paid the driver and sent him off.

"Shall we get ice cream afterward?" Clara smiled at her sisters. She wanted to make this afternoon as lovely as she could, a lovely summer party for the three of them to remember, a farewell party of sorts.

Euphora took one of Clara's hands and one of Izzie's and led them both through the thicket of people. She picked a spot behind one of the benches. They were too late to find seats, but Euphora got them close enough to see and hear the musicians.

The conductor introduced himself, Mr. Harvey Dodworth, and announced that the musicians would start with *Friends Jubilee Galop*. When the horns struck up, Euphora swayed between her and Izzie, bouncing off her shoulder, then Izzie's. Then Euphora took their hands and nudged harder against Clara and Izzie until they began to sway along with her.

Euphora and the music were contagious. Clara's worry about wrangling with Izzie drifted away. She thought about Papa being gone and how he couldn't hurt her or Euphora and how her little sister could go home with Izzie now. Clara turned her gaze away from the band shell and looked at Izzie and Euphora enjoying the music. For a short moment, she felt happy for them, but then when she thought of telling Euphora she wasn't going to Rochester, her heart sank back down. As soon as Euphora understood it had to be this way, she'd be thundering miserable.

Before Izzie went back home, Clara would make her swear never ever to let Papa steal Euphora away. Swear. Swear on twenty-five stacks of Bibles. Swear by all the saints in heaven. Swear forever and ever.

The band played *Fly My Skiff*, *Lurline Quickstep*, a waltz, and *Viva l'America*. Then they played selections from an opera. Through the entire concert, Clara grasped Euphora's moist hand.

When the concert was over, Clara suggested they walk for a while. The crowd spread out in all directions, many people heading south with them along the Promenade with its poor little parched elm saplings.

"You'll be one of the cooks at the Upper Falls Water-Cure, Euphora. When you are older, maybe even the head cook." Izzie put an arm around Euphora's shoulder. "It's vegetarian mostly. You'll have to learn some new things."

"No meat?"

"Only if the patients request it."

"Clara, what will your job be? Will you and Izzie be Spiritualists together again?"

Feet dragging, Clara looked down. "I'm not going, Euphora. I'm staying here in New York City."

Euphora scraped to a stop and spun toward her. "What?"

"I'm staying. I have employment here and I have my friend Hannah. And I've decided I want to be an actress. If you want to be an actress, you must start in New York City."

"Bring Hannah to Rochester. You can be an actress there."

"No, I want to stay here. Rochester doesn't have Laura Keene's Theatre, or Wallack's, or the New Bowery. But, I'll visit you as often as I can."

"Yes. Bring Hannah. Clara, of course you can bring Hannah. I'm sure Mac would agree. She could stay with us at the Water-Cure Institute for a while," Izzie said.

Clara started walking again into the flow of the crowd. Izzie and Euphora fell in step with her. For a moment, she considered the idea of bringing Hannah to Rochester, but Hannah "staying for a while" wasn't long enough. And then there was Mary Johnson and the others and being an actress. She didn't want to leave it all.

"Please, Clara. We should all be together," Euphora said.

"I can't."

"Well, if you won't go, I won't go. I can stay at Mrs. Hogarth's and Izzie can visit us."

"No. You have to go with Izzie. I want you to go with her. I'll be all right. You'll be happy there. It'll be much better than Mrs. Hogarth's. It'll be sweet summer cherries."

"Clara, please come. There are actresses in Rochester," Izzie said.

"Not famous ones."

"I'll hate you for the rest of my life." Crossing her arms, Euphora kicked at the gravel.

Tears welled in Clara's eyes. She stared at Euphora a moment. "Please don't hate me. I'll write. I'll visit."

Euphora embraced her. "I don't want you to stay here."

"I don't either." Izzie placed a hand on Clara's shoulder.

"Let's not talk about it anymore now," Clara said. "Let's enjoy our stroll. I know where we can we get ice cream."

Before Izzie left, there would be a tarnal awful fight between them, but she didn't want it to be right then, not with Euphora there.

THE NEXT MORNING, with the door to her bedchamber open at Mary Johnson's, Clara had the collywobbles. She was listening for Izzie's knock downstairs at the front door. Izzie was coming to talk to her again about going to live with her. It would be hard as hell-fire to stand her ground against Izzie's older-sister clout, but there was nothing that Izzie could say that would make her want to work as a lady's aide in a Water-Cure Institute and there was nothing that could make her want to leave Hannah and Mary Johnson and the others or her new life in New York City or her new dream of becoming an actress. She belonged here. That was truly, sure-as-rain, final.

They would wrangle and Izzie would give in, and then they were to take Euphora to Barnum's Museum and then tomorrow morning Izzie and Euphora would leave on the train without her.

The door knocker clanked. She raced toward the stairs hoping to be the one to let Izzie in, but she heard the door open and Mary Johnson's voice greeting Izzie. Her stomach flipped over like a pancake. She wanted to keep Izzie away from Mary Johnson and Hannah or anyone else that Izzie could talk into making her go to Rochester. What if Izzie and Mary Johnson had a heart-to-heart talk and then Mary Johnson decided it was best for her to leave? Then what choice would she have if Mary Johnson booted her out? *Damn.* Why couldn't Izzie meet her at the St. Nicholas Hotel like she had asked? "No, I want to see where you live and meet your friends," Izzie had said.

Clara skipped a few steps to catch up to them at the door.

"Lizette, I mean Clara," Mary Johnson said, "has told me so much about you, Izzie. Would you like to come into the rear parlor for tea?"

Oh, *Double rot.* Clara didn't want to be with Izzie in that room. That was where they met the men and were chosen at night.

"My sister and I have so much to talk about and so little time," Clara said.

Mary Johnson glanced at her. "Why don't you both go in the rear parlor then? I'll have Lettie make tea and I'll stay but a few minutes then let you two jabber to your hearts' content. I would like to speak to your sister briefly, Lizette."

Before Clara could say a word, Mary Johnson darted off for the kitchen. *Damn.* A few minutes between Mary Johnson and Izzie could be enough to ruin her life. Clara led Izzie through the front parlor past the piano and into the rear room. In the big gilt frame mirror that hung over the fireplace, she glimpsed Izzie whose brow was furrowed and mouth slightly open. Was she shocked? Was it the nude woman in the painting or was it that everything was so fancy?

"Does your madam know I want you to come home with me?" Izzie asked.

"Probably. You won't try to convince her to boot me out, will you? I want to make my own decision."

Izzie looked away, then began to pace about the room, winding her way through the sofas and chaise lounges.

"I told you I'll visit," Clara said. "I want to see you and Euphora whenever I can."

"Clara." Izzie approached her. "You know I'm the closest thing you have to a parent now that Papa is gone. You're only fifteen."

"All right, girls. Lettie will have tea for us in a minute." Mary Johnson strode over to them and stood near Izzie. Even Izzie seemed short next to the madam. "Now, Izzie, what are your plans?"

Izzie blinked just once. "I want Clara to come home to Rochester with me. I have work for her at my husband's Water-Cure Institute."

"Well, that's plain enough. You know I'm fond of Clara and proud of her. She's been through a great deal and she is a strong young woman. She stood up to your father. She told you that? She's proved she can fend for herself in this world."

Clara calmed as she felt Mary Johnson fold an arm over her shoulders.

"I was telling Clara I feel I am her guardian now with our father gone," Izzie said.

"She needed that sort of thing from you long ago. I doubt Clara would be here if you had tended to her sooner."

Izzie blinked. "I know. For that, I hope someday she'll forgive me."

With the two of them starting a debate for themselves, Clara was starting to feel small. Maybe she should go outside for a walk and see what they decided when she came back. Here was Izzie, her older sister, standing with Mary Johnson, her madam. They were looming over her. Her collywobbles were coming back.

Lettie arrived with a tray and set it on a marble table. She poured tea from a blue ceramic pot into three cups.

When the third cup was full, Clara looked straight at Izzie. "I'm not leaving."

Izzie and Mary Johnson stopped talking and both looked as though they suddenly realized someone else was in the room.

"I'm not leaving."

Lettie scurried away.

"Clara, you can't stay here. I won't allow you to do this with your life. You'll regret it."

The tone was familiar. Izzie was getting riled. Even though Clara had missed Izzie's brass for such a long time, she wished she didn't have to stand up to it now.

"Izzie, I believe Clara has already made her own choice. I will say it again. Any girl who can get up the nerve to get herself and her sister away from a man like your father and come all the way to New York City on her own and find her way, even if you don't approve of that way, can make her own decisions." Mary Johnson crossed her arms over her waist. "If she says she wants to leave, I'll help her pack her things up and I'll escort all of you to the depot. If she says she wants to stay, she stays."

Izzie's face went hard like a big, flat rock. "I'm her sister, Miss Johnson. I am responsible now."

"I don't think you are responsible," Clara said. "I can take care of myself."

"You want to … you actually want to be a prostitute?"

The word came at Clara like a sharp, bitter arrow. She couldn't speak or move.

"I take care of my girls. As long as she stays here with me, I will take care of her." Mary Johnson stared straight at Izzie like she could see right through to her other side.

"How can you take care of her? Look what she does every night? What about syphilis and gonorrhea? What about abortion? Is that how you'll take care of her?"

"I can't listen to you say these things," Clara said. She turned and headed for the double doors.

"Clara, wait. You must come with me. Please." Izzie stretched a hand in her direction.

"I can't. This is my home now, Izzie. I'm sorry."

"Clara, you must. I insist."

Mary Johnson nodded solemnly at Clara.

"What time will you collect Euphora at Mrs. Hogarth's? I'll come and say goodbye." Clara felt the tears flood up, but she held them back.

Izzie's face grew cold. It was an awful face. Clara was thoroughly nauseous now.

"Six-thirty in the morning. What about today? What about the American Museum this afternoon?"

"Tell Euphora I have a fever. Tell her you couldn't make me change my mind, but I'll visit in a month or two."

Her stomach jumping up and down like a leather ball, Clara left Izzie there by the big mirror with her madam. As she climbed the stairs, she heard Izzie and Mary Johnson quarreling. They could argue all they liked, all morning and afternoon. She belonged here and she was going to stay.

CLARA WOKE WITH THE FIRST LIGHT. Foggy-headed from the night's champagne, she felt like she had hardly slept at all. Beside her, a young sporting gentleman was snoring quietly through his long brown mustache. The young ones who didn't have wives and children to return to often stayed the night, especially if they were pickled like this Russell something or other from Georgia. He said he hated everything about the north, but not the women. He loved northern women. He told her she was like a cool deep well he could drink from.

Clara's night had been easy. He was not one of the imaginative ones and he didn't smell much. She got up from bed, combed her hair, and tied and pinned it up on her head. It was a mess, but no one would see it under her summer bonnet. Slipping into a light blue day dress, she decided to walk to the Hogarth's on Nineteenth Street. It was too early for anyone to heckle her. At this hour, she'd be left alone to walk in peace.

The sky was gloomy, but it was the kind of sky that only teased at rain. It wouldn't really rain. It would just feel sticky and hot all day and once in a while there would be thunder far off.

While she walked across Washington Square Park, she thought about her sisters leaving without her. Maybe she should change her mind. Maybe she should go with them. She slowed her pace. What would happen if she never became an actress? What would happen if Hannah married one of the sporting gents and left her? She couldn't think of these things. Anything could happen. She only wanted to think about today.

Later on she would join Hannah, Abbie and Carlotta on a two-hour steamer ride to Coney Island, to wade in the blue rolling waves of the Atlantic Ocean. She was excited to see the ocean for the first time. "If your name is LaMer, you must know the ocean," Carlotta had said.

When Clara arrived at the Hogarth's, Izzie and Euphora were already waiting on the sidewalk with their bags. Mrs. Hogarth was with them. Her red hair down below her shoulders, Euphora saw Clara first and ran toward her.

"You have to come with us, Clara. I don't understand."

"I told Izzie I'd visit. I will."

"Are you sure, dear?" With worried eyes, Mrs. Hogarth arrived at her side. "You're so young. I don't think my cousin Emma or your mother would have approved." Mrs. Hogarth's hand with the missing fingers twitched at her side.

"I'm going to stay," Clara said.

"You'll visit me even with Euphora gone, I trust." Mrs. Hogarth embraced Clara. "Tell me if you need help with anything, anything at all," she whispered into Clara's ear.

"We're going to walk to the depot. Will you come along?" Izzie asked.

Euphora took Clara's hand and dragged her over to Izzie.

They said their good-byes to Mrs. Hogarth and set off to the west for Tenth Avenue. As they walked, Euphora clutched Clara's hand so tightly that Clara nearly yelped with pain more than once. Euphora asked about how often Clara could visit and told her how much she would miss her and then told her again, and then again, until they were saying the same things over and over. Izzie was mostly quiet, except to direct them when to cross the streets and which direction to take. Surely she must have more to say than "right here, left here, straight now," thought Clara. Perhaps Izzie was so ashamed of her that she didn't want to speak to her. Perhaps the last few days of seeing Clara and her life at Mary Johnson's had sunk in.

At the depot, Izzie purchased two tickets on the train bound for Albany where they would change to another train for Rochester.

Then the three of them stood with a small crowd of people and their cargo at the door of a rail car. Tears streamed down Euphora's face and Izzie's eyes were watery too.

"All aboard the Hudson River line for Albany." A man paced along the platform repeating his instruction.

She could get on the train with them right now. She didn't need her things. Someone at the parlor house could ship her dresses to her. Would it be so terrible being a lady's aide at the Upper Falls Water-Cure? She could be with her sisters. She could leave all the men and their strange, complicated needs behind.

"I'm sorry for those things I said to you yesterday." Izzie squinted as though feeling a burn. "I'm sorry, Clara. You are my dear sister and I love you. I will love you always no matter what you choose to do with your life."

Even though Clara had managed not to cry until now, this broke her and tears flooded out.

"Change your mind and come with us. Please," Izzie said.

Clara took Billy's red bandana from her pocket and held it over her mouth. She couldn't go. She shook her head.

"You can change your mind later. You are welcome anytime. Euphora and I will keep a place for you and Billy too, if he comes back."

"And Hannah," Euphora said.

Clara embraced Izzie and held her a long moment, then Euphora. Her two sisters turned together and climbed onto the train, then looked back at Clara with tear-soaked faces and waved. It was as though the three of them had one heart, one big broken heart. Finally they disappeared into the rail car.

She decided to stay there on the platform by the rails to see if she could see her sisters through the window. In a moment or two, the train would hiss and whistle and clang away along the tracks. It was more than she could bear. She spun and ran away. Heart beating hard, she shoved and dodged her way through the throngs of passengers and well-wishers until she was out on the street. She ran to Twenty-Eighth, Twenty-Seventh, Twenty-Sixth, then slowed to a walk. The sky was gray and sullen. Breathing in the smell of the river, she decided to walk south along Tenth Avenue and then West Street.

Ships lined the docks and slips as far as she could see. She started to count sails. Three on one ship, five on the next. Eight total, then eleven total, then fifteen. At four hundred and ninety-four, she ran out of ships. She looked around her. Where had she been? Where was she now? That was Brooklyn across the East River. Without realizing, she had followed the ships all the way down the Hudson River to the Battery then along South Street to the East River. *Lawks.* How had she done that?

Izzie and Euphora were on their way to Rochester, she thought. They were sitting close together on the train, leaning into each other and telling each other about the past year. Clara felt like someone was squeezing her heart in a double-handed grip. She coughed.

A small sailboat slowly rowed out of its slip and drifted by her sailing into the East River. She watched it until it was out of sight. She thought about Billy on his ship to China. Was he safe? Would she ever see him again?

Then it seemed it must be time to walk back to the parlor house and see Hannah. Hannah would just be waking up with the rest of the girls. She'd sit with Hannah in her room and tell her everything that had happened since Izzie had arrived. She'd tell her that she was staying. Then in the afternoon, they'd go to the Atlantic Ocean.

Forty-Nine

"THE CHANGE CAME WHEN I DECIDED not to be afraid of the voices. Once I let them talk through me, my own soul calmed down and I was able to listen to them in an orderly way. Usually orderly." Izzie laughed.

"You must at least write an article, perhaps a book. Have you read mine?" Isaac Post asked.

"I have."

"What did you think of it?"

"I am interested that all the spirit voices that you transcribed were of famous men, like Benjamin Franklin. All the spirit voices I hear are simple, ordinary people in the other spheres."

"I invited those men to speak through me. I selected them."

"My voices select me, I think."

Post rose from his chair and took his straw hat from the rack near Izzie's office door. "The editor of the *Banner of Light* is a dear friend. He's visiting in two weeks. I'll bring him by. Perhaps we can hold a special circle when he is here, a Grand Circle." Post grinned. "I'll bring my wife, Amy, and invite Mr. Stebbins and Mrs. Edgeworth."

The term "Grand Circle" reminded Izzie of the terrible moment at Ada Coan's when she broke down into a blithering, screaming idiot. She silently cringed with embarrassment.

"Wouldn't a Grand Circle be superb? And perhaps we could even bring in a few of the other really well-known mediums from Boston or New York," Post said.

She nodded. Perhaps it would be different than her last Grand Circle. Perhaps if she wasn't obsessed with finding her sisters, it would be interesting, even exciting.

"Good. I'll write to a few of our medium friends. And you must start writing now about your experience with hearing voices. Include the story of your mother, too. When my friend comes, we'll show him what you are working on."

"You really think people would be interested?"

"That's precisely what I am telling you."

After their chat, Izzie walked Isaac Post out to the front door and waved to him as he departed in his carriage. She stood a moment in the driveway and watched him ride away. The September sun was already low in the sky, but the sunlight was crystal clear and strong and it shimmered on red and orange leaves along the street. She breathed in the cool air.

It wouldn't be long before the ground froze. Her tulip bulbs were bundled by color in burlap sacks near the new side garden, the one visible from Mac's office. How lovely it would be for those staying at the Upper Falls Water-Cure to stroll among red, white, and purple flowerbeds in the spring. The sun wouldn't set for another hour or so. She had time to do a little planting.

She rushed upstairs to change into her homespun gardening dress, apron and shawl. Once outside at the garden beds, she pulled on her heavy cotton gloves and opened the sack labeled "white." She reached inside and grabbed a handful of bulbs. Mac's aides had helped her with the beds, a circle divided into quarters with paths cutting across. In the center of the larger circle was another smaller one where a wood bench would rest.

She studied the design. Should she plant each quarter section all one color or blend them? It would be too mundane to make them all the same by quarter, she thought. It should be more random than that, and something with curves, and she wouldn't count the bulbs out in tidy rows like Clara or Billy would. She stepped into the loose soil in one of the sections and bent down. Then she began to set the white bulbs in the shape of a droplet. After the droplet was done, she took purple bulbs from their sack and set them on the ground in another droplet shape cradling half the white. On the other side of the white she laid out red.

As she picked up her trowel from her wooden toolbox, she glanced up at Mac's expansive office windows. He was there watching her. He waved and smiled. She returned the gesture, then he vanished into the dim of his office.

Izzie knelt down and jammed the trowel into the ground. She lifted the earth out in several clumps, placed a bulb in and covered it over. The work was easy and fast since the soil had already been turned. Even so, by the time the first droplet was planted, the sky was just beginning to glow with pinks and reds. Soon it would be dark. She had promised Euphora she'd help her with a dozen apple pies for tomorrow's supper so she clapped the soil off her gloves and trowel and closed the sacks up.

As she collected her things, the rumble and clatter of a carriage on the stone drive drew her attention away from her garden. Drawn by two black horses, a closed carriage approached the Water-Cure Institute entrance. Mac or his aide would greet the new arrivals, she thought. No need to run over there a dirty mess to welcome arriving patients.

A moment later, with her garden toolbox hooked over her arm, Izzie started down the path that led around the back of the building where the shed was.

"Wait! Izzie!"

Lawks. It sounded like Clara. Two women hustled toward her from the direction of the carriage. Was it? Izzie set the box down and rushed toward them.

"Clara?" Izzie cried.

As Izzie got closer, she saw that the other woman was Hannah, or at least she guessed it was from Euphora's descriptions of Clara's blond friend. She threw her arms around Clara and held her tight a long joyous moment, but as she held Clara she felt her sister seemed too slender, too frail. She could practically feel her ribs through all their clothing. There was no flesh at all on her.

"Are you visiting? You didn't write me," Izzie said.

"No—we're staying. That is, if it's all right with you and Mac?"

"Yes. Yes. Lawks. Yes. Oh my, Clara, yes." Izzie turned to Hannah. "And you're Hannah. You're welcome, too." She reached for Hannah.

As Izzie received the warm clasp of Hannah's two hands, she noticed the shape of Hannah's dress draped over a large belly.

"There are three of us," Clara's lips grew taut, her brow pinched. "Is it all right?"

From the quiver in Clara's voice, Izzie sensed her sister was weary, even afraid.

"Of course. We have plenty of room and plenty to do." Izzie beamed at them as hard as she could, but Clara's expression stayed worried and pinched and she was very pale.

"Come on. Let's go find Euphora. She's in the kitchen. She'll be ecstatic that you are here." Izzie linked arms with Clara to lead her back toward the front entrance.

Izzie began to chatter cheerfully about how she had just been making a garden and how Clara would have counted the tulip bulbs if she had been there. But while Izzie spoke, she became aware that Clara— whose arm felt boney interlocked with her own fleshy forearm—was almost dragging behind her. Then, even as Izzie was happily describing which bedchamber the girls could stay in, her mind was racing ahead. Clara might not stay very long.

Some part of her beautiful sister had disappeared. Was there a way to get her back? Clara had seen and done things Izzie couldn't imagine. Why was she so skinny and pale? And how could Clara ever want to stay in a Water-Cure Institute after a fancy, fast life in New York City with champagne and theatre and gorgeous dresses? Izzie turned to catch Clara's eye, to see if she could find a hint of what was to come, but Clara's thin face was pointed down toward the path. Izzie glanced over her shoulder at Hannah, whose blond hair had the soft pink of sunset on it.

Was that a slight, hopeful gleam in Hannah's blue eyes? Perhaps Clara would stay because of her friend and the child. That child of Hannah's won't be born for a few months and then there will be an infant to care for. Clara would stay a good long while for that. Wouldn't she?

Trying to slow her thoughts, Izzie inhaled deeply. She shouldn't let herself leap so far ahead with notions about what Clara would do or wouldn't do. She was here. *She was here.* Squeezing Clara's arm as tightly as she could, she led the girls into the Institute, their new home, and directly to the kitchen.

When she drew open the heavy kitchen door, she called, "Euphora! Come see what I've got."

Acknowledgements

Many thanks to my fine writer friends who gave me the gift of their insights while I developed *The Spirit Room's* story and characters — Daniel Becker, Stacey Bennetts, Sherry Brummel, April Caron, Lynn Dixon, Michelle Furtado, Florine Gingerich, Gabrielle Herkert, Betsy Herring, Ed Ratcliffe, Carla Saulter, and Harold Taw. Also, thank you to Pam Goodfellow and Skye Moody for inspiring and guiding me. A special thank you to Barbara Bailey, Thatcher Bailey, and Phil Kovacevich who provided me with many "writer retreat" days and nights, as well as delicious sustenance, at Chevy Chase Beach Cabins in Port Townsend. And thank you, of course, to Margaret, my beloved, who has always believed in, and supported, me.

Hundreds of places, references and resources provided me with the detail and inspiration for this novel. I am particularly grateful to the Rochester Public Library and the Geneva Historical Society for use of their archives and collections and to the following authors for their excellent non-fiction work about women in the 19th century: Barbara Goldsmith, *Other Powers, The Age of Suffrage, Spiritualism, and the Scandalous Victoria Woodhull,* Alfred A. Knopf, 1998; Christine Stansell, *City of Women, Sex and Class in New York* 1789-1860, University of Illinois Press, 1987; and Janet Farrell Brodie, *Contraception and Abortion in 19th-Century America,* Cornell University Press, 1994.

A mid-19th century work, *New York by Gas-Light and Other Urban Sketches,* University of California Press, reprinted 1990, by George G. Foster, a reporter for the *New*

York Tribune, was invaluable for its detailed portrayal of New York life during the era.

About the Author

The Spirit Room is Marschel Paul's first novel. Born in New York City, she lived the first part of her life in Pennsylvania, Connecticut, New Hampshire, Massachusetts, and New York. Though she is still a Yankee at heart, she currently lives in Seattle with her beloved partner.

CPSIA information can be obtained at www.ICGtesting.com
Printed in the USA
BVOW070502150513

320755BV00001B/111/P